DO YOU REALIZE?

DO YOU REALIZE?

Kevin A. Kuhn

BEAVER'S POND
PRESS

Lyrics used with permission—Crowded House. "She Goes On." By Neil Finn. Los Angeles, CA: Capital. *Woodface*. 1991.

Edited by Kellie Hultgren

ISBN 13: 978-1-59298-695-8
Library of Congress Catalog Number: 2016918807
Printed in the United States of America
First Printing: 2017
21 20 19 18 17   5 4 3 2 1

Book design by Athena Currier

 Beaver's Pond Press, Inc.
7108 Ohms Lane
Edina, MN 55439–2129

(952) 829-8818
www.BeaversPondPress.com

For Melinda

PROLOGUE

Who'll Stop the Rain?

September 23, 2015

George hated Oak Lawn cemetery. It was stark and organized, with perfect rows of granite headstones. Even in the September rain, with scattered leaves and wet brown grass, the cemetery felt too groomed and artificial.

We don't live our lives with this much order and control. To represent them in death like this is a lie. A proper cemetery should have big, gnarled trees among crumbling angels and weathered tombstones arranged haphazardly. The grass should be littered with clover and worn down to dirt in places. Not like the manicured, rootless sod in this place.

George read the name on the headstone and felt a wave of emotion wash over him. He looked up and let the rain pour over his face. He was mad at the universe—no, *mad* wasn't the right word; *furious* was a better choice.

It's not fair that I have to go through this. No man should have to make this choice. I didn't ask for any of this. I wish I'd never met him.

The cemetery was empty, and he felt cold and alone. He glanced at his watch, which felt heavy on his wrist. He turned and walked back to his car.

CHAPTER 1

What Is Love?

June 2, 2014

George's alarm woke him at 5:15 a.m. *Oh God, not another Monday.* His mind immediately filled with meetings, issues, and all the things he had been worried about while trying to fall asleep the night before. Sleep seemed to come harder and harder each year, especially when his work problems were so excessive. Feeling his stress level rising already, he made a conscious effort to clear his head.

He looked over at his wife. She looked peaceful. He loved her smile, but it was her big hazel eyes that had hooked him long ago. He still remembered the first time he had seen those eyes. He was staring at her in a high-school hallway, and when she glanced back he felt butterflies as big as birds in his stomach.

She's still beautiful after all these years.

He loved Elena, but he missed the days when they were intensely in love.

We are very comfortable with each other.

As he sat up, Elena's eyes fluttered open.

"What?"

"Oh, sorry; nothing, just remembering back to high school and missing your long hair."

Elena yawned and frowned. "That's how you wake me, criticizing my hair?"

She always wakes up in a bad mood.

"I didn't mean to wake you, and I wasn't criticizing. Go back to sleep, grumpy."

"I haven't had long hair for twenty years, George. I cut it short the year after we married."

"I know. Your hair is cute, it's fine. Forget I said anything."

"Go to work, George; you're just digging yourself a deeper hole."

George boarded the 610 Union Pacific Northwest Metra train in Crystal Lake every morning at 6:13 a.m. This put him into the Chicago Ogilvie Transportation Center, or OTC, at 7:22 a.m. It left him plenty of time to walk the four blocks to his office building before 8:00 a.m. Some mornings he even treated himself to a second cup of coffee along the way.

Today, as usual, he boarded a car in the middle, avoiding the crowd of regulars at the front and back of the train. While he was somewhat jealous of the camaraderie of people who made life-long friendships on their morning commutes, he'd never been able to muster up the courage to break into one of those groups.

George picked one of the empty bench seats. Looking around the train, he recognized a few passengers who seemed to share his approach to the morning commute. *Head down, eyes forward, avoid eye contact, and build a mental wall defining personal space.*

In a minor victory, by the time the train lurched forward, no one else had joined George.

Today is my lucky day.

Four minutes later they reached Cary Station, and as the new passengers filed down the train car, George couldn't help but look them over. He liked to pick out people he thought would or would not take the spot next to him. Over the years, he'd gotten pretty good at predicting his seatmates.

One person stood out as he eyed the row of people: a man with a full beard, slightly overweight and dressed in worn jeans, a T-shirt, and an ill-fitting tweed jacket with patches under the elbows. His shirt bore the letters *SISOMSO*, which made no sense to George. He had small brown eyes with well-defined crow's-feet. His unkempt hair and disorderly eyebrows gave him an out-of-control look. George pegged him to be in his early forties. A pair of large headphones encircled his neck.

Oh, Christ, look at this guy. Don't sit here. Keep moving.

George watched the man shuffle toward him. He was about to look away when they made eye contact. The man gave a slight smile, and George knew it was over. He immediately turned away, but a moment later he felt the seat move and stole a quick glance to his left confirming his seatmate's identity.

I had a bad feeling about this morning.

He quickly raised his morning paper and began reading. He got through a couple of sections before the inevitable interruption.

"How are you?" asked his new seatmate. George thought about ignoring him but couldn't summon the courage. He lowered his paper and said the first thing that came to his mind.

"Do you really want to know, or are you just making small talk?"

"I really want to know. How are you?"

George thought about trying a quick "fine" and returning to his paper, but to his surprise he heard himself confess, "Well, my job sucks, I'm balding, I seem to put on five pounds every year, and I think my wife and I are falling a little more out of love every day. And to boot, the world is overheating, running out of resources, and getting more violent."

There, now you know how I am. Happy?

The man looked at him squarely in the eyes and asked, "What is love?"

George was more than a little pissed at himself for falling into this conversation. Half of his brain searched for a way out while the other half searched for a name. After a moment he replied, "Who are you, Haddaway?"

The man laughed. "That *is* an addictive song—a real earworm. I'm serious, though: if you think you're falling out of love, you should make sure you know what love is. So let me ask you again, what is love?"

Caught off guard—this man did not seem the *SNL* type—George forgot how crazy it was to explain his personal definition of love to a complete stranger and instead thought, *What the heck is love?* "I guess it's when two people care for each other."

His seatmate laughed loudly again. "So this thing that has brought down empires and is responsible for about half of all the music, literature, and art on the planet just boils down to two people caring for each other?"

This wasn't the sort of conversation you have on the Metra. George suddenly felt embarrassed. But the background noise on the train was loud, and as he scanned the car he realized no one seemed to have noticed their conversation. He looked at his seatmate and admitted, "I suppose it's a little more complicated than that."

The man stared at George as if waiting for more. George leaned back in his seat and thought. He had just watched a *National Geographic* TV show that explored different animals' approaches to love and mating.

"How's this? Love is an evolutionary construct developed over time to support the propagation of the species by encouraging breeding and child-rearing. Tribes that had this construct were more successful and carried on the trait more often," George replied smugly, surprised at the way his answer flowed off his tongue.

His seatmate didn't seem impressed. "So if love is due to millions of years of evolution and has developed successful breeding and child-rearing, then why do people cheat?"

George again glanced around the train; most people were sleeping, reading, or working. No one seemed to care about or even notice the strange discussion he was having. Somewhere in the back of his mind, he decided he might actually be enjoying the conversation.

"I suppose that, for evolution to be successful, it needs gene mixing and variety. So . . . love is . . . a mix of commitment and faithfulness to encourage child-rearing, and a dose of cheating to stir up the gene pool on a regular basis," said George.

"Okay, now we're getting somewhere. So, it's just evolutionary programming that tricks people into propagating the race and raising the young, while adding a little variety to mix up the chromosomes? Sounds miserable! So why do people break up and divorce—what's the evolutionary purpose in that?"

"I don't know. Maybe there isn't one?"

"Then why?"

George breathed in deeply. "Whew, a thousand different reasons, I'm sure. Infidelity, stress, boredom . . . I guess after the romance is over, people find they just aren't that compatible. And just so you know, I have never cheated on my wife and I love her. I just said our love seems to be a little less intense each day."

The man looked into George's eyes. "Okay, dude, wake up. You just need to know that love is the most precious thing in the universe, and it's the only thing that matters. It's more than just evolutionary programming. Do you realize that love is a natural painkiller? Do you realize that when two people in love stare into each other's eyes, their heart rates synchronize? And men who kiss their wives in the morning can live up to five years longer than those who don't? And that people's blood pressure is lowest when they're with their lovers? And most people, when questioned at the end of their life about happiness and fulfillment, state that love is the only thing that mattered? And man, if you feel like you're letting go even a tiny bit of it, you ought to think about it. Friend, my advice is to spend a little more time thinking, wondering, and appreciating and a little less time worrying and stressing."

He caught George's perturbed expression and smiled. "Sorry, man, I don't mean to preach. Have a great day—this is my stop."

He pulled on his headphones and left the train. George was somewhat stunned, but as the man put on his headphones, he could just make out the faint sound of Haddaway's "What Is Love" playing. George looked at his watch; it was 7:08 a.m.

CHAPTER 2

Imitation of Life

In the last fourteen minutes of the train ride, it finally came to him, the meaning of *SISOMSO*: reverse osmosis. *Physics humor,* he chuckled to himself. He wanted to be annoyed with the stranger, but he realized he had enjoyed the conversation. And the man was correct: he needed to worry less and appreciate life a little more.

The walk from the OTC to his office building was pleasant. It was a warm June morning, and even at 7:30 a.m. the temperature was nearing seventy degrees. As George navigated the crowded sidewalks and the never-ending downtown construction, he tried to relax and enjoy the morning. He felt happy and upbeat until his office building loomed ahead. Without conscious thought, his mood shifted in response to the problems he was about to face.

George arrived at the office at about 7:50 a.m., according to his watch. He quickly settled in and checked his schedule; it was nearly full of conference calls and meetings. About a dozen e-mails had arrived overnight.

Don't these people ever let work go?

Within fifteen minutes he was in work mode, responding to e-mails, completing approvals, and dealing with issues as best he could.

A bit later, Carl stopped by and asked, "Hey, George, how you doing?"

"Living the dream," replied George. Carl worked for George, but George thought of him as more of a friend than a direct report. He was one of the few people in the office George felt he could completely confide in. Lately, they had been playing the who-can-complain-more game.

"That bad, huh?"

"You know, I used to take work a year at a time; then, at some point, it became a month at a time, and now I'm just trying to get through a day."

"Hey, at least you're the boss! You get to assign your crappiest tasks to me. I just have to eat it," Carl said.

"I'm the boss? I'm a cog! At least you only have one boss. We are so matrixed now, I can't even keep track of all my bosses. All I know is that if I see an ass, I'm kissing it."

This got Carl laughing. "How long have you been here?"

"I don't know, like sixteen years?"

"Seriously, George, you seem pretty unhappy lately. Have you ever thought about quitting?"

"All the time. The problem is I got a mortgage and two kids to put through college. How am I going to make it through another seven to ten years around here?"

"Why don't you go somewhere else, a different insurance company?"

"Ah, it would be the same crap, just at a different place. I love to complain about this company, but I think it's probably as much about me as it is the company," George said.

"What about doing something completely different?"

George looked around the office. The gray cubicle walls depressed him. A tear in the carpet, a couple of fluorescents that were out, a broken copier in the corner—the whole floor felt depressing. "I've spent some time thinking about that; something like teaching, coaching baseball, or even bartending. But I'm afraid I would eventually get bored again, and then I'd still be unhappy, just making a whole lot less pay."

"It always comes back to the money thing, doesn't it? I'm probably here until I die. I got four kids. I can't even afford to *think* about quitting," Carl said.

"Okay, you win. Hey, I'm supposed to be inspiring you. Instilling you with the 'thrill of accountability.' What do you say we use our systems thinking to go redesign some value streams to fully realize business benefits?"

This got another laugh. George knew he could count on Carl to get his sarcasm. He was glad to have someone he could commiserate with, but he still felt paralyzed and trapped.

But George, like time, marched through his day, conference call by conference call and e-mail by e-mail. He didn't believe he was doing a poor job, although he was fairly certain his declining attitude was beginning to show through. He had tried to push the reset button a few times and throw himself into the work, to change his negative mindset by sheer willpower. None of his attempts had lasted a day— not even a few hours, really. He would start the day with optimism, have a few good meetings, and then along would come a soul-crushing e-mail from on high or some stressful personnel issue. He just couldn't turn off his frustration.

"Hello, this is George, United Property Insurance."

"Hi, Dad, it's Alex."

"Hey, how's my favorite son today?"

"Fine, Dad. Hey, can I skip baseball practice tonight? There's some other stuff I want to do."

"What? No. You can't skip practice. You're on a team, you've made a commitment. Besides, the way you've been playing lately, you need the practice. You need to show your coach how hard you're working."

"Don't you even want to know what else I have tonight?"

"Not really, Alex, that's the point: you have a commitment. Unless it's life and death, you have to honor your commitments. What's so important, Alex?"

"Never mind."

The phone went dead.

Oh, that boy. He's so damn lazy; I hate the teenage years.

George felt a tinge of guilt for not asking him about the "other stuff," but he quickly put it out of his mind. *I'll talk to him tonight.*

On his walk back to the train station, he recounted his morning encounter with the bearded man. Something about him was intriguing. He hadn't come across as particularly brilliant, but his questions had gotten George thinking. He wondered what the odds were of running into him again. He couldn't remember at which stop the man had gotten off the train, and he made a mental note to check his transit schedule to see if he could figure it out.

At 5:20 p.m. George arrived at the OTC and quickly made his way to the Union Pacific Northwest Line, where he boarded the 5:33 p.m. train that would arrive in Crystal Lake at 6:49 p.m. He grabbed an empty seat on a car in the middle of the train and put his briefcase on the seat next to him. Spreading out was frowned upon, and most people were not afraid to ask you to make room, but there would be some available single seats, and George was hoping to get lucky again.

The train pulled away right on time at 5:33 p.m. He scanned the schedule for the first couple of stops and learned that not all the trains stopped at the first few stops. The 5:33 p.m. train skipped the first five or six stops, and George realized he would not have another chance encounter with his morning seatmate. He was surprised at his disappointment. Eventually, a nondescript businessman took the seat next to George and promptly went to sleep.

God, I hate my job. I need to snap out of it. I'm letting it affect my relationship with Elena. My mood is dragging the whole family down. Tonight. Tonight I'll have a real conversation with Elena. We'll open a bottle of wine and talk about life for a while.

CHAPTER 3

Home Sweet Home

It was 6:50 p.m. when he stepped off the train and onto the platform in front of the quaint brick station. George walked to his car and made the ten-minute drive to his house, where his daughter Amanda passed him on her way out.

"Hi, Daddy, can you take me and a friend to Northwestern this weekend? We want to tour the campus."

"Northwestern? Jesus, do you think you can get in there?" *How much would tuition be there? More than I can afford, that's for sure. Add a few more years to that retirement plan.*

"I don't know, Daddy, but my friend probably can, and you told me I should start visiting some colleges," she said as she put on some sandals.

George had described Amanda as *precocious* as a child and then changed to *stubborn* when she hit ten. Elena preferred *strong-willed* and later *independent.* Amanda had also inherited her mother's good looks; she just didn't know it yet, which suited George just fine. Her hair and complexion were a shade darker, but she had the same big eyes and cute, upturned nose as Elena. While Amanda had dated few boyfriends in high school, George had no doubt she would soon figure it out.

"Okay, well sure, I guess—I have to check our schedule." As his daughter opened the door, his mind was still swirling with thoughts of outrageous tuition costs. "Hey, wait, where you going?" he barely got out as the door shut. Before he could follow her, his wife called out from the other room.

"Honey, is that you?"

He put down his briefcase and walked into the family room. "Yeah, hey, where is our daughter going?"

"Out with some friends, it's fine. I'm glad you're home; there's some Chinese food on the counter. After you eat can you pick up Alex from baseball? His practice is done at seven thirty. And the engine light is on in my car. We've got some bills to pay as well. I've got book club at eight, but I should be home a little after nine."

"Uh, sure," he replied, a little overwhelmed.

"Sure to what, honey?" She gave him a condescending look, as if she didn't trust he had processed it all.

". . . Um, sure to picking up Alex from baseball."

"Okay, great. What about the engine light in my car?"

"Uh, I don't know. What do you want me to do?"

"Well, I don't think I should be driving with an engine issue. Can you take a look at the car?"

"Elena, I doubt it's anything I can fix." *Now I'm a mechanic?*

"I certainly can't either," she countered. "When am I going to be able to take it to the dealer?"

He sighed. "It should be fine for the week. Drive it the least you can. How about we take it to the dealer on Saturday together?"

"The least I can? Have you seen the calendar this week? We are running fifty different directions every night. And Alex has a baseball game on Saturday morning. We have a graduation party on Saturday night. I'm not sure when you think we can get to the dealer."

He rubbed his temples and sighed. "Okay, I guess I'll have to miss Alex's baseball game. I'll take the car in on Saturday morning, and you go cheer on Alex. Does that work?"

"I suppose, but I hate driving the car knowing it could break down at any moment. You sure it's okay to drive this week? Maybe it's getting to the point where we are going to have lots of issues with it? It just needed new brakes last month, and the dealer said it's time to start thinking about new tires."

"It won't break down; it's probably just a loose gas cap or something. I think that car has a good five more years before we need to replace it. It's fine." He tried to sound confident, but the last thing he needed was a breakdown while Elena was driving the car. She would never let him hear the end of it. And the thought of another big expense opened a pit in his stomach.

Add another year onto the retirement plan.

George barely had enough time to eat some of the Chinese food before it was time to pick up his son. When he returned home, Elena had already left for her book club. George changed his clothes and paid the bills.

So much for the wine and talk.

George was upstairs in his bedroom, beginning to get ready for bed, when he heard his wife come home. A quick glance at the clock told him that it was 9:43 p.m. Both kids were home, the kitchen was clean, and the house was picked up. George still was hoping to talk some with Elena, and he didn't want her to be grumpy.

She came strolling into the bedroom, humming some unintelligible music. George rightly guessed that she'd had a few glasses of wine. She seemed to be in a good mood.

"How was book club, honey?"

"Oh, fine. As usual, we didn't talk much about the book. They were mostly bragging about kids and gossiping," she said as she took off her jewelry. "But it was still fun."

"Hey, I did get the bills paid and Alex said his baseball practice went well. There's still some Chinese left, so I just put it in the refrigerator. Oh, and Amanda wants me to take her to Northwestern with a friend this weekend to tour the university."

"It's great she's starting to show interest in her college search, but I don't know how you are going to find time to run her down to Northwestern this weekend. Who knows how long my car will be in the shop, and you promised me we would take care of some yard work on Sunday. What friend, and what did you tell her?"

"I think I said maybe, and I'm not sure which friend it is."

"How in the world did you think that would work? She needs to understand that something like that needs a little more planning. You need to tell her no right away so she can tell her friend." Elena sounded a little frustrated.

"Okay, no worries; I told her maybe. I'll tell her to pick another weekend tomorrow."

Elena walked into the bathroom and shut the door behind her. Elena's bedtime ritual was precise and comprehensive, and it took a solid ten minutes. It would be after ten o'clock before they had a chance to talk. George climbed into bed and waited for her.

Almost exactly ten minutes later, Elena emerged from the bathroom, turned off the lights, and climbed into bed.

"Elena, what do you think love is?"

"Oh, honey, I'm too tired for lovemaking tonight. It's been a long day. Amanda and I had another big fight this morning."

"What about?"

"You know what? I don't even know. I think it started with me telling her to get off her phone. It went south from there; she can get really nasty. When I told her she needed to pitch in more around the house, she had the nerve to say that was my job because I don't have a real job."

"Wow, I'm sorry to hear that. When she gets defensive she goes on the attack." *And she gets that from her mom.* "By the way, I wasn't asking to make love. I want to know what you think love is."

"I think it's when a husband is willing to make sure his beautiful wife is driving a safe car that's not on the edge of breaking down."

"Okay, okay, I get it. We'll look into a new car. But, seriously, what do you think love is?"

"George, you know I love you. I think love is when two people know each other well enough to know when the other is really, really tired and really wants to go to sleep. That's what I think love is."

George thought about trying one more time, but he knew Elena was genuinely tired and he was as well. He leaned over, kissed her, and went to sleep.

CHAPTER 4

Everybody Wants to Rule the World

June 3, 2014

George was on autopilot the next morning, preparing for another day of battle at the office but preoccupied with yesterday's strange encounter. *He was just some quirky guy—he said nothing particularly profound. Am I so starved for real conversation that this man has me obsessed? There is a good chance I'll never see him again! I should forget about it.* The next thing he knew; he was boarding his morning train to downtown. He sat down in the nearest empty seat and pulled out the morning paper.

World events were grim. Russia was screwing around with the Ukraine, and there were new reports of ethnic atrocities in Sudan. George was surprised that a new world war had not broken out in the last few years. Domestic news wasn't any better. More headlines about racist police brutality, another gang rape at a major university, and a rash of car break-ins right at home in Crystal Lake. Even the weather and financial sections contributed to the misery. A long article discussed record highs in global temperatures and the likelihood of several mass extinctions due to the climate change. The financial section featured fresh reports of growing debt in several countries and the increasing likelihood of a global recession. *Jesus,* thought George, *can things be any worse?* He unconsciously began to bite his fingernails. It was a bad habit he was continuously but unsuccessfully trying to break.

"What do you fear?" said a voice.

George about jumped out of his skin. He had been vaguely aware of someone sitting down, but he was unprepared for the random question. He took half a second to regain his composure before lowering the newspaper.

Somehow he knew even before he looked that it would be the man he had met the day before. *So much for getting the weirdness out of my head.*

"This about sums it up," George stated, presenting the daily paper. "Violence is on the increase, global warming is cooking the planet, and we're on the brink of a global financial crisis."

"Is violence increasing?" the man asked.

Despite being surprised, George felt a little more prepared for this morning's discussion. He put his paper down, turned to the man, and smiled.

"Okay, before I answer that, I would like to know your name. You caught me so off guard yesterday, I never asked."

The man extended his hand. "My name is Shiloh. Pleased to meet you."

George shook his hand and chuckled. "Isn't that what Brad Pitt and Angelina Jolie named their daughter?"

Shiloh appeared embarrassed. "Yes, but it was mine first. And it can be male or female."

George regretted his attempt at humor. He classified himself as a bit of a geek, but this guy was such an easy target. "Sorry, Shiloh. It's very nice to meet you. My name is George. I thought we were discussing love?"

"Well, we started with love, but you can't understand why it's important unless you start to understand other emotions. So, do you think violence is increasing?"

George sensed he was being set up, but he replied anyway. "Yeah, I believe violence is increasing every day. If you read the paper, watch the news, or check the Internet, I think it's pretty obvious."

"Actually, you're wrong. There is documented, scientific evidence that worldwide violence has been decreasing since 10,000 BC. There has been a continuous decline in war, murders, and other violent crimes. And even slavery has been nearly eliminated. Do you realize you are living in the most peaceful period in the existence of our species?"

"I have a hard time believing that," George said.

"It's true! Check the facts. Take murders: in the Middle Ages there were about a hundred murders for every hundred thousand people per year, while today some European countries have about one murder for every hundred thousand people per year. Overall, murder rates have dropped by about one hundred times from the Middle Ages to today," Shiloh said.

"I don't know how anyone could know how many murders there were during the Middle Ages. Where did you find this, some random page on the Internet?" asked George, glancing out the window.

"No, I read a book by Steven Pinker, called *The Better Angels* or something like that. He's credible; look it up. And

23

despite the fact that people think war violence is increasing, there has been a ninety percent reduction in war-related deaths since World War II."

"All right, Shiloh, for the sake of argument, I'm going to assume you are correct, and if so, that's pretty surprising," George conceded.

"Good. Now, are you concerned about carbon?" Shiloh asked.

Again George felt he was being set up, but he forged ahead. "Yeah, I'm concerned. We're pumping more and more of it into the atmosphere and it's destroying the environment and overheating the planet."

"You do realize they're talking about carbon dioxide, not carbon monoxide. Carbon monoxide is a noxious, poisonous gas, but carbon dioxide is the elixir of life. It's the one element that all life on Earth is based on. It's what every plant on the planet needs for life, and what they need to produce our oxygen. Scientific evidence suggests that the increase in carbon over the past forty years has led to a 'greening' of the planet." Shiloh was on a roll.

The conductor walked by, checking passengers, and George and Shiloh flashed their monthly passes. As George watched the conductor punching tickets, the process designer in him kicked in.

There has to be a better way to collect fares. How are they still hand-punching tickets this day and age?

Shiloh continued, "Now, we should be worried about the greenhouse effect of carbon, as there is pretty good evidence that it has some impact on global atmospheric and oceanic temperatures. However, it's difficult to understand exactly what is the impact of carbon and what is natural variability."

George was making mental notes for some Google searches later, but Shiloh's stream of facts seemed to ring true. "I'm still skeptical, but I'm intrigued. Maybe the world isn't on the brink, but I still think things are pretty bad."

Shiloh shifted back in his seat. "George, I'm not saying we should stop trying to reduce violence or lower carbon emissions or improve the earth. I'm just saying that most of the planet lets their lives be driven primarily by fear. Do you realize that the University of Cincinnati found in a study that eighty-five percent of what we worry about never comes true?"

"Actually, I do think I have heard that. But it's easier said than acted on."

"Also, do you realize that life expectancy has more than doubled in the last one hundred and fifty years? Or that poverty levels have dropped dramatically? A century and a half ago, seventy-five percent of the world population lived in extreme poverty. Now that number is under fifteen percent. And developing regions realized a forty-two percent reduction in the number of undernourished people in the last twenty-five years. There's still an incredible amount of work to do, but do these facts line up with your worldview, George?"

Where does this guy get this stuff, and how does he remember it all? I can barely remember my wife's birthday. "Not really. It seems like everything, including violence, poverty, and hunger, has been getting steadily worse. Why is that, Shiloh? Are you sure you have your facts right?"

"It's about attention, money, and power. In these modern times, what's the easiest way for people in power to control the masses? If one party is losing control, what's the simplest way to regain their power? It's fear. It's the easy way out; it's the lowest common denominator. How does a country convince its populace to go to war? It's through terror. Everyone has to stop letting their lives be managed by fear. You, George, you have to stop letting your life be led by fear and worry. Do you realize that you're fifteen times more likely to be killed by falling coconuts than by a shark? Everyone is worried about home invasions, sharks, and hurricanes. You know what they should be worried about, George?" Shiloh only paused for an instant. "Car accidents, television, and junk food, that's what they should be worried about. But those aren't as newsworthy, are they?" Shiloh shifted forward in his seat. "I'm preaching again, aren't I?"

George looked at him and said, "You know what? It's all right. I'm enjoying it. So, do you hate government? Are you an anarchist?"

"Oh no, we all need the structure and some level of control. It's just the laziness of governing and driving change by fear that pisses me off. Trust me, good governance is essential for our civilization. We need our government, our legal system, and our public-safety organizations."

"Really? We need bloated government agencies, ridiculous national debt, frivolous lawsuits, and law-enforcement agencies that can't seem to stop shooting innocent people? We need all of that?"

"George, the reality is that some set of the population is always going to turn to sin, violence, and crime. But that's a good thing—or, I should say, a necessary thing."

"Wow. You have to help me understand why that's a good thing."

Shiloh leaned forward again. "Sins and immorality create ethics, social mores, customs, and beliefs. Revolutions create constitutions and governance. Wars create treaties, accords, and alliances. We would never have the belief systems, the democracy, or the peace we enjoy today without humankind's history of violence. George, the murders and crimes you read about every day help advance our laws and law enforcement. Even frivolous or dishonest lawsuits create sophistication and flexibility in our laws. It's taking too long, but it's necessary. Do you understand?"

"I understand what you're saying. You believe we're only going to work it out through trial and error. That our government and our legal system will only get there by evolution."

"Exactly, you get it!"

George crossed his arms. "I said I understand what you're saying. I'm not sure I completely agree with you. It seems like we should be able to think it through and design the right structures without all the trial and error."

Shiloh was shaking his head from side to side. "Nope, it's not going to happen. Life and people are too complex. We have to go through the growing pains; we have to go through the journey."

"I hear you. I'll have to think about that." George glanced at his watch.

"Let me give you some more to think about. You believe that we set our own destiny, right? You believe the politicians, scientists, religious leaders, and business leaders make the difference in our future. Actually, a growing number of scientists and thinkers believe that our destiny isn't controlled by individual conscious thoughts and decisions. Instead there's *evolutionary epistemology*. This phrase means that human knowledge itself evolves by natural selection. It means that all of our accomplishments and progress come not from great thinkers or scientists, but rather through natural selection."

George tried to process this. "But it's still the individuals who are discovering the new idea or inventing something new, right?"

"For some time people have been analyzing the concept of multiple discovery or simultaneous invention, where multiple individuals or groups of individuals independently made simultaneous or near-simultaneous discoveries. The polio vaccine, calculus, the telephone, the discovery of oxygen, jet engines, powered flight, and the lightbulb are all well-documented multiple discoveries." Shiloh took a breath.

George wondered if there was some point on the autism spectrum that allowed for a savant with Shiloh's level of assertiveness. This guy recited facts like some sort of computer.

"Some sociologist named Merton has made a case that multiple discoveries represent the common pattern in science. The thinking is that discoveries and advancement happen not due to original thought, but because humankind as a collective is ready for that idea. It's simply a series of inevitable steps in an evolutionary process," explained Shiloh.

"So, in the big picture, our future is predetermined. We have no control over it. Is that what you believe?" asked George.

"No, individually we have free will. For instance, we have the ability to destroy our entire planet. But if we avoid that, we will most assuredly grow and progress. Let me give you one more example. If you study the structures and processes of modern government, religions, and legal systems, you will discover that no one person designed them. They clearly evolved over time, and there's good evidence that they evolved using a form of natural selection. Humans will become less violent and more cooperative over time. It's an outcome in the process. But it may take hundreds or even thousands of years. More mistakes have to happen to drive the selection. But as long as we don't destroy ourselves, we will get there. In the end, only one thing matters: love. If we love each other, the universe will take care of everything else."

"Ah, there's the tie-in to love. Very interesting, Shiloh," admitted George.

"George, I'm wondering if you would do me a favor."

George's emotional walls immediately went up. *Here it comes. I can't believe I let this guy pull me in. He's about to sell me something, probably a timeshare or some scam. What the hell was I thinking, talking to this guy?*

"I have a small side business—more of a hobby, really," Shiloh said. "I'm beta testing smart watches for Apple and developing applications for them. I'm wondering if you would be willing to try one for me."

George gave Shiloh an uncomfortable smile. "I'm not sure I've got the time to get involved with something like that."

Shiloh smiled back. "No strings attached, I promise. Apple sent me ten of them, and I need some people to try out the application I'm working on. The watch would be yours to keep. All I ask is that you learn to use watch and test my application when it's ready."

George's mind raced. *This has to be a scam.* "I really don't think I'm interested."

Shiloh pulled a small, white cardboard box out of his pocket. He opened it, revealing a sleek, black-faced Apple Watch with a leather strap. "Please, you would be doing me a big favor. You're a busy guy; I saw you have an iPhone. You're exactly the type of person I need for beta testing."

George couldn't take his eyes off the watch. He had always been a gadget guy, and he was intrigued by Apple's new watch. The possibility of having one roughly nine months before anyone else was nearly impossible to pass up. He managed one more protest. "I don't know."

Shiloh took the watch out of the box and handed it to George. "Just try it for a while. If you don't like it, give it back to me the next time you see me."

George examined the watch and looked at Shiloh. "Are you sure?"

"You'd be doing me a favor. Just use it for a while, and I'll let you know when my beta application is ready," Shiloh said, looking out the window. "Oh, wow, that time flew by. This is my stop coming up, and I've got to run." He handed the box to George and put on his headphones.

As George tried to sort through the questions that were stacking up in his mind, he heard himself ask, "What are you listening to?"

"Ah, let's see . . . oh, it's Tears for Fears, 'Everybody Wants to Rule the World.'" As the train slowed and then stopped, Shiloh turned and asked, "George, what's the only thing that can conquer fear and hate?"

Feeling silly and confused, George smiled and said, "Uh, I don't know, education?"

"Love, George, the answer is love."

Shiloh stood up, and his jacket gaped open over a T-shirt reading, *Screw "lab safety," I want superpowers.*

George was flustered and starting to panic. "Wait, how do I reach you?"

Shiloh must have turned up the volume, for he never turned back. He walked off the train in the crush of other passengers. All George could do was pay attention to the station: Clybourn. He looked at the Apple Watch; it said the time was 7:09 a.m.

CHAPTER 5

What a Wonderful World

"So I go to this work happy hour the other day. We're having a good time, and I've had a few drinks. I go up to the bar and order another round, and sitting there is this drop-dead gorgeous blonde. She gives me this look. You know, that 'I want to make breakfast for you' look?" said Cade, leaning back in the booth.

George laughed. "No, Cade, I don't know that look. I wish I knew that look."

Cade was a neighbor and George's best friend; the guy George would think of first whenever he got sports tickets or had the rare window to go golfing. Cade also worked downtown, at a financial institution, and he and George tried to have lunch together at least once a month. They both enjoyed escaping from work for a bit, getting caught up on sports and each other's kids, and flirting with the waitresses.

"Well, anyways, I smile, grab the drinks, and bring them back over to my buddies. But every now and then I glance back over to her. She's still staring at me. And now it's the bacon, eggs, toast, and coffee stare. I'm starting to wonder if she thinks I'm someone else. Or maybe I've got something in my teeth."

Cade took a drink of his iced tea and continued, "So next thing I know, she's coming over to me. And when she stood up, oh man, she had a body that wouldn't quit—legs that go all the way down to the floor. She walks right over to me and starts talking. We hit it off right away. Next thing I know, we're talking about music and life and everything. Then it starts to get weird. She asks me how many kids I want. So I can't help myself, I tell her I'm married and that I have two kids. I actually show her my wedding ring."

Cade held out his hand, showing George his wedding ring.

"So, after I show her my ring, she grabs my hands, interlocking our fingers, and leans in and kisses me. Now this is no peck on the cheek. This is a full-on, open-mouth, hint-of-tongue kiss."

George had been enjoying the story, but now he was beginning to get nervous for Cade. Cade loved to flirt, but as far as George knew, he had always been faithful to his wife, Lynn.

"Now I'm really in trouble. I've had way too many drinks, and this beautiful girl is just staring into my eyes. Then I think of Lynn and the kids, so I tell her I can't do this. George, she doesn't care. She asks me to dance with her. She hugs me and starts to sway. I mean, there isn't even any music. So now I'm freaking out. I'm trying to pull away from her arms, but she won't let go. I'm pushing her and backing away, but she's got a vise grip on me. So she slips and goes down to the floor, but she's still holding on to me. She's got my leg and she's pulling it. She's pulling it hard, just like I'm pulling yours."

It took George a couple of seconds to realize that the whole story had been a joke. Slowly a smile came to his face.

"Oh man, I got you good, George. The look on your face was epic."

"All right, maybe you got me a little."

Cade made his finger into a hook and pulled his cheek with it. "Hook, line, and sinker. Hook, line, and sinker."

"Okay, okay, you got me good. I should have known a beautiful blonde would never fall for you," countered George.

George thought about telling Cade about his strange encounters on the train with Shiloh and the new Apple Watch, but he couldn't come up with a way to discuss him that didn't sound weird.

"Cade, do you ever feel trapped in your life?" asked George instead.

Cade paused and smiled. "What do you mean?"

"I mean . . . I feel like I'm just headed down a path I can't change. It didn't happen all at once. It crept up on me. First you get a house, then the kids come along, and suddenly I've got major responsibilities. And one day I wake up and my life is half over. I mean, my life hasn't been horrible, but I feel like I'm just along for the ride."

"Dude, if you want a couch session, we're going to have to talk about my fees."

"I'm sorry, Cade, I don't mean to get all heavy on you during lunch."

"No, it's okay. Seriously, it can be a grind some days. You need to make some more time for yourself. You should get out golfing more; it seems like you hardly ever go anymore. You and I should get out a few times before the summer is over. Hey, we also need to check out that new brew pub in Crystal Lake."

"Yeah, you're right, Cade. It's just tough, with work and the kids' activities and everything. I just keep telling myself to take it one step at a time."

"Sometimes one step at a time will get you up the mountain. Other times it might just get you further down the wrong path." Cade's face lit up. "Hey, that's pretty damn deep. I'm going to have to charge you for that."

The rest of the afternoon went by quickly. George spent some time figuring out the Apple Watch. He cranked out a couple of assignments, conducted a few meetings, and next thing he knew, it was 4:30 p.m. He hustled through a few final items so he could leave early and make it to OTC by 4:57 p.m. He had noticed that the 5:06 p.m. express departure from Clybourn Station arrived in Cary at 5:58 p.m. This train, he surmised, was the most likely train for Shiloh's return trip.

George easily made the 4:57 p.m. train, found an empty seat, and spread out to discourage anyone from claiming the rest of it. As the train pulled away, George found himself hoping that he had picked the right train and the right car.

As the train pulled into Clybourn Station, George again found himself thinking about Shiloh. *Is he for real, or is this going to turn out to be some elaborate scam?* As passengers filed onto the train he spotted Shiloh through the window lined up for the same car. *The good news is he's as predictable as I am.* Shiloh had his headphones on and was messing with an iPhone or iPod or something as he walked down the train car. When he looked up, George saw that Shiloh was wearing black-framed glasses with plastic shields on the sides.

George had to yell "hey" and wave his hand to get Shiloh's attention. He smiled, sat down, and pulled off his headphones.

"Hi, George."

"Shiloh, hello. I didn't know you wore glasses?"

Shiloh snatched the glasses off his face. "Oh, I forgot I was wearing them. They're my lab safety glasses." He glanced around the train, looking embarrassed.

"I was hoping to run into you. I didn't get to thank you for the Apple Watch."

"Yeah, no problem! Have you started using it?"

George showed his wrist. "Well, I can tell the time. I'm still figuring everything else out. What are you listening to?"

"Right now I'm listening to Joey Ramone singing 'What a Wonderful World.' It's a tremendous cover."

"Is rock and roll your favorite music?"

Shiloh's eyes widened. "I love all types of music: classical, country, contemporary—but yes, no doubt, rock and roll is my favorite."

"This is great, Shiloh. Today I get to ask the questions! Why is rock and roll your favorite kind of music?" George asked with a smile.

Shiloh seemed almost giddy, shifting around in his chair. "First of all, it's the perfect representation of life."

Perfect representation of life? "I'm not sure I understand what you mean."

Shiloh seemed ready to burst out of his skin and began to talk fast. "Okay, so life succeeds when it finds the right balance between order and chaos. Plants, animals, and even humans thrive on a thin line between structure and variety. The more diversity there is in life, the better its chance for success. Remember our discussion the other day about love? You said life needs some variety to evolve, but also needs enough structure to thrive. Well, you're right, if a species is too perfect—if it faces no challenges—it will devour its resources, say, its food supply, and it will perish. But if there is a balance, another predator species or some sort of system that keeps it on the edge between success and failure, it will not only survive but also develop. It will improve. It's not intuitive, but too much order is as destructive to life as chaos. Too much order doesn't allow for adaptation. It doesn't allow life to grow, to change, and to succeed. Do you understand, George?"

"I think I get it, but I might have to think about that a little. But, um, I thought we were talking about rock and roll?"

"Yes, yes, YES. People love music, and they particularly love rock and roll because it walks that line between order and chaos. They love music because it represents our need to find that balance. Have you ever listened to a two-year-old bang away at the piano? It's annoying. It's way too much chaos, no structure and no rhythm. On the flip side, have you ever practiced scales, George? It's dreadful. It's tedious and soul crushing. For me even classical music has too much structure. Despite its wonderful complexities and varieties of instruments and sounds, I believe it's often still too ordered. Only the best—maybe Mozart and Beethoven and a few others—are able to still surprise within that structure, inside those complexities. But rock and roll, it finds that balance with such simplicity, three or four instruments, along with a voice or two. Its very name conjures images of order and chaos. Rock is the structure, and roll is variety. Despite everything we do to create order, laws, norms, and morals, down deep we know—we know we need variety and chaos as well. And man, do rock stars give it to us. Kurt Cobain found that edge. And if Jimi Hendrix playing guitar isn't the perfect example of walking an almost impossible line between order and chaos, then I don't what is. Think of the Beatles or the Stones: great rhythm, harmonies, and order in their songs, but oh, what perfect surprises! A change in direction, a twist of a phrase, an unexpected transition. The music is masterful, pure beauty. We recognize that balance, that blend, and we admire it—we crave it. It's the sound of life's struggle to succeed." Shiloh finally took a breath, staring at George as if to say, *Is this as earth-shatteringly important to you as it is to me?*

"Wow, Shiloh, that is a cool take on music and life. I'm not sure I know what to say. I'm kind of blown away."

"Yeah, I've thought about this a lot, and it kind of gets me excited," Shiloh replied. "Hey, George, thanks for listening to me. Not everybody does. Few people get me."

"I have to be honest, Shiloh: I underestimated you. That first day, I was hoping you'd pass me by, but I'm glad we met. I've enjoyed our conversations. People don't talk enough about things that matter."

"Exactly! Like love, fear, and rock and roll," Shiloh said. "Hey, I did kind of finish my first beta release of that Apple Watch app. You want to give it a try for me?"

"Um, sure, I'm happy to test it for you. What does it do?"

"It's a time-adjustment application."

George thought, *according to the instructions, the Apple Watch already does that pretty well*, but decided not say anything. "Okay, thanks! Is it on the Apple Store?"

"No, it's in beta, remember?" Shiloh pulled out a business card and wrote a URL across the back. "Just go to that URL on your iPhone and it will download first to your iPhone and then to your Apple Watch. Let me know how it works out. Oh, here's my stop," he said.

"Okay, thanks. Do you ride the same trains every day?" asked George as the train pulled to a stop.

"Most days, but thirty-three trains run on this line; that's why I gave you my cell number."

Shiloh pointed to the business card, smiled, and left the train. George looked at the business card, it said:

Shiloh Adams
Physics Teacher
Cell: 312-555-8463
Twitter: @ShilohAdams42

There was no school name or address. He flipped it over, read the URL, and then put it in his pocket. *What a strange dude.* Not long after, he surprised himself with another thought: *I sure hope I run into him tomorrow morning.*

CHAPTER 6

Borrowed Time

June 4, 2014

On Wednesday, Shiloh was not on the morning train. George wondered if he might have taken another train, or if he was in a different car. It was pretty long odds that he had run into Shiloh three times already. With the number of trains and cars, he might never run into Shiloh again. At least he had his cell number. He thought about calling but he didn't want to appear too interested.

George struggled to stay focused throughout the morning. He tried to concentrate on his work, but his mind kept drifting back to Shiloh, their discussions, and this Apple Watch app.

"Carl, you know more about technology than me. Do you know anything about the Apple Watch?"

"Uh, a little, I read an article on it in *Wired* magazine."

"Does it handle time-zone functionality out of the box? It has to, right? It's a damn watch."

"Oh, yeah, it's going to be awesome for that kind of stuff. That's one thing Apple really focused on. It uses GPS to know where it is and adjusts time zones automatically. You never have to set it because it's always using the servers to keep perfect time and to handle things like daylight saving time."

"Any idea what a 'time-adjustment' application would do?" George asked.

"Hmmm. Well the article said it has 'time-travel functionality.' Maybe it has something to do with that."

George scowled. "What?"

Carl laughed. "Well, it's not really time travel. I think it's a cool way of flipping back through your watch's history. You know, like your calendar, appointments, and things. Why do you ask?"

"Oh, I have a friend who's developing an application for it. I'm just wondering what the hell it does."

At lunch, against his own better judgment, George navigated to the URL on the back of Shiloh's card. George knew it was a bad idea to directly open a random URL on his iPhone. Despite the fact that he was potentially exposing his phone to malware or, worse, a virus, he had to know more about Shiloh's app. The web page took a moment but then popped up. It was a simple page with a link in the center to download the code that would eventually be transferred to his watch. Below that was a sample of the watch interface.

What the hell? There were no other instructions or links.

"Is it more of a date adjuster?" George wondered aloud and laughed.

Is he so slow that he doesn't believe Apple didn't handle dates well on their flagship watch? What could the application possibly be? Maybe he's just learning to code Apple Watch applications and he's experimenting with controlling some simple features. How do I tell him it's useless?

He put his phone down and walked over to the window. He had started navigating the Apple Watch interface to see how Apple handled time-zone changes when his watch began to vibrate. It told him that Elena was calling; he decided to call her back later and tapped Ignore. Just as he returned to the watch interface, another call from his wife popped up. A little frustrated, he tapped Ignore again. *Chill, I'll call you back in five minutes!*

A few seconds later, his watch vibrated again. This time a text scrolled across the Apple Watch: *911 PICK UP MY CALL Amanda in serious car accident, in intensive care!!!*

CHAPTER 7

Lightning Crashes

The next hour was unbearable. George left his office without saying a word to anyone and called Elena the moment he was out the door.

"George?"

"Elena, I got your text, I'm on the street looking for a taxi. How is she?"

"Oh God, George." He could hear her crying, and he had to fight back his own emotions.

"Elena, please, I'll be there soon. Please talk to me. Tell me what you know." He could hear her taking deep breaths as she tried to get herself under control.

"I don't know much. They said she's in serious condition. I don't know what that means, George. She's in intensive care, and they're evaluating her to see if she needs emergency surgery." Elena began to cry again.

My God, are we going to lose her? How did this happen?

"Stay with me, Elena. What else did they tell you?"

"She has a broken leg, a broken collarbone, a lacerated eye, and possibly other internal injuries. I don't think they know yet, George. What I heard was what the EMT driver told the nurse. I haven't been able to speak with the ER doctor yet."

"Is she going to be okay?"

"I don't know. No one is talking to me." George could hear the frustration in her voice.

Stupid question, George.

"Okay, I'm sorry. Do you know what happened?

"Sort of. A state trooper spoke to me. I'm not even sure— it's all happening so fast. He said something about distracted driving. Her friend Tami was driving."

Damn it. I bet Tami was texting. I warned Mandy about that.

"So Tami was distracted? Was she texting or something?"

"No, not Tami, it was the other driver. The other driver ran a stop sign and broadsided them. Amanda was in the passenger seat."

"Is Tami okay?" asked George.

"Yes, thank God, they said she only has minor injuries. I haven't seen her yet."

"Did they tell you anything else?"

"No. They want me to do the stupid paperwork. I can't even think, how am I supposed to do the stupid paperwork?"

"Okay, Elena, I just flagged a cab. I'll be there soon. Try to do the paperwork, but if you can't, I'll do it when I get there. If you hear anything, please call me right away."

"Okay, but if I get to go into intensive care I'm not supposed to use my cell phone. Get here soon, George."

"I will. I be there as fast as I can. I love you. Hang in there."

He felt shocked and lightheaded. He explained to the cab driver that his daughter had been in an accident and was at the hospital. George hoped it would get him there faster. The ride to Good Shepherd Hospital in Barrington seemed to take forever. He wanted to call Elena back, but she had already told him everything she knew. He would just upset her more.

After a few moments of silence in the cab, his mind began to wander. He thought of Amanda's birth. Elena had gone through fourteen hours of painful labor, mostly at home. When her contractions were finally close enough to go to the hospital, Amanda had come quickly. The delivery was pure chaos, and the doctor arrived just in time. When the doctor handed him his beautiful, crying baby girl, George experienced the most intense joy of his life. But it was short-lived, for as the nurse was cleaning up Amanda, she stopped breathing. The delivery room returned to chaos as the doctor, who had been stitching up Elena, rushed over to Amanda. A quick slap on the feet was all it took for the baby to begin breathing again. The doctor explained that Amanda had swallowed some fluids during the birth. The nurse told them they needed to get the baby to the prenatal intensive care and that she would return soon. George had gone from indescribable happiness to complete terror in just a few moments. He and Elena were left alone in the delivery room for the longest half hour in their lives, feeling terrified and helpless. When the nurse finally returned, she saw the look of fear on their faces and immediately apologized. She told them that their baby was just fine; she was under observation, and they were giving her oxygen, but the fluid would naturally drain over the next several hours. She was perfectly healthy, and they would be able to see her after the doctor returned and finished with Elena. George felt great relief, but he also remembered feeling a profound sense of responsibility. A new life was now in his hands, and she seemed so fragile.

When the cab finally pulled into the emergency room entrance, George took a deep breath.

Just be strong for them. All you can do is just help keep it together.

When George saw Elena in the waiting room, he ran to her and hugged her. They held on to each other and cried for a couple of minutes before they recovered some control. Other people in the waiting room stared at them, but George told himself to ignore it. He looked into Elena's eyes and asked, "How is she?"

"I don't know any more," replied Elena. "The doctor is supposed to be out any minute. It's been too long, George; something is wrong."

"Elena, she's going to be fine," he replied, trying to convince himself as much as his wife. "This is a great hospital. Did they say why she might need surgery?"

"They said they were worried about internal bleeding. And I'm worried about her eye. Oh God, why was I fighting with her?"

"She knows you love her. Did you see her yet?"

"No, she's been in intensive care since I got here. I got a call from the state police and came right over. An officer spoke with me briefly, and one of the nurses told me what I already told you. That's when I called you. No one has spoken to me since. All I've done is fill out the damn insurance paperwork! Why aren't they talking to us, George? I can't take this."

"You stay here; I'm going to go ask the station nurse. We'll get someone to talk to us. Hold on, Elena, I'll be right back."

But every nurse he saw was helping someone else. It was maddening; he wanted to interrupt and demand an update on Amanda. Finally, a man in light blue scrubs returned to the main desk, and George pounced. The man listened to George and asked him to hold on. He disappeared into the intensive care ward, and George waited as patiently as he could. After a few more minutes, the man returned with what George assumed was the doctor.

"Mr. Hartdegen?" she asked.

"Yes, I'm Mr. Hartdegen. Call me George," He said, extending a hand. He resisted the urge to blurt out, "How is she?"

She shook his hand. "I'm Doctor Beranger."

"My wife is back in the waiting room."

"Okay, let's go find her," said Dr. Beranger. When they reached Elena, she looked as pale as the ER curtains. George introduced the doctor, and they moved to an empty exam room.

"Your daughter was in a serious car crash. She has significant injuries, but she's absolutely going to live. She's sedated now and stable."

George and Elena looked at each other, not sure whether to be happy at the news or even more distraught that it had been a life-or-death situation.

"She has several broken ribs, a bruised spleen, a broken fibula, and a broken collarbone—all serious injuries, but they will all heal fine with time. Her internal bleeding is minimal, so there's no need for emergency surgery." Dr. Beranger paused for a moment, gathering herself, before she continued. "Now—and I'm sorry I have to tell you this—there is a high likelihood that Amanda is going to lose her left eye. It was severely damaged, and from my perspective it can't be saved. However, we do have a specialist on the way in. He should be here shortly, and we will have a definitive answer within an hour or two."

"Oh my God, not just her vision, but her whole eye?" gasped Elena. She buried her face in her hands and sobbed. George felt like he was on a rollercoaster.

"When can we see her? When can we talk with her?" asked George.

"Not until after the eye surgeon examines her and we finish with her eye," explained the doctor. "Do you have any other questions?"

Elena and George were both too stunned and upset to think of additional questions. The doctor agreed to meet with them again within an hour. She promised they would do all they could and left in a hurry.

"How do we tell her she lost her eye?" asked George. It was the wrong question again, and Elena buried her face in George's shoulder and cried. George put his arm around her but let her cry. He felt tired and numb, still trying to get his head around it all.

Somehow they composed themselves enough to check on Alex and update some immediate family members. Then it was back to the waiting game. George realized he was going from numb to angry.

I can't wait to find out who did this. Somebody is going to pay.

He wanted to contact the police, but that would have to wait. George looked at his watch; it was 2:54 p.m.

CHAPTER 8

Accidents Will Happen

As George turned onto another Chicago suburban street, he couldn't seem to get his bearings. He was lost.

Where am I? Whose car is this? I don't recognize any of these streets. No navigation? Who doesn't have GPS in their car these days? If I could just find a familiar street.

He accelerated, not knowing or caring about the speed limit. His iPhone rang, and he saw it had fallen to the floor of the passenger seat. He leaned down to pick it up, and as just as he wrapped his fingers around it, there was an explosion of sound and glass. He was thrown forward against the steering wheel and dashboard. Leaning over had put him at an awkward angle, and now he felt searing pain in his lower back. Warm liquid crept down the side of his face—his own blood. Confused and stunned, he sat up and wiped it from his face the best he could. The hood of the car had crumpled upward, so he could not see what he had hit. Smoke billowed out from under the hood. He tried to open the car door, but it seemed to be jammed. He pulled back the handle and drove his shoulder into the door. He felt sharp pain in his back, but the door snapped open.

He gingerly stepped out of the car. It was deathly quiet, and a thick haze surrounded the accident site, making it difficult to see. As he took in the scene, his confusion changed to unease, then panic. From the position of the cars, it appeared that he had run a stop sign and broadsided a passing car.

What the hell did I do?

He walked through the thick smoke toward the passenger door of the other car. The damage emerged through the mist; the entire passenger side of the car was pushed in at least a foot. The windows were gone—either down or completely blown out. The passenger appeared to be unconscious, head down on the console.

"Hello?"

It took too long to close the short distance to the other car. It still felt too quiet, and the mist continued to thicken. Long hair covered the passenger's face—it was a woman—and he couldn't tell if she was injured. He put his hand on her shoulder, and she didn't respond. Using both hands, he eased her back into the seat and laid her head against the headrest. He gently pushed her hair aside and stared into the bloodied face of his daughter.

Mercifully, the Apple Watch woke him from his nightmare. He'd been trying to scream, but nothing was coming out. He was sweating and cold; his hands went immediately to his face, and he checked them, half expecting to see blood. He couldn't shake the feeling of panic and terror until he sat up, slid over, and put his feet on the floor. He shut off the alarm and tried to clear his head. It was shaping up to be a wonderful Monday.

"Hello, Hartdegen residence."

"George, it's Carl from work. Is this an okay time?"

"Yeah, actually it's perfect. A break in the action."

"I got your e-mail; glad to hear you're back tomorrow. How is she?"

"It's been rough, Carl. The eye specialist was able to save her eye, but not her vision. I guess we're over the worst of it, though."

"Man, that has to have been the longest two weeks ever for her and for you."

"It's crazy—it's been both fast and slow. Watching her go through this, some of the days have dragged on forever."

"I'll bet. So she doesn't need an artificial eye?"

"No, her eye will look normal, but she'll never see out of it again. The retina was severed and couldn't be repaired. And her concussion was so bad that they basically kept her sedated the first couple of days. They wouldn't even let us talk to her for more than a half hour at a time. They only let her start watching television a few days ago."

"Jesus," Carl said.

"Yeah, apparently the brain heals better if it has complete rest. She literally slept for a week. I mean, she would come to now and then, but they had her on so much medication. . . . It wasn't until they started to dial back the pain killers that she woke up."

"Has she been in a lot of pain?"

You have no idea, he thought. *I bet even she won't remember how much pain she was in. But I will.* But he said only, "Yeah, she has. Even with the painkillers. It's so hard to see your kid in pain. I mean, serious pain. Luckily, she doesn't remember the accident at all. I bet she doesn't even remember her first couple of days in the hospital."

"That must have been hard."

George shook his head. "You know, the worst part for me was being there when the doctor told her she'd lost her vision in one eye. I could tell she was so scared. I've never felt more helpless. They laid it all on her. All her injuries, her eye, the painful rehab she gets to go through. The doctor felt it was better to get it all on the table so she can start the healing process. I'm not so sure that was the best way to handle it."

"How much have you been at the hospital?"

"Either Elena or I has been here all the time. One of us sleeps in her room every night. They tried to get us to go home and get a good night of sleep, but Elena wanted one of us to be there whenever she woke up. I guess we both wanted that."

"You guys must be exhausted. Did you find out any more about the other driver?"

"Yeah, I've spend a lot of time talking with the state police. They arrested the other driver. Turns out it was a seventy-three-year-old lady. Apparently, she had just purchased her first cell phone and was trying to use the navigation feature when it slid from the passenger seat to the floor. When she reached over to grab the phone, she ran the stop sign and struck Amanda's friend's car. They charged her with reckless driving. She probably going to lose her license and maybe even serve some jail time. She's also in the hospital, recovering from her own injuries, which are less severe than Amanda's despite her age. They told me she's a sweet old lady who's horrified about the accident and Amanda's injuries. I guess they're treating her for depression and having a hard time getting her to eat."

"Well, at least you know who did it. I mean, at least it wasn't a hit and run."

"I guess. Actually, Carl, it pisses me off. I so badly wanted to be mad at someone. But how did you get mad at some depressed little old lady who made one mistake. Why couldn't it be some arrogant businessman? At this point, I'm more pissed at God, or the universe or something. She's already been through so much pain, and the doctors are telling us the worst is yet to come with her rehabilitation. I just don't know what kind of impact this is going to have on her long-term. Is it going to impact her self-confidence?"

"Hey, George, I'm sorry, I've got to get back at it here. Things have been piling up without you. Let me just say, I'll be very happy to have you back tomorrow."

Great, that means I'm walking into a disaster.

"Oh, all right. Sorry, didn't mean to go on like that. Yeah, I'll be in bright and early tomorrow. I can't wait to see the phone messages and e-mails waiting for me. But compared to what my daughter is facing, it's nothing."

"I hate to even ask this, because we need you, but are you sure you're ready to come back?"

"Yeah, I thought about family leave, but I can't stay away forever. I need this job and my insurance now more than ever. The medical bills are piling up. At least our company has good insurance."

"All right then, I'll see you tomorrow, George."

"See you tomorrow, Carl."

CHAPTER 9

The Question

June 16, 2014

When George was seated on the train, he set aside his reservations and just texted Shiloh what train and car he was on. He needed to talk to someone who would go below the surface. He barked, "It's taken," when some stranger tried to take the seat next to him. He was in no mood to mess around.

Shiloh arrived right on cue. Today's T-shirt read, *Solid, Liquid, Gas, they all matter.* George noticed what looked like crumbs in his beard, but he decided not to say anything. Shiloh took his headphones off as he sat down, staring at George the whole time.

"Hi, George. I got your text. I haven't seen you for a while. Did you try my app?"

"No, Shiloh. My daughter, Amanda, was in a car accident," George said, his voice cracking.

"Oh no! Is she okay?"

Is she okay? Would I text you, would I be telling you about it if she was okay?

"No, she's definitely not okay. Another car broadsided her car, and she was in the passenger seat. She had multiple broken bones, some internal injuries, and a serious concussion, and she lost her vision in her left eye. And Shiloh, I'm so damned pissed off. I just don't know why the hell this happened. She's a good kid. She shouldn't have to go through this. The last two weeks have been hell, and I think the next two months might be just as bad." George glared straight ahead, struggling to keep control of his emotions.

"It sounds like she's lucky to be alive."

Lucky? Unbelievable. God, I need more coffee. "Oh, yeah, she's goddamn lucky, Shiloh. She's lucky to spend the next month in the hospital. She's lucky to go through three months of physical therapy. She's lucky to never see out of her left eye again. And who knows what kind of good fortune that will bring her? I don't even know what she can and can't do, I don't know what kind of limitations she now has. Tell me again how lucky she is?" He finally looked over at Shiloh.

"I didn't mean it that way. But I'm not sure you understand how rare and fragile life is."

"Okay, Shiloh, why don't you tell me how rare and precious life is?" He wanted to be angry with someone, and Shiloh was stepping up to the plate.

Shiloh missed the sarcasm. "Have you heard of the Rare Earth hypothesis? It's from a book by two professors at the University of Washington. It's a good book, George; you should read it. And what you learn is that the conditions for life are so precise that it's almost impossible. You need the right kind of galaxy, in the right location, with the right orbit in that galaxy. An area that's not too close to the center of the galaxy, because the center of a galaxy has too many stars and therefore too much radiation or gravitational perturbation. And not too far, because if the star and its surroundings are not complex enough, the elements for life don't exist. You need a galactic location just on the edge of order and chaos." Shiloh paused to take a breath.

George leaned back in his seat and rubbed the back of his neck. *This isn't the conversation I wanted. But I asked for this. How do I cut off someone who thinks he knows the answer to "Why me?"*

"And you need the right star: not too big, not too little. And it has to be in the right time of its lifespan. Now, once you get the right star, then you need the right planet. Well, the right arrangement of planets. The ones that have life need to be the right size and the right location and orbit from their sun. That planet has to be largely rocky and needs to have an abundance of water. It's also likely that the conditions for life greatly benefit from having a large moon and a molten core. The moon helps keep the orbital tilt stable, and the molten core provides a magnetic field that protects life from harmful radiation. Are you following me?"

"Shiloh, has anyone told you that you're a walking Internet search?" Shiloh's goofiness and excitement were dissipating George's anger.

"So maybe life isn't as probable as Carl Sagan thought it is. But even after life is created, there are a million ways for it to end. Let's see, there are super volcanoes, asteroid impacts, geomagnetic reversal, global pandemics, nuclear war, rogue artificial intelligence, runaway biotechnology, and oh, of course, honeybee extinction."

"Yes, of course, honeybees, but you forgot about zombie apocalypse," offered George.

"Oh yeah, and zombie apocalypse," said Shiloh. Then he paused and said, "That's probably already covered by global pandemic." Once again he had missed the sarcasm.

George gave up on being angry with Shiloh. It was like fighting with an encyclopedia.

"Okay, I get it. Life is rare, and life is precious. I agree with that. You make a great case. But I don't think it's fair, Shiloh. I don't think life is fair."

"Personally, I think we're lucky we have *one* day. And for those of us that have a lifetime, it's like we hit the cosmic lotto. George, she may have lost an eye, but she has *life*. She can live her life, she can explore, she can create, and she can love. She can have a family. Once she overcomes this, life will be so much more precious for her. George, I think she's going to have a *great* life."

George closed his eyes for a minute. He tried to think about Amanda in five or ten years. *I don't want to admit it, but he's right. She'll heal; it's just a matter of time. She'll move on, and God willing, she'll be happy. It just takes time.*

"George, I know you're focused on your daughter right now, but how are you doing?"

"Oh, I don't know. Taking things one day at a time."

"Have you ever been on a river cruise?" asked Shiloh.

"A river cruise?"

"I took a river cruise in Europe once. It was nice to take in the scenery, and it was comfortable because you always knew were you were going. But after a while, I realized it was too predictable. I saw some places I wanted to explore, but I couldn't. I got bored. There were no diversions, no delays, and no changes in the itinerary. So I went back a few years later and went backpacking. I had a plan, but it completely changed. I ended up in a small French village, drank some fantastic wine, met some amazing people, and had three of the best days in my life." Shiloh paused and looked at George. "Do you understand?"

George sucked in air. "It's not that simple, Shiloh. I need my job more than ever now. My daughter's in the hospital. My family needs stability."

"I'm not just talking about your job. You need to let go of your fears. Fear should be an advisor whose counsel is weighed carefully, not a leader whose commands are followed blindly."

"Who said that?" asked George.

"I did. I just made it up. It's time to get off the river, George."

"It's easy for you to say that, Shiloh. Do you even have any responsibilities?"

"This isn't about me. I'm just asking you to think about it."

"I'll think about it."

"Awesome," said Shiloh as he got up to exit the train. "Hey, you promised you would test my application."

"I will." George watched him adjust his headphones and walk away.

Christ almighty! Supervolcanos and bee extinction, and I'm the one with fears? My daughter's in the hospital, I've got a right to be worried. What the hell am I doing getting advice from this guy?

CHAPTER 10

Working Man

George's first half hour in the office was filled with coworkers stopping by to inquire about his daughter. The office had sent flowers and a nice card to the hospital the prior week. George was a little surprised at the flood of heartfelt words. Everyone seemed to find a way to ask about Amanda, offer hopes for a quick recovery, or even ask George how he was doing. George was happy to put off his inevitable mountain of voice mails, e-mails, and to-do's.

George's watch notified him that he had a meeting with his manager at 9:00 a.m., so he left his desk. After accepting well wishes from the administrative assistant, George entered the corner office. His manager stood and came around his desk to shake George's hand.

"George, great to see you. We missed you around here. How's Amanda?" he asked.

"It's a slow process. She's stable and getting a little stronger every day. But she has a long road ahead of her, in terms of both healing and physical therapy." He was about to go into more details, but his boss was staring at him. George knew that stare. It was the I'm-very-interested stare that his boss used when he wanted to get on with his own agenda. So George paused.

"Great, great, George, I'm glad she's on the mend. That's excellent," he said, settling back into his chair. "It's great news, because we need you back at it. There's a big meeting this Thursday, and I need you to take point on it."

George struggled to maintain the smile on his face. *I hate "big meetings." It's such an ugly dance. The politics of who gets invited, the PowerPoint decks that accentuate the positives and hide the negatives, the "pre-meetings" to ensure the right support is in place. It's all a game. Why can't we just talk through the issues like real humans?*

George looked over at his boss, wondering if his distaste was showing.

You can't let me ease back into work? Just for a couple of days? My daughter's still going to need attention and the medical paperwork is piling up.

"I'm your man, sir," he heard himself say.

George's boss stood up. "Wonderful to have you back, George. Let me know if you need anything. And tell that lovely wife of yours that I send my best wishes."

George returned to his desk and began the gargantuan battle with two weeks of e-mails and voice mails. He made good progress up until lunch and then grabbed a sandwich, which he wolfed down at his desk before getting to work on his big meeting. He made a call to Carl to get more background. When he hit a wall, he did a few hundred more e-mails and then decided to take off an hour or so early. He was surprised at how productive he'd been; despite everything he was dealing with. With Monday down, the rest of the week might be a little easier. He realized it had been a good way to get away from the accident's aftermath and his worries about his daughter.

Can you say ironic?

The downside of leaving early was that he wouldn't run into Shiloh on the train home. He made his way to the station and onto the platform. George always felt a little nervous waiting there, with nothing between him and the oncoming train but a thin yellow line.

What was that guy's name? Pagino or Pagano or something. He was the executive director of the whole Metra system. Got himself in deep trouble—unauthorized bonus or improper vacation pay, something like that. Decided his best way out was to step in front of one of his own Metra trains. How bad does it have to get for a guy to decide to end it like that?

George felt the wind and heat of the train's rushing arrival before his brain processed the sight of it. He boarded, found a seat, and fell deep in thought again.

CHAPTER 11

Take Me to the River

The boy strapped on his backpack and called, "See ya, Mom."

"Be careful and be home by dinnertime," she replied. By the time she finished her sentence, the front screen door had slammed.

The boy was off like a rocket, cutting through backyards on the shortest route to Bobby's house. Neither his skinned knees nor his collection of mosquito bites slowed him a bit. He was wearing cutoff jean shorts, a red tank top, the sandals that he could get wet. The boy was tan and his hair was almost blond from playing outside nearly every day of the summer. Today was the day they'd been planning forever—or at least a week. They were setting out on their epic trip. They had played near Hickory Creek, behind Bobby's house, all summer long, and one day Bobby had come up with the idea to raft down the three or four miles to the St. Joseph River. There they would paddle across the river to a restaurant where they would call

Bobby's mom, who would come pick them up. They had talked about it for a couple of days before getting up the nerve to ask their mothers' permission. Bobby's mom had said yes right away, but it was only after the moms had spoken to each other that the boys got the go-ahead.

The boy arrived at his friend's house and knocked on the front door. "He's around back," yelled Bobby's mom from the kitchen. He ran around the house and found Bobby inflating the raft with a foot pump.

"Here it is, the SS *Bobby*."

The raft looked like a small inflatable dinghy, but it was really a cheaply made pool raft. It had two small plastic oars.

"She's a beauty."

"What did you bring?" asked Bobby.

The boys both got out their backpacks and compared supplies. They each had small pocketknives, a towel, and a lunch. Bobby also had a compass, his slingshot, a matchbook, and a couple of firecrackers.

"Wow, where did you get the firecrackers?"

"My brother's room. If he finds out, he'll kill me." Bobby repacked his backpack. "You ready? We need to get going!"

The boys strapped on their backpacks and then hoisted the raft over their heads for the trek down the to the creek. They could walk that path with their eyes closed—they knew every twist and turn, every rock and root. They made quick time, their excitement building with every step. When they arrived at the creek, the set down the raft and stood over the water.

"Holy cow!" said Bobby.

There had been a daddy of a thunderstorm the night before, and it had continued to rain hard all night. The creek was swollen and moving fast; it did not at all resemble the creek they had played around the rest of the summer. The boys looked at each other, a little wide-eyed.

"You wanna back out?" asked Bobby in a hushed voice.

"N—no. But it's okay if you want to back out."

"I'm not afraid. It's just a creek," Bobby replied.

It was a delicate process to step onto the raft, since it wanted to take off downstream as soon as it touched the water. But soon they were floating down the creek, oars in hand. They had only gotten their feet wet in the surprisingly cold water, and the bottom of the raft was relatively dry. The current spun the raft, and the boys paddled furiously to keep it pointed downstream and facing the right way. It took a while for them to get the hang of it, but eventually they got into a rhythm.

It was still early, and despite the exertion of carrying the raft down the creek, both boys shivered from the cold. But as they relaxed, they both began to enjoy the trip.

"I'm glad it rained! This is fun, and we're going to make record time," Bobby said.

"Woo-hoo!" said the other boy.

As they came around a bend in the creek, they struggled to keep the raft straight against the swirling current.

"Whoa," Bobby said.

They both looked ahead to a large tree that had been struck down by lightning. The trunk angled down into the creek from a twisted stump on the left bank. The water rushed violently over the partially submerged tree.

"I think we can fit under the log, over there."

Both boys paddled toward the opening. The fast-moving water moved them quickly along but pulled them away from the opening.

"It's no good, head for the other side!" yelled Bobby. Despite their frantic paddling, the current pushed them right into the log. The SS *Bobby* crumpled, and both boys fell out. The raft was pushed under the log and popped out the other side, along with Bobby. The current trapped the other boy against the log, his face just inches below the surface. He struggled to push himself up the trunk, but the current kept him pinned squarely in place.

Bobby had reached the side of the creek and was trudging slowly through the knee-deep rapids toward the fallen tree.

"George, George," he called. "Are you okay!?"

George struggled against the tree and the current; it was maddening to have his face an inch or two from the surface, but not be able to take a breath. For a moment a ripple in the water exposed his face and he gasped, but took in half air and half water. Now he was coughing and panicking. Suddenly, he understood that he could die from this. He relaxed, almost ready to accept his fate. Just then a thought entered his head: *Push down.* He had been pulling up the whole time, trying to get his face up the inch or two out of the water. He pushed down instead and almost immediately slipped under the log. The current shot him downstream, and his head burst out of the water. He took a huge breath and got his feet under him. It was shallower, and George stood, his hands on his knees, coughing up water.

"Oh God, George, I thought you were a goner!" called Bobby from the side of the creek. "Are you okay?"

George was only able to give him a thumbs-up as he panted and spit out creek water. Then they retrieved the raft, the oars, and their backpacks, threw it all on the bank, and then laid down on their backs, gazing up at the perfect summer sky. After a moment George said, "I almost died."

"Yep, you almost bit it. You almost met the big guy. You were almost pushing up daisies." Bobby giggled.

"I'm alive. I'm alive! I'm ALIVE," George yelled.

"Oh crap," Bobby said. "Both the firecrackers and the matchbook are ruined!"

They sat on the bank for some time. George kept talking about his near-death experience, and Bobby kept making jokes about George's rotting corpse. The day warmed up quickly, and soon their clothes and supplies were nearly dry. The raft required a little good old-fashioned hot air, but other than that, it was surprisingly in good shape. Realizing that quitting would mean having to walk the raft upstream all the way to Bobby's house, they decided to carry on with the expedition. They also made a pact to never tell their parents about George's mishap. They were third graders, so they were smart enough to know that it would severely limit their unsupervised play at the creek.

They shoved off again, and to their relief the creek widened and the current slowed down. They were uneasy at first, but they calmed down as the rafting became easier. Bobby maintained a constant chatter about whatever popped into his head. Why Hershey's with almonds was the best candy bar ever, who was better—Cubs versus White Sox—and how he was going to raise Seeing Eye dogs for a living when he grew up. Eventually, faced with a combination of George's silence and the sheer beauty of the creek, Bobby slowed down and then stopped talking. For a while, they just floated in silence. Everything seemed bright and amazing to George. The scenery alternated between deep forests and wide-open meadows. He listened to the cicadas chirp and the birds sing. He watched water bugs dance on the water and saw a large spider web hanging over the creek, decorated with dewdrops. He smelled wildflowers on the wind as they floated past another meadow.

George had just laid back and closed his eyes for a moment when Bobby shouted something about a giant fish. George looked where Bobby was pointing but saw nothing. Bobby had a habit of embellishing stories, so George was skeptical about both the size of the fish and its very existence.

When they came around another bend in the creek, Bobby pointed and whispered, "Hey, George, look."

George looked up and saw the largest heron he had ever seen standing in the shallows. It looked at the raft and then turned its attention back to the water; a second later it stabbed its head into the water and came up with a small fish in its beak. It paused for a second, seeming to adjust the fish for a better grip, and then, in a movement both awkward and graceful, it spread its enormous wings and took off right toward Bobby. Bobby ducked, but the heron cleared him and the raft easily. George turned and watched it follow the path of the creek and disappear around the bend behind them.

Not long afterward, they heard turbulent water up ahead. They paddled furiously for the bank, neither wanting to repeat the events of the morning. Just as they reached the edge, a large entanglement of logs and branches appeared downstream. Bobby stepped out and pulled the raft to the bank. Then George stepped out, and together they dragged the raft fully up onto the shore. They walked along the bank toward the entanglement.

"Cool, it's an old beaver dam!"

One side of the creek was obstructed with large logs, and in the middle was a well-made, but clearly old and deteriorating, beaver lodge. On the other side, the water rushed and frothed over some barely submerged logs. As they inspected the dam and the lodge, George caught a flash of silver out of the corner of his eye. He didn't say anything, thinking it was just the sun glinting off the water. But as he watched the water flow over the logs, he caught another glimpse of a much larger flash of silver. His brain finally figured it out, and he yelled, "Bobby, fish! Great big fish!"

A moment later several fish leaped out of the water and cleared the submerged logs. They were big fish, and George and Bobby were shocked to see them in their little creek.

"They're salmon, and they're spawning," Bobby said.

"What's spawning?"

"I have no idea, but I just heard about it on the Mutual of Omaha's *Wild Kingdom*. And George, when the fish spawn, it attracts bears," Bobby announced in a serious voice.

"There are no bears in these woods. Do you think our moms would let us play in woods by ourselves if there were bears?" replied George.

Bobby and George settled in to watch the salmon jump the logs. They laughed and cheered when two jumped at the same time. They were astonished that the fish could leap completely out of the water while going upstream.

When they pulled out their lunches, they were surprised to find that they both had dry sandwiches, thanks to their moms and Dow's Minigrip plastic bags. "Baloney has never tasted so good!" George proclaimed. When they grew tired of watching the salmon, they carried their raft past the beaver dam and continued their journey.

The rest of the trip was pleasant but uneventful. The creek grew ever wider and deeper, the further downstream they went. A snapping turtle about the size of an extra-large pizza swam underneath their raft at one point. They were both thankful they were not dangling toes in the water. As Bobby had predicted, they made good time, and by early afternoon, they spotted the St. Joseph River ahead.

As they neared the mouth of the creek where it fed into the river, they were both nervous. The river seemed enormous. A little further downstream they could see four gigantic cement silos. The boys had watched the cement barges bring in their loads to deposit them in the silos. It was something almost every dad in town took their kids to watch at some point. George hoped they would not see a cement barge when they tried to cross the river.

"What happens if we miss the restaurant?" Bobby asked. The boys looked at each other nervously. But the creek didn't give them much time to think about it. The current picked up and dumped them into the river without time for a decision. Bobby and George paddled furiously toward the far shore of the river.

"I see the restaurant," yelled Bobby. "Keep going."

The river's current was slow. Still, both boys breathed sighs of relief when they dragged the raft up onto the river bank. They turned to each other, laughed, and exchanged their secret hand-shake—a relic of Bobby's secret-agent period. Later, after they called Bobby's mom on the payphone to be picked up, they stood on the bank and skipped rocks. George told Bobby that he was about the best friend a guy could ever have, and Bobby told George to go kiss a snake. They renewed their pact to never tell their parents about the incident at downed tree.

As Bobby's mom pulled up, George said, "This was the best day of my life."

"Yeah," Bobby replied. "And it was almost the *last* day of your life."

CHAPTER 12

People Get Ready

The passenger next to George stood up as the train stopped. George felt a moment of panic as he realized he had no idea which stop they were at. Luckily, they hadn't reached Crystal Lake yet, and George relaxed. The memories had come rushing in and felt so real that he almost believed he was there.

How long ago was that? Thirty-odd years—I haven't even thought about that in at least fifteen years. I wonder what happened to Bobby? Let's see, he married and had a kid; then Mom told me she heard he was divorced. I wonder if he's happy now.

They had been inseparable all through elementary school, but they'd drifted apart in middle school, when George became obsessed with baseball.

I wish I could enjoy every moment like I used to as a kid. When did I lose that? Is this the point that Amanda changes, when she realizes what real life is? With the loss of an eye and months of pain, she's going to be feeling anything but an appreciation of life. George looked around the train. *So many people and so few connections . . . .*

About half the people had ear buds in, and the other half were reading, sleeping, or just staring into space.

Not a single conversation . . . what a waste. He laughed under his breath. *George, you are some kind of hypocrite.*

He glanced at his watch. It was 4:17 p.m. He had enough time to give Shiloh's app a try, so he got out his iPhone, went to the link that Shiloh had provided, and tapped on the link for the download. The download took less than a minute—it was a surprisingly small, simple application. Then he navigated to the application on his iPhone that allowed him to download the app from his phone to his watch. The transfer took only about thirty seconds. George tapped on the watch to access additional applications and found the new icon. It was a simple hourglass that didn't even spin. He tapped on the icon, and a bare-bones interface appeared.

TIME ADJUSTOR

Adjustment Date:
06/16/2014
Adjustment Duration:
01

START

Adjustment Count:
01/10

George tapped on the Adjustment Date field, and it highlighted. He twisted the crown on the side of the watch. When he scrolled up, nothing happened. When he scrolled down, the date decreased a day at a time.

I guess you can only adjust backward.

He tried tapping the Adjustment Duration and the Adjustment Count, but neither seemed to be active. Finally, he changed the Adjustment Date back to today's date, 6/16/2014, and tapped Start, expecting the application to take him to another screen.

Nothing happened.

Well, almost nothing . . . .

The Adjustment Count changed to 2, and "working . . ." appeared below the start button.

George waited for a few minutes, but it appeared frozen. The application still claimed to be working. He tried swiping left and right, with no results. Eventually, he grew tired of waiting and exited the application. The rest of his watch's functionality seemed to be working normally.

It seems like the beta release is a complete failure. I can't quite decide if Shiloh is someone special or just a guy with a photographic memory who spends too much time surfing the Internet. He has kind of grown on me, though, and I'm not looking forward to telling him his app is useless. Do I like this guy, or do I just need someone to talk to this desperately?

I'm pitiful.

As the train slowed for George's stop, he resumed autopilot mode and prepared to leave the train. He was anxious to get home and catch up with Elena. It was his first day without seeing Amanda, and he wanted to hear about her progress.

CHAPTER 13

Monday, Monday

George's alarm woke him as normal. He felt groggy, almost as if he had a few too many drinks the night before. He groaned and slid out of bed. As George began his morning ritual, though, several things threw off his routine. Some of his toiletries were in different spots, and his toothpaste was a different brand than the one he had used the last few days.

Elena must be reorganizing and cleaning up. She's so damn retentive.

He shaved and showered as usual, but his unease grew when he found the clothes in his closet in a slightly different order.

Elena again. Except nothing's particularly clean or reorganized, just different. Okay, this is just plain weird.

He shook off the unease and focused on psyching himself up for his workday. Tuesday would be just as hard as Monday was, if not worse.

He arrived at the train station right on time, boarded, and found an empty seat. He got a paragraph or two into the front page of the paper . . . and stopped.

I've read this before. It's Monday's paper. They delivered yesterday's paper again—unbelievable.

He checked the watch; the welcome screen read *Monday, 6/16/2014.* Then it came to him—*Shiloh's app!* He looked at his iPhone and saw the same date.

Oh, great, now Shiloh has the date on my phone and my watch screwed up. How do I reset it? Ah, I'll fix it later. I really need to just close my eyes for a bit.

He leaned his head back and had nearly fallen asleep when the train stopped at a station. Someone sat down in the empty seat next to him. He opened his eyes, half expecting to see Shiloh, but it was a complete stranger. George closed his eyes again and promptly fell asleep.

George was trying to get off the train, but he couldn't get up out of his seat. He couldn't tell if he was belted in or if his body just wouldn't work, but no matter how he struggled, he couldn't get up. He felt a strange hand on his shoulder, and voice said, "Sir, sir—"

He awoke with a start. It was one of the conductors.

"Last stop, sir. You need to exit the train."

George stared at him, wild-eyed, and gathered enough wits to give him a nod and collect his belongings. He exited the train, feeling woozy, almost like he had taken some strong cough medicine. The walk to the office helped, and he stopped into a coffee shop for a second cup of coffee.

Today is a good day for a second cup.

He was finally feeling like he was getting his feet under him. As he waited in line, though, he read a sign that knocked him right back off balance: *Monday Trivia—Get 10 cents off your coffee!* The feeling of unease returned.

Is it really Monday? Did I get drunk last night? I don't remember drinking last night.

He clearly remembered yesterday's trip into the office, seeing his coworkers for the first time in two weeks, the e-mails and the meeting with his boss. He thought about asking the person in line behind him what day of the week it was, but he was afraid of what the answer might be. Impossible thoughts rolled around in the back of his mind. He chose to push them aside and ordered his coffee.

Don't think.

George cleared his mind as he walked to the office, sipping his coffee, but he felt numb and absent when he arrived. His temporary equilibrium was obliterated when he entered the office. He coworkers welcomed him back to the office and inquired about Amanda. The feeling of déjà vu was overwhelming, and George found it increasingly difficult to breathe. He made his way into a stall in the men's room. He was unable to ignore the thought that he was living the same day over again. He forced himself to simply focus on breathing until he regained some control.

What the hell is happening? Shiloh's Time Adjustor doesn't change the date on my phone and watch; it actually changes the day I'm living. No, bullshit. It has to be some sort of elaborate practical joke. Maybe I dreamed yesterday? No way. Am I hallucinating right now?

He felt queasy.

None of that is right. I'm living the day over again. Jesus.

Part of his mind was trying to move on to wondering, *What next?* But he was still struggling to deal with the impossibility of the situation. A thought popped into his head, breaking the stalemate.

Call Shiloh!

George pulled out his cell phone and found Shiloh on his contact list. He tapped the screen and waited for it to ring. He heard static and then the unmistakable tone of a disconnected line. Sure enough, a recorded voice came on.

"The number you have dialed is not in service. Please hang up and try your call again."

George did just that, but got the same message. He tried three more times in rapid succession before giving up on Shiloh.

Call Elena? How do I explain this to her? How do I even start?

George navigated to Shiloh's application on his Apple Watch. It looked the same as yesterday, still showing 6/16/2014 and "working . . ." He tried tapping, swiping, and using the crown button, but nothing worked.

Delete the application? Wait, that might be bad. Calm down. Just get back to your desk before someone notices. Slow down and give yourself time to think.

He left the stall, went to the sink, and splashed a little water on his face. It felt good. He walked back to his desk as quickly as possible while trying to appear normal. A few people welcomed him back, and he was able to get out "Thanks" without too much trouble.

Okay, just get through the next couple of hours. I have to be missing something. I just need some time.

He dialed in to his voice mails, but after listening to the first message three times and still not comprehending it, decided to switch to e-mails. They weren't much better. He found a few he could delete, but when he ran into any that required serious thought, he couldn't focus. His mind kept drifting back to the impossibility of his situation.

I am living the same day twice. Every time he heard the phase in his head it brought him a little dread, like the feeling you get when you are completely and hopelessly lost.

He checked his calendar and learned he had his meeting with his boss at 9:00 a.m. He didn't want to have a discussion with anyone in his current state, much less his manager.

One step at a time.

As he approached his manager's office, the sense of déjà vu hit him again like a punch. He said a quick hello to his manager's administrative assistant and then leaned into his office. His manager stood up from his desk and looked at George, expecting him to enter.

"George, great to see you! We missed you around here. How's Amanda?"

"It's a slow process. She's stable and getting a little stronger every day. But she has a long road ahead of her, in terms of both healing and physical therapy."

"Come on in, George, and close the door."

Just bail. Get out of here.

"Um, I need to tell you that I'm really not feeling well. I think I need to go home and fight this off. I don't want to come in and get you sick."

"All right, George." His boss looked disappointed. "You go home and get better. But we need you back at it soon. Get some sleep, George; you probably just haven't had enough sleep."

"That's probably it. I'm sure I'll be back in tomorrow." George felt relieved to be headed home.

"And tell that lovely wife of yours that I said hello." His manager sat down and began to tap away at his computer.

Probably trying to figure out who else gets the "big meeting."

George left as quickly as he could, stopping only to update Carl. He hailed a taxi and gave the driver his address. He was exhausted.

CHAPTER 14

Dazed and Confused

George tried to call Elena on the way home, but she didn't answer.

Maybe she's already at the hospital, visiting Amanda? I still don't know what to say to her, anyway. I want to sleep, but damn, this taxi smells odd. It's making me even queasier. I'll just text to tell her I don't feel well and I'm coming home.

When he arrived, Alex was in the kitchen, making himself breakfast.

"Hey, Dad, why are you home?"

"Ah, I'm not feeling well today, might be a touch of the flu. I'm going to lie down for a while."

"Okay, I'll stay away. Feel better, Dad."

George went up to his bedroom, changed out of his suit, and lay down in his bed. He thought about heading over to the hospital, but he was listless and didn't want to interact with anyone. After a few minutes he fell asleep.

George awoke to the sound of the front door opening. He was feeling better and less groggy. He could hear his wife downstairs. It sounded like she was putting away groceries and cleaning up the kitchen. George sighed; Alex must have left a mess.

After a while, Elena came up the stairs. "George, I got your text, are you sick?"

Should I tell her? How?

"Sort of. I just couldn't handle work today."

"You couldn't handle work? Did you quit, George? I know you're stressed at work, but we need this job right now, with Amanda's situation."

"No, I didn't quit, Elena. I just came home sick. I'm kind of dealing with something serious." *You would never believe how serious.*

Elena was in a bad mood. Things must not have been going well with Amanda at the hospital. "You're dealing with something serious, George? No, *Amanda* is dealing with something serious. This isn't the time for you to feel sorry about yourself at work. We need the medical insurance. We need the money."

"I know, Elena, but this is something different, something that's hard to explain."

"Jesus, George, this isn't the time for middle-aged crazy. We are all struggling here. All you've done for the last two weeks is visit Amanda. I'm the one keeping the family going here. I'm the one sorting through the bills, calling the health insurance company, fixing the dinners. George, you need to snap out of this. I need you to be strong for Amanda."

George gave up on the idea of trying to tell her what he was experiencing. "Okay, Elena, I'm sorry. You're right; this accident threw me for a loop. But honestly, I don't feel right today. I think I might be coming down with something."

"Fine, George, go back to sleep. But when you feel better, you need to start pitching in around here."

"Okay, Elena, I'm sure I'll feel better tomorrow."

"I hope so, because they are going to change the bandage on Amanda's right eye tomorrow. She might need our support."

Right eye?

"Wait, what's wrong with Amanda's right eye?"

"George, are you joking? She lost the vision in her right eye in the car accident. Are you really that sick, or are you that clueless?"

George tried to appear calm, but inside he was losing it. He was sure it was Amanda's left eye.

What the hell is going on?

"No, I just got confused there for a moment. Sorry."

"Go to bed, George. You're a mess," she said as she left the room.

If I tell anyone I'm living the same day twice, they'll think I'm crazy. So could I actually be crazy? Is this what it feels like to have delusions? How would I know? Maybe I have some sort of tumor or brain cancer. Seems more likely than the alternative. If nothing changes tomorrow, I'm telling Elena. If she tells me to meet a shrink, I will. I'll let it be someone else's problem.

Another wave of dizzy exhaustion hit him.

If this is real, then I've traveled back in time one day. Why does that make more sense to me than living the same day over? It's the same damn thing.

Thinking about it was making his head spin. He leaned back in the bed and quickly fell into a deep sleep.

George's watch alarm woke him at 5:15 a.m. He rolled over and tapped the screen.

Tuesday, 6/17/2014.

I slept all the way though to morning. It's Tuesday—at least I'm not living the same day over and over again. Maybe it's all been a dream. I already feel better; the dizziness and nausea are gone.

He checked Shiloh's app, which no longer flashed "working" under the start button. He walked into his bathroom.

Everything is back to normal. My toiletries and even my toothpaste brand are right. What the hell happened? Did I really relive the day? Shiloh has some explaining to do.

George found the business card, went downstairs to his home office, and furiously punched in Shiloh's number. He heard some static, but then it rang three or four times. In a faint voice that sounded far away, he heard, "Hello?"

"Shiloh, what the hell is going on? How is this possible? Is this some kind of magic trick, some sort of illusion?" George was nearly yelling.

"Who is this?" asked Shiloh.

"It's George, the guy from the Metra, the guy you gave the Apple Watch, the guy who thinks he might be going insane."

"Oh, hi, George, cool, so the app worked?" asked Shiloh. His connection seemed to clear up.

"*Yes*, Shiloh, it fucking worked. I just did my damn Monday twice in a row! I just TIME TRAVELED, I just did some impossible thing and I'm losing my mind here, Shiloh. How is this possible? WHAT IS GOING ON?" He sucked down a few deep breaths, trying to get control.

"Settle down, George, you're stressing me out. I can't tell you how it works."

"I'm freaking out here. You have to tell me—what's going on? Why can't you tell me?"

"You wouldn't understand. It would take too long."

"Why don't you try me? I got all day, I got all week if needed. Tell me how you can get a damn Apple Watch to transport me back in time, when I know that time travel isn't possible."

"I'm sorry, George, but even if we had fifty years I couldn't explain it to you. It's basically a cheat."

"A cheat?" replied George, exasperated. He caught himself biting his fingernails.

"Yeah, it's kind of a universe-level hack. It's not really time travel; time travel isn't possible. Well, it might be, but it requires too much energy."

George took a deep breath. "So what *is* this, Shiloh?"

"I'll explain as best I can. You've heard of string theory, right?" He didn't wait for a reply. "The only way you can reconcile Newtonian physics with quantum mechanics is with string theory. The math implies multiple dimensions and multiple parallel universes. Are you following, George?" Again Shiloh didn't wait for an answer. "Those parallel universes all have slightly different timelines; we simply query for highly similar universes that have timeline offsets equal to the date you put in the Apple Watch. Then we project your consciousness, using quantum entanglement, into that parallel universe, into that world's version of you."

There was a moment of silence while George tried to process what he heard and find the right, next question. "Who is 'we'? Who or what are you? Are you from the future? Are you an alien? What, Shiloh?" George's volume increased again.

"We? Oh, did I say, *we*? I meant me." Shiloh paused. "And no, George, I'm no alien. I'm just a man. And I can't tell you any more than I have."

"How could an Apple Watch do this? How can you just drop something like this on me? How am I supposed to deal with this?"

"It's, uh, more server based-ish. The Apple Watch is just the mechanism to capture the request; your watch is nothing special. But its GPS and other features are helpful for the tracking. It's partly why you can't return if you go back more than twenty-five years. And George, I'm sorry, I didn't mean to put you through anything rough. I thought this would help you. I still do think it will help. But it's up to you. You can delete this application off your watch and forget it ever happened. If you're not comfortable, you don't ever have to use it again."

"Okay, Shiloh, let's just say, even though I'm still not believing this, that all this is true and I accept it. How can you try this out on me? How do you know this is safe? How did you know this wouldn't have killed me?"

"Oh, it's perfectly safe; there's no transfer of matter, only energy. Well, other than the watch. But I'm not transferring your body or anything, just your consciousness. Actually, it's not even really a transfer, more of a flip. And the Apple Watch tracks the duration and triggers the flip back," Shiloh said.

"First of all, I'm kind of attached to my consciousness. Second of all, what if something happened to the Apple Watch during my, uh, travels?"

"Oh, they are well made. Really, really sturdy. But yeah. You, uh, need to take care of the watch. If you lost it or broke it, you wouldn't be able to return."

"So I would spend a lifetime trapped in a different life? How could you expose me to that risk without explaining it to me? What if I turn you in, Shiloh? What if I tell the government about this?"

"Do you think the government would believe you? There's nothing special about the app. They'll never believe you—that I can promise. As to you, it's the same answer; you would have never believed me. Also, I thought we were friends."

George took another deep breath; he was still trying to sort out his thoughts.

"We barely know each other, Shiloh; you're basically a stranger to me."

"I understand. Just delete the application, and keep the watch. I'm sorry. Hey, I got to go. See you."

George started to say something, but the connection was lost. He thought about calling Shiloh back, but he needed to do some thinking first.

CHAPTER 15

Ordinary World

June 17, 2014

George desperately needed something ordinary and decided to head into work.

Just go on like it's a normal day? If work can help me forget about Amanda, it might help. I just need a couple of normal hours, and then maybe I can get my head around this.

As he took the train downtown and read Tuesday's paper, a curious thought came into his mind. *It's nice to be living in tomorrow and not yesterday.* He sighed.

He was relieved to see that everything he had accomplished the first Monday had still happened. The voice mails and e-mails he had deleted were gone. The preparations he had completed for the big meeting were still in place. It was if the second Monday had never happened.

I can almost make myself believe that. Almost. But down deep it'll be there, gnawing away. I'm going to have to deal with it sooner or later.

He tried to call Shiloh a couple of times, but he didn't even get voice mail. The line just continued to ring. He sent several texts, but received no replies.

He threw himself into his work. He revised the Power-Point he'd been working on until he felt it was passable. He tried to avoid his coworkers as much as possible. He didn't feel very conversational anyway. They left him alone. He guessed they felt he needed some space.

He had lunch at his desk and continued to catch up on many of the things that had piled up from his time off. He hadn't felt this productive in a long time. It was a good day, and before long he was heading for the train.

I was rough on Shiloh. But how could he do something like this without warning me? He's right, though: I would have gone right to thinking he's crazy and probably never spoken to him again. I should apologize, but he's got to understand. How can he be doing this? Who the hell is he?

Shiloh did not appear on the train. George found himself wanting more and more to talk about what had happened. He thought about Elena, but she was dealing with a so much already. Instead, when he got home, he called Cade.

Cade answered, "George, what's up?"

I hate caller ID. "Hey, can you get together for a beer? I need to talk."

"Sure, you want to meet at Duke's?"

"Yeah, see you there in ten minutes."

Duke's was Cade and George's favorite hangout in Crystal Lake. They had great food and more than 150 different beers. It was a great place for conversation as well. George arrived early and ordered them both a beer.

"Are you all right, George? How's Amanda?" asked Cade as he joined George in a booth.

"Amanda's doing great. I'm fine. I just need to talk with someone besides Elena."

"Dude, are you having an affair? You're having an affair with that waitress from the restaurant downtown, aren't you?" joked Cade. "I knew I should have paid the bill! They always go for the guy who pays the bill."

"Funny, Cade." *How the hell do I tell him this? I have no proof other than a normal Apple Watch. He's never going to believe me.*

"Seriously, what's going on?"

George panicked, but another thought popped into his mind just in time. "I think I'm going to quit my job. I just can't take it anymore."

"Really? Have you found something else?"

"No, that's what I'm struggling with. If I go to another insurance company, it will be the same bullshit for less pay. And I'm not qualified to do anything else at my salary."

Cade looked at George and cocked his head. "Is it really that bad? I mean, I think everybody hates their job. You got two coming up on college. You ought to think this through."

"Yeah, I know. I'll probably stay. I'm just in a funk at work."

"I know exactly how you feel. It sucks, man."

They both glanced around the bar for a few moments over their beers. Cade looked like he was searching for more to say. George let him off the hook. "Cade, have you ever thought about time travel?"

"Wow that was out of nowhere. Uh, no, it's not something I'm typically thinking about."

"What would you do if you could travel back in time?"

"I would go back twenty years and invest in GE, Coke, and Microsoft, of course. Then I would sell it all at just the right time and buy an island in the Caribbean."

"What else? What if you could go back ten times?"

"Let's see. I would probably meet Jesus Christ, kill Hitler, hunt a dinosaur, and then use my last seven times trying to get in Marilyn Monroe's pants. Why are you asking—did you find a time machine?"

George chose his answer carefully. "No, it's just with work, and getting older, I've been thinking about my life and how things might have been different if I had made different choices."

"Ah, that makes sense. Yeah I think I would probably change some things about my own life if I had the chance."

"Like what?"

"I don't know. Man, you're going to have to get me drunk if you're going to ask me questions like this. Are you okay, George?"

"I'm a little out of sorts lately; Elena says it's middle-aged crazy." Which reminded him . . . . "Speaking of Elena, I need to run over to the hospital and see her and Amanda. Thanks for listening to me. Sorry if I'm a bit odd lately."

"No problem—always up for having a beer with my friend George, especially when he buys. Tell Amanda I said get well soon, and tell Elena to hang in there for me."

"Will do. Talk to you soon, Cade," George said. They walked out of the pub together and then went their separate ways.

CHAPTER 16

When Tomorrow Comes

George was unfortunately familiar with the hospital at this point. He knew the best places to park, the quickest way to Amanda's room, and where to get a decent cup of coffee. When he arrived, however, Amanda's room was empty. As he stepped out to find a nurse, he saw an orderly pushing Amanda in a wheelchair. Elena was walking beside her. Amanda's face was red.

"Hi, George," Elena said. "Amanda started some light physical therapy today. She did awesome."

"Amanda, great job, I'm so glad to hear that."

"It sucked, Dad. It's been like two and a half weeks since the accident, and I'm still sore and weak. They physical therapy really hurts."

George could see tears forming in both of her eyes.

I forgot to ask about whether she would still have tears. Well, there's my answer.

"Honey, the doctor said it was going to be hard at the beginning, but it's going to get better every day."

They all went into the room, and George helped the orderly get Amanda back into her bed. "I hate this place. When can I go home?"

George looked at Elena, who said, "Soon, honey. The doctor said you just need to get a little stronger. And your eye doctor is coming tomorrow to do a final checkup on your eye."

"You mean my useless eye?"

Elena frowned. "Amanda, didn't we talk about staying positive?"

"I think I have the right to be a little negative, Mom."

George could sense they'd spent a little too much time together the last two days. He suggested that Elena head home to eat dinner with Alex. Elena resisted but eventually gave in.

George said, "We'll have dinner together, Mandy, you and I. I'm buying; the best hospital food money can buy."

Amanda sighed. George was watching for her usual eye roll, but it didn't come. He wondered if it hurt, or if she was unable to move her eyes that much, but decided not to ask about it.

The dinner was not quite as pleasant as George had hoped. He was allowed to wheel Amanda down to the cafeteria, so she didn't have to eat in her room. However, that didn't seem to lighten her mood.

"Honey, the worst of it's behind you. From now on, every day is going to be better."

"Today's worse than yesterday." She stared at him, looking for an argument.

"It's your first day of physical therapy. Give yourself a chance."

Amanda picked at her food.

"You are going to heal. You're going to get past this. Someday it will all seem like a bad dream."

"My eye will never heal."

Oh man, queen takes rook, and checkmate. I guess she learned it from the best. She's my daughter.

"Amanda, it could have been a lot worse. In some ways you're lucky to be alive."

"Sorry, Dad, I'm not feeling lucky right now."

I bet Shiloh's Rare Earth story would just piss her off. I'm not playing this game; she just needs time.

"Yeah, I'm can see that. All right, finish your dinner."

George stayed till bedtime, watching some late-teen TV drama with Amanda, who seemed to just want to escape into her show. So George stayed quiet and decided that being there would have to be enough. Eventually, he helped Amanda get ready for bed. When she was all set, he kissed her goodnight and left her alone in her hospital room. He hated leaving, and he hated seeing her go through the pain.

On the ride home it hit him like a runaway train. *I'm such an idiot! It's so obvious. This is why he said it would help me!*

He rushed home filled with a combination of hope and dread. His watch said it was 9:30 p.m. When he came in, Alex was playing video games and Elena was already asleep. He tried to talk with Alex, but he was too engrossed in his game. He told Alex not to stay up too late and went up to get ready for bed.

Elena must have been very tired to be asleep already. It's good that she's getting some rest. She has been carrying the heavier load, and I'm going to help to fix that, one way or another.

After he was ready for bed, he tried to call Shiloh again. It went to voice mail again, and he decided to leave a message. "Shiloh, it's George from the train, I'm sorry about earlier, but I'm going to try your app again. I just thought you should know." He hung up.

He pulled up Shiloh's application and changed the Adjustment Date to June 4, the date of Amanda's accident.

I think I'm going crazy. Do I really believe it's all real?

George's finger hovered over the start button, but he hesitated, feeling a pit in his stomach.

I should probably wait until I can talk with Shiloh again.

He sat there for almost a full minute, staring at the watch. Then he reached down and tapped the start button. The application updated.

George assumed he would wake up on Wednesday, June 4. Part of him expected nothing to happen, but he was still nervous. What would happen if he stayed awake all night? After tossing and turning over an hour, George finally drifted off to sleep.

CHAPTER 17

Master Plan

June 4, 2014

George awoke feeling disoriented and queasy again. A quick glance at the watch told him it was 5:15 a.m. Just as he started to lower his arm, he remembered. He took another look at his watch and saw the date: Wednesday, June 4.

"Oh my God, it really is time travel," he said as he sat up in bed. Elena stirred but did not wake.

I am a damn time traveler!

George pulled back the covers and put his feet on the floor. He still felt groggy, but it didn't seem to be as bad as the last time. He grabbed his phone off his dresser—Wednesday, June 4. He threw on his robe and went downstairs to his office. Once he got to his desk, he noticed the differences again. There were items out of place on his desk, and some of the mail piled there unfamiliar.

This is nearly two weeks ago. Maybe I'm just misremembering.

He checked the computer and the Internet: Wednesday, June 4.

I'm either completely insane, with incredibly sophisticated delusions, or this is happening. I could actually do what Cade was joking about. I could invest in a stock or bet on a football game.

Just about when his mind was about to run off in a million directions at once, one thought rose to the surface.

Amanda, I need to focus on Amanda.

He collected himself. *I need to remember back to that day—well, today. Jesus, if I'm not crazy already, thinking about time travel is going to make me crazy. Let's see, I headed into work, hoping to run into Shiloh, but he wasn't on the train. I arrived at work, and I was through most of the morning before I got the text from Elena. It was just before lunchtime; how much earlier was the accident? Damn, I should have prepared more before coming back. I should have studied the accident report. I really haven't thought much about how I would save her.*

He'd had some vague image in his head of arriving at the accident site early and blocking the other woman's lane, before she crashed into Amanda's friend's car. He calmed himself down.

I've got plenty of time: relax. How do I save her? I don't need to do anything dramatic at the accident site. I just need to stop her from going with her friend.

It seemed simple, but he was still worried. He had this feeling that something was going to happen to Amanda no matter what he did. He wished he had taken more time before traveling back and felt concerned that he had been so impulsive.

I have been dealing with a few things.

He remembered some horror movie, where a group of teens had cheated death. Through the rest of the movie the teens experienced horrible deaths one by one, as the Grim Reaper or fate restored what was supposed to have happened.

You're overthinking this, George. Shiloh wouldn't have given you this opportunity if there wasn't a reason. Take it slowly, and work out a plan.

The first thing he did was call his boss. He had no intention of going into work today. He left a message that he wasn't feeling well and wouldn't be in. The house was quiet; Amanda, Alex, and Elena were still asleep. The rest of the plan would have to wait.

CHAPTER 18

Lost Cause

"No, Amanda, you cannot go with Tami to the lake today," George said. He was still a little rattled from seeing a healthy, happy Amanda join them at the breakfast table. He couldn't stop staring at her perfect eyes.

"I don't understand, Dad. I've been planning this for a while, and Mom said it was okay."

"I took the day off today to spend time with you. You and I are going to hang around the house, and we are going to figure out some options for college. We'll do some Internet research together, make a list of potential colleges, and decide which ones you should visit."

"Dad, I don't mind doing that with you but not today. I already made plans with Tami; I can't just tell her I'm not going. Mom, tell Dad he can't just do this to me. We're meeting a bunch of friends, and I've been looking forward to this for a long time."

"George, I don't understand why this has to be today. Amanda told me about her plans last week, and I told her she could go. And I don't understand why you didn't tell me about it, either. I would like to be part of her college planning as well, and I need to run a bunch of errands today."

Once Elena joined in, George knew he was losing the battle. Amanda's debating abilities were surpassed only by Elena's, and when the two teamed up he had little chance. He abandoned his plan and searched desperately for alternatives.

"Amanda, you can't go today. I know it's not fair and I know it doesn't make sense. I'm sorry, and I'm going to find a way to make it up to you."

"Dad, I'm going. This isn't fair at all. You've always told me that I need to keep my commitments, and I'm keeping my commitments with my friends today. Why don't you spend the day with Alex?"

Elena opened her mouth, but George jumped in, talking fast, "Amanda, after we do the college planning, I'm taking you to the mall to shop at your favorite store. You can buy a couple of outfits, and we'll go to lunch together. And I'm going to allow you to have that party at the house you've been asking to have. Mom, Alex, and I will go out to dinner, and as long as you follow some ground rules you can have the party at the house all alone." He turned to Elena. "It's important for me to be with Amanda today."

Elena looked puzzled. George hadn't wanted to leave the house with Amanda, but he had to stop her from leaving with Tami. He gave Elena his best "please support me" look. Amanda turned to her mother, seeking help.

"I'm sure you can plan another trip to the lake with your friends, Amanda. I know when your Dad has made up his mind. Tami will understand. And besides, I think you'd better jump on the shopping and the party offer. I never would have thought your father would agree to that."

George was relieved, but he knew from Elena's stare that he would have some explaining to do later.

One step at a time.

"Fine," exclaimed Amanda before she stomped off. George guessed that the offer to have a party at the house had worked, but she still wanted him to think she was mad.

After she left the room, Elena gave him another puzzled look.

"You have to just trust me here, Elena. I need to keep an eye on Amanda today."

"Did you find out something about Tami or her friends? I hope this isn't just because they're meeting boys at the lake today."

"That might be reason enough, but no, this is more important. Let's just say I had a strong premonition that something was going to happen to Amanda today."

"That doesn't sound like you, George. Are you sure there isn't something else you're not telling me?"

"I honestly just have a bad feeling about today, and I want to spend the day with my daughter. And we do need to make some progress on the college planning."

"Okay, I'm going to trust you, but you'd better have a good reason for all this. I'm taking a shower, and then I'm off for my errands. You owe me one."

She always sees right through me.

The college planning went by much faster than he'd planned. Within an hour, he and Amanda had talked through a number of college options and picked three or four to go visit. He had wanted to stall and keep Amanda in the house as long as possible, but now he was starting to think they should just get to the mall and stay there.

The drive there was terrifying—at least for George. He took back roads as much as possible and was extremely careful going through every intersection, each time expecting a car to come from nowhere and broadside them. By the time they pulled into the parking lot, he had to pry his hands off the wheel. He carefully escorted Amanda into the mall and then breathed a sigh of relief.

The shopping, though excruciating for George, was successful. After visiting seven different stores and sifting through what seemed to George to be hundreds of clothing racks, Amanda had found three outfits. Of course, none were on sale, and George was shocked at the prices. Amanda was making him pay dearly for changing her plans. George led the way to the nicest restaurant in the mall and they had a wonderful lunch.

"So, Amanda, how's school?"

"Fine."

"Oh no you don't, I just spent a small fortune on three outfits and lunch. I get more than 'fine.'"

"Um, it's okay, I guess. I like Spanish, but it's my hardest class. I don't think I can ever become fluent without living somewhere where they speak Spanish."

"Well, let's get one thing straight, I'm not sending you to college in Barcelona. Although, I bet the schools in Tijuana have pretty cheap tuition. Okay, you convinced me, we'll look at a few schools in Mexico."

"Funny, Dad. Calc is hard, but I'm pretty good at math, so I'm doing pretty good. Digital photography is all right—kind of tedious, though. Like I said, it's all fine." She gave him one of her fake smiles, turning her head slightly.

"Have you thought about a major? That would help you narrow down a college."

"I have no idea."

"Come on, you must have some idea? Accounting, nursing, teaching—what interests you?"

"I'm being totally honest, Dad. I have no clue."

"Well, spend some time thinking about it. It doesn't have to be set in stone, but you should have some sort of plan going into college."

"Is it normal not to know what you want to do with your life? My guidance counselor wasn't exactly thrilled with me either. He said I need goals."

"Oh, Mandy, I don't think it's that unusual. You'll figure it out."

"I'm not all that excited about college, either. I like high school. I like my friends. I don't want to start all over."

Whoa, this is more than I bargained for. "You're going to love it. I think college is going to be the best time of your life."

"That's depressing: four years, and then it's all downhill from there? My friend's older sister got homesick and quit after three months. What if that happens to me?"

"It's not going to happen. You make friends easily. And you're so independent. Your mom would love to hear that you don't want to leave the nest. But trust me, by the time it rolls around, you're going to be ready for it."

"It will be nice not to be nagged all the time. And not to have Alex poking around my room. I guess we'll see."

"Hey, you've got time. Why don't we go see a movie?"

"Deal, but I get to pick."

Anything to keep you out of the car and off the streets. A movie should get us well past the time of the accident.

Amanda picked a new teen romantic comedy, and George was in such a good mood that he found he enjoyed it. He got a little nervous when Amanda went to the ladies' room but relaxed as she hurried back to her seat. The movie ended around 2:30 p.m., around the time that he and Elena had first met with her doctor.

Despite the time of day, George was still ridiculously careful on the car ride home. He confirmed with Amanda that she did not have any plans to go that night. Later, as they had dinner as a family, he listened to Amanda actually brag about her day to Alex.

"Dad, are you going to let me have a party at the house too?" asked Alex.

"Maybe I will—in a couple of years, when you're her age." George sensed that Alex was jealous and made a mental note to have a similar outing with Alex. He and Amanda had both enjoyed the day, and he was glad they had spent it together, no matter the reason.

It wasn't the superhero car-crash rescue I first envisioned, but it was a pretty good day. Maybe I'm getting the hang of this time-traveler thing.

CHAPTER 19

Under the Milky Way

June 18, 2014

George awoke anxious and apprehensive. He checked his watch—it was 5:45 a.m. on 6/18/2014.

I'm back to the present. This is happening. This is real. Holy shit. I've got a lot to think about. Something still seems not right. What am I missing here? Amanda: I need to check on her. Make sure.

He forced himself out of bed and walked to Amanda's room. Her door was closed, and he paused. *Moment of truth.* He slowly opened the door and quietly stepped inside. The room was perfectly clean and the bed was made and empty.

"Where is she?" he whispered to himself. He left the room to search the house, but his mind was already saying, *She's still at the hospital.* He did a quick search and ended up in his office. He looked at the pile of medical statements and bills.

It still happened—somehow it still happened. Damn Shiloh, what is going on? You better answer your phone!

The phone rang four times, and then a soft voice answered, "Hello?"

"Shiloh—it's me, George, something is wrong with your app. It didn't work, it didn't take. I need you to make it work."

"Wait, what? What are you talking about, George?" asked Shiloh. George heard him yawn into the phone.

"I used your app to travel back to the day of Amanda's accident. I prevented it, but she's still in the hospital. It still happened. What's going on?"

"You can't change the past. Once it's done, it's done. Remember I said it's not really time travel? Remember the multiple, parallel universes, George? You're temporarily visiting an alternate universe. You're not actually time traveling; it's a hack."

George put his free hand on his forehead and closed his eyes. "What? I'm temporarily visiting an alternate universe? What does that even mean? This is so insane; I can't believe I'm even talking about it. What is the point, Shiloh? Why did I go back and save Amanda if it doesn't even matter? Why are you doing this to me?"

"George, this is important: it does matter. You saved that Amanda from the accident, just not your Amanda. It's still important."

"There are two Amandas? It doesn't make any sense. And if I didn't save my Amanda, why do I care? Shiloh, I don't care about parallel worlds! Here's the thing, if you can send me to another parallel world, you can save Amanda from the accident. Don't tell me you can't." George felt more and more frustrated.

"I can't. I can't change the past, and I can't save her eyesight. I'm not a doctor. You have to move on from her accident, George. She lived. She's going to be okay. She just needs time."

George sighed; he had wanted so badly to save her, to make her whole again, to make her happy again.

"As to caring, you *need* to care, George, because all the realities matter; all the worlds count. We're all on this journey together, and everything you do, no matter which universe you're in, matters."

"Shiloh, in all honesty, I have no idea what you're talking about. I was just starting to get my head around time travel. Now I'm not time traveling, I'm visiting another world or universe. You can't expect me to understand this."

"Meet me on the train, George. I'll explain more. You may not understand it all, but I'll try. I'll tell you more about the journey you're on . . . the journey we are on. Meet me on the train. And George, Amanda is going to be fine."

George threw his iPhone onto the carpet. He put both of his hands in his hair. *Time travel, parallel universes, multiple Amandas: I'm losing it. I have to be losing it. This is nuts. Pull it together, George.*

He picked up his phone and headed upstairs to get ready. He was still going to meet Shiloh; no way was he going to miss that train.

Thirty minutes later, Shiloh was sitting down next to George on their regular train.

"Hi, George," Shiloh said, as if nothing was out of the ordinary. He was wearing the same jacket and khaki pants, and today's T-shirt read, *When you're not looking, I'm just a waveform.*

George offered him an angry stare.

"I know this is difficult. But if you just hear me out, I'll try to help. There are multiple parallel universes; actually, an almost infinite number of multiple parallel universes."

Shiloh looked at George, who maintained his glare.

"You can look it up, George. Read anything recent by any theoretical physicist, like Hawking or Brian Greene or Michio Kaku. They all talk about parallel universes; it's the thing that makes string theory work. And while there are almost an infinite number of parallel universes, a limited number of them are very similar to our universe, similar enough to be useful for travel. Now, many of the parallel universes have alternate timelines; remember that time is relative—Einstein. I'm just flipping your consciousness over to one of the other similar universes. Many are very, very similar, but they do have minor differences. Did you notice minor differences when you traveled?"

"Yes, little differences."

"Good, okay. So I use quantum entanglement to flip your consciousness over for one day, George, that's it. You're not time traveling, you're not changing the past, and you're not going insane."

"Why only ten times, Shiloh, and why only one day each?"

"There are limitations on the math, in the physics. I told you it was a beta release. I might be able to expand it—I don't know. Oh, also, if you go back more than twenty-five years, you can't return. After that the entanglement gets too wonky."

There goes meeting Jesus or stopping Hitler.

"I'm not sure I'm ever going to understand any of this. But I did experience it, so I guess I believe you. What about the journey you were talking about?"

Shiloh smiled. George already knew that smile meant he was excited.

"You, me, everyone, the stars and all the parallel universes; we're all on a journey together."

"What kind of journey?"

"It's a thirteen-billion-year journey of complexity. It started at the dawn of time with the big bang. In the beginning the universe was incredibly simple. There were no stars, no galaxies, and certainly no planets or life. Five hundred and sixty million years after the big bang, the first stars formed. They were basic—mostly just hydrogen—and they were very, very large. These first-generation stars quickly used up their fuel and went supernova, creating the first twenty elements in the periodic table. The dust from these stars gathered to form second-generation stars, which became white giants or red giants, or went supernova themselves, creating more elements. Finally, third-generation stars appeared. These were more likely to form surrounded by planets and solar systems. Our sun is a third-generation star. So, if you've ever heard the phrase 'We are all made of stardust,' it's true. We are made of elements that can only have been made from the destruction of several generations of stars."

"Shiloh, it's fascinating, it really is. But I'm not sure what this has to do with my experiences and with Amanda."

"Hang with me, George, it's important you understand this. Now, our galaxy of second- and third-generation stars was formed about nine or ten billion years ago. Our solar system formed about four and a half billion years ago. Then, just under four billion years ago, life formed on Earth. It was another step of complexity: life. Evolution then took over and created more and more complex organisms. About two hundred and fifty thousand years ago, *Homo sapiens* appeared. Are you with me so far?"

Shiloh paused until he got a nod from George. "But it doesn't stop there. Now humans take over the complexity journey. We form more and more complex societies with the advent of things like speech, agriculture, and law. These structures allow us to develop math and science and technology. This brings us to today, thirteen point eight billion years after the big bang. The things we have created—the space shuttle, the Internet—these are some of the most complex things in the solar system. But they're not the most complex things. You know what the most complex things are? Humans. Our brains, our nervous system, our circulatory system. We are most complex thing in the solar system. But not for long, George; soon the things we create will become more complex than our bodies, our brains. We will create the next step in the journey. You see, stellar evolution, galactic formation, birth of the solar system, creation of life, human evolution, industrial revolution, technology transformation—we tend to think of all of them all as separate events. But they aren't; they're one story. They're a continuous stream of development of higher and higher orders. That's the journey of complexity we're on. An amazing teacher named David Christian explains it better than me—look him up sometime. He calls it 'Big History.' I think it's a TED talk."

"I want to understand where you're going with this," George said, "but I'm still not sure I get the point. Where do we go from here—technology and computers, artificial intelligence?"

"Great question. Remember how I talked about life needing that balance of chaos and order to progress? Computers and AI are a dead end without our humanity. This is a danger of letting computers bringing too much structure to our world. We have to keep our edge and hold on to our humanity. We have to stay connected to nature and music and the arts. We have to be the creative force that carries on the complexity journey."

"Okay, I think I understand your point, but I'm not connecting it back to the multiple universes and all of them being so important."

"You're right, this is difficult to explain. Our universe is on the same journey as all of the other parallel universes. It's all probabilities. The universe wants entropy. It dislikes complexity and structure. It takes a bit of magic to get complexity. And so all the parallel universes are on the edge of a knife. They have to be. Many of them will fail. But we just need one to succeed, just one. And every little action makes a difference. And, while you saving the other Amanda might not change what happened in this universe, it might change you."

"Who are you, Shiloh?"

"Just remember, Amanda is going to be fine. I don't think she's the one you need to worry about. It's my stop. I've got to go."

Shiloh got up and put his headphones on.

"Shiloh," George said, "what are you listening to?"

"A tremendous band named The Church. Give them a listen sometime," he replied, speaking embarrassingly loud. He left George to his own thoughts.

Great. Who should I be worried about? Elena? Me? I thought Shiloh told me I worry too much anyway.

CHAPTER 20

Another Day

George forced himself to settle into his workday. While thoughts about parallel universes and stellar evolution kept creeping to the surface, he made it through a respectable number of tasks. At lunchtime he did a little Internet research to see how much of Shiloh's information was accurate. He wasn't surprised to find that most of what he remembered of the conversation was true. He even found information about parallel universes when he searched on the physicist that Shiloh had mentioned. Nothing was proven—it was all theory—but the best minds in the world were working on multiple theories similar to what Shiloh described. They referred to it as the multiverse or "many worlds interpretation."

Maybe I'm not going crazy. He thought about Shiloh's app and whether he should use it again. In some sense it seemed wildly dangerous, but he had used it twice already and survived.

Where in time would I go in the last twenty-five years? I have to admit I'm intrigued.

His iPhone rang, and his watch told him it was Elena. "George, I have great news."

"Well, spill it; I could use some great news!" She sounded giddy.

"Amanda gets the final bandages off her eye and gets to come home a week from Saturday! I want to throw her a surprise coming-home party."

"Great idea, Elena," George said, thinking the exact opposite. He was constantly finding himself in this same predicament. He wanted desperately to support his wife, especially with something as positive as a party for his daughter. But being the expert worrier that he was, he had a gut feeling that Amanda was not ready for something so big and so social. It seemed that Elena was thinking about what good it could do Amanda, while George immediately went to what could go wrong.

"We will invite our friends and neighbors, and all her friends. It will be just the thing to cheer her up. Do you want to do a cookout, George, or should we have something brought in?"

"I'm happy to grill, but don't you think we should first see how she is feeling a few days before she comes home?"

"George, she's already made great improvements, and this will be over a week from now. She's going to keep getting better every day. The doctors wouldn't be sending her home if she wasn't ready. And it's not like we are going to have her dancing or playing baseball. Besides, if we are going to have a party, we need to start planning it now."

"All right, just let me know what I need to do," George said.

"I'll make a list. Honey, she is going to be fine. I'll see you tonight. Love you."

"Love you, Elena," said George before he hung up the phone. *Everyone keeps telling me that.* But it wasn't just this accident; what upset him the most was that anything could happen to Amanda, to Alex, to Elena, and he couldn't stop it or change it. He'd spent the last ten to fifteen years worrying about his kids, making sure they had the right crib and the right car seat, and even that Elena was cutting up their hot dogs the right way. Now, in ten seconds Amanda had lost her eye and almost her life. It bothered him deeply.

George battled all afternoon to keep the thoughts of Amanda, Elena, and Shiloh with his parallel universes out of his head. He mostly won the battle. He conducted several fruitful pre-meetings to make sure his boss's Thursday meeting would go without issue.

I don't have to win every battle. I just need to win the war.

He wrapped up the final agenda and PowerPoint and sent it to his boss for final review. It wasn't his best work, but he felt he'd been going through a great deal. He spent the last hour of his day catching up on the last of the e-mails from his time off. It wasn't a perfect day, but at least it wasn't the same day over again.

There was no Shiloh on the train home. Despite the fact that he had more questions, George was ready for a regular evening. He decided he wouldn't mind a few days off from Shiloh and his craziness. He needed to get his regular life back in order before he dealt with what had happened.

When he got home, no one was there. He guessed Elena was at the hospital, but he had no idea where Alex was. He texted Elena that he was home and that he would be there in an hour or so. He sent Alex a text asking where he was and if he needed dinner. The house was a mess; while Elena had been at the hospital all day, Alex had been a one-man wrecking crew. George followed the trail of clothes, dirty dishes, and empty Gatorade bottles through the house. It took him a good thirty minutes to clean up. Just as he finished, he heard Alex come home.

Perfect timing.

He went downstairs and found Alex standing at the refrigerator with the door open, staring inside. "Where were you?"

"At my friend Jeff's," answered Alex, providing the least amount of information possible, as usual.

"What were you and Jeff up to?"

"We were playing video games. I got your text and yes, Dad, I need dinner. I'm starved."

"Alex, you can't just play video games and mess around with your guitar all summer. When I got home the house was a disaster. You had clothes and dishes and bottles all over the house. With me going back to work and your mom at the hospital, we need you to pitch in more."

Alex stared at the ceiling. "Okay, what about dinner?"

"Why don't you come over to the hospital and have dinner with Amanda? You've hardly visited her lately."

"I hate the hospital. The food is terrible there, and it's boring."

"You know what? Why don't you just make yourself one of the frozen dinners your mom bought. And you still need to get over to the hospital more this coming week. It may seem boring, but you need to support your sister. She's going through a great deal. And when I get home, you had better have cleaned up after yourself."

"Frozen dinner, really?"

George stared down his son. "Yes, really. And I'm serious about the cleaning up."

Alex half stomped, half moped off up the stairs to his room. A few moments later George heard a door slam. He headed off to the hospital.

On his way in, George stopped at the gift shop and picked out some flowers. He pulled one out of the bunch, and when he got to Amanda's room, he handed one flower to Elena and then set the bunch on table next to Amanda.

"Flowers for the beautiful ladies." He gave them both hugs. "How was your day, young lady?"

"Hi, Dad, did you hear I get to go home next week? I still have to come back every day for physical therapy and some check-ups, but I get to sleep in my own bed!"

George thought it might be the first time he had seen his daughter smile since the accident. "Yes, your mom told me. That's wonderful news, honey."

"She did great in her therapy today. It's amazing how much progress she's making every day," said Elena. "How was your day?"

"It's a war, but I'm winning the battles one at a time. Then I came home to an Alex tornado, it took me thirty minutes to clean up after him."

"I'm sorry, George, between meeting the doctor and the therapy session, I didn't even have a chance to check in on Alex. I feel bad we're having to leave him alone so much lately, with you going back to work."

"He was at Jeff's playing video games most of the after-noon. I don't think you should feel sorry for him," said George.

"I still feel bad. But thank you for fighting the good fight at work, and for cleaning up at home and for the flowers. They are beautiful, right, Amanda?"

"Yeah, thanks, Dad."

It was a nice evening. The hospital food seemed better, and Amanda was much more talkative. After dinner they took Amanda for a long walk outside in her wheelchair. She loved to get outside when she could.

That evening, at home, George tried one more time. "Are you sure about this surprise party? What if she isn't ready for something like that?"

"Did you see her tonight, George? In another week, she is going to be fine. You worry too much."

"Somebody has to," replied George, winking at Elena. But he *was* worried—about Amanda, about his job, and, in the back of his mind, about his experiences with Shiloh. He wanted to talk to Elena about it, but he couldn't imagine trying to explain it all. He tossed and turned for a good hour, then drifted off to a troubled sleep.

CHAPTER 21

War

George crouched even lower into the trench as the explosions continued. With one hand, he pulled his helmet tighter to his head. The other hand held a rifle. He looked around the trench. It was difficult to see through the smoke and dust that hung low in the air, but he could still see debris everywhere. It seemed like someone had left in a hurry. There were boxes of ammo and MREs, backpacks, and even a frying pan. Another explosion crashed nearby. The trench shook, filling with more dust and smoke. George almost screamed when another soldier jumped down a few feet from him. George raised his gun and pointed it at the man.

"Put that down," yelled the man. As he took another step closer, the smoke cleared enough that George recognized Shiloh. He lowered his rifle. "We got 'em on the run," Shiloh barked. He was wide-eyed and grinning.

"Jesus, get down, Shiloh," George yelled. He was still shaking from Shiloh's entrance and the explosions. Shiloh knelt down next to George. They both seemed to be wearing the same uniform, with the US flag on the sleeve. Shiloh had a star on his helmet and was carrying a small machine gun.

"What war is this?"

Shiloh cocked his head to the side. He looked puzzled. "It's the Second World War. Are you shot or something?"

George looked down at his chest arms and legs. "No, sorry, I'm just a little confused."

"No worries, it's just a little shell shock. You'll be fine. I think they've pulled back even more. You need to take that next trench."

"What?" asked George.

Shiloh leaned in and yelled, "You need to take that next trench."

"I'm not going anywhere. I'm certainly not taking the next trench by myself," yelled George.

"I think they've pulled back even more. I think the next trench is empty. They're losing the will to fight, and we need to keep them on the run."

Another explosion hit nearby. George could hear the sound of machine-gun fire and tanks in the distance. "It doesn't sound like they're losing the will to fight."

"It's just cover fire for their retreat. You need to move now, soldier."

George worked up the courage to turn and peer over the rim of the trench. It was difficult to see through the haze, but George saw enough to crouch back down. It was a wasteland of barbed wire, fire, and bodies. He coughed smoke from his lungs.

"I'm . . . not . . . going . . . anywhere," he sputtered.

Shiloh grabbed the front of his uniform. "George, we have to keep moving. We have to get Hitler. We've come so far, and we are so close."

"Hitler?" George said, now even more confused.

Shiloh turned George toward the edge of trench and put his hand on his back.

"Yes, Hitler. Take the next trench, soldier. That's a direct order. Don't make me shoot you in the back."

Incredibly, George found himself crawling out of the trench. He saw a tank rolling away from him about three hundred yards to the left. It was green, and he couldn't tell which side it was on. The smoke was still thick, but he thought he could make out another trench about a hundred yards straight ahead. There was a barbed-wire barrier about halfway. George looked back; Shiloh had his machine gun pointed directly at him.

He crawled onward. He was shaking, and his eyes were tearing up from the smoke. He squinted at the trench ahead of him, but the smoke made it difficult. From what he could see, it appeared empty.

Another explosion hit to his right. It seemed far away, but a moment later, dirt and debris rained down on him. He heard Shiloh yell from behind, "Move faster!" George rose to a crouch and tried to run. He made it about twenty feet and then fell forward onto his face. It took him a moment to regain his wits. His face was scratched, and he felt blood trickle down his cheek. Another explosion hit to his left. It seemed to be closer, although this one was behind him.

George scrambled to his feet and sprinted for the barbed wire. As he approached the barrier he saw that while it was about six feet tall, it did have a small opening at the bottom. He didn't slow down; he just continued his all-out run until he was just short of the barrier. George put his rifle out in front of him and dove headfirst under the barrier.

I knew all those years of baseball would pay off someday.

George slid about halfway under the barbed wire and then abruptly stopped. He tried to crawl forward, but his backpack was firmly caught on the wire. He tried to crawl backward, but it wouldn't come loose. Just then George heard machine-gun fire and saw the dirt explode off to his left. He put his head down, heard more fire and the sound of bullets passing just overhead.

If I don't die, I'm going to kill Shiloh.

He worked his shoulders and arms out of the straps of the pack and crawled forward. He was free. As soon as he cleared the barbed wire he jumped to his feet and began to run again. He heard machine-gun fire but didn't see where the bullets were hitting. He ran serpentine, expecting to be riddled with bullets at any second. The edge of the trench was up ahead, but he couldn't seem to get any closer—at one point it even seemed to get farther away.

Finally, George reached the trench and leaped into it. He landed awkwardly and crashed into the back wall, helmet first. Stunned, he rolled onto his side and groaned. His back to the wall of the trench, he looked down a seemingly identical, smoke-filled cut. But as his senses returned, he made out a man's face. Still groggy, he realized that the man was much older and seemed vaguely familiar. He wore a helmet different than George's and Shiloh's. And the man had a pistol in his hand and was pointing it at George.

George became aware that he still had his rifle in his hands and that it was also pointed straight ahead. He felt his rifle go off in his hand. The soldier slumped back against the other wall of the trench. Blood began to seep from his chest, and his eyes glazed over. George was horrified.

Shiloh jumped into the trench in a surprisingly athletic manner. He turned left and then right, and then yelled, "Clear." He kneeled down at George's side. "Are you hit?"

"No, b–but he is," stammered George.

Shiloh walked over to the other soldier. "He's German, and he's dead. You got him. Wait. Oh no. Oh, George, this is bad."

"What?" said George.

"Oh no. You killed your great-grandfather. George you killed your own great-grandfather."

George gasped. "What? No." The mist was thickening, billowing into the trench. George started to feel strange, lightheaded. He looked down at his hands, and they become transparent.

Shiloh yelled, "George, George!" The mist had filled the trench. George watched as Shiloh walked across the trench waved away the smoke and mist from where George had been sitting. All he saw was George's empty helmet and uniform.

George awoke, sweating and panting for air. He felt his chest and legs, the dream still fresh in his memory. He had a splitting headache. He couldn't recall remembering a dream for years, other than the night he dreamed about Amanda's accident. But this dream had been more vivid than any dream he could ever remember.

It felt like I was there, the explosions, the fear. But killing my own great-grandfather, really? That's so ridiculous. Where does my subconscious come up with this stuff? Although, I was truly terrified at the feeling of fading away. That was full-on disturbing.

George hurried into the shower, anxious to shake the feeling of the dream. He turned the water to hot, hoping to burn away the oddness. Steam filled the bathroom. The shower helped dissipate the dream, but it didn't shake the headache. He grabbed a couple of aspirin on the way out the door.

I hope Shiloh's on the train. I want to tell him about the dream. Obviously, the battle represents my job, but does it mean more? Why my great-grandfather, whom I've never met? Does that mean I'm really just fighting myself?

But Shiloh's stop came and went, so George turned his thoughts to work. It was the day of the big meeting. George felt a sense of dread about both the meeting and his job in general.

He arrived at his office right on time. The aspirin and coffee had taken the edge off his headache, but it was still there, a dull ache that made it difficult to concentrate. His meeting was at 10:00 a.m., so he spent some time reviewing the agenda and the PowerPoint.

I'm not as prepared as I usually am. I cut some corners, and I really haven't connected with everyone I should have. Hopefully, everyone knows what I've been through. They'll cut me some slack.

Despite his ever-present headache, he got through his eight thirty meeting and then prepped for the big one. He had the copies of the agenda and the PowerPoint ready to go. He killed a little more time by reviewing e-mails. As he was gathering his materials to go, his phone rang. It was Elena. He thought about letting it go to voice mail.

Last time I let it go to voice mail it was Amanda's car accident.

"Oh, George, thank God you answered," Elena said.

"What's going on?"

"My car broke down. I was on my way to shop for supplies for Amanda's party, and it started running rough. Then it just quit."

"Oh shit. I'm sorry, honey, you told me the engine light was on. It's just with Amanda and all . . . ."

Elena let him off the hook. "It's okay, George. It's been crazy for all of us. Do I just call the insurance or a garage?"

"Call the insurance. There should be an option for towing. Have them take it to Ed's Auto Repair near our house."

"How do I get home?"

"Ed's will have a shuttle, or maybe the repair will be quick."

"It's never quick. How will I get to the hospital today?"

George looked at his watch. "I don't know, Elena. Maybe ask the garage if they have a loaner? I've got a meeting right now that I have to get to."

"Fine, George, I'll figure it out myself, but I have to get to the hospital today. Amanda is going through a whole new set of exercises for physical therapy. It's going to be rough, and she's going to need me."

"Elena, I'm sorry, but this meeting is important. I'll call you right away afterward." He felt awful.

"Go to your meeting. I'll figure it out. Bye." Elena hung up.

George glanced at his watch; it was 10:01 a.m. He hustled to the meeting room, all eyes were on him as he walked in about five minutes late, out of breath. His manager gave him a *WTF?* stare. George apologized and started the meeting. It was a disaster. A leader that he hadn't taken the time to meet with pointed out a gap in his plan. His boss threw him under the bus, and it went downhill from there. George did the best damage control he could and ended the meeting fifteen minutes early. On the way out of the room, his boss told him to stop by his office in the afternoon.

He gave himself five minutes back in his office to regain his composure and his dignity. Then he called Elena.

"George, I'm at Ed's, I'm going to give you their number. They've listed about five or six things wrong with the car, and they want to know if we want them all fixed. It's going to take days. They're telling me our insurance doesn't cover a loaner and it's going to be forty-five dollars a day."

George took the number and called Ed's back. Despite the outrageous costs, he told them to fix everything and to give Elena the loaner.

Some days you just have to pay the piper.

He called Elena back and explained it all to her. She was merciful and just seemed to want to get off the phone and get to the hospital. George let her go.

The rest of the day followed suit. George had an awful lunch at this desk and struggled through the early afternoon. He stopped by his manager's office at 2:00 p.m.

"Is now a good time, sir?" he asked.

"Come on in, George, sit down," said his manager. "How's your daughter?"

"She doing well, I think. They told us she can come home a week from Saturday." *You don't care, you're just asking to be polite.*

"Great, great, I'm glad to hear it. How long have you been working here, George?" he asked.

Oh crap. "Over fifteen years. It's only my second job."

"You've had some excellent years here. You've accomplished a great deal. I mean that." He paused. "George, it's going to get difficult around here. The company is struggling, and senior management needs us to take it to the next level. We've only got room for people who are totally committed. I know you've been through a lot with your daughter lately, but even before that it seemed like your commitment was slipping."

"Honestly, I have been a little burned out," admitted George. "But I think once my daughter's out of the hospital I'll be able to get back on track."

"I hope so, George. I hope so, because I like you. You've always been dependable. But we can't have anything more like we had today, right?"

Just keep it simple, George. "Right."

George's manager looked him over again. "Okay, George, we're going to forget this meeting today ever happened. Now that your daughter's on the way home, I'm expecting to see the old George back."

"Count on it, sir."

The old George is a pushover, same as the new George.

Later, on the train, George went back over the conversation.

How many more conversations like that can I take? Everyone's working their butts off already . . . . What is this "take it to the next level" bullshit? Between Amanda's medical bills and Elena's car repairs, I'm going to need to work another ten years. But I'm not sure I can make it another month.

Shiloh didn't appear, but the train arrived in Crystal Lake right on time. George drove straight home. When he walked into the house he wondered if he'd traveled back a day again. The house was a disaster.

"Alex, are you home?" he yelled. He waited for a couple of moments. There was no response. "Alex, are you here?"

A few minutes later Alex walked down the stairs from his room. "Hey, what's up, Dad?"

George was furious. "Alex, we talked about this yesterday. This house is a mess."

"Yeah, Dad, I was going to clean it up after a while."

"No, Alex, you're going to clean it up now. And next time I come home, I'm not going to walk into a disaster. Do you understand me?"

"Okay, Dad, chill. I said I was going to clean it up."

The word *chill* only fired him up more. "And, Alex, you and I need to sit down and discuss what you're doing for the rest of the summer. Baseball will be over soon. I have a few projects around the house for you."

"But Dad, it's my summer."

"Alex, your summer isn't just about comic books, guitar, and video games. You need to pitch in around here, especially with your sister's accident."

"I heard you yesterday, Dad. All you and Mom care about is Amanda. I'll just be cleaning, don't worry about me," mumbled Alex.

Could this day be any worse?

George stomped upstairs to change. When he descended again, he found Alex cleaning. "I'm going to the hospital. Your mom and I will be home later."

Alex ignored him. George grabbed his car keys and left for the hospital. When he arrived, he found Elena and Amanda in her room. They both seemed tense.

"Hi, honey," Elena said.

"Hey, guys, what's going on?" he asked.

Amanda jumped in. "Physical therapy sucks. I'm not doing it anymore."

"Amanda, stop saying that. You can't 'not do' physical therapy. You have to do it to get better. You did fine today," Elena said.

"It's pointless and it hurts. I'm not going tomorrow."

Elena looked at George. George sat down on the bed next to Amanda. "Amanda, I know it's hard and it hurts. But it's the only way to get better. Don't you want to come home next weekend? Don't you want to be back one hundred percent before school?"

"What, so everyone can call me One Eye? No, thanks, I'd rather rot in the hospital!"

Okay, this is crazy. I'm in no mood to be a counselor. "I think we all need to get something to eat," George said.

They wheeled Amanda down to the cafeteria and ate a mediocre dinner. George told Elena about his day while Amanda stared off into space, uninterested. Elena seemed concerned about his job situation and asked a number of questions. Eventually, they made their way back to Amanda's room, where Elena tried to get Amanda to play cards with her and George, but Amanda refused. They ended up watching television together until visiting hours were over.

"Get some good sleep, honey, and you'll feel better in the morning," urged Elena. Amanda rolled her eyes. George took that as a minor victory—her eye was healing properly.

Later, as they got ready for bed, George sighed and said, "This has to have been one of my top ten worst days."

"I'm sorry to hear that. You know, it's not been easy for any of us."

Maybe I should tell her. "I know, Elena, but I'm really struggling with some things. I don't think I can handle my job for too much longer. And I'm even dealing with some bigger things."

"Do you think you're the only one growing older, George? You think I don't struggle with my purpose in life? You don't think I wonder what would have happened if I had kept working? I mean, grocery shopping, housecleaning, cooking, and homework aren't exactly the most fulfilling responsibilities."

"Whoa, whoa, whoa. You do a lot more than cooking and cleaning. You're raising these kids, and you volunteer. If you didn't do what you do, I could have never been successful at work. I thought this is what you wanted. I thought this is what we agreed to."

"It is what I wanted. But I still struggle with it, all the time. You aren't the only one in this family who is dealing with challenges."

I can't tell her about Shiloh and everything now. "I'm sorry. I have been pretty focused on feeling sorry for myself. I do realize this is a tough time for all of us."

"You don't have to apologize. You just need to understand that Amanda has a tough road ahead, and I'm pretty sure Alex is feeling neglected. It's got us all a bit down. But tomorrow will be better, it's Friday," Elena said.

"Oh, thank God. And then the weekend. I'm kicking back and doing absolutely nothing this weekend."

"I hate to be the bearer of bad news, but that isn't happening this weekend. First of all, we'll still be back and forth to the hospital. Second, the lawn needs mowing. And Alex has a baseball game on Sunday. I'm afraid you won't be doing any kicking back at all this weekend."

George just groaned. He desperately needed a break. After Elena turned the lights off, he couldn't fall asleep. Everything was rolling through his head, his job, Amanda, the insanity with Shiloh.

It's all too much. I deserve a break. If I could only . . . wait. I am going to get a break. Yeah, why not? To hell with saving the world. I've got to save myself.

He set Shiloh's app, then his alarm. Ten minutes later he was fast asleep.

CHAPTER 22

One

The watch alarm woke him early at 5:00 a.m. He felt groggy, but he wasn't sure whether it was from the Adjustment or just from it being so damn early.

Through his job, Cade had somehow scored tee times at one of the most exclusive country clubs in the northern suburbs. George dressed quickly and made the drive in less than thirty minutes, just like the last time. It was Saturday morning, and there was no traffic. As he pulled into the parking lot of the county club, the sky was just beginning to lighten up, but it wasn't quite sunrise.

Let's see, if I remember right, the sun will rise while I'm on the practice tees.

He pulled up to the club drop-off sign.

Okay, last time the attendant surprised me when he took my clubs and shoes to clean them. And it was definitely an awkward moment when he refused my tip.

This time, George acted as if he belonged. Before he knew it, he was out on the practice tees, watching the sunrise. The clubhouse and the practice tees were elevated, which provided an amazing view of the back nine. The grounds and course were deep green and lush. Something about the hypnotic pulsing of the sprinklers got George thinking.

I forgot how beautiful this course is, despite this hot summer. After driving through all the brown, burned fields on the way in, they are unnaturally green—like, black-magic green. Of course, it's not magic: it's money and hundreds of gallons of water.

George looked back at the grand clubhouse.

This isn't your middle-class country club. It's an old-money, upper-upper-class country club. After my hole in one, I was in the bar . . . walnut paneling, crystal chandeliers . . . this place just oozes wealth. It was seductive; I was the center of attention, drink after drink, the flirty waitress, everyone congratulating me, giving me business cards, telling me to give them a call. When I arrived I felt out of place, but by the afternoon it all felt attainable. If I would just give myself over to the altar of business. Put all I've got into work, business connections, and finances. Then I wouldn't be stuck in middle management. Maybe this time I should . . .

"George, my man, isn't it a glorious morning?"

"Cade, you surprised me, I was just remembering . . . something. Hey, you just missed the sunrise! I'm not sure I've ever seen that shade of purple before."

"I saw it from the parking lot. It was incredible, but you know, I'm kind of partial to sunsets, preferably on the beach, with a beer and a babe," Cade said. "They paired us with a couple of members. The starter said they were good guys, not too stiff. That okay with you, George?"

"Absolutely. Trust me, this is going to be an amazing day. A day to remember."

A few minutes before 7:00 a.m., Cade and George pulled their cart up to the first hole, where a couple of other golfers were waiting. "Are you guys the seven o'clock tee time?" asked Cade.

"Yup," said one of the golfers. "Are you our other two?"

Cade stepped up and put out his hand. "Name is Cade, and my partner over there is George." George stepped over, and the four men all shook hands.

"I'm Harry," said the first man.

"And I'm Steven. I don't recognize you boys, are you guests?"

"Yeah, a business partner of mine hooked us up," Cade said. "Looks like a magnificent course."

"Guests are only supposed to be going out with the member that invited them." said Harry. There was an awkward pause. "But I guess we can look past it this time."

George tried to change the subject. "You guys get out much?"

Steven responded, "I golf eighteen holes, four days a week, from opening day till the last day in the fall."

"Wow, how do you get your wife to agree to that?" It was the perfect setup for Steven.

"I wake her up every morning at six and ask her, 'Golf or sex, honey?'" It got a big laugh out of George and Cade, but it seemed Harry had heard it before. It was enough to break the ice, and the starter let them know they were good to hit.

They all teed off on number one, and it seemed like they were pretty well matched. George could feel the humidity rising off the well-watered fairway.

I should be able to remember how this round played out. I've got the scorecard framed at home in my office. But the only hole I remember is my eagle on seventeen. I just remember being dialed in that day. The round was my personal best by far, a seventy-nine. Not bad for a difficult course I'd never played.

The morning was perfect and they all started well. George relaxed, and when they all reached the green on two, Cade began to tell a story.

"I was golfing a couple of days ago. I went out by myself, and they paired me with this drop-dead gorgeous lady. Not only was she beautiful, but she was a fantastic golfer. We were getting along great, she was flirting with me, but I started getting frustrated that she was outscoring me. Anyway, we get to the back nine and she's beating me by a stroke or two and it's pissing me off. She can tell I'm upset so she leans over in the cart and starts making out with me. I can't believe it. To make a long story short, we finish the round, and sure enough she beats me by three strokes. Then she asks me to her place, but tells me there's something she has to tell me first. You won't believe this, but she tells me she's really a man. I was so furious. I told her, I can't believe all round you've been hitting from the red tees!"

Cade's joke got Harry and Steven laughing out loud. George had heard it the first time he had lived this day. He laughed along anyway. Harry and Steven both missed easy putts, and George wondered if the timing of Cade's joke was intentional.

Everything continued as well as George remembered, and he finally relaxed enough to enjoy himself. The morning was beautiful, his golf was as good as it gets, and he was looking forward to his big moment. They arrived at hole number sixteen, a 167-yard par three. It was a beautiful hole with a large pond that surrounded the green.

If you go left, right, or deep, you're wet. Most people aim short and hope the ball trickles up onto the green. They're content with a long birdie putt. But not me, not on this day. For some reason I'm fearless.

I go right at the hole. I can still picture it. It hits about five or six feet short, takes one small hop, and then rolls dead center into the hole. I wonder what made me decide not play it safe that day.

Cade had honors; he teed up his ball, took his standard two practice swings, and then stepped up to the ball. He swung hard, and the ball shot skyward.

He must have underclubbed it and then swung hard.

The shot was fading to the right, catching the light breeze blowing across the fairway. George thought it might have a chance, and it did get to the green, but Cade had put so much backspin on it that it shot back off the green and down back to the fairway.

"You're dry—that's what's important on this hole," said Steven. From the way Cade strode off the tee box, George could tell that he wasn't happy with just being dry.

Harry was up next; he approached the tee box carefully.

Seem like a perfectionist to me. Golf must be frustrating for him. Even for a pro, golf is anything but perfect.

After a single practice swing, Harry took a relaxed, easy shot. It took a flatter trajectory than Cade's but also drifted right. It hit a good fifteen yards in front of the green, skipped a couple of times, and then rolled the remaining distance onto the front right edge of the green. Harry picked up his tee and walked off the green. "And that, is how you play number seventeen."

George was up. He took a deep breath.

This is my moment. How many practice swings did I take? What was I focusing on? Don't overthink it. Just picture the shot—ball tracking dead on, hitting the fairway, and hopping onto the green. Then the slow roll up to the hole, hesitating for half a second before the ball disappeared.

George paused for a moment to clear his head, focusing on aiming just slightly left. The breeze had pushed both Cade's and Harry's balls to the right. He felt good, in the groove. George stepped up and teed up his ball. He took a couple of relaxed practice swings.

"Go for it, George," Cade said, just like last time.

George took one last look at the flag and then refocused a foot or two to the left. He looked down at his ball and swung. He connected perfectly, and everything felt right. Just as the ball took off, George felt the breeze stop. The foursome tracked the path of the ball, its arc was somewhere in between: higher than Harry's, but flatter than Cade's. It seemed to have the right distance. It hit about six feet in front of the green and made one hop onto it. It rolled up the green, pin high, and stopped about two or three inches to the left of the hole. George was stunned.

"Great shot, George!" Cade shouted.

"You know what?" said Steven. "If that breeze hadn't quit, I think that would have gone in the hole. Just think, if you had hit that ball five seconds earlier or five seconds later, you'd be buying us all drinks in the clubhouse."

George just stood there in disbelief.

What the hell? That felt perfect, just like last time. Steven was right, it was the stupid wind. If I hadn't paused right before I hit . . . . I know little things are different. But it wasn't a little thing, it was the whole reason I picked this day.

Cade came up behind him and put his hand on George's shoulder. "Hey, that was a beautiful shot, it should have gone in. Come on, you need to let Steven hit." George walked off the tee box, still in a daze.

Steven found the water on the right, just like before. George pulled himself together enough to make his birdie putt, but he fell apart on seventeen and ended up with a double-bogie. He carded a bogie on eighteen, which was enough to push him past his personal best score, and he went into the clubhouse dejected.

They ended up in the bar, and George consoled himself that Steven was right: at least he didn't have to buy everyone a drink. Harry and Steven brought over four Bloody Marys but only stayed long enough to finish the drink. George couldn't get his mind off hole seventeen.

Everyone should be gathered around me right now. I felt like a superhero. Even Elena seemed impressed. Gust of wind, and it goes from one of the top ten days of my life to an ordinary day. How did I consider that one of the great accomplishments in my life? I don't belong here anyway. Even with the hole in one, by the next morning I was back to regular George.

CHAPTER 23

We Are the Champions

June 20, 2014

George watched Shiloh walk down the aisle toward him. Today's T-shirt read, *I'd be unstoppable, if not for physics.*

"Good morning, Shiloh. How are you?" asked George, not quite sure where to start. He didn't want to jump right into his transgression and sought a way to ease into it.

"Morning, George. I'm fine."

"Being a teacher and so into science, do you think sports are trivial?"

"By no means, I think anything that celebrates life or appreciates humankind's struggles against the universe is wonderful," Shiloh said, clearly excited about the topic.

"What's your favorite sport?" asked George, a little relieved to hear Shiloh's response.

"Easy, it's football."

"Really? I would not have guessed football. Do you have a favorite team? Let me guess, the Green Bay Packers?"

"No, the other football, you know, soccer."

"Oh, that makes more sense. Why soccer?" questioned George, still wanting to delay his confession.

"Obviously, it best represents life's struggle between chaos and order."

"Obviously," George replied.

"Seriously, a top soccer club has to have great organization, and players need to have a strong base of fundamental skills. But it's the teams and players that are creative and thrive in chaos that win the championships. That's why they call it the beautiful game. It's a true team sport. A year ago I was watching a game in the English Premier league. It was just a regular season game: Arsenal versus Norwich City, back in 2013. Arsenal's on the attack, and Norwich has eight men back defending. A midfield named Cazorla slots a pass to the French player Giroud, who flicks it over to Jack Wilshere, the Englishman, who flicks it back to Giroud, who one-times it forward to Wilshere, who finishes. I think there were seven perfect passes in a row. It was perfect creativity amid chaos: pure beauty. You should watch it on YouTube some time. You just don't see that in any other sport."

George considered an objection, but choose to remain silent.

"I don't mind other sports, but they all have their issues. I don't know a lot about baseball, but it seems way too dependent on traditions and statistics with little opportunity for creativity. You can almost predict every situation. While soccer has to rely on a general shape and a team philosophy, then the best teams operate freely inside of those structures," said Shiloh.

George smiled, happy to let Shiloh carry on.

"Now hockey is too chaotic for my tastes, unless it's at the highest level. The most skilled professionals have the talent to play with that same creativity inside of a game plan, like soccer. And it's even faster. But at any other level, the ice creates a little too much randomness from my perspective."

"What about American football or basketball?"

"American football certainly has it chaos. But it's actually a highly structured game that is largely about individual strength. Like baseball, its plays are set and organized, at least on offense. I see it as more of a representation of battle or war. I understand why people like it—it's all about momentum and emotion—but for me it lacks the creativity and flow of soccer or hockey. Did you realize the average actual play time in an NFL football game is around eleven minutes?"

Shiloh paused and smiled at George, enjoying himself.

"That can't be right," said George. "They are only playing for eleven minutes?"

"It's right, look it up. Now basketball, it's actually a fairly ordered game. Teams can be creative, but most of the chaos is all about the shot. Putting the ball in a hoop while you have a six-foot-eleven, two-hundred-sixty-pound monster leaning on you is no easy task. There is some randomness and luck with rebounds and loose balls. But ultimately, it's too controlled for me. Players have such skill in handling the ball and their passes that good teams control the game. Upsets are rare. Although there are some magical moments in basketball, like NCAA tournaments or game seven of the NBA finals."

"Can you relate everything to your philosophy on life?" asked George. *You're stalling, George. Tell him you traveled. Tell him where you went.*

"Pretty much."

"Shiloh, I traveled again yesterday." George finally blurted it out.

Shiloh was not surprised. "I know."

"How do you know?"

"I can see the request come in on the server. I'll be able to see every time you travel and to what month, day, and year."

"Can you see where I go or what I do?"

"No, but it's your choice anyway. You can only go ten times, but you get to choose," Shiloh said.

"What if I used one to do something fun? I mean, you've never explained why you've let me do this or what I'm supposed to do. With such an earth-shattering invention, should you be using it for something significant? Like preventing a war or finding a better way to harness energy?"

"Nothing you experience on your travels will change what happens here. The parallel worlds that get picked have to be extremely close to this reality. And you never know what events will change a life; in that world or this one. You need to decide how to use them."

"My travel was to golf. I went back to the day I hit a hole in one. Only it didn't happen this time. I wasted a travel."

"Did you learn anything?" asked Shiloh.

"I guess I learned that what I thought was one of the most important days in my life wasn't all that important."

"Then you didn't waste it. Then it was worthwhile."

"Great, I'll stop feeling guilty about it then," George said sarcastically.

"Even more important, you went. You were brave, and you trusted me. I like you, George. I hope you keep traveling, and I hope we can be friends."

Brave or stupid, I'm not sure which. An idea sprung into his head. "Hey, can you travel with me?"

"No, it doesn't work that way."

George thought for a moment. "Okay, well, if we can't travel that way together, someday would you be willing to go to a baseball game with me? I want to show you why I think baseball is a great sport, despite what you've said."

"Sure, I've never been to a live baseball game."

"Great, because the beauty of sports that are a little more structured, like baseball and basketball, is that despite the odds, sometimes the underdog wins. Have you ever seen the movie *Hoosiers*?"

"Yes, and I see your point. I'd love to go to a game with you. Let's not wait too long. You know how time flies."

CHAPTER 24

Everybody Hurts

June 22, 2014

"Strike three!" called the umpire. George watched Alex hang his head and shuffle back to the dugout. Alex threw his bat against the chain-link fence and his batting helmet to the ground. Alex had struck out looking to end the game. A few minutes later George saw the coach talking with Alex. The coach did most of the talking, and Alex just seemed to nod. After they finished, Alex gathered up his gear and started walking toward the car. George met him there and opened the trunk. Alex was silent.

> *I think I'll just give him some space.*

As they were pulling out of the parking lot, George asked, "Where do you want to eat, Alex?"

"Don't care."

"What about the burger and malt place?"

"Sure."

Alex sunk down into his seat with his arms crossed. George waited until they arrived at the burger joint and ordered before he spoke again. "Rough game, huh?"

Alex scowled. "Coach said he's moving me from shortstop to second base and back to six or seven in the batting order."

"Really? You struggle in one game and he's already moving you?"

"Dad, I went zero and four, and I had an error. And it's not been one game; I haven't had a good game in two or three weeks."

"You're just in a slump. You'll come out of it."

"No, Dad. It's not a slump. I suck. Just because you played in college doesn't mean I'm going to be a good baseball player. Kids are passing me up; I'm just not a good baseball player anymore."

"Alex, you're a great baseball player! Just last year your batting average was third or fourth on the team."

"Yeah, okay, and the year before I was first and this year I'm probably last on the team. Dad, I don't think I want to play baseball after this season," Alex said as he stared out the window of the restaurant.

Where is this coming from? He's just not willing to work harder.

"Whoa, Alex, wait a second. You don't quit just because things get hard, you work harder. When's the last time you got out in the yard and practiced?"

"That's not going to help me, Dad, I'm not ten anymore. We practice plenty as a team. Besides, I really don't want to play anymore. I don't enjoy it."

George felt his blood pressure rising. "Alex, we let you drop basketball last year because you wanted to focus on baseball. Now you're going to drop sports altogether? What about your buddies? Seems like you're a little shy on friends these days."

"Thanks for pointing out I don't have any friends," Alex said. "But that's the thing. I'm not friends with anyone on the team anymore."

"We just talked about this. You just can't spend all your time messing around on your guitar, reading comic books, and playing video games."

Alex shook his head. "They're graphic novels, not comic books."

"Whatever, it's the same thing. You need to do something more productive. I still think you're on track to make the high school baseball team. It's important to have some school activities when you do college applications in a few years."

"Dad, I'm worried about school too."

"What do you mean?"

"You and Mom made me sign up for all those Advanced Placement courses. There is no way I'm going to be able to keep up this year."

"Alex, you had all A's last year, I think you've had all A's every year. How in the world can you be worried? Yeah, it's going to get a little hard. So what? You need to push yourself. Besides, it doesn't sound like you'll have anything else to spend your time on; it might as well be homework."

"Dad, I just get A's because I do my homework and extra credit. I suck at tests, and extra credit is not going to be enough next year. It's so much easier for everyone else. I study twice as much as my friends and I still do worse on the tests. Look at Amanda: she does the bare minimum for homework and she barely studies, and she still gets straight A's."

"Alex, I don't know when this all came about, but you've just lost a little confidence. Hard work can get you good grades. You might have to work harder than others, but that's going to make you better in the long run."

Now Alex was struggling to keep himself from crying. "Better for what? So I can get into a college, where I still have to work twice as hard as everyone, so I can get a crappy job like yours, Dad?"

Ungrateful brat. "Hey, my crappy job puts food in your mouth every day and a roof over our heads," George said.

"Yeah, I get it, Dad, it's all about money. But I see how miserable you are at work. You come home angry every other day. And I can tell Mom's not exactly thrilled to be spending her days cooking and cleaning and going to book club. Is that my life, work my ass off in high school, then in college, so I can get a job that I hate for the next thirty years? I don't want any of this. I don't know if I even want to go to college."

Unbelievable. He'd be damn lucky to do as well as I have. I don't remember questioning this when I was a kid. Parents say work hard in school, I worked hard. Coach says more effort in sports, I give one hundred percent. Go to college, I went to college.

"Alex, I don't know where to start. Yeah, I don't like my job right now, but it hasn't always been that way. And, yes, your mother gave up a lot to take care of you guys, but she wanted to. Yes, some days it sucks, and we complain, but none of it is as bad as you're making it seem. It's just tough right now because of Amanda."

"No, it's not just because of Amanda's accident. Dad, you were miserable long before the accident. Our whole family was. Don't take this the wrong way, but I don't want to be you. I don't want to live your life."

The waitress saved George from saying something he would regret by bring their food.

"Alex, I think you need to eat. I don't understand where all this is coming from. I know I've brought home my work problems, but our lives are better than most. A lot of people would love to have our lives."

"I was wondering when you'd bring up the starving kids in China or Africa."

"Alex, you need to change your attitude. This is ridiculous. You *do* live like a king compared to most people in the world. And just because you went zero and four today is no reason to whine about our lives. We're not worried about where our next meal is coming from; we're not worried about where we are going to sleep tonight. And while your sister is in the hospital in pain every day, you have no business complaining. Now, eat your food."

That was pretty much the end of the conversation. They both focused on their hamburgers for a while, and when George tried to talk more with Alex, he got one-word responses. George decided he was going to need Elena's help this time.

Jesus, how did it go from a baseball slump to not wanting to go to college? When did he go from a fun-loving kid to an angst-ridden teenager?

CHAPTER 25

Where Is My Mind?

June 23, 2014

George awoke on Monday morning vaguely aware of some quickly dissipating dream. He remembered panic and struggling against several pairs of arms, but the more he tried to recall the dream, the quicker it went away.

Another Monday. At least it has to go better than last Thursday.

He had spent Friday doing damage control, but he still needed to be at the top of his game this week. He still had to dig out of the hole he was in.

At 6:12 a.m. George boarded the 610 Union Pacific Northwest Metra train. Four minutes later, Shiloh boarded and sat down next to George. Shiloh's shirt read, *Think like a proton, stay positive.*

"Good morning, George."

"Good morning, Shiloh. What are you listening to today?"

"It's one of the best punk bands to come out of Boston, The Pixies. Kurt Cobain said they were the inspiration for his biggest hit. How's your family?"

"Amanda's doing better every day. It's my son, Alex, that has me worried now. He seems depressed. We were talking about him dropping out of baseball, and the next thing I know he's saying that he's not even sure he wants to go to college. And to top it off, he went out of his way to tell me he doesn't want to grow up to be me. I don't know what is going through that boy's brain," George said.

"The brain is fascinating. Do you realize that the average human brain is about three pounds, and pound for pound it's the most complex object in the solar system, maybe the universe?"

George wanted to tell Shiloh that he had already told him about the brain's complexity, but when Shiloh got on a roll, it was difficult to get a word in.

"Even a fruit fly's brain has one hundred and fifty thousand neurons. But the human brain, it has around one hundred billion neurons and exponentially more synapses. And even with all that complexity, it only consumes about twenty watts of energy. Do you realize it's more active when you're dreaming than when you're awake? And do you realize that in a lifetime you spend about six years dreaming? Oh yeah, speaking of dreaming, did I tell you that you may experience some vivid dreams as a side effect of the traveling?"

George sighed. "No, Shiloh, you didn't tell me about any side effects. But I have had a few strange dreams. You were in one. We were in World War Two, and we were trying to kill Hitler, but I ended up killing my own great-grandfather."

"Interesting. That is a weird dream," said Shiloh. "You may have a few more; it's just your brain adjusting."

Why the hell does my brain need to recover from the traveling? At least it explains the crazy dreams. But just how dangerous is "flipping" my consciousness to another dimension or parallel universe or whatever the hell it is? Maybe Shiloh keeps telling me not to worry about my kids because it's me I should be worried about.

"Fantastic," George said. "I don't have enough weirdness in my life. Are there any other side effects I should know about?"

"No, I don't think so. George, do you understand the power of positivity?"

"Who are you, Tony Robbins?"

"No, seriously, there has been an incredible amount of scientific research on the effects of positivity on the brain. It shows that positivity has a scientifically measurable impact on the hormonal, cardiovascular, and immune systems. It actually has a role in increasing hormones like oxytocin, which leads to many positive health impacts such as lowering blood pressure and the ability to handle stress."

"I believe you, but Alex is a teenager. They're negative by default. It's probably a stage. Every kid goes through them," replied George.

"It's not Alex who needs to be more positive."

"Huh?"

"It's you, George. You need to be more positive with him. Have you ever heard of the Gottman index?"

George crossed his arms and leaned back. "No, I haven't."

"It's based on a number of studies, but it boils down to the fact that it takes at least five positive interactions to make up for one negative. Alex needs positive reinforcement. He needs to hear what he's doing right. You have to go out of your way to point out the good things he's doing."

George smirked. "That's a bit difficult right now. He's a slob around the house, he's in a major slump in baseball, and all he does all day is read comic books and play guitar. I don't know what I'm supposed to praise him about."

"You have to figure it out. Maybe you can connect with him through music. The teenage years are important. Things can spiral either way—up or down."

"I just wish he'd put more effort into baseball. He used to be such a great player; he was a joy to watch. I think he could be a great player. I just don't know what happened to him."

"I know you have a love of baseball, but maybe he doesn't. Maybe he worked hard and succeeded to please you, to spend time with you. He's not you, George."

Jesus. It's not like I'm asking him to work in the salt mines. I'm asking him to honor a commitment by playing a game. "Okay, okay. Have you spoken with my wife? I feel like the two of you are ganging up on me. It's just that all his issues came out of nowhere. And now he's talking about skipping college. I guess I could get over baseball, but college—nothing is more important than education."

"There are lots of kinds of education and lots of careers, George. Make sure you understand what he wants from life. What's important to him? You can't help him if you don't understand him. Besides, you probably think scientist and engineer and business leader are the most important careers."

"Well, yeah, those *are* important careers."

"I believe that artist, musician, teacher, and most historians are the most important."

"Why's that?"

"Because technology is already advancing too fast, and we need our humanity to keep pace. And, more importantly, we need to learn from our mistakes. We can't learn from our mistakes without great historians and teachers. People have lost touch with our past, which is a huge problem. It's essential that we learn from our history. The saying is right: those who cannot remember the past are condemned to repeat it. George Santayana, the Spanish philosopher, said that way back in 1905. One hundred and nine years later, we still don't get it."

"I'm not sure how you can say that. They teach history in school, and history is getting more popular in our culture. Take the History Channel, for instance. I think people are paying attention."

"No, people aren't even coming close to understanding enough about history. They only think only in terms of the last one hundred years. I bet most people have no idea that during the Han Dynasty, the Chinese were drilling for natural gas and transporting it through pipelines two hundred years before Christ. Or that ancient Roman people developed the formula still used for concrete today over two thousand years ago."

Is there anything this guy doesn't know?

"Let me ask you this, George. What came first, the extinction of woolly mammoths or the building of the first Egyptian pyramids?"

"I have no idea. I guess the extinction of woolly mammoths?"

"Thank you for proving my point. The early Egyptian pyramids were built before the woolly mammoth went extinct. So you see, we don't pay enough attention to history. If we did, we wouldn't keep making the same mistakes. People have no idea that Oxford University predates the Aztec civilization or that Harvard University was founded before calculus was invented."

"I'm not sure I understand why it's so important."

"Oh, George, it's everything! Our most challenging issue is that while we aren't learning from our past social or ethical mistakes, we're accelerating our technological development. It took us over one hundred thousand years to learn to fly, then just sixty-six years more to reach the moon. Our advancements in genetics, bioengineering, nanotechnology, robotics, and other scientific disciplines have grown at an exponential rate. Think of all the world-altering technologies just on the edge of major breakthroughs: technologies like fusion reactors, quantum computers, artificial intelligence, and 3-D printers. Significant advances in any one of these spaces have the potential to disrupt every aspect of our lives."

"But isn't that good?"

"Not if we're not ready for it. Our ability to solve social issues is moving at a snail's pace. We need to advance our humanity as fast as our technology; otherwise it's all going to end. Do you realize that a ruler who lived around a quarter century before Christ banned slavery, the death penalty, animal cruelty, and deforestation? He was Emperor Ashoka, a Buddhist who ruled in India. He even supported gender equality in education and religious institutions. But still it took two thousand one hundred and seventy years for the women's suffrage movement to finally win out. And there still isn't gender equality in many countries, and the death penalty is still used throughout the world. Hell, France was still using the guillotine for execution in 1977. Can you see the problem, George? It isn't Muslims or China or even North Korea. It's all of us. It's our fears, our greed, and our hate."

"Okay, I see your point."

"So, if your son wants to become a historian or a teacher or an artist, just support him. Hey, my stop is coming up. Think about it, George."

"I will, Shiloh, but this isn't easy for me."

As Shiloh stood up to leave, he replied, "Nobody said it would be. But suck it up, George, your son is worth it."

He goes straight for the jugular. Of course Alex is worth it. But I swear, if he's a history major, I'm going to be supporting him for the rest of his life. I can never retire.

His arrival at work wiped away his concerns as he tried to throw himself back into his job. He was having a pretty good morning and took a break to call Elena.

"Hi, George."

"Hey, baby, we've hardly seen each other lately. What do you say I come home at lunch and we do some serious making out?"

"Funny! How's work?" she asked.

"It's a jungle, but I'm hacking through it. I'm still taking it a day at a time. How's our daughter?"

"Oh, she's still struggling. I suppose it's normal, but I don't think she's over the loss of her eye. I think she's still sort of hoping they're going to take off the bandages and she's going to be able to see out of both eyes. And she gets so frustrated with the physical therapy. But she's doing really well. Even the staff says she's doing awesome. I just can't wait to get her home."

"Well, I'm sorry to throw more at you, but on Sunday Alex told me he wants to quit baseball and might not want to go to college."

Tag, you're it.

"The baseball part doesn't surprise me much; I think he's been losing interest for some time. But I'm worried about college. What else did he say?"

How does she think she knows more about his baseball than me? "I'm probably just blowing it out of proportion. I think he's going through a phase. I need to spend some more time with him working on baseball. Then maybe he'll reconnect with his baseball friends instead of Jeff."

"I'm not sure that's the answer. George, you need to make sure that Alex is playing baseball for himself, not for you. I'm worried about him. It's driving me crazy that I haven't been able to spend more time with him. But this is a critical week for Amanda. I think we have to divide and conquer here. I'm going to focus on getting Amanda home this week and getting ready for her party. Maybe we should think about getting Alex into some sort of counseling."

George raised his eyebrows. "What? You mean like a psychiatrist? Elena, don't you think that's a bit extreme? All boys go through phases. That might mess him up even more." *No way is he going to psychiatrist.*

"It doesn't have to be a psychiatrist. It could just be a school counselor. Someone trained to listen and understand what he is going though. He might open up more with someone else instead of you and me."

"I don't think he needs that. Let's see how he does after we get Amanda home."

Elena paused for a second. "Okay, but I need you to concentrate on Alex. Listen to him, George. Make sure you understand everything that's going on with him."

What am I, the backup parent? Second string?

"I got it, honey. You take care of Amanda. I'll talk with Alex. Everything just seems out of whack with Amanda at the hospital. It'll be fine. I've got to get back to the jungle."

"Love you," Elena said.

"See you tonight."

George called Cade, and they agreed to meet for lunch. He arrived at the restaurant first and, since it was a cloudy, dreary day, he made the call to sit inside. Cade arrived a few minutes later.

"George! My man, my man, how you doing? Do we have the same waitress? If so, I'm buying today!"

George smiled. "Not bad, Cade. No, I think she's off today, but you can still buy anyway. I have a feeling our waiter is going to really like you."

"How's your daughter? She must be doing well—Lynn and I got an invitation for a surprise homecoming party for her."

"Yeah, the doctors say she's doing great. We're still worried about her, not so much her recovery but more about how she is dealing with the loss of her eye. I'm still not sure she'll be ready for a big party on Saturday, but Elena is hell-bent on it."

It was Cade's turn to smile. "Has Elena ever been wrong?"

"That's a great point. Will you and Lynn be able to make it?"

"Try and keep us away. How's your job, still awful?"

George scowled. "Thanks for reminding me. Yeah, it's bad. I royally screwed up a meeting last week, and now I'm just trying to make up for it."

"Hang in there. Just remember, everybody hates their job these days. It's a jungle out there."

George laughed. "That's just what I was saying to Elena. Anyway, it's hard to feel too sorry for myself with all the things Amanda and Alex are going through."

"Alex? What's Alex going through?"

"Oh, I guess just a phase. He wants to quit baseball. It seems like he's has no motivation for anything." *Why did I bring up Alex?*

"Quit baseball? Really, that's his sport! He's a great ball player, just like his dad."

"I know. I'm trying to reason with him, but he's just in this funk."

Cade seemed concerned. "He'll snap out of it, it's just typical teenage boy stuff. He's probably just struggling with you and Elena having to focus so much on Amanda. You guys need any help with anything?"

"No, we're okay. Everything is getting a little better every day. I'm just looking forward to getting things back to normal," George said. Just then their waiter arrived and they ordered. "Hey, Cade, remember the other day when I asked you about time travel? I have another question."

"Marilyn Monroe, remember? That's your best bet," Cade said.

"Yeah, that's solid advice. No, what if you could only go back twenty-five years or so, and it was more about going back and reliving a day in your own life? And you could only go ten times?"

"Hmmm, I'd go back to all ten times I've slept with Elena," teased Cade.

"Funny, man. Like you'd ever have a shot with her."

"Your right, she's way out of both of our leagues. How you ever ended up with her, I'll never understand."

"I do agree with you there. I don't understand it either. But seriously, what would you do?"

"Let see . . . I'd go back to that time that I had the game-winning jump shot in that game against Barrington High."

"That was you? I don't remember that," joked George.

"You're just jealous. Everybody remembers that!"

"I hate to tell you, Cade, but it was more than twenty-five years ago. Okay, what else?" asked George.

"I don't know, maybe a couple of vacations in Mexico or one of the cruises that Lynn and I took in the Caribbean. I would go back to that party Lynn threw me for my fortieth birthday—that was a fun day," Cade said.

"What about your wedding or the birth of your son?"

"Ah, I'd probably skip the wedding and childbirth and pick the honeymoon and conception instead," replied Cade with a smile.

George laughed. Another thought came to Cade, "Oh, I know, I'd go back and not crash my 1971 Mustang Mach 1. Then I'd still have it."

"Lynn would have made you sell that by now."

"Damn, you're probably right. What about you George? When would you go back to?"

"I don't know, the same kinds of things you've been thinking of, but I'd go the wedding and the births."

"That's why Elena picked you; you're such a pushover. Hey, what about the day you had a hole in one?"

Ah, see, I wasn't crazy for picking it!

"Yeah, I don't know. It was a fun day, but I'm not sure it's in my top ten," he replied, hoping his face wasn't giving up too much. The waiter arrived with their food.

"Hey, what about that time we went to Rosa's Lounge and Big Time Sarah pulled you up on stage to sing with her? That was about the funniest thing I've ever seen. What was the song she sang with you?" asked Cade.

"It was 'Meet Me with Your Black Drawers On,' and that is not a day that I would pick. It was terrifying. It was pretty funny, though, I have to admit," George said. He hadn't thought about that in a long time.

"I just remember her pushing your face down into her chest. The whole place was busting up." Cade got serious. "Hey, what about that time in South Chicago. Would you go back to that day?"

"I try not to think about that. Thanks, Cade, why did you have to bring that up?" George didn't tell Cade that it was a battle he lost regularly.

"Because I think if you'd talk about it more, you might be able to get over it. You've been beating yourself up about that for years." Cade looked George straight in the eyes.

"Yeah, well, thanks but no thanks. And the answer is no, I would not go back to that day. I should have never told you about it."

"Sorry. Seriously, I'm not trying to give you a hard time, just a chance to talk. That's what friends do. I know it bothers you."

"I'm over it. Okay? Finish your burger, I've got to get back to work," George said, now wanting the conversation to be over.

Cade paid for lunch, and they said their good-byes along with a fist bump on the way out. George settled into an afternoon of conference calls but couldn't stop his mind from wandering to his past. In particular, he couldn't stop thinking about a certain day in his past on the South Side that he wished had never happened.

CHAPTER 26

We Are Family

"Alex, how about we go to the park and I hit you some fly balls?" asked George.

"Dad, really? I just got home from baseball practice. I'm tired and hungry."

George put his hands on his hips. "Maybe this weekend then?"

"Doubt it. It's Amanda's stupid party, and I have a game on Sunday."

"Okay, Alex, I get it. Are you up for going to visit Amanda tonight?"

"As much as I love the hospital, I'd rather not," Alex said.

George looked at him and said, "You know what? Tonight you're going. You haven't seen your sister in a while, and I want the whole family to eat dinner together."

The ride to the hospital was quiet. George asked a few questions but barely got grunts for answers. He was a little relieved when they arrived.

"There are my boys," Elena said. "How are the men in my life?"

"Don't ask," George said.

"Ah, bubbling over with positivity and family fun are you?"

George gave her a stare. "Let's just go to dinner."

The Hartdegen family had arrived on meatloaf night. After much analysis, the ladies chose chef salads and the gents chose turkey sandwiches, all from the premade section. They found a table for four in the corner of the dining room and sat down.

"Who wants to say grace?" asked Elena.

After a long pause, George replied, "Grace."

"Wow, the kids can't even be bothered to participate in their favorite dinner joke?"

"Apparently not," said George. "Okay, who wants to jump in first on family discussion?"

Surprisingly, Amanda spoke up. "I hear you're quitting baseball, Alex. You're going to get picked on at the high school if you're not in any sports."

"Don't care," replied Alex.

"Really, Amanda? I told you that in confidence, not so you could tease your brother," Elena said. "Honestly, what is wrong with this family?"

"It's sort of true. Kids are brutal at high school. And good luck with your two AP classes; you're not going to have any time for sports anyway."

"At least I don't have one eye! I guess we're both going to be freaks at the high school."

Well, that escalated fast. "Alex, I can't believe you just said that. Seriously, you two, you're family. You don't treat each other this way," George said, his voice rising.

Amanda pushed her food away. "I want to go back to my room."

Elena shot a look at Alex and said, "Amanda, you have to eat. The doctor told you how important your nutrition is right now."

"Fine, I'll bring it back to the room," Amanda said, tearing up.

Elena looked at Amanda and then George. "All right, I guess family dinner was a bad idea tonight. We'll see you boys later."

She gathered up their salads and plopped them on Amanda's lap. Then she wheeled her off toward the exit.

Divide and conquer. Good strategy, Elena.

"Alex, this is unacceptable."

"She started it."

"You went too far—way too far. What she's dealing with is serious."

"Yeah, it's always my fault, never Amanda's," Alex said.

George was out of things to say, so they cleaned up their table and headed for the car.

"I don't know what is wrong with these kids," George said later on, in bed.

"They're both going through a lot. These are tough years for kids, don't you remember? They're both nervous about school, especially when things are so out of sorts."

"Yeah, but why do they have to be so mean to each other? They're brother and sister, for Heaven's sake."

"Who else are they going to lash out at? They have to express their feelings and their fears. They are easy, safe targets for each other," Elena said.

"Well, it's ugly," George replied.

"Tell me about. It took a good hour for Amanda to settle down."

"Let's change the topic, Elena, if you could go back and relive ten days in your life, which ten would you pick?"

"You can't ask me to pick just ten. I want them all, every day."

"What? Bullshit. You just told me the other day that you struggle being a stay-at-home mother," George said.

"No, really, I would relive every day. I miss my childhood. I want to fall in love with you again. I want to fit in my wedding dress again. I want every day of the pregnancies, even when I was miserable. I want to hold my babies again. I want to watch them learn to talk and crawl and walk. I want to laugh when they laugh and hold them when they cry. I want to watch you teach Amanda to shoot a basketball and Alex to catch a baseball. And yes, even though I wonder, I'd relive the last ten years at home, too."

"What about days you were sick, or just bad days? What about high school? Don't tell me you would go back and relive high school?"

"High school wasn't that bad. Sure, some days were better than others, but I don't think there's a day I wouldn't live over again. We're so lucky to have lived such great lives. Think about what other people have experienced in their lives—prison, war, abuse—now *they* have a reason to skip some days."

"Sometimes your positivity drives me crazy, Elena. You spend the days cleaning up after your caveman son. I don't know where you get your patience."

Elena smiled thinly. "Well, I'd say I live with two cavemen. Have you seen your closet lately? But okay, maybe there are some days I'd list at the bottom, but there are certainly thousands I would repeat in a second. I don't think we appreciate what a great life we have had."

"Even today?" asked George.

"Even today. Our kids are going to get past this. We have to help them overcome their fears. It's hard to grow up."

George mused on that for a few minutes. When he looked over, he saw that Elena had fallen asleep.

How does she fall asleep so easily when it's such a struggle for me? These kids have to be driving her as crazy as me. Well, she doesn't have bills, college tuition, and the mortgage chasing around her head. And relive every day? Come on, I'd miss more than I'd live if I had the choice. Maybe instead of counting sheep, I should count years till retirement.

CHAPTER 27

Welcome to the Jungle

George waited behind Shiloh, who hacked at the deep underbrush with his machete. The heat and humidity were unbearable.

I can't catch my breath. How is Shiloh working so hard in this heat?

Shiloh wore khaki pants, a long-sleeved khaki shirt, and heavy boots. To make it worse, he carried a full pack, along with binoculars and a pith helmet. George had a simple animal pelt slung over this shoulder and somehow fastened at his waist. With his arms and legs fully exposed, he swatted constantly at the mosquitoes and black flies that swarmed him.

Shiloh paused and said, "Shhh. Look, George." He pointed with his machete. George looked but saw nothing but the thick vegetation. "Look right there," whispered Shiloh, reaching out further with his machete. He seemed to be pointing a large stick on a larger branch. As George peered into the jungle, he saw the stick move. It had legs.

That's a walking stick. Bobby and I used to find those in the woods by the creek. But look at the size of that thing! It's almost a foot long.

It moved slowly up the branch and then froze again. When it stopped moving it was nearly impossible to see. Shiloh smiled and said, "Cool, isn't it?"

Shiloh returned to hacking while George watched the walking stick and scratched his full beard. It was a tangled mess and seemed to be full of brambles. Shiloh paused again and turned to George.

"You really stink, George."

George took a breath and decided that Shiloh was right. He opened his mouth to reply but was only able to get out a garbled sound. He tried again with the same result. It felt like trying to speak at the dentist through a full dose of Novocain and a mouthful of dental tools.

What's wrong with me?

Shiloh laughed at him and returned to hacking away at the jungle. He cleared away enough to push through the thick brush and step into a clearing. George followed him, nearly losing his animal skin on a branch. The clearing had no underbrush, but a canopy of trees overhead blocked the sky. As they stepped inside, Shiloh again paused and hushed George, gesturing with his machete.

"Watch this," he whispered.

Shiloh was pointing at a large plant with a large, long, vaselike structure at its center. At the top, a tube turned to the side with a six-inch round opening. George could see liquid inside the tube. It looked syrupy, like honey or nectar. A small bird was fluttering around the opening. George didn't recognize the bird, but it seemed like a cross between a hummingbird and a small finch. It was brightly colored in yellow and red. The bird darted back and forth, and then finally perched on a ridge at the bottom of the opening. The little bird looked around the clearing carefully. Just as it reached down to the syrupy liquid, the opening snapped shut. George gasped. The plant was just transparent enough that George could make out the shape of the bird inside, struggling. After a few moments it stopped.

"Now that's something you don't see every day."

George tried to reply again but only got out a grunt. Shiloh moved through the clearing to the other side and started hacking away at another wall of vegetation.

Soon Shiloh had broken through the other side of the clearing. They stepped out into bright sunlight, blinking at a large expanse of grassland stretching as far as they could see. George saw smoke in the distance and followed its trail across the horizon to a large mountain. It was a long way off, but George thought he could see glowing red at the top of the mountain. George pointed and grunted.

"Yep, a volcano. I see it, George," said Shiloh, in the tone you would use to talk to a small child. George grunted again in frustration. Shiloh turned away from the volcano and walked across the grassland toward a ridgeline. George looked down and noticed it wasn't grass; it was some type of fern. The jungle was on their left. George followed Shiloh.

As they neared the top of the ridgeline, Shiloh slowed down and then stopped. "There," he said, pointing off to the right. Two . . . no, three large animals were now visible, grazing on the ferns. George's eyes took a moment to focus.

Those are some sort of dinosaur. Wow, they must be about the size of a city bus. Their heads look like horseheads.

George grunted again in surprise. Shiloh lifted his binoculars to his eyes. "*Saurolophus*—herbivores. Cool, I don't have this one." He put down the binoculars and pulled out a small notebook. George couldn't take his eyes off the creatures. Even from this distance, they seemed too big to be real.

Shiloh put his notebook away. "Let's see how close we can get." He motioned for George to follow him. They first walked back toward the jungle and then angled toward the dinosaurs, staying close to the treeline. As they moved closer, the *Saurolophus* seemed even larger. Nervous now, George grunted at Shiloh.

"Don't worry, they're plant eaters. They won't care about us," said Shiloh.

Shiloh was right: even when they got within a hundred yards, the dinosaurs didn't seem to notice or care.

Good God. I don't care if they're herbivores; they're so large they could kill by stampede or with a swipe of a tail!

Shiloh, fearless as usual, approached the dinosaurs directly. George followed, keeping the jungle in sight. One of the *Saurolophus* lifted its head from the ferns and snorted.

They finally see us.

The others stopped grazing as well. They shifted their weight and made strange sounds, seeming agitated. George made a slow step backward toward the jungle. Then a terrible crashing sound echoed from the tree line further down—trunks snapping like twigs. He froze. A few seconds later something charged out of the jungle toward the *Saurolophus*, which all took off directly toward Shiloh and George. George was thinking that the impossibly large dinosaur looked like a *Tyrannosaurus rex* when Shiloh raced past him.

"Run!" yelled Shiloh.

George snapped out of it and chased Shiloh toward the jungle. As they neared the treeline George heard the *Saurolophus* thunder by. They had to be no more than twenty yards away—it sounded and felt like a large train was passing just behind him.

As Shiloh leaped into the jungle, he yelled, "You're probably thinking it's a *Tyrannosaurus rex* chasing them, but it's not. I believe it's an *Albertosaurus.*"

George didn't much care about which dinosaur it was. As they entered the jungle, a thick mist rose up around them. They were about twenty feet into the trees when George heard more crashing behind him.

"Move faster, he has your scent!" yelled Shiloh. Shiloh cut more to the right, and George stumbled straight ahead. The undergrowth thickened, and after about five more steps George was tangled in vines and bushes. The mist swirled as the crashing behind him grew louder. George struggled against the vines, but they seemed to wrap around him even tighter. He heard a terrible snarl and made one more push to break free. The mist was so thick he could no longer see the jungle in front of him.

The next sound he heard confused him so much he went limp.

George blundered into consciousness and turned off the alarm on his Apple Watch. He sat up in bed and ran his fingers through his hair.

I half expect to pull out a leaf or a twig. Jesus, Shiloh wasn't joking about the vivid dreams. I'm so relieved to be awake. That feeling of being chased and immobile in the vines was horrible. God, my dreams are crazier than my travels. So what does that mean? My

*troubles are too big to solve? I'm trapped and I can't escape? To hell with
Alex, I'm the one who needs a psychiatrist.*

He searched for Shiloh on the train, but the stop came and
went without any sign of him.

*So who is Shiloh? It doesn't seem possible that a community
college physics professor has stumbled on a universe-level hack by himself. He said he wasn't an alien, and for some reason I believe him. So .
. .what, some sort of government program or highly advanced research
corporation? It doesn't make sense. I can't see an organization like that
selecting that guy. What if he is from of one of these alternate universes?
Maybe his watch broke? Or he's some sort of time-travel tourist? It feels
crazy just to think about this. Time castaway or tourist, I need a theory
just to stay sane. If he was a tourist, he could only stay for one day, so
let's go with castaway. Why is he helping me? To somehow get himself
home?*

He looked around the train at all the people on their way
to work. Almost all of them were absorbed in their phones, news-
papers, or books. The stranger sitting next to him was focused on
his laptop. He appeared to be in his early sixties, but as George
looked at wrinkles on his face, he guessed the man had been living
with stress for many years.

*That's me in ten more years. Who needs time travel? I can see
my future in his face.*

The man caught George staring. George quickly turned
away.

*Just look normal, George. How am I ever going to get back to
"normal"? Will I ever be normal again? Maybe I just need time, and to
make the best of it. I still can't imagine telling anyone else about this,
not even Elena.*

At lunch George grabbed a sandwich from his company
cafeteria and went back to his desk. As he ate he made a list.

First travel—done
Save Amanda from accident—done
My hole in one—done (wasted one)
~~Bears Super Bowl win~~ —too far back
~~Wedding day~~—too far back
1995/1996 Chicago Bulls Championship
St. Maarten vacation
~~Sky diving~~—once was enough
Kids' births?
~~Promoted at work~~—blah
~~Incident in South Chicago~~—no
Alex's first tee-ball game
See Mom & Dad again
~~Berlin Wall goes down~~—too far to travel in one day
~~Stop 9/11~~—too risky

George tapped his pencil on the paper and reread the list. He got up from his desk and looked out the window. Then he walked back to his desk and looked at the list again.

I'm probably forgetting things. Have the last twenty-five years of my life been that meaningless? Would most people struggle like I am, or are they more like Elena? It might help if I could go all the way back to my childhood. Maybe I should I forget about my past and literally try to be a superhero? Prevent disasters? How do you stop 9/11 in one day? How do you convince people it's going to happen without being implicated yourself? The authorities would want to know how I knew about the terrorists' plans? Would I ruin that other George's life? What if stopping a major event has other unintended negative consequences?

George ran his fingers though his hair, leaned back in his chair, and stared at the ceiling.

I could just keep it simple and relive a Disney World vacation or a birthday. Not really top ten–worthy, but safe. Maybe my best days were just ordinary days? Lazy Saturdays in the yard playing with the kids. Or watching the kids learn to walk and talk. Back when we used to have family game night or movie night. Or enjoying the excitement of the kids' last day of school. I remember picnics with Elena in the park before we had kids. Those were pretty great days. The more ordinary the better.

But how do I pinpoint those days? I don't want to pick a day at random and end up accidentally picking a bad day. Like that weekend the whole family had the flu. Oh hell no. I guess I just need to take it one travel at a time. Maybe as I experience more it will help me decide what to do next. Wow, it's past lunch hour. I guess my cross-dimensional time-travel planning will have to wait.

He kind of enjoyed losing himself in his daily routines. It wasn't until he was trying to fall asleep on Friday night, with the rush of preparations, that he started to worry about the surprise party and Amanda's reaction. As he lay there, he decided to cross one more travel off his list. He set Shiloh's app and an alarm. It would be an early start.

CHAPTER 28

Play the Game

June 14, 1998

The alarm woke him at 5:00 a.m. The traveling hangover, as he had started to call it, wasn't as bad, but it was there. He quickly got out of bed, made some coffee, and headed down to his office to make preparations. He spent a solid hour figuring everything out and making reservations before he dialed Cade's number.

"George, morning. Three things: number one, it's Sunday, number two, it's six a.m., and number three, I'm still hungover from last night, so this better be good," grumbled Cade.

He's not going to believe this.

"Get in the shower, Cade, we have to be at O'Hare by seven. We arrive in Salt Lake City at ten thirty."

There was a moment of silence, and then Cade said, "You're joking."

"Get moving, Cade, we're going to game six. I'm buying. We're taking the red-eye home, so you'll be back in time for a quick nap and work on Monday morning."

"George, wait. All that money! What if they don't win? Why don't you wait and see, and then we can go to game seven at the United Center? Even if the tickets are more, it will still be cheaper without airfare."

"Cade, I can pretty much guarantee that there isn't going to be a game seven. The Bulls are going to win today, it's going to be one of the greatest games ever, and you and I are going to see it. Get in the shower."

Can I really guarantee that they'll win? After the hole in one?

"I don't know how you got Elena to agree or where you got the money, but I'm all in! I'll see you at the gate," said Cade before hanging up.

Cade was easy to find at the gate. He was six foot five, and he was wearing a Bulls jersey along with a white headband. George walked up to Cade laughing. "Are you going to watch the game, or are you planning on playing in it?"

"Oh man. Pippen, Jordan, and I would be unstoppable. It would have been over in four games," joked Cade.

George handed Cade a boarding pass. "Here's your ticket to ride. Sorry I couldn't swing first class."

"My man, I don't care where we sit on the plane, but we are first class all the way. I don't know how to thank you. I'm going to owe you for years. I guess that's your plan, huh?"

"You don't owe me a thing; it wouldn't be the same without you. Let's get on the plane," George said.

They both got a little nervous when the pilot announced a fifteen-minute delay due to traffic, but ten minutes later they were on the way. Cade bought them a couple of Bloody Marys, and the rest of flight went well. They spent the entire flight discussing the first five games of the playoffs and the Bulls' game plan for today. George found it difficult not to talk about what he already knew about the game. He understood that there might be minor differences, but he was hoping the outcome would be the same. Cade was giddy with excitement, and George found it to be contagious.

In Salt Lake they went straight from the gate to the taxi stand and told the driver to take them to the bar nearest to the arena. The driver explained to George and Cade all about Salt Lake City's liquor laws, private clubs, membership dues, and 3.2 percent beer. They settled on a small pub downtown that opened at noon. A friendly Utah Jazz fan "sponsored" them, so they were able to have a couple of beers. They had fun sparring with the home fans about the upcoming game. Cade was impressed with George's confidence about game six.

Tip-off was at 2:30 p.m., so Cade settled the bill and they headed for the Delta Center around two. George picked up the tickets at will call, and Cade profusely thanked him again. They made it to their upper-deck seats in time for the national anthem and pomp and circumstance of the starting lineups. George and Cade hooted wildly for Jordan and team in a largely Jazz crowd.

"Cade, did you notice that Scottie Pippen injured his back when he missed that dunk in the first period?"

It's playing out exactly the same.

"I was wondering why he was on the bench so much."

The Bulls were down by three at the end of the first quarter and by four at the end of the half. Michael Jordan was keeping them in the game with twenty-three points, but Karl Malone had twenty points and the Jazz were leading by four.

"I'm not sure this is the game we wanted. I just don't know if Jordan can keep carrying them all game. I'm nervous, George."

George smiled at him. "All that matters is the final score. Relax, take it all in, and enjoy the moment. This is going to be special."

"I never thought you would be the one telling me to relax. It's usually the other way around. All right, George, I'll trust you, but if the Bulls break my heart, I can't afford to buy us tickets to game seven."

"There isn't going to be a game seven," said George as the players took the court for the second half.

It was intense. The Bulls went down by five at the end of the third quarter. Jordan started off the fourth quarter by missing six of eight shots. Cade groaned with every miss. The Bulls managed to tie it up until John Stockton made a three-pointer with just forty-two seconds left in the game. Then the Bulls' coach, Phil Jackson, called a timeout. The whole stadium was standing. Cade was so nervous he was hopping up and down.

Michael Jordan caught the inbound pass and went end to end, scoring over several Jazz defenders. The Jazz still had the ball and an eight-six to eighty-five lead. They got the ball over midcourt and passed to Karl Malone in the low post. Dennis Rodman tried to deny the pass, but Malone outmuscled him and caught it. Jordan snuck in behind Malone and stole the ball. Jordan then took it up the court himself and paused at the top of the key. Ten seconds left. Jordan started right, then crossed over left and sunk a perfect eighteen-foot jumper. There were still 5.4 seconds left on the clock when John Stockton missed a desperation three-point shot. The Bulls won their sixth title.

George and Cade were screaming, hugging, and jumping up and down. "You were right, George! You were right! This is the greatest moment of my life!" yelled Cade. They hung around for the award ceremony and the Finals MVP award that everyone— not just George—knew would go to Michael Jordan.

Later, standing outside the arena, waiting for a cab, George said, "That was glorious. I needed this. Thanks for sharing it with me, Cade." *And it happened just the same. Hallelujah.*

"Are you kidding me? I wouldn't have missed this for anything. It's what makes it all worthwhile," replied Cade.

"Yeah, sometimes the universe finds a way to show you that there is still magic."

They both slept the entire plane flight home.

As they split up at the airport, Cade thanked George one final time. "See you later, George."

"Or someone that looks just like me. Take care, Cade."

On his drive home, he thought more about the traveling. He was still exhilarated from the experience.

I can't believe I pulled that off. Six more travels . . . maybe I should just be a time-travel tourist? Shiloh says it doesn't matter, I get to decide. But somehow, I think I'm supposed to figure out that it's more than just tourism. Okay, step it up a notch, but this one . . . this one was worth it.

CHAPTER 29

A Sort of Homecoming

June 28, 2014

"Good morning, sweet cheeks," George said.

"I prefer honey buns," Elena replied.

"Oh, I could go for a honey bun or a donut right now."

"There are fruit and yogurt in the fridge."

George gave her a hug. "You're no fun."

Elena patted his tummy. "You're the one who keeps saying you want to lose weight."

Elena got two mugs out of the cabinet above the coffee-maker as it burbled through a fresh pot.

"The problem is I only say it. My only exercise is jumping to conclusions and running my mouth." *And traveling to other dimensions!*

Elena laughed. "Don't worry. I'm going to work you like a dog today. Speaking of today, are you ready?"

No, it's going to be a disaster. "Honestly, I'm still nervous. You've been around Amanda more; is she ready for this?"

"Her friends have been stopping by almost every day. Did you know that Cade and Lynn stopped by the other day as well?"

"Nope, remember I'm slaving away downtown every day?"

"George, she's ready. She needs to get out of the hospital. She needs some fun and excitement."

"I get the coming home part. I'm just not so sure about the excitement."

The coffee finished brewing. Elena filled both mugs and handed George one.

"It's going to be great. Stop worrying. Can I tell you how the day is going to go?" asked Elena.

"Sure, fire away, I'm ready." *As ready as I'm ever going to be.*

"Okay, I need you to get the house ready this morning. Bring up the table and chairs, move the furniture like we have for other parties, stuff like that. I cleaned and vacuumed yesterday, so you're just arranging. I'll be off running errands for most of the morning. I need to pick up decorations, wine and beer, that kind of stuff."

George snuck in a few words. "Got it."

"Later this afternoon, I'll be cooking and putting up decorations, and I need to be here when the caterers arrive. Hopefully, I can get Alex to help with the decorations and such. So, as soon as you finish arranging the house, you need to get over to the hospital. There's some paperwork that has to get done before Amanda is discharged. Also, her eye doctor will be there to remove her bandages today, and she'll see her regular doctor for a final checkup before she's discharged. Guests are arriving between four thirty and five, and we're expecting you two between five and five thirty."

George took a deep breath. "What are the chances that everything is going to go on schedule at the hospital? What if we're late?"

"I've checked and double checked. If anything, you're going to be early. If you are early, you just need to stall her until five."

"Okay, well, I'm fantastic at procrastination, so I should be pretty good at stalling. I got it. Fingers crossed."

Elena looked at him through the corner of her eye. "Do I need to write it down for you?"

"Nope, I'm good. Sounds like you get the brunt of the work anyway."

George made himself some fruit and yogurt while Elena took her coffee upstairs to get ready. While he ate, George went back over Elena's game plan in his mind. It seemed like a long shot that everything would go as planned. But he did believe in Elena—she had a way of pulling everything together.

By the time George finished his leisurely breakfast, Elena was heading out the door. "Alex is still asleep. Wake him up before you leave, and fill him in on the plan. Tell him I need his help this afternoon. I'll see you around five."

They kissed, and Elena disappeared out the door. George cleaned up his breakfast and started to arrange the house. He couldn't quite remember all they had done for the last few parties and almost called Elena on her cell phone, but he stopped himself and just made his best guess. It took longer than he expected, but when he felt like everything was ready he headed upstairs to shower.

On his way to the hospital, he remembered that he'd forgotten to check on Alex.

I'll call him from the hospital. Let the boy sleep; he needs to be in a good mood tonight.

He found Amanda in her room, dressed and sitting in her chair, watching TV. "There she is! Ready to go home today?"

"Yes! I can't wait. I can't wait to sleep in my own bed tonight. I can't wait to get out of this place. Why can't we leave earlier? Like now?"

George laughed. "It's great to see you excited, Amanda. You've got a couple of appointments today, and I've got some paperwork to get done. One of them is to get the bandage off your eye permanently."

"I know, but it's not like I can see out of it anyway. Why does the eye doctor have to take it off? Why can't one of the nurses? I just want to be done and go," Amanda said.

"He needs to examine it and make sure everything has healed up properly. Trust me, you're going to be happy to have the bandages off."

"All right, then, get the paperwork done. Anything to be one step closer to going home!"

George took off to finish the paperwork. He was relieved to find out that both of Amanda's appointments were on schedule. After what seemed like far too long, he finished and headed back to Amanda's room.

"They're bringing my lunch, but I'm not even hungry," she declared as he walked in. "The nurse called it my last meal. I think she's glad to see me go. She was really nice at first, but she kind of got mean over time."

"I'm sure you haven't been a joy to be around lately, Amanda. You need to eat your lunch. Who knows what time we'll have dinner tonight, with all the excitement of you coming home. I'll go grab a sandwich and eat with you."

They still had some time before Amanda's appointment, so George wheeled her outside for a walk. It would still be some time before Amanda could trade her hard cast for a walking cast. It was a beautiful day, and they both enjoyed the break.

"I'm going to spend all of Sunday afternoon lying in the sun on the deck," Amanda said, her face turned toward the sun.

"Are you sure that's a good idea?" George asked. "Do you want a tan line from your cast?"

Amanda smiled. "I just want to be in the sun for more than ten minutes."

"Well, then, lots of sunscreen, Snow White," George said.

They made their way back to Amanda's room and killed some time watching TV. Her eye appointment was at 3:00 p.m. and her final check with the doctor at 4:00 p.m. George didn't understand how Elena thought they could be early.

According to George's watch, it was 3:07 p.m. when the eye doctor arrived. Amanda's nurse accompanied him.

"Good afternoon, young lady. How are you feeling?"

"Fine" was all he got from Amanda.

"Are you feeling any pain around your eye?"

"It's hard to tell with the bandages, but it's always seemed sore."

"She's only been off the painkillers for a week or so," explained the nurse.

The doctor carefully began removing the bandages. Once he had them off, he examined Amanda's eye. He asked her to blink both eyes, then to look up, down, left, and right.

"Overall, I'm very happy. You're lucky we were able to keep the eye, Amanda. I understand that you may not appreciate that right now, having lost the vision. However, there can be many long-term issues with glass or acrylic eyes. And even though they're more realistic these days, there's nothing like the real thing. Your eye is functioning properly in every way other than your sight.

Other people will not be able to tell that you have a damaged eye. You can cry, wink, and even roll your eyes."

He gently turned Amanda's chin until she was looking at him. "However, we do have a small problem. While the healing is nearly complete, a small infection has just started up in the corner of the eye. The good news is that the eye and tissue around the eye heals quickly. So we'll get some antibiotics and some topical cream, and I expect it will be healed up in a few days. In the meantime, it's important that you wear an eye patch for a few more days. We don't need a full bandage, but you need to keep a patch on the eye until the infection is cleared."

"Seriously, an eye patch? I'm going to look like an idiot. Can't I just wear it at night or something? I really don't want my friends to see me in an eye patch," Amanda said.

"I'm sorry, but you need to wear it for three or four days, until the infection is gone. I suppose we could bandage the eye again."

"Never mind, I'll just hide in my room for a few more days."

"I think there are a few color choices these days. They even have pink, I believe," offered the doctor.

"I'm not twelve. I'll stick with basic black," said Amanda, whose mood had clearly changed.

The doctor finished his exam and paperwork and then sent the nurse off to get the eye patch. She arrived about ten minutes later, and the doctor adjusted the patch and put it on.

"It's a perfect fit." He looked at the nurse. "Let's get another appointment on the schedule for next Wednesday to take another look at the eye and get Amanda out of her stylish eye patch." He turned back to Amanda and George. "And you'll need to stop by the pharmacy on the way out to pick up this prescription." He slipped a paper to George, issued a few final instructions to daughter and father, and then left along with the nurse.

Crap! Don't freak out, George. Look like everything is fine. Think calm.

"It's no big deal, honey. It's just a couple of days," he said. "Hey, I need to give your mom a quick call. Can you hang out and watch TV for a bit? I'll be right back."

"Sure, Dad."

George casually walked out of the room and then hustled down the hallways until he found a spot he could use his cell phone. He dialed Elena, and when she didn't answer he tried the home phone. He got the answering machine. He called Elena's cell phone again and left a voice message. "Elena, you have to cancel the party. Amanda's okay, but she has an infection in her eye and has to wear an eye patch for the next couple of days. She thinks she looks like an idiot. Please call me or text me right away."

When George walked into Amanda's room again, she looked at him. "What?"

"What do you mean?"

"You seem upset, and you're looking at me funny. What's wrong?"

"Nothing. Everything is fine. You're just like your mother," he said.

Amanda gave him one more glance, as if she didn't believe him, and then went back to watching TV. George kept checking his cell phone, but he received nothing from Elena. He sent a text to Elena to listen to her voice mail. Amanda's doctor arrived and asked about her eye and eye patch. She asked Amanda a series of questions, and George could tell Amanda was answering with whatever she thought would most likely get her home. They walked through Amanda's physical therapy schedule and upcoming appointments. The doctor explained the time frame for getting the cast removed and stressed the importance of not walking on the hard cast.

"As soon as we can, we'll get you in the walking cast. Are you ready to go home, Amanda?"

Finally, the smile returned to Amanda's face. "Yes, please," she said.

The doctor smiled. "Okay, let me finish up my paperwork, and we'll get you out of here."

By the time they gathered up Amanda's things it was 4:35 p.m. George began wheeling Amanda out of the hospital. He felt like he should be thrilled, but instead he was terrified. As they got to lobby, he told Amanda he had to use the bathroom before they left. In the bathroom he checked his phone again. He had a text from Elena.

I got your voice mail. It's okay. Party is still on. Will be fine. Bring her home!

George left the bathroom, pushed Amanda out of the hospital, put her in the car, and headed home.

CHAPTER 30

Get the Party Started

George tried his best to act normal and make small talk with Amanda in the car. But no matter how hard he tried, he still felt like he sounded awkward and nervous. Amanda didn't seem to notice.

She's so excited to be leaving the hospital that she probably wouldn't notice much of anything.

George stopped trying to make conversation, and as he glanced over at Amanda, his thoughts began to wander through brief flashes of memories. One-year-old Amanda in her high chair, toddler Amanda in the pink princess dress that she loved to wear, five-year-old Amanda heading off to kindergarten—one by one, they passed before George's eyes. He began to tear up and felt thankful that Amanda was looking out the window.

She hasn't seen much besides her hospital room, so I imagine the scenery is quite the treat right now.

They pulled into their neighborhood, their street, and finally their driveway. The house looked quiet, and George saw no additional cars around. If the party was still on, Elena had gone to great lengths to preserve the surprise.

I'm not so sure that's a good idea. It would be better if she had a moment to prepare herself. I can't ruin the surprise, though.

George helped Amanda out of the car and into her wheelchair. She was starting to get strong enough in physical therapy to use crutches, but the doctor wanted her to use the wheelchair for a little while longer.

He began wheeling her up the walk to the front door. "I'll come back for your suitcase and your other things once you're settled. Getting you up to your bedroom later will be an adventure, right?"

"The house looks empty. Where are Mom and Alex?"

"Ah, not sure. Maybe they went to pick up something for dinner. You know your mom, she probably wants to do something special for dinner tonight," said George, trying to lie as little as possible.

He pushed Amanda up to the front door, stepped in front of her to unlock it, and opened the door. Everything was quiet—he could see no sign of a party. He stepped back behind Amanda and prepared to push her into the house. As they crossed the threshold, George began to wonder if Elena had changed her mind and canceled the party.

Just then chaos broke loose.

"SURPRISE!!!!!!" yelled Elena and what seemed like a hundred other voices. George struggled to take everything in as he pushed Amanda further into the house. Lights came on, and a crowd of people spilled into the living room as the noise grew to a nearly deafening level. Senses on overload, George noticed that everyone was wearing an eye patch. Then he realized that many of the guests were dressed in pirate attire, and a few were even wearing pirate hats. To the left was a large banner that read, *ARRRGGG! Welcome home, matey!!! We love you, Mandy!*

George began to regain his composure.

A pirate theme! Leave it Elena to pull off something like that at the last moment. But if it's this overwhelming for me, I can't imagine what it's like for Amanda.

Several of her friends had rushed over to her, but through the crush he could still see her. Tears streamed down her face, and she still looked shocked. He waved at the crowd, as if trying to get her further into the house, but then took a moment in the bubble that opened to kneel down beside her.

"Amanda, are you okay? Do you want me to get you out of here for a moment? Do you need a little time?"

She looked up at him, tears still streaming down her face. "Oh my God, Dad, I'm just so happy. I'm just so happy to be home and to see my friends."

George was trying to decide whether to wheel her back out the front door or to lift her out of her chair and carry her up to her bedroom when she began to smile. The meaning of what she'd said finally hit him.

He smiled back. "Are these happy tears?" It was a phrase they had used when she was little.

"Yes, Dad, happy tears. I'm shocked, but happy—very happy."

"Okay, Mandy, welcome home. Enjoy your party." He was feeling a little choked up and embarrassed. He maneuvered her into the living room to greet the rest of the party. Her friends swarmed her with gentle hugs, and they launched into conversation and laughter.

He heard Amanda say, "This is so crazy! How long have you guys known about this, and why didn't you tell me?"

Someone turned on the music, and conversations broke out all around the room. A neighbor congratulated him on having Amanda home and handed George a beer. "Looks like you could use one. You seemed more surprised than Amanda."

"Thanks! Yeah, I nearly wet my britches, or whatever pirates call their pants."

George took one more look at Amanda, who was smiling and surrounded by her friends. Two of them were having a sword fight with plastic swords.

George searched the room and spotted Elena talking with the parents of one of Amanda's best friends. As he crossed the room, they gave Elena a hug. Elena thanked them for coming and turned to greet more guests. George stepped in and gave her a long hug. When he let go, Elena's eyes were wet.

"Arrrgghh! Hiya, matey," Elena said.

"Well, as usual, you did it! How you came up with a pirate theme and pulled it off in hours is beyond me. Amanda seems thrilled and not the least bit self-conscious," said George, shaking his head.

"You had me a little scared, George, but I think Mandy is a little more self-assured than we know. I'm just glad it turned out okay and she's happy."

"I'm just glad I trusted you," George said.

Elena gave George a big smile and said, "Okay, we've got a big party to attend to. Can you help me make sure everyone has drinks and knows where the food is?"

"Aye, you mean attend to the carousers with grog and grub?"

"You scallywag, you're a better pirate than I. Get attending!" she said as she handed George an eye patch.

George spent the next hour handing out drinks and making his way through the party, thanking folks for coming. Everyone seemed to be having a great time, and the noise level and energy never seemed to drop.

"How'd ya like to scrape the barnacles off me rudder?" said a voice behind him.

He turned around to see Cade and Lynn, both in full pirate getup. Lynn gave George a hug. George replied to Cade, "Ah, me wooden leg has termites."

"Mandy looks great, and she seems so happy. It's great to see her home," Lynn said.

"Thanks—and thanks for visiting her at the hospital. Elena told me you both stopped by."

"Yeah, we're so happy she's doing so well. She's such a great kid," Cade said.

"Thanks," George said. "I was worried that she wouldn't react well to a surprise party, but it's been great. I should never have doubted Elena."

"No you shouldn't," Lynn said.

"Speaking of Elena, I love her low-cut pirate dress, cuz me treasures her chest," joked Cade.

Lynn slugged Cade in the shoulder. "Do I have to cut you off already, Cade? Come on, let's let George mingle with his guests. I'm going to cast Cade in irons."

"Promises, promises," Cade said as Lynn dragged him off toward the food.

After George felt he'd spoken with all the guests, he helped Elena restock the food and then emptied the trash. He was feeling tired and decided he'd earned a quick break. He snuck out of the house and walked to the end of driveway. Other than the rollicking sounds of the party, the neighborhood was quiet.

Thank God everyone in the neighborhood is at the party and can't complain! It's such a beautiful evening. I can't remember the last time I saw this many stars in the sky.

George looked back at his house. It stood out not only for the sound, but also as well-lit, compared to the rest of the neighborhood. It felt so full of life and joy that George found himself tearing up and smiling at the same time. He took a deep breath and enjoyed the moment.

We're lucky to have so many neighbors and friends who genuinely care about Mandy. I haven't felt this happy in a while. Now this is a day I'd travel back to. Maybe Shiloh is right, maybe I worry too much. Things do have a way of working out.

When he returned to the party, a neighbor told him that Elena was searching for him. He found her in the kitchen. "Hi, honey. Were you looking for me?"

"Yeah, have you seen Alex?" she asked.

"No, I haven't seen him since we arrived at the party."

Elena frowned. "He helped me prepare for the party, but at some point he just disappeared. Did he text you?"

"No, I haven't heard from him since this morning. I can't believe he skipped out on his sister's party, especially without telling us."

"I'm worried about him. Can you text him?" Elena asked.

"Yes, I'll text him. I'm less worried and more pissed off. I'm going to make that boy walk the plank," George replied.

"Go easy on him, George. He's jealous of all the attention that Amanda is getting."

George sent Alex a text and got a reply after about five minutes: *At Jeff's, home soon.* George told Elena, who seemed relieved.

The party began to wind down. A steady stream of people stopped George, Elena, and Amanda to thank them for the party and to say good-bye. There were lots of hugs. George caught Alex when he returned and told him they would discuss it tomorrow. Alex shuffled off to his room, head hung low. Later, Amanda asked if she and a couple of her friends could go up to her room.

"I can't wait to see my room. I never thought I'd say that, but I miss it so much," she said.

Since nearly everyone had left, George agreed and helped get her up to her room. When he returned downstairs, Elena, Lynn, and Cade were cleaning up, and the last few other guests had left.

"I guess it's just us bilge rats, left to swab the poop deck," George said.

"Oh, please, no more pirate talk. I've had enough to last a year," Lynn said.

"Hang her from the yardarm for sedition," Cade replied.

They finished cleaning up, and the four of them sat down for a last drink at the kitchen table. They talked for half an hour or so, laughing about the party, before Amanda's friends finally came down and said good-bye. After Lynn and Cade left and Elena went upstairs to get ready for bed, George was struck by how quiet the house had become. He felt melancholy and tired. He was upset with Alex, but there would always be something to be upset about. Amanda was home, and she was happy.

CHAPTER 31

Sunday Morning Coming Down

June 29, 2014

According to his Apple Watch, George woke at 6:52 a.m., which was about two hours earlier than he wanted. He tried to force himself back to sleep, but after about five minutes, he knew it wasn't going to happen. No matter how tired he was or how late he'd been up the night before, he couldn't seem to sleep past seven.

He got up, went downstairs, and made himself a cup of coffee. The rest of the family had no difficulty sleeping in, so the house was quiet. Still, the morning was beautiful, so he went out on the deck to drink his coffee. The neighborhood was quiet again except for the birds and squirrels, which were already busy and vocal.

I'm so glad that went well and that Amanda's happy. Now I can relax and enjoy the morning . . . except for work, Alex, and Shiloh. Jesus, George, just clear your mind . . . or deal with them one at a time.

Okay, first I'll have a discussion with Alex—besides, something came up last night that might help. Second, work isn't getting any better, but with everything that's going on, now is not the time to make a change. Finally, this little Shiloh thing, traveling to alternate dimensions. I feel like I've sort of compartmentalized it. That's a good thing.

George finished his coffee and went back inside. With the party and all, he had been neglecting the bills and mail, so he sat down at his desk. He set aside all the medical bills and pulled out an envelope bearing his company's letterhead. He opened and read the notice. His mouth dropped open, and he read it again.

Holy shit!

It was a notice that his coverage included a benefit of one hundred thousand dollars for a family member who loses sight in an eye. George was stunned. The letter said that after he completed and submitted a required form, a check would be mailed within four to six weeks.

That could cover not only all of the co-pays and out-of-pocket medical bills, but also a sizable amount for Amanda's college. Add that to what the neighbor told me at the party last night—that Amanda's disability along with her grades would help her qualify for more scholarships and financial aid programs. . . . I would still give anything to restore the sight in her eye, but I'm amazed that some good might come out of the accident. What a crazy world.

He leaned back in his chair and put his hands behind his head. Then he heard sounds coming from the kitchen. Somebody had finally woken up. He set the notice aside and headed into the kitchen, where he found Alex standing in front of the refrigerator with the door open, staring blankly inside.

"Good morning, Alex," George said. "Are you going to pick something or just let all the cold air out?"

"We never have anything to eat," Alex said.

How can he manage to piss me off in thirty seconds?

"There is plenty to eat: yogurt, eggs, and toast, to name a few. And cereal and oatmeal in the pantry."

Alex shut the refrigerator door. "Like I said, there's nothing to eat."

"What do you expect, you open the fridge and pancakes pop out at you? If I make you a bowl of cereal, will you sit down and talk with me?"

"I guess." He poured himself a glass of milk and sat down at the kitchen table and began to check his phone.

George got out a bowl for Alex and a bowl for himself. He poured the cereal and then the milk from the gallon that Alex had left on the counter. He put the milk away and the brought the bowls over to the kitchen table. Alex set down his phone and began to eat.

"Alex, you know you should have gone to your sister's party, right?"

"I guess. It's just that I didn't really know anybody—it was all adults and Amanda's friends. Amanda probably didn't want me there anyway."

"Alex, we're family, and you support your family no matter what. You should have been there to welcome her home. She's been through a great deal. I don't care if you would have been bored. It's not always about you."

"It's never about me."

George rolled his eyes. "Come on. What were you doing at Jeff's anyway?"

"I don't know, goofing off. We were messing around on our guitars, playing video games, and talking."

"You know, son, your friends have a big impact on your thinking and your choices. Is Jeff someone you think you should be hanging out with?"

"He's fine, Dad. I thought we agreed you weren't going to pick my friends."

"I just want you to think about it. You're just so negative and moody lately. I miss when you were hanging out with all your baseball friends. You guys seemed to have a great time. In fact, I was talking with Kyle's dad at the party last night. He said Kyle was having a bunch of kids over tonight and that you were invited. You should go."

"Dad, I've told you, I'm not friends with those guys anymore. If Kyle wanted me at his party, he would have invited me. I'm not going," Alex said flatly.

Can't you tell when I'm doing you a favor? he thought. "Alex, you are going to go. This is a great chance to reconnect with those guys. Think of it as punishment for not going to your sister's party. They're having pizza, and I'm betting once you get there you'll have a great time."

"No, Dad, it would be so awkward."

"It's not an option. And you need to change your attitude," George said, looking Alex directly in the eyes.

"Whatever," said Alex. He stomped off to his room, leaving his half-eaten bowl of cereal on the kitchen counter.

George sighed and placed his bowl next to Alex's, intending to wash both after he used the bathroom. When he returned, Elena was at the kitchen sink washing both bowls.

"You boys left me a present this morning."

"I was just about to take care of those," George said.

Elena gave him one of her looks. "I can see that."

George was about to protest but decided it was futile. "Can I get you a cup of coffee?"

Elena smiled and said, "That would be great, honey. Thanks."

George made the coffee, and Elena joined him at the kitchen table. "Mandy's up already. I helped her get to the bathroom. She seems in great spirits. We talked for quite a while. Her girlfriends were already texting her this morning. They all want to take her out to dinner tonight."

"She's going to be in better spirits when she finds out she's one hundred thousand dollars richer."

"What?" asked Elena.

"One of the benefits I have at work pays out one hundred thousand dollars for the loss of eyesight to me or my dependents. I didn't even remember! Somehow—I guess because of the medical claims—they sent us the forms we need to complete to get payment," George said. "Pretty impressive company I work for, huh?"

Elena seemed shocked. "You're kidding me. That's amazing, but I'd give it all back in a second to get back Mandy's vision."

George laughed. "I thought the exact same thing. I think some of the money needs to cover medical bills, you know, co-pays and anything that's not covered. But I think that will only be five to ten thousand. The rest can go right into her college fund."

"I guess that makes sense. How about we give her a little spending money now to do some shopping? I bet her girlfriends would love to take her shopping before dinner tonight," Elena suggested.

"Sure, I've got five dollars on me," said George, smiling.

"Funny man."

"And get this: I was talking with Tom from down the block, he was telling me that losing sight in an eye, even one eye, classifies Amanda as disabled. He thinks that will increase her chances of getting into any college she wants and qualifies her for a bunch of special scholarships and financial aid programs."

"When God closes a door, he opens a window," Elena said. "It's nice to see some good come of all of this."

"And . . . I lined up something for Alex tonight, so, how about you and I do a little celebrating? I'll take you out to dinner," George asked.

"That sounds wonderful. What did you line up for Alex?" she asked.

"At the party last night, I was talking with Mark—you know, his son Kyle plays baseball with Alex. Kyle is having a bunch of friends over tonight for pizza, and Alex is invited."

"And Alex wants to go?" Elena asked.

How does she know these things?

"I had to cajole a little. But that frees us up for a night out."

Elena gave him a sideways glance. "But Alex agreed to go?"

"Yes. What time would you like for me to make the reservation for?"

Elena smiled. "How about seven o'clock?"

"Seven it is—consider it a date!"

CHAPTER 32

Comfortably Numb

George's Sunday was clicking along fantastically. The whole household seemed to be in a good mood—or at least he, Elena, and Amanda were. He hadn't seen much of Alex. He had finished some chores, watched some sports and was enjoying feeling happy for a change. Amanda was settling back into the house. Getting her up and down the stairs was a chore, but she seemed almost giddy about going out with her girlfriends. Elena was spending a lot of time with her, helping her rearrange her room and sorting through her clothes to determine what worked best with the leg cast. Amanda seemed surprisingly unimpressed about the insurance money, but intrigued by the possibility of more college options. Though she was pretty thrilled about having some "serious shopping cash," as she called it.

The next thing George knew, everyone was showering and getting ready for the evening. George gave Amanda her shopping money and Alex some money to offer for the pizza. George stared into his empty wallet.

Good thing for credit cards.

He headed upstairs to get ready himself. Amanda's girl-friends arrived, and George helped her out to her friend's car. He looked her friend in the eye and asked her to drive carefully. She smiled and told him not to worry.

Okay, THIS I get to worry about.

When he got back inside, Alex was on his way out to walk over to Kyle's. George stopped him and said, "Alex, thanks for not fighting anymore about this. I think it's going to work out fine. Just give those guys another chance."

"Sure," muttered Alex as he left the house.

George went upstairs to finish getting ready. Elena was putting on makeup. "Did the kids leave?"

"Yeah, with all my money."

"Hey, be nice. You might need to take a loan from Amanda someday," said Elena.

"Good point!"

George washed up and changed, and when he came out Elena was just putting on her earrings.

"It almost feels like things are returning to normal. And you look beautiful," he told her.

She gave him a peck and the cheek and whispered in his ear. "Play your cards right tonight and you might get lucky."

They headed out to the restaurant about thirty minutes before their reservation, and after checking in with the hostess, they found an open table in the bar. George ordered them each a martini.

"What a crazy couple of months, huh?" he said.

Elena sighed. "I'm just happy to have Mandy home. They did a great job at the hospital, but I'm so glad we're not spending every day there anymore."

George leaned in. "Hey, I just want to thank you for keeping everything together. You somehow were there for Amanda, Alex, and me all at the same time. I don't know how you did it, but I just want you to know that you're amazing."

"You are playing your cards right," Elena replied.

"I mean it, and not just because I'm trying to get lucky—which I am, by the way. But on top of Amanda and work, I'm dealing with some other things as well," admitted George.

Elena nodded. "I've noticed. I've been guessing it's kind of a minor middle-aged crazy on top of everything else. But I appreciate that you haven't purchased a sports car and started dating a twenty-year-old. You're not dating a twenty-year-old, are you?"

George laughed. "If you find a twenty-year-old willing to date me, let me know. No, seriously, Elena, you know you're the only girl for me."

Do I tell her? More importantly, how do I tell her? She'll think I'm crazy. I probably am crazy.

His cell phone, which he had set face down on the table, began to vibrate.

"Let it go to voice mail," he said. "I don't know if it's middle age, but I do feel a little like I'm going crazy. Work is insane; I'm still just trying to make it through day to day."

"If it's that bad, you should leave. You'll find something else, and I can go back too."

"Yeah, I know, I just don't know what else I can find that won't be more of the same. I'm just not sure how much of it is work, and how much is me." George took a deep breath. "And there is something else that's I've been struggling with."

Here goes . . . .

Elena pulled her cell phone out. "Now mine is ringing. It's got to be the kids. I'd better answer."

George nodded. "Go ahead."

Elena answered it. "Hello? Yes, this is Elena Hartdegen. I'm sorry, who is this?" Elena's face went from confusion to concern.

"My husband is right here with me. We are out at a restaurant."

What now?

"Oh my God." Elena looked shocked, and her eyes began to tear up. "Oh no, where? We will be right there. We're about fifteen minutes away." Now barely able to get the words out, she managed, "Yes, my husband can drive. Okay. Thank you. Goodbye."

Elena hung up her phone and stood up. "Come on, we have to go."

George stood up. "What the hell is going on, Elena? I don't have any cash to pay for the drinks."

Elena was crying now, fumbling in her purse for her wallet. She threw thirty dollars on the table. "Come on, George," she said and walked out of the restaurant.

Don't let it be Amanda. Not another accident.

George followed her out into the parking lot. "Elena, what's going on? Where are we going?"

"To the hospital. Get in the car."

George complied and began to back out. "Please don't tell me Amanda was in another accident."

"No, it's Alex. He has alcohol poisoning. Oh God, George, the police said he's in critical condition." As soon as she got the words out, Elena began crying, her body going limp.

"Oh God, no. If I find out that he went to Jeff's and this happened, I'm going to raise holy hell! I mean, how much alcohol do you have to drink to be in critical condition?" George pulled out onto the street, going a bit too fast.

Elena took a couple of deep breaths and dug through her purse for a tissue. "Let's just worry about Alex right now," she said. "Focus on driving, George."

"You're right. I just can't believe this is happening. Oh, Alex."

George tried to keep his emotions in check. Elena went quiet and stared blankly at the road ahead. It all felt eerily familiar, like déjà vu.

George remembered a day when Alex was a toddler. They were shopping at a department store for a present for Amanda, and Alex wouldn't let them put him in the cart. He wanted to run. He ran down an aisle, and George had to chase after him. He was late to crawl and walk, but once he figured it out, you couldn't stop him. Alex turned it into a game and kept stopping to let his dad catch up and then running off again just before he was within reach. After three or four rounds, George decided to let him go, figuring that once Alex saw he wasn't being chased, the game would be over. He went back to Elena and they picked out the present, expecting Alex to come running back—but he didn't.

George and Elena searched for Alex, their frustration turning to unease turning to sheer panic. They enlisted other shoppers, and finally the store manager made a storewide announcement. No one could find Alex. George felt like an idiot for letting him go. A few minutes later they called the police, who arrived within ten minutes, and Alex still hadn't been found. The police questioned them about what Alex had been wearing. When they asked for a recent photo, Elena started crying.

After what had seemed like an eternity, a store clerk found Alex fast asleep inside a circular rack of clothing. He had apparently hidden and then fallen asleep waiting to be found. George remembered feeling like a horrible parent even though the police said it happens more often than they might think.

Why can't I protect my kids? he wondered angrily. *Damn, why us, why all at once? Calm down. Just focus on your driving. Here's the hospital. I hate this goddamn hospital.*

George pulled into the hospital emergency room parking. After a short wait in the lobby, a doctor arrived and shook their hands.

"Mr. and Mrs. Hartdegen, pleasure to meet you. Sorry it's under these circumstances. I'm Doctor Lavinch, and I've been on point with Alex. Let me start by saying that Alex is going to be fine. He was in bad shape when he arrived. We measured his blood alcohol at about point two four percent, which is extremely dangerous, particularly for a boy as young as Alex. He was unconscious and had respiratory depression. That means his breathing was less than eight breaths per minute. We pumped his stomach, gave him oxygen and fifty milliliters of a fifty percent dextrose solution and saline flush. After about fifteen minutes his body responded well, and his respiratory system seems to have returned to normal. At this point, we'll continue to monitor him for eighteen to twenty-four hours, but I expect him to be fine."

Alex was .24? Oh my God.

"Oh thank the Lord," Elena said. "What a relief."

George added, "Thank you, doctor."

"Now, you should know this was a serious situation. Alex could have easily experienced liver damage, brain damage, or even death. He's lucky he was brought in as quickly he was and that we were able to treat him right away. This level of alcohol consumption at the age of fifteen is a serious warning sign."

"We understand," said Elena. "We are shaken and shocked. As far as we know, this is the first time that Alex has been drinking. Can we see him? Can we talk to him?"

"Soon, but first we would like for you to meet with Dr. Rao, who is our resident psychiatrist. Also, just so you know, the police may ask you some questions as well. They're investigating the incident to determine if there are legal implications."

"Is Alex in trouble with the police?" asked George.

"He could be charged with minor intoxication, but I think that's unlikely. I believe the police are more interested in how he obtained the alcohol and who might have provided it to him."

"Well, we're happy to cooperate with both the police and the psychiatrist, whatever we can do. Do you know what exactly the psychiatrist needs to discuss with us?" asked George.

"I'd rather leave that to him. I'll page him now, and we'll find a room for you to meet. Hang tight for a few minutes. It was nice to meet you. I think Alex will be fine, but I hope you get him the help he needs after his physical recovery."

"I can promise you, we'll do everything in our power to help Alex. We love him very much, and I can't tell you how worried we are about him," said Elena. George nodded in agreement.

"Great, I guessed as much, but I'm happy to hear you say that. Dr. Rao is fantastic and will take care of things from here. Best of luck with Alex. I hope I never see him again!" said Dr. Lavinch with a wink. He walked off briskly.

George and Elena hugged. "The most important thing is that he's going to be fine," said Elena.

"Yeah, first I want to hug him, and then I want to kill him."

"George, let's make sure we completely understand what happened before we make any judgments."

"You know I'm not serious. I just want to know what happened and why it happened. What do you think the psychiatrist wants?"

"I'm sure he wants to know why Alex would do this to himself."

George nodded. "That's a great question, and I can't wait to ask Alex it myself."

"Okay, we know Alex is going to be fine. Now we have to be patient. Let's just take things one step at a time here," said Elena.

"I just can't believe we're back in this hospital, now with our other child. Why is this happening to us?"

Just then their names were called over the hospital loudspeaker. They made their way to the emergency room desk, and an orderly walked them to a consultation room.

A short, brown-skinned man met them at the door and gestured them in, saying, "Mr. and Mrs. Hartdegen, I'm Dr. Rao, the staff psychiatrist. I need to talk with you about your son, Alex."

"Of course, Dr. Rao, thank you for talking with us," Elena said. She and George perched on a pair of gray upholstered chairs as the doctor seated himself in a rolling desk chair, manila folder in hand.

"First, I need to know that you both understand that this was a serious situation. Alex's life was in danger. Do you both understand the gravity of this event?" asked Dr. Rao.

"Yes, we do. Dr. Lavinch basically told us the same thing, about how lucky Alex was to receive treatment quickly. We're concerned about him and can't wait to see him," replied George.

Dr. Rao nodded. "Good. Okay, I'll explain the situation as I understand it. I've been working with the police, and the other youth who were involved and the family that hosted the event have cooperated fully. My understanding is that Alex arrived at the party alone. The other teenagers all were paired up as couples, so I believe that put him in an uncomfortable position right away."

Elena looked at George, questioning.

"I had no idea—oh, he must have been mortified," said George.

"Yes, we understand that an older brother supplied one of the boys with a half-liter of high-proof whiskey. The parents were unaware of this. Shortly after Alex arrived, they pushed Alex to drink a shot of the whiskey. I understand he resisted at first, but eventually he tried to drink the shot. I am guessing he's had little to no hard alcohol before, because he apparently gagged and spit out the shot. The group laughed, as you might expect, and I'm guessing that Alex was extremely embarrassed. He left the party, taking the whiskey bottle with him. A couple of the kids tried to go after him, but they stated that he ran off before they could talk with him." Dr. Rao paused for a moment to let the words sink in.

Oh God. I want to crawl under the table. I could not be a bigger idiot. I had no idea that girls were invited. I forced Alex into that situation. Any boy would be horrified. And the kids I'm pushing Alex toward are drinking.

"After a period of time, maybe an hour, they began to worry about Alex. They went outside into the yard and found him passed out in a treehouse in the backyard. He had drunk around half of the bottle of whiskey. When they couldn't wake him, they alerted the parents, who immediately dialed 911, and you can guess the rest. Do you understand what happened?"

George was the first to reply. "Yes, that makes sense. I feel awful and somewhat responsible, but I understand the sequence of events."

"Good, I need you to understand because you need to consider a couple of aspects of this incident. First, a question: do either of you have any knowledge of any prior drinking by Alex? Not just hard liquor, but beer or anything?"

"As far as we know, this was his first time," Elena answered.

"Okay, that was my guess as well. Have either of you ever tried cheap, high-proof whiskey?" asked Dr. Rao.

"Yeah, it's awful, it burns," George said.

"Exactly, so imagine a teenager, drinking for the first time or at least one of his first times. Even a mellower alcoholic beverage such as beer is distasteful; drinking a large amount of this high-proof whiskey is difficult. It must have been quite the effort. He had to have forced it down."

George and Elena shared a glance.

"So, I need to ask you, has Alex been dealing with other issues? Has he ever done or said anything previously that would lead you to believe he is suicidal?" asked Dr. Rao.

Suicidal? Elena physically flinched at the word.

The doctor couldn't help but notice how distraught they were. "I'm sorry to have to ask you this. But if you examine the situation, it's plausible that Alex was trying to kill himself tonight."

"No, I can't imagine it, I can't believe Alex would do such a thing," Elena said.

"He has been dealing with some things, but nothing serious enough to consider suicide. He had a best friend move away last year, and now he's struggling to fit in. He used to be a star baseball player, but he's been in a slump lately. I pushed him to go to Kyle's house tonight to see if he could reconnect with some boys that he was growing away from. But I think—or maybe I hope—that he was just embarrassed and wanted to escape," George admitted.

"Unfortunately, there is no way to tell how any given situation or issue will affect another person. What seem to you, as parents, to be relatively minor challenges can seem like life-or-death situations to a teenager. I have seen kids show suicidal tendencies over less. Young adults—in fact, even toddlers—can experience depression, clinical depression."

Clinical depression?

"So, first, I would like to keep Alex here for at least the next twenty-four hours. During that time, I will meet with him several times and do an assessment. Based on the assessment, we'll either admit him to a facility where he can be safe and get treatment, or, if my assessment is more positive, we'll release him and schedule him for follow-up care."

"I'm sorry, doctor, but this is all such a shock. I think Elena and I are having a difficult time processing it. Alex has been grumpy, frustrated, and a little withdrawn, but we never would have imagined he would be suicidal." George struggled to say the words.

No way he's tried to kill himself. Please don't let it be true.

"In the end, you may be right. However, I hope you see the logic in being careful with Alex. All I'm asking at this point is your permission to do a couple of psychiatric evaluation sessions and to keep him here at the hospital till at least tomorrow. Does that make sense?"

"Yes, please, I don't want to take any chance of losing Alex," Elena said. "Take all the time you need, do all the evaluations you want. I think he's going to be fine, but if he needs help, let's get him help." She looked at George, and he nodded in agreement.

"Okay, I'll start the paperwork. We'll talk a few more times before we make any decisions past the next twenty-four hours," Dr. Rao explained.

"Can we see him now?"

"Yes, you can, but I have a few conditions. At least for the first visit, as it will be before my first evaluation," Dr. Rao said.

"What conditions?" asked George.

"First, you are to listen to him only. Don't question him about the incident. Don't push for details. Please don't scold him for the incident, even indirectly. And don't ask him if he's suicidal."

"I'm sorry, doctor, but what *can* we say?" asked George.

"Support him. Tell him you love him. Ask him if he's okay. If he wants to talk about it, listen to him. Tell him you're here for him and that everything is going to be okay. Can you do that?"

"Yes, we can do that," Elena said.

CHAPTER 33

We Can Work It Out

A nurse met Elena and George and confirmed they'd spoken with both doctors. Alex had been moved out of the ER and into a regular room and was awake but feeling quite ill. She told them they could spend about fifteen minutes with him, but then they needed him to sleep for the night. They'd be able to talk with him again in the morning. Elena asked if they could spend the night, and the nurse agreed, but there was only room for one person, and only on an uncomfortable fold-out chair. In addition, a nurse would be checking vitals every couple hours, so whoever stayed would likely not get much sleep. The nurse led them to Alex's room, showed them in, and shut the door.

George took a deep breath when he saw Alex. He still had an IV in his arm and thin oxygen tubes under his nose. He looked pale.

"Hey, Alex, how are you doing?" George asked.

"I feel really bad, like when I had the flu last year, but maybe worse," Alex croaked.

"Does it hurt to talk?" Elena asked.

"A little."

"The doctors say you're going to be fine. You scared us, Alex," George said.

"I'm sorry," replied Alex. Elena shot George a look.

Strike one.

George tried again. "It's all right, Alex. We just couldn't wait to see you. We love you. We're here for you, and everything is going to be okay."

"You just don't know how it is, Dad, I was just so . . . ." Alex struggled for words and began to tear up. "I just wanted to escape."

"Okay, buddy, I understand. Hey, I just want to tell you I'm sorry. I've been a bad listener lately, and I promise I'm going to do a lot better from now on."

"It's not your fault, Dad. I just don't want to be around those guys any more. All they want to talk about is baseball, drinking, and girls. And the way they talk about girls, it's just not right."

"I get that now. I'm sorry I forced you to go to the party. I didn't understand, Alex."

"When can I go home?"

"First they want you get a good night's sleep. I think you're going to be here till tomorrow night. They just want to keep a close watch on you and make sure you're okay. If everything goes well, you might be able to sleep in your own bed tomorrow night," Elena said.

Alex scowled. "Is everyone I know at school going to hear about this? I bet Kyle and his friends told everyone—it's probably all over Facebook already."

"Maybe, honey. I know things seem rough right now, but it's going to be okay. Your dad and I are going to help you get through this."

Alex seemed unconvinced. "I don't care, anyway. I don't care about all the stupid kids at school."

There was an awkward pause. *I don't know where to go from here. Just keep it zipped, George.*

Elena saved them. "Alex, do you mind if one of us spends the night?" she asked.

"No. That's fine."

"Okay, are you tired?"

Alex nodded. "Yeah, I'm real tired."

"All right, Dad and I are going to talk for a moment, and then we'll help you get ready for bed. Be right back."

"Okay," Alex said.

Elena and George stepped into the hallway. Elena checked her phone. "Amanda sent me a text. She's going to be home in about an hour. I'll stay here with Alex. You head home and help Amanda. She's probably exhausted."

"Are you sure? I can stay."

"No, I got this. I still have an overnight bag in the car from Amanda's visit. You need to help Amanda get settled. Are you going to work tomorrow?"

George hadn't even thought about work. "I don't know. I'm out of vacation days. But I suppose if I spoke with my boss."

"You should go to work tomorrow." Elena thought for a moment and rattled off, "Here's the plan: you take care of Amanda tonight, and tomorrow make sure she eats breakfast and is set for the morning. I'm going to spend the night, talk with Alex in the morning, and then take a cab home around lunch. I'll get Amanda lunch and make sure she's okay. Then I'll come back here for Alex.

Maybe you can come home a little early and check on Amanda, and I'll try to schedule something with the psychiatrist that you can make around six or seven p.m. Oh, be sure you carefully explain all of this to Amanda. She needs to know, but try not to freak her out."

"Jesus, Elena, are you sure?"

"Positive. You might need to take some time off another time. Who knows where this is all going to lead? Let's save any extra favors from your boss. This is going to work."

Once she has a plan in place, there's no changing it.

They told Alex that Elena was staying, and George kissed Alex goodnight. He was nearly asleep anyway. Elena walked George to the car to grab her overnight bag. They agreed to keep each other up to date with texts and kissed. Elena headed back into the hospital, and George pulled out of the parking garage. He wanted to beat Amanda home.

Man, can Elena switch gears from distraught to quarterback in a flash, George mused as the blocks rolled by. He could make the drive in his sleep at this point. *She must think I'm an idiot. Hell, I think I'm an idiot. All that worrying about Jeff, and it's Kyle and friends I should have worried about. I know where Alex gets the escaping through alcohol. How many times have I come home from and said, "What a crappy day, I need a beer"? But was Alex really trying to kill himself? I can't believe it. He was just looking for a way out. No matter what, I'm responsible. I have to do better by Alex.*

CHAPTER 34

Fix You

June 30, 2014

"Hey, George, it's been a little while. How's Amanda?"

Shiloh had been the first to board at his stop. This morning his shirt read, *Never trust a subatomic particle. They make up everything.*

George pursed his lips. "Amanda's wonderful, but you were right, she's not the one I need to worry about."

"What happened?"

George took a deep breath and let it out. "It's Alex. I forced him into an awkward situation at a teen party, and he decided to nearly drink himself to death. He spent yesterday and last night in the hospital, recovering from alcohol poisoning. He could have died."

"But he's going to be okay?" It was somewhere between a question and a statement.

"Yes, he's going to be fine. But the psychiatrist believes that Alex may have intentionally tried to kill himself. Wow, this is hard for me to say out loud. He thinks Alex may be suicidal and that he needs some serious psychiatric treatment. Shiloh, it's been over twelve hours, and I'm still having a hard time processing this."

"I can imagine," Shiloh said. "George, do *you* think he tried to kill himself?"

"No. Well, probably not. I do see the doctor's point, but I just can't imagine that Alex feels that way. He's such a bright kid—he has everything in front of him. But I do remember how difficult it was to be a teenager. Even the littlest thing could seem like your life was over. So, I guess I don't know. I'm just hoping he's okay. I want to ask him about it, but the psychiatrist wants to talk with him first."

"George, do you realize that alcohol is the leading drug used and abused by youth in the United States, more than tobacco and other illegal drugs? Some studies have shown that over thirty-five percent of high school students have tried alcohol. And youth who begin drinking at age fifteen are five times more likely to develop dependency issues later in life."

"Shiloh, do you realize you're not helping me? You're supposed to be calming me down. I know how serious this is, and I know I've been horrible about modeling alcohol as an escape. I've been beating myself up over it. I'm sure Alex has noticed that every time life gets rough, I grab a beer or head to the bar with my friend Cade. I tend to forget what a problem alcohol is and all the lives it destroys. I guess the government needs to do more to control it, especially with teens."

"Actually, I disagree," Shiloh said. "I think anything that is focused on vices like drugs, alcohol, infidelity, and obesity is missing the point. It's impossible to fight a war on drugs, alcohol, prostitution, or unhealthy foods. You're just throwing money away on symptoms. You have to attack the root causes, things like ignorance, abuse, and poverty. People turn to drugs, alcohol, affairs, and other unhealthy behaviors because they want to escape from reality. Long-term happiness seems impossible to them, so they turn to short-term pleasure. They lack positivity, they lack hope, and they lack love. And the key about solving these root causes is that the more individual or personalized the approach, the more successful it will be. A government program will never be successful in solving obesity, alcoholism, or drug addiction. Billions have been spent on this, and what comes out? Brochures, medicines, agencies, programs, and procedures. None of this will heal people; they need care, education, understanding, and love. They don't need brochures and ten different prescriptions. We have to help people become better, more positive parents. We have to teach not only math and English, but also emotional intelligence. We have to help children become more self-aware, more self-regulating, and more mentally resilient. We're losing hundreds of thousands of brilliant minds because they can't handle relationships, they can't practice self-control, and they can't manage stress. No one taught them, no one helped them, and no one loved them."

George just stared at Shiloh.

"Oh, I'm sorry, George, I kind of got off track there, and you hit a chord with me. I wasn't talking about Alex. Alex is going to be fine; he's not the one you should be worried about. I know you love him and you've been doing the best you can as a parent. But let me ask you this: if he's not interested in sports and he's not excited about school, what is he interested in?"

He's not the one I should be worried about either? "I don't know. I just feel awful. I've been a horrible parent."

"How so?" Shiloh asked.

"Despite you and Elena telling me, I wasn't listening to Alex. I just wanted him back in baseball and back with his old friends. I want him to be the perfect student. I made him go to a party where he didn't fit in. There is nothing worse for a teenager than not fitting in. And honestly, I don't know what he wants from life. I only know what I want for him." George was rubbing his temples again.

"Don't you think you should understand what Alex wants from life?"

"Of course, Shiloh, I get it now. Please don't make me feel any worse than I already do. I learned a long time ago from Elena that when she came to me with a problem, she didn't want me to solve it, she wanted me to understand and listen. I don't know why I can't translate that to my kids."

"Brain research is sort of a hobby of mine. You should understand, George, that although the greatest period of brain development is in infancy, adolescents experience a second neuronal blooming from about age fifteen until they reach roughly age twenty-five. In this time period, their decision-making ability is still developing, and they may make decisions that are irrational or emotional. This is because their brains rely more on the limbic system than the more rational prefrontal cortex. In addition, part of this additional brain development is a new, profound ability to consider what others think about them. That's why peer pressure is so powerful at this age."

"I was a teen once myself. Trust me, I'm not upset with Alex, and I'm not going to screw up with him anymore," George said, reassuring himself as much as Shiloh.

"I know you won't, George, I just want to make sure you have all the facts. One more thing. The hormonal changes caused by puberty increase the creation of more receptors for oxytocin.

This can lead to more emotional sensitivity, particularly around self-consciousness. This is why they feel like everyone is watching and judging them."

"Thanks. But seriously, how do you remember all of this?"

"I have sort of a photographic memory. It's a blessing and a curse. I do have a bunch of facts rolling around in my head, but some people find it annoying."

I knew it! "It can be a lot to take in, Shiloh, but I do enjoy our conversations. A photographic memory is a gift. You've taught me a lot. It's been a tough couple of months, and I appreciate your friendship. I think if people don't appreciate you, it's their loss."

"You're a good father. Alex is going to be fine, trust me. Try to enjoy listening to him. I think you're going to be pleasantly surprised. Here's my stop." Shiloh stood and began walking down the aisle, and then, rather awkwardly, turned back and waved. George smiled and waved back.

Elena sent him several texts throughout the day. She was doing a masterful job of juggling Amanda and Alex. The psychiatrist had met several times with Alex and was ready to talk to them. Elena had set up a six o'clock meeting, and George was anxious to hear his suggestions. He wrapped up work around three and headed for an early train.

The ride home was uneventful, and he wasn't in the mood to talk anyway. He was feeling anxious about meeting with the doctor. Elena had sent George a text that she and Alex would eat at the hospital, so he should pick up something for Amanda and himself on the way home. George retrieved his car at the Crystal Lake station and stopped at Amanda's favorite sub shop on the way home.

At least I'll be a hit with Amanda.

When he arrived home he found Amanda in front of the television. "Hi, Dad. How was work?"

He handed Amanda her sub. "No tomatoes, extra mayo. Work was fine. How are you holding up?"

"I'm fine. I'm just worried about Alex. Are you really mad at him for drinking?"

Amanda opened her sub and inspected it for tomatoes. She seemed satisfied and reassembled it.

"No, I'm not mad at him. I'm mad at myself. I haven't done a good job of listening to him, and I think I've only added to the pressure he's been feeling. I just want him to be happy."

"Mom said she was worried that you'd be blaming yourself. I was kind of feeling guilty too, because I haven't been that nice to him either."

Amanda took a bite of her sub.

"At least you have an excuse. You went through a lot. You deserve to be a little grumpy now and then. I, on the other hand, have no excuse."

George leaned forward and brushed some breadcrumbs off Amanda's cheek.

"Mom says Alex has to see a psychiatrist. Isn't that kind of overboard? I mean, a lot of kids his age have gotten drunk. I know he screwed up, but it's not like Alex is crazy or anything."

I wonder how much Elena has told her? "No one thinks he's crazy, but he was very sick. Everybody just wants to make sure he's okay. Honey, a lot of people see psychiatrists. It doesn't mean that you're crazy. Sometimes it just helps to have someone who can talk through your problems and help you think about how to handle them. But speaking of Alex, I need to get over to the hospital to see him. Are you going to be okay? Do you need anything before I go?"

"No, Dad, I'm fine. Mom got me a movie, and Tami is coming over to watch it with me."

George changed, ate his sandwich, said good-bye to Amanda, and headed to the hospital.

Boy, reassuring Amanda didn't really help me reassure myself. Am I about to be told that Alex has serious mental issues? Is he going to have to spend time in an institution or see someone for years? I hate that it's not a wound you can look at to check whether it's healing. It's not something I can just put a Band-Aid on.

At the hospital, he found Alex sitting up in his bed with Elena perched on the side. They were both trying to answer *Jeopardy* questions. Alex Trebek had just asked about a 1997 movie based on a Carl Sagan book. George snuck into the room and said, "What is *Contact*?"

Elena smiled and said, "I was just about to say that. Hi, honey. How's Amanda?"

George gave Alex and then Elena a hug. "She's great. She's eating her dinner, and Tami is on the way over. How are you, Alex?"

"I'm bored and ready to get out of here."

That seems like a good sign? "There's the Alex I know and love." George looked over at Elena.

"Like I said, Alex, your dad and I will meet with Dr. Rao in a little bit, and he'll tell us when you get to go home."

"How was Dr. Rao?" George asked Alex.

Alex turned to his mom but replied, "Fine. I didn't think I'd like him, but he's pretty cool."

"Well, it's about time for us to find Dr. Rao and find out if you can go home tonight. Do you need anything before we leave, Alex?" asked Elena.

"No, just convince him to let me go home tonight. I feel fine now."

George handed Alex the TV remote. "Hey, if he doesn't let you out, we'll find a way to break you out of here. We'll tie some bedsheets together and go out the window. Or maybe have Mom bake a cake with a file inside."

Elena sighed. "You're not funny, George. Come on, we have to go. It's going to be fine, Alex, just hang in there."

After they were in the hallway and out of earshot, George asked, "Well, how is he, really?"

"He seems fine. Like our normal Alex. But I've been following doctor's orders and trying not to pry. I've just been here for him. It sounds like the sessions with Dr. Rao went well, but let's go find out."

George and Elena arrived at consultation room number two about five minutes early, and Dr. Rao was about ten minutes late. For George it was another agonizing wait. Finally, he arrived and sat down across from them.

"Good evening, George and Elena. You both seem tense, so let me start by saying that I had two excellent sessions with Alex. You have a bright and creative son. In fact, he has a very high emotional intelligence for his age. Personally, I found him to be an amazing young man."

Both George and Elena breathed a little easier. "So what does this mean?" asked George.

"I'll get to that, but let me dive a little deeper first," Dr. Rao said. "Alex opened up to me. Teenaged boys are typically difficult to connect with, so I was thrilled that Alex was so open, so quickly. The good news is that he is advanced in this thinking about his sense of self and his future. Most teenagers are not thinking more than the next week, or even the next day, in front of them. They live in the now and don't spend much time thinking about their future or what they want from life. Alex has spent a great deal of time thinking about his life, his future, and the implications of his choices."

A thought hit George like a lightning bolt. "Wait, is Alex gay?"

"Would you be okay if he were, Mr. Hartdegen?"

"Call me George, please. Honestly, it would be difficult for me. But I guarantee you that I love him no matter what. So is he?"

"No, he isn't gay. But it's interesting you asked that. Alex has a similar challenge. He's sensitive, creative, and artistic. And he has a great deal of respect for you, George, and as much as anything, he desperately wants your approval. He is feeling a great deal of anxiety about it. He also knows that his easiest path of acceptance in high school is sports and hanging around other boys in sports. But, more importantly, he knows you value athletics and hard academic subjects, like science and math. But he doesn't want that."

I never said that. Where is he getting this?

"I'm not trying to force him in any direction. I just want him to be involved and successful."

Don't defend yourself; just listen.

"I'm sure you do, George. But remember, this isn't about your intentions. It's about what Alex thinks you want from him. He believes the path set for him is athletics, good grades, and hanging around with the popular crowd. Part of him wants to head down this path to please you and because it's safer and easier. His struggle is that he already knows that it's not what he wants from life. He doesn't want to become an accountant or a scientist, he wants to be something much more creative, like a musician or an artist."

But there's no money in being an artist. Oh, stop being a stereotypical parent, George.

"It's rare for an early teen to already have such an advanced viewpoint on their future. I believe he's motivated and, if supported, he'll be successful. So, let me cut to chase. I don't find Alex to be suicidal. He was embarrassed, feeling sorry for himself, and attempting to escape the moment. But I don't believe he was trying to kill himself. Nor do I believe he is a risk going forward."

"Oh, thank God," Elena said.

"Yes, it's good news. I'm happy to sign his release for tonight. I'm sure he would love to sleep in his own bed," Dr. Rao said.

"Yes, he'll be thrilled."

"Now, I still would encourage you to line up some counseling. I believe Alex should have a minimum of three to four more sessions over the next two months. After that, a decision can be made as to the need for any future counseling. I'd be happy to continue on with him, or you're free to line up another psychiatrist. In addition, I encourage both of you to have several conversations with Alex as soon as possible. Ask him about his interests and goals in life. Make sure he understands that you support him, especially you, George. And help him make adjustments in his life that make him happy."

"He seemed to like you, Dr. Rao, so we'll work on getting four more sessions scheduled with you," Elena said.

"And I'm going to force myself to just listen to Alex if it kills me. We appreciate your help, doctor," George said.

After they got home, Elena told George she was anxious to talk with Alex. "That's fine, honey, I'll tell him good night, but you go first. I'm going to save my discussion till tomorrow night," George said.

"Why?" Elena asked.

"I just need to think about it for a while."

George stopped in Alex's room. "Glad to be home, son?"

"Yeah. Are you really mad at me, Dad?"

"No, I'm just glad you're okay. And I'm afraid I haven't been a great father lately. I've made some mistakes, like forcing you to play baseball and to go to that party. I'm sorry, Alex."

"It's not your fault, Dad. I don't know what's wrong with me. All you're trying to do is to help me."

"You know what, Alex? Nothing is wrong with you. I've been trying to turn you into another George, and you're not another George. You're Alex, and that's a good thing. Hey, I think your mom wants to talk with you tonight, and then you need to get some sleep. You and I will talk more tomorrow night. Goodnight, Alex. I love you."

"Good night, Dad."

George told Elena she was up. After she left their bedroom, George navigated to Shiloh's application on his watch. He set the date to Thursday, December 12, 2002.

CHAPTER 35

Golden Years

December 12, 2002

With some trepidation, George walked up to the front door. He simultaneously knocked and opened the door, announcing himself. His parents still never locked their house.

It's a miracle they never got robbed. Although, based on my discussions with Shiloh, it's probably not a miracle. My parents lived with a lot less fear than I do.

"Hi, Mom and Dad. It's George."

Childhood memories came flooding back. He and his buddies had played so much Wiffle Ball in the backyard they'd worn base paths into the grass. It was a house that all the kids came to, and his mom was always bringing out Kool-Aid or cookies or something. George and his friends would play night games like kick the can or ghost in the graveyard. The boundaries were a six-house rectangle, and neighbors didn't seem to care that kids were hiding, running, and screaming in their yards.

Today people would pull a gun or call the police.

He saw his mother first, and even though he'd prepared himself all day, it was still a shock. He smiled and gave her a hug. "Happy birthday, Mom! How old are you today?" he asked, even though he knew the answer.

"Of course I'm twenty-nine," Martha said, pausing. "Again. And, Georgie, you should know better than to ask a lady her age. Where are your manners? How are my little granddaughter, Mandy, and your beautiful wife, Elena?"

"They're both great, Mom, and they're looking forward to this weekend when we celebrate your birthday. I just wanted to stop by on your actual birthday and see you. I can't stay long."

If I stay too long, I'll lose it.

They both sat down on the living room couch. "It's sweet of you to stop by. Your father is cooking me his famous fried chicken. It's the one day a year he cooks, and cleans the dishes too."

"Hi, George, be out in a minute," came his father's voice from the kitchen.

"Hi, Dad, no problem. Finish cooking your chicken," George replied. He turned to Martha. It was still difficult to comprehend that he was seeing her again. "Hey, Mom, do you remember that time that Bobby and I rafted down Hickory Creek?"

"You boys lived down by that creek for a couple of summers. You used to come home filthy and mosquito-bitten every night."

"Yeah, but do you remember the time we took Bobby's raft and went all the way to the river?"

"Yes, George, I remember that. I worried the whole day. Bobby's mom wasn't worried in the least bit, but I had a bad feeling about it. I was so happy when you walked in the door that evening," she said.

"Huh, I had no idea you were worried. Not to freak you out or anything, but I almost died that day. I fell out of the raft and got pinned against a log underwater."

"Oh my, I wish you hadn't told me that, George. I guess we never should have let you go."

"No, I brought it up because I'm glad you did, Mom. I was thinking about it the other day. It was the first time that I fully appreciated my life. From then on, I kind of knew that life was special. I think moments like that help shape your outlook on life. I just wanted to thank you for letting me be a kid and learn some lessons on my own. I think it made me a better person. You gave me a lot of freedom, but you and Dad were always there to help me and guide me. I'm worried I won't be able to do that as a parent."

"Why would you say that? You're already a great dad. You worry too much, George," Martha said.

"Yeah, that's my problem. I'm not sure I know when to let my kids make their own mistakes and when to not."

"That's the beautiful thing about being a parent. Mostly you get to watch your kids learn and grow from everything they experience, but every now and then, you get to help them avoid the hard lessons. You get to prevent some frustration or pain or sadness. But I think they learn best when they make their own mistakes, so I think you try to find that middle ground. And you know what? At least half the time you think they're going to make a mistake, it turns out they don't."

"But how do you know? How do you know when to let them make their own mistakes? How do you know when to push them down the right path?" he asked.

"You let them make their own mistakes, as much as you can take. You put the cup of milk in front of them, even though you know they're going to spill it. And, George, you don't know the right path for them. They have to find their own way."

"What's all this serious talk?" said Jonathan as he walked into the room.

"Oh, I was just giving George some bad parenting advice, telling him to let Mandy spill her milk more often. You know, George, when you were little there was no such thing as a no-spill sippy cup."

"She's right, George. It's your job to let her make mistakes and then to be there to clean up all the messes. But, just to be clear, as grandparents, it's our job to coddle her and spoil her and generally make your job twice as hard."

George looked around the room, taking it all in. The nostalgia was overwhelming. *God, I miss this house. So many memories.*

"Oh, you're both already doing a great job of that. Hey, Dad, did I always want to play baseball? Did you ever have to push me to stay with it?"

"Oh, heavens, no. You were obsessed with it all the way through. But before you came along, I hated baseball. I always found it to be a slow, boring game. I learned the game through you, through your passion. And now your mom and I go to a half dozen Cubs games a year. We'd go to more games if they'd win every now and then. But force you to go to baseball? Never," said Jonathan.

It doesn't get any better for the Cubs, Dad. Wow, I really miss them. I didn't realize how much I miss them. The hardest thing is not being able to just pick up the phone and tell them about the kids.

"Yeah, I didn't think so, but I was just checking."

"We did try to push you into music, though. Remember the piano lessons?" Martha said.

"Yeah, I remember the piano lessons," George replied.

"You mother wanted you to stick with piano. Your teacher even told us you had serious potential. You picked it up so fast. But you hated it. It killed your mother, but we both agreed to let it go. It just wasn't something you had any interest in."

"I just think music is important for anyone," Martha added. "We tried everything—school band, choir, any private lessons you wanted. You weren't even interested in guitar. I finally had to admit that it just wasn't for you. But I was surprised how passionate you became about baseball and how valuable it was for you. Making friends, being part of a team, it made you happy, so that was what was important to me."

"And, most importantly, it paid for your college. Hey, George, can you stay for dinner? I made my fried chicken, there's plenty," Jonathan said.

I need to leave. I can't believe I've held it together for this long.

George stood up. "No, I've got to go. I promised Elena I'd come home for dinner. I think she's ready for a break from Mandy. I'm glad I got to stop by, though. Happy birthday, Mom."

Martha stood up as well, and George gave her a hug. "I love you, Mom," he said, fighting back tears.

"Well, I love you too, George," Martha said.

George's dad stood and offered his hand. George took it, but stepped forward and hugged him instead. "I love you, Dad."

"You too, slugger," Jonathan replied.

I never said I love you often enough.

George made it out the front door before the tears came full on. He sat in car and bawled. Two months later they would both be gone. A semi would hit a patch of ice and cross the four-lane highway, killing them both instantly. They would never see Amanda graduate from high school, and they would never even meet Alex.

George got himself under control, backed out of the drive-way and headed for home.

Good-bye, Mom and Dad.

CHAPTER 36

Dream On

July 1, 2014

George awoke and checked his watch to confirm he was back in 2014. It was another working day, and for once George wasn't dreading it. He lay in bed a while, thinking about his mother and father.

I was so angry when they were taken from me. I was angry they didn't get to enjoy their retirement. But more so, it was about me. I was angry I didn't get to say good-bye and angry I never thanked them for my childhood. I know they weren't my real parents, but it still helped. It helped to see them and tell them I loved them. It doesn't bring them back, but I'll take it.

On the trip downtown, his thoughts danced all over the place, but mostly around Alex.

I just need to apologize and do whatever it takes to make Alex happy. But what if I'm being too soft on him? He hasn't exactly been the model son lately, and it's not like anyone forced him to get drunk. If I'm easy on him now, where does that put us in two years?

By the time he reached his office, he was more confused than when he left. He threw himself into his work to avoid thinking about it. The day went by quickly, and before he knew it he was back on the train. Shiloh did not appear, so he forced himself to think about Alex again.

There's an easy answer: just listen. No speech, no perfect words of wisdom, and no tough love. Just listen. It's simple, and it's what everyone is telling me. I just want to fix things so badly. To tell Alex exactly what to do. I'm afraid he'll make the wrong decisions. What did Mom say? You let them make their own mistakes, as much as you can take. I'll just listen.

When he arrived home, Elena and Amanda were watching TV together. He greeted them both. George couldn't tell if it was a soap opera or a reality show, but there was certainly a lot of drama. Elena joined him in the bedroom as he changed out of his work clothes.

"The kids are doing well, but it's been a pretty lazy day. Both Amanda and Alex slept almost till noon. They both ate a good lunch and seem fine. Alex and I talked for a while, and now he's up in his room. Amanda has physical therapy tomorrow and Thursday. Also, she'll get her eye checked and hopefully lose the patch. I'm thinking she will be back to school on Monday. I'm going to call the school to see if they have anything she can work on the rest of the week to start to catch up. As for Alex, he has an appointment Wednesday with Dr. Rao. I think he should go back to school on Monday, but we'll see what Dr. Rao says tomorrow. George, you should talk with him tonight or at least tomorrow, before he sees Dr. Rao." Elena finally paused.

"I'm planning on it. It took me a whole day of thinking to decide to say nothing. I'm just planning on listening to him."

"Right on, hubby. I know it's not your natural instinct, but you got it. I think it took two or three years of marriage for you to stop telling me what to do."

"I'm pretty sure you let that last about a month. You were never shy about helping me understand when I was being rude."

"I had to train you in right away." She laughed. "Hey, spaghetti for dinner. We eat in about an hour."

"Okay, I'll be up in Alex's room, having our conversation," George said.

"Good luck."

George made his way to Alex's room and knocked. Silence. He knocked again, louder, and said, "Alex, it's Dad!"

"Enter."

George opened the door and walked in. Alex was in the corner, sitting in a beanbag chair with his guitar, which was plugged into an amplifier. Alex pulled down the headphones he had plugged into the amp.

"What's up, Dad?"

Don't screw up, George.

"I just wanted to talk." He looked at the guitar, and a thought came to him. "Hey, will you play for me?"

Alex looked a little sheepish. "I don't know, Dad. I'm still trying to figure it out."

"Come on, Alex, I want to hear."

Alex shrugged and leaned over to unplug the headphones from the amp. George thought he saw a little smile on Alex's face. A high-pitched squeal came from the speaker, and Alex quickly turned down the volume. He glanced down at the strings and began to play.

George was mesmerized as he watched Alex's fingers effortlessly move up and down the frets. Alex played for a couple of minutes, then paused and looked at his father.

"Wow," was all George was able to get out.

"It's a song called 'Heartbeats' by José González. I can't play it perfect yet, but it's really fun to play."

"Alex, that was amazing. How in the world did you get so good at guitar?"

"I don't know, it's just fun. It kind of helps me forget about school and baseball and stuff. It was hard for a while, but then it just started to get easier and easier."

"Is it just that song, or can you play lots of songs?"

Alex began to play again. This time George recognized the tune immediately, and it brought a smile to his face. "Ah, 'Yesterday,' by the Beatles. That's fantastic."

"It's your favorite, right?"

"Yeah," George replied, still trying to get his head around Alex's ability. *He took the time to learn my favorite song.*

"I only know five or six by heart. But if I have the tabs, I can sort of play almost anything."

"Tabs?" George asked.

"Guitar tabs, it's like music shorthand. You can get them off the Internet. Jeff showed me—he plays guitar too."

"Is that why you've been hanging out with Jeff?"

"Yeah, sort of, we both like guitar, graphic novels, and a bunch of the same stuff."

"Graphic novels?" George wrinkled his face. "Oh, you mean comic books."

"Yeah, I guess. But Dad, graphic novels are more than just comic books now. They are a legitimate art form. Did you see *V for Vendetta*? That was a graphic novel. Or how about *Watchmen* or

300, or *The Walking Dead?* They were all graphic novels before they were movies or TV shows."

"You'll have to loan me one, son. It's not that I don't believe you, I'm just completely out of the loop," George said. "So that's why you want to hang out with Jeff instead of the guys on the baseball team?"

"Well, it's more than that."

"So what is it?"

"It's complicated," Alex said.

"Come on, Alex, I want to understand."

"Okay, the guys on my baseball team and that whole crowd are idiots. All they want to talk about are sports, drinking, and girls. And Dad, you should hear the way they talk about girls. Like they aren't even people, like they're objects. It's just a big contest to see how far they can get with any girl. They don't care about them. Ever since Danny moved away, everything changed, and I just don't want to be around those guys anymore. And Jeff's different—it's not just that we both play guitar, we talk about real stuff. Like what we're going to do after high school. And how messed up the world is."

Hey, maybe there is something to listening thing. "Alex, I'm so glad you told me this. And I'm so sorry I didn't listen to you earlier. I don't want to *make* you do anything. Especially not hang around with those kind of guys. And it sounds like Jeff is a pretty good guy. I just thought I had heard that he got in trouble at school for alcohol."

"Yeah, he did. His dad's an alcoholic, and he put some liquor in his backpack to hide it from him. He was going to ditch it after school, but someone saw it and told on him. Jeff hates alcohol because of his dad, but they wouldn't believe him. You have it completely backward, Dad, Jeff doesn't drink, but most of the boys on my baseball team do."

George rubbed his temples. "Boy, you must think I'm an idiot."

"No, Dad, it's just that sometimes I don't know what I want. I probably should hang out with the guys on the baseball team. It would make things easier in high school. And I know I should probably focus on math and science. I've heard you say that artists don't make any money."

"You know what, Alex? You need to do what makes you happy. If you work hard, you can make a living doing anything. The real trick is to find something you love. And that goes for friends also. Hang out with the people you like, with people you can talk to. High school comes and goes."

"I guess," Alex said.

"I've spent a lot of my life worrying about what others think and being afraid of failing. I'm just now starting to figure that out. You're fourteen, and you're already figuring it out, even with me constantly telling you what to worry about. You can't be afraid of failing or what others think. Basically, ignore everything I've told you the last couple of years."

"Dad, come on."

George wanted to keep it going. "I'm serious. Follow your instincts, take some risks. And speaking of risks, are you and Jeff going to try to perform?"

"Maybe, but neither one of us has the guts to sing. And I think you have to have a singer to be successful."

"Maybe you have to find a singer. Or maybe you just need to get some guts. I think you've got talent, at least with the guitar, kid."

"We'll see," Alex said. "I'm kind of busy with something else too."

"What's that?"

"Nothing, it's kind of stupid."

George could sense it was something Alex wanted to tell him. "What is it, Alex?"

"Remember the graphic novels I was telling you about? I kind of want to write one and illustrate it," Alex said, looking away.

I hope I haven't teased him too much about comic books. "Wow, you are full of surprises. So do you have an idea?"

"Yeah, I do. But it's kind of weird—it's science fiction."

George leaned in. "Okay, let's hear it."

"It starts with an archeological expedition finding these alien ships that are about a hundred thousand years old. The scientists figure out they had damaged each other in a battle and both crashed on Earth. Despite being so ancient, they're in amazingly good condition. They uncover enough information to learn that one alien race was in a galactic battle to save the universe from another totally evil race that was spreading like a cancer across the universe. That race is pure evil and only cares about its own survival. The other race is great warriors and the universe's last chance to stop the evil ones. The scientists discover some preserved DNA and believe we're descendants of one of the races of aliens. Eventually they restore one of the ships enough to travel the stars—and here is where the time travel comes in. They decipher enough information to learn that not only were the aliens were able to time travel, but they used the ship to make the time travel work. However, because part of its navigation system is damaged, they can only go back to shortly after the ships crashed. The main character volunteers to go back in time. They send him back, and he witnesses an epic battle between the two ships' pilots after the crash. One looks humanoid, and the other is a large, black spider-like creature. The main character helps the humanoid pilot destroy the other creature. The plot twist is that the humanoid creature, not the black spider-like being, turns out to be the evil race. We are the evil race."

"Wow, I love it."

"Do you want to hear the rest of the ending?"

"Sure," George said. "But that would explain the human race, wouldn't it? We would be the ones that go out and create death and destruction, just to spread mankind across the universe."

"Right, but there's one final twist to the story. The main character figures out that the humanoid pilot is the evil race. So he kills the pilot as he is attacking one of the prehistoric women. And since the main character saves her, she falls in love with him. The time traveler ends up being the father of modern humans."

"Wow, that's a humdinger of an ending. I guess it's hopeful, even if it's a bit of a paradox. Alex, it's awesome, you should go for it."

"I pretty much have the whole story figured out, but the illustrations are going to take a long time."

"Wait, you're illustrating it too?"

"I'm trying. I've sort of roughed out the first part, and I just started drawing the first few frames for real. I think I might need to get some computer software to eventually bring it all together."

"Can I see?"

Alex put down his guitar and went over to his desk, where he sat down pulled out a sketchbook. George followed and leaned over his son's shoulder as Alex flipped through the sketch book. George saw page after page of drawings: aliens, spaceships, scientists, and then a drawing of a girl. Alex flipped by that page quickly.

"These are mostly practice drawings. Okay, here's the layout."

Alex had turned to a page that was boxed in, like a comic book. The drawings in each frame were rough, but George was still impressed.

"Amazing! This is very cool. Where did you learn this?"

His head was spinning. He felt like a fool for knowing nothing about Alex's talents. He was relieved to know he was going to be okay. And pride was swelling up in him.

"Remember how Mom got me that book on how to draw a graphic novel for my birthday?" Alex turned the page. "And this is my first attempt at drawing an actual frame. You draw it large and then you shrink it down on the computer."

The page was drawn from a point of view behind the shoulder of a group of workmen digging with heavy equipment. They had broken a large hole into a massive cavern. Inside it was beautiful, with large, broken rocks, stalactites, and stalagmites. On either side were intricately drawn spaceships, one looking sleek and fast and the other more heavily armored and weaponized.

George reached down and picked up the sketchbook.

"Careful, it can smudge," Alex said.

"Oh, Alex, this—" George let out an incredulous laugh. "This is fantastic."

Alex looked up. "Thanks, Dad."

"I have to be honest with you. I thought you were spending your whole summer in your room playing video games, watching TV, and reading comic books. I mean, to get this good with your guitar and drawing, you've been working hard."

"It really doesn't feel like work. And I have been playing some video games now and then."

George set down the sketchbook and laughed again. "I don't know what to say, Alex, other than I'm sorry for being a jerk, and I'm so proud of you." He leaned down hugged his son, once again fighting off tears. Alex was quiet, and George couldn't see his face.

"Hey, who's that girl that you drew? Is she a character in your novel?"

Alex glanced away again. "No, she's just a girl at school, a friend."

George instantly knew there was more to the story, but decided to let Alex off the hook, for today, at least. There was a knock at Alex's door.

"Hey, boys, spaghetti is ready," Elena called.

George walked over and opened the door, and Alex scooted out past them both, clearly in a hurry for dinner. George looked at Elena and smiled.

"You have an amazing son."

"I already knew that, dummy. You're just figuring it out?

"No, I knew. I just didn't understand how incredible."

They both headed downstairs for what would be a lively, cheerful dinner.

CHAPTER 37

Kashmir

George's boots crunched through the crust of the ground with each step, but he couldn't hear or see it. His space suit shut out sound, and thick mist covered the ground. His space suit had limited peripheral vision, but he could still see Shiloh walking next to him. For some reason it didn't strike George as odd that Shiloh wasn't wearing a space suit. Shiloh was in his normal tweed jacket, khaki pants, and a T-shirt that read, *May the (Mass × Acceleration) be with you.* What did strike George as odd was how hard it was to walk. The slight hill they were climbing wasn't steep enough to explain the difficulty he was having. George began to struggle with his breathing. It felt like his suit wasn't providing enough oxygen. He stopped walking and began to take fast, shallow breaths. Shiloh walked over to him and peered into his visor.

"You're fine. Your oxygen's fine. You're just having a panic attack," yelled Shiloh through his suit's intercom. "Slow down your breathing."

George forced himself to take slow, even breaths, and it seemed to help. His visor fogged slightly from the heavy breathing. George looked up into bluish-green sky, still focused on his breathing, but felt panic rising up again as he saw the three suns low above the horizon directly ahead of them.

"Isn't it wonderful?" said Shiloh. "It's the only system in the universe—actually in the whole multiverse—that has three suns in this configuration. The two smaller suns are in a near-perfect orbit around the larger sun. It is highly improbable for this configuration to form—as close to impossible as you can get. But it's one of a kind, which is why we chose it. We call it Kashmir. The planet orbits all three stars. Its orbit is much more distant than our Earth's is from the sun, but the extra energy from the three stars creates a reasonable temperature."

Shiloh pointed at the ground below them.

"This planet is two point three percent larger than Earth, which is why it's difficult to walk—more gravity. But we have to keep moving. It's just over that ridge."

"What is over the ridge?"

"Something awesome. Come on! All will be revealed."

George noticed that Shiloh was wearing his large, white headphones. "What are you listening to?"

"Led Zeppelin. 'Kashmir,' of course." He began to sing along with the music as they hauled themselves up the hill. Off to the left, large, rocky spires colored in a vast spectrum of reds and purples rose out of a roiling blanket of mist. Overlapping shadows from the three suns accentuated their varied tones against the contrast of the blue-green sky. There was no vegetation, nor any other sign of life forms.

As they crested the slope, George stopped abruptly. He wiped at a smudge of fog on his helmet visor, but realized it was on the inside. They were on the edge of a vast, circular crater. Awed, George looked around—twisting his whole body first to the left, then to the right, because his helmet didn't turn—to take it all in. The inside of the crater was filled with machinery. Unable to take in the sheer size of it, George instead focused on the nearest collection of machinery, which seemed to be some type of vats surrounded by thick mist. The vats were in groups of three, connected by tubes and wires. Each group of three connected to two other groups, and so on—they were all interconnected. George estimated that he was looking at tens of thousands of vats, maybe hundreds of thousands.

"Isn't it awesome?" asked Shiloh. "They're in groups of threes. Have you ever noticed that tragedies always come in groups of three, George? It's weird. Let's keep moving. They're waiting for us."

George asked the first of several questions that had appeared in his head. "What is it?"

"It's the most complex machine in the multiverse. You wouldn't understand, George, but think of it as the largest, most advanced computer possible."

He led the way down the edge of the crater toward the machinery. As they got closer, George spotted movement—some sort of creatures tending to the vats. He noticed only a few at first, but eventually he made out hundreds, then thousands of the creatures. The light glinted off them as though they were made of metal, like the machinery, but they walked upright. Soon George could make out their shapes, like human-sized, robotic praying mantises. The scurrying horde give him the chills.

Shiloh motioned to George to keep walking. At around fifty yards from the nearest vats, George could make out the contents of the vats. It looked like humans suspended in water or some other liquid.

"Are those people?"

"Yes, they are," Shiloh said. "They're part of the machine. Think of each of them as a CPU in a massively parallel brain. It's beautiful. It's the perfect creation."

Something about the humans in the vats seemed familiar. As he got close enough to see their faces, his curiosity turned to horror. "They're me! They're all me. Oh my God. Are they clones, Shiloh?"

"No, they are all the Georges from hundreds of thousands of parallel universes. You see, they all need to be compatible. This is what we've been working to create. This has been billions of years in the making, and this is the final step in our journey. You are the last George we need. You are the final puzzle piece that will complete the machine."

Two of the praying mantis creatures scurried through the mist toward George. He backed away and tripped over something in the fog—Shiloh's tweed jacket. He turned to Shiloh and screamed. Shiloh was tearing the skin off his face to reveal the same metallic insectoid head. Led Zeppelin's "Kashmir" echoed through his suit's intercom. He screamed again as the mist rose up, covering him completely.

George awoke with a shudder, the image of Shiloh tearing his face off still fresh in his mind.

Okay, that officially wins my Weirdest and Creepiest Dream of All Time award.

He glanced at his watch: 4:53 a.m. He sat up in bed. It was too close to his usual alarm to try to go back to sleep, but he'd gone to bed late and he knew he'd miss the extra sleep later. He tried to remember what Shiloh had said to him in the dream, but it was already beginning to slip from his memory.

It's probably a combination of traveling and thinking about Alex's sci-fi story. Maybe it's just about fear, about being scared. Or maybe it's just a stupid nightmare.

George gave in and got ready for work. His normal routine got him to the train station fifteen minutes early, and he made the earlier train. It felt strange, like he was an intruder. George decided it was a ridiculous thought, as even his regular train was filled with strangers. Between the lack of sleep, the nightmare, and being slightly off his normal schedule, George slid into a foul mood. He tried to think about being positive with Alex, but his thoughts kept drifting to darker things like losing his parents, his job, and the frustrations of traveling.

I can travel to the past, but I can't change anything! While it was great to see my parents, what would really be useful is to have them back again in this life. It's reminding me what a hole their deaths left in my life. Ever since they've been gone, it's like the safety net has been pulled away. Everything is for keeps now. If I screw up, there's no one to pull me out of it but myself.

George smelled breakfast, someone was eating on the train.

Bacon and hot sauce? I don't mind the smell of fresh bagels on the train, but hot sauce in the morning? Jesus, I feel queasy. Where was I? Oh yeah, feeling sorry for myself. So, assuming that Alex pulls out of this and things go back to normal, then what? Become a better parent, listen more, keep my job or find a new job? Is everything going to be better then? Maybe Shiloh will give me a few more speeches about the meaning of life and it will all be clear. A little less fear, a little more love, be more positive, and everything will fall into place. It all sounds good, but is it going to change anything? Christ, what is that smell, some sort of breakfast burrito?

257

Mercifully, the train pulled into the OTC and relieved George from his self-pity session—at least for a moment. It was a perfect July morning, but even the walk couldn't lift him from his self-induced funk. His office building loomed ahead. He pictured it as a dark tower with ominous clouds and black crows circling.

He arrived at the office, shut his door, and turned on his computer. About halfway through his unread e-mails, he ran into a sledgehammer: an e-mail from his boss explaining a new initiative to cut the bottom 10 percent of their workforce.

This is crazy. We're understaffed as it is. We can't even hire good employees, and now we're going to fire ten percent? My team is working their butts off covering for me. They're working evenings and weekends because I've been out so much. Who do I let go? Sure, some are stronger than others, but there is no dead weight on this team. So, now I have one month to decide whose reward for the late nights and stress is a paltry two-week severance and a handshake?

George went through the rest of his day in a stupor. He kept his door closed and ate lunch at his desk. He thought about walking into his boss's office and quitting. Deep down, he knew it was a bad idea. He at least owed it to Elena and his family to find another job first. Even that seemed daunting: updating his résumé, poring over job-search websites, and finding time to interview. It had been so long since he'd hunted for a job that he didn't even know how to prepare these days.

Just do it, George. Anyone you lay off will land on their feet. This kind of thing happens all the time. They'll be the lucky ones. Everyone left here will have even more work and stress. Just buy yourself some time, and once your family is back to normal you can start looking for another job. You just make a list, figure out the curve, and sit down and explain it to them.

Oh, Christ, who am I kidding? I can't do this.

At the end of the day, he drafted an e-mail to his boss and copied his boss's boss, Mr. Kirkpatrick. He made it as respectful and positive as he could. He made his case about being under-staffed and explained his viewpoint that there was no dead weight. He made suggestions about how they might be more efficient and productive with the staff they had. He knew he should have the discussion in person with his boss instead of sending an e-mail, but right now he didn't have the strength. And he knew it wouldn't go well. His boss would listen and then explain why it had to happen and that George didn't have to agree with the decision, but that he had to support it. George also knew that he shouldn't copy Mr. Kirkpatrick. It would likely get him fired. At a minimum, it would put him on rocky ground with his boss. And, in the end, it probably wouldn't change anything.

He reread the e-mail and made a few small wording changes. Then he hovered his cursor over the delete key.

Just delete it, George. Or just save the draft, wait a day, and consider it again tomorrow. That's the right thing to do.

George read the e-mail again.

No. Stop living your life in fear. I've been on rails for too long. I need to stop being a passenger and start driving my own life. Send it!

He clicked the send button, shut down his computer, and packed up. Shocked at himself, he made for the train.

CHAPTER 38

All You Need Is Love

July 1, 2014

George boarded his usual train and slumped in a seat.

I could use a drink. It feels like it's already been a long day. I think lack of sleep is catching up to me. I don't want to think about anything—especially not my job or traveling.

At Shiloh's stop, George saw Shiloh boarding. He was listening to music on his headphones and had a large grin on his face. It annoyed George. Shiloh's T-shirt said, *Resistance is not futile, it's voltage divided by current.* This annoyed George even more.

"Hi, George. How's Alex?"

George remembered slivers of his dream from the night before and examined Shiloh's face carefully. It seemed normal, and he felt silly for thinking about it.

"You know what? He's good. You were right. I do think he's going to be okay. I've been listening, and I'm learning things about him I never knew. He's a special kid with a great deal of potential. I think I just need to let him be himself."

"That's wonderful," Shiloh said.

"I've also learned what an awful parent I am. You know, Shiloh, I should be happy. My kids have both come through these things, and I should be thrilled. And I am—for them—but I'm still not happy. I still hate my job and want to quit. It's not even the crazy traveling. It's that I can't even pick ten days in my life that matter. I went back and visited my parents, which was amazing, but there is nothing that *I* have accomplished in my life that's worth reliving. I went back to a day where I hit a hole in one in golf. It's sad that I used to believe that was an important moment in my life. I'm struggling, Shiloh—struggling to find meaning in my life."

"George, I believe the meaning of life is two things. The first one is balance. It's about finding the edge of everything but never going over. If you're an athlete, it's the edge of your endurance; if you're a lawyer, it's about finding the edge of beliefs and mores; if you're a guitarist, it's the edge of creativity. Artists can't take their creativity so far that it becomes unintelligible or unrecognizable to others. They must find that middle where they stretch people's thinking without losing them. If you're a parent, you have to find that balance between pushing your children to grow without pushing them away. None of it's easy. It's always a struggle, but that's the key. All the clichés are true. It's not the destination, it's the journey. Why do we climb the mountain? We climb it because it's there." Shiloh looked at George to see if he was following.

"Shiloh, you're the first person I've ever met who believes they understand the meaning of life. I appreciate your confidence, but I'm not buying it. It's easy to talk about it, but it's hard to live it every day. So how do you live above the everyday? How do you make life special when you're working and parenting and dealing with people who make you angry? How can you be positive when there is so much sickness and death in the world?"

"You're right, it's not easy. When you surf, you don't get to ride the wave until you paddle out. You have to get through the paddling, George. But when you do, and you find that perfect wave to ride, it's so gnarly. You do have to deal with the everyday, but you have to find moments every day to remind you of what's special about life and love. You have to experience chaos, disorder, death, and destruction first. You're lucky to have experienced tragedy and come through the other side so well."

"Really, Shiloh? I'm lucky because I lost my parents, my daughter lost her eye, and my son almost killed himself?" George felt anger rising up in him.

"Do you think the universe has taken more than it has given you, George? Do you realize how many positive things have happened in your life? And do you understand that everything negative that happens to you is an opportunity? It's okay to have negative emotions. They're part of what makes you human. But when you do feel anger or self-pity or hate, you have to let them go quickly, and you have to learn from them. Each one is chance to grow, to learn, and to change."

"I can't accept that all the bad things that have happened in my life are good for me," George said.

"I'm not saying they're good. But it's half the equation, and without it there is no happiness or joy. You also need to do the things that connect with the balance in the universe as often as you can. Enjoy your kids, love your wife. Watch a soccer game, listen to more music, take a walk in nature, and appreciate how far the universe has come. Seek out the things on the edge, the things in balance. There's a reason why we see beauty in the sunrise and the sunset, in the change of the seasons, and where the land meets the sea."

"And what's the second thing? You said there were two things."

"It's love, of course. Love is the thing that keeps us headed in the right direction. It's the thing that makes us more than individuals. In the end, it's the only thing that makes life worth living. It's not easy either, George—no one ever said it was. We have to rise above the fear, the pride, and the jealousy. But when you do, when you find love, you've found the meaning of life."

"But if we all end up dying, what does it matter?"

"We all matter, George, and everything we do matters."

"You have it all figured out, don't you, Shiloh?"

"Actually, it's quite the opposite. Once you understand the journey of complexity we're on, once you let go of fear, you find out you're just getting started. When you realize that all the technical breakthroughs and advances are going to happen regardless and when you realize the things that really matter—tolerance, happiness, and love—are what are important, you're just at the beginning of your own journey. Remember, we're all contributing to the universe's journey of complexity. With every generation, every life, every action, we're all taking a step on that journey. The stars started it, George. They started this quest. But life took over, and life is what must take it to the end. Because the stars, as beautiful and powerful as they are, don't have love. And love is what is going to carry us through the chaos and the destruction and the hate. McCartney was right—all we need is love."

"And balance," George said.

"And balance," Shiloh repeated. "All you need is love and balance. It wouldn't have made as good of a song, though."

George couldn't help but smile.

George was in a better mood when he pulled into his driveway. It was still a beautiful summer day, and he was glad to be home.

I don't know if Shiloh really has it all figured out, but at least he's trying. Half the people on this planet have given up. I think the best thing he said was that it's the journey, not the destination. It's about trying to live a better life, not having the perfect life. That, I can get my head around. So how do I tell Elena about my e-mail and my job, or potential lack of job?

As George entered the house he could hear his family in the kitchen. It sounded like they were sitting around the kitchen table. "Hey, Daddy, I'm getting married," called out Amanda.

That caught George a little off guard—not that he believed her, it just wasn't something he was expecting to hear. As crazy as his life had been lately, anything was possible.

"What?" was all he was able to get out.

"But you'll be thrilled to know that I'm going to college," Alex said.

Elena joined in. "And you'll be even more thrilled when I tell you about our third child."

"Okay, what's going on?" George said as he walked into the kitchen with a large smile on his face. While he knew he was being teased, he still relaxed a little when he saw his wife and kids sitting around *The Game of Life*.

"Ah, it warms my heart to see my family struggling through the trials and tribulations of household finances, employment, and legal matters. I've never understood why anyone finds that game fun, but maybe you'll all better understand the pressures I'm under every day."

"Seems pretty easy and fun to me," Amanda teased.

"Hey, where's the eye patch, Captain Hook?" George asked.

"She got the all-clear today. Her eye infection is completely cleared," Elena said.

George looked at Amanda. "Aw, I miss my pirate girl."

"It's really weird now, not to have the patch but to still only see out of one eye. I think I'm starting to get used to it," Amanda said.

George examined her; she didn't seem to be upset. He was amazed at how quickly she was adjusting. He turned away, so as not to be caught staring, and asked, "And how's the rock star?"

"Look, Dad, no straitjacket!" Alex said. Elena shot him a glance. "What? I'm just trying to be funny."

"The doctor continues to be impressed with Alex. He still wants one more session tomorrow. Amanda gets her walking cast on Thurday," Elena said. She gave George her thank-God look.

"That's great news."

George went upstairs to change his clothes while the rest of the family resumed their game. When they finished, George helped Elena prepare dinner. It was taco night. George enjoyed the relative normalcy of a fun family dinner.

Later, as they were getting ready for bed, George asked Elena, "So, did both appointments really go that well?"

"Yeah, it was wonderful. I think Dr. Rao wants to adopt Alex. He all but told me that tomorrow's session is just protocol. He thinks Alex is a normal kid going through some tough changes in his teen years."

"So what's next?"

Elena turned her head to one side. "I'm not exactly sure. I get the feeling that's it. I suppose they have us keep an eye out for any unusual behavior and probably some sort of three- or six-month checkup. I guess I'll find out tomorrow."

"I guess that's great. But honestly, after that kind of scare, it almost seems inadequate. I don't know whether to be happy or worried. Ah, hell, I'm just going to go with happy."

By the time Elena was in the middle of her evening ritual, George had summoned up some courage. "Hey, honey, I need to tell you something about work today."

"What's that?" she replied before splashing water on her face.

"To start with, my wonderful boss has decided it's time for some cutbacks," George said.

"I thought you said your team was shorthanded?"

"We are, but since when do reality or common sense matter at work?" George said. "So I got pretty upset today and wrote an e-mail explaining why that's a bad idea. But I was very polite."

"That doesn't sound that bad," Elena said.

"I sent it to my boss's boss," George admitted.

"Hmmm, won't your boss be upset about that?"

"Yeah, I'm pretty sure he will be. I just couldn't help it."

Here it comes. Let me have it, Elena.

Elena looked at George, washcloth dripping in her hand. "Maybe it's time you moved on. You've been unhappy for a long time, and it's not changing."

"You're not mad?"

"No, I'm not mad. You'll land on your feet. Or maybe it's time I went back to work. One way or another, we'll work it out," Elena said, and then bent back to the sink.

"You don't know how relieved I am to hear you say that. Because I think it might be over at United."

Elena just moved on. "You do need to go to the doctor with me next Thursday. He said he wants to talk with both of us. I had my checkup last week, and he had me come back this morning for some tests."

"Are you okay, Elena?"

"I'm fine, I've just had some bloating and cramps, and I've missed my last period. I'm sure it's nothing. Hah, maybe I'm pregnant." She laughed.

Pregnant? She's joking right? Please be joking. "Jesus, you couldn't really be pregnant, could you Elena?"

"No, George, I'm forty-nine years old. It's more likely that we're going to get a speech on early-onset menopause from the doctor."

"Oh, *oh*. Really? Menopause, I thought that was something women get when they turn seventy."

"No, it can happen a lot sooner. But don't worry, everything will be okay. The doctor will explain it all to you," Elena said, sounding a little patronizing.

"Why didn't you tell me you went to the doctor last week?"

"You typically don't like to hear about my womanly issues. It's not a big deal."

"How have you even found time with the kids?"

Elena pointed to herself. "Uh, Superwoman, did you forget?"

"Let's see, super hearing, x-ray vision, and the ability to jump to conclusions with a single bound. Yep, it all adds up."

"Hey, knock it off, or I'll use my superpowers on you!"

"That's what I'm hoping," George said as he hopped into bed.

CHAPTER 39

Work It Out

July 2, 2014

"Are you getting the fried egg on the fried egg?" George asked, extending his hand. Cade was a fried-egg maniac. George had never seen him pass up an opportunity: huevos rancheros, fried-egg sandwich, or even a fried egg on a burger. If a fried egg was on the menu, Cade was ordering it.

Cade smiled and shook his hand. "You might have something there. But I'm getting the corned beef hash, which does happen to have a couple of fried eggs on it. But you're the one who picked a restaurant called Yolk. What am I supposed to do? Besides, I've gone at least three or four days without, so cut me a break."

George laughed, sat down, and read the menu. When the waiter arrived, Cade ordered his corned beef hash and George ordered pancakes. The waiter poured them both coffees.

"How are Alex and Amanda?"

George was caught off guard. "You know about Alex?"

"Sorry if that's on the down low. But I think Elena has been leaning a little on Lynn. We haven't told anyone else."

"Oh, no problem. I don't mind you and Lynn knowing. Lynn's a good friend to Elena." George paused. "Thanks for asking. They're both doing great. I think Amanda is supposed to get her hard cast off today and get a walking cast. Alex is going to be fine. He gave us a good scare, but he's all right. It's these damn teenage years and the crazy peer pressure and all."

"I get that. High school is tough on everybody. And hey, the only difference between Alex and me is that I never got caught," Cade said.

Ain't that the truth! "The amazing thing is that I've learned a lot about Alex. I mean it feels like I hardly knew the boy. He can draw like you wouldn't believe, and he's a good guitar player. But I think baseball's over for him—he's just not into it."

"Hey, that's okay. If he can play the guitar, he's going to have to fight the girls off," Cade suggested.

"Oh man, one thing at a time! I'm not ready for girl trouble. Even Amanda doesn't date much yet, thank God."

"As far as you know," Cade said. "Seriously, I'm happy they're doing well. They're great kids. Hey, speaking of the kids, are you guys up for going to the Crystal Lake fireworks tomorrow night? Lynn is planning to make it a big deal—get there early, spread out some big blankets, and bring some snacks and beverages."

The waiter arrived with their food and then refilled their coffees.

"Sounds awesome," George said, unrolling his silverware. "I need to check with my boss—you know, Elena—but I'm sure we're in. It sounds like fun."

"I think the ladies have already been talking."

"Well, then, we're in for sure. I'm looking forward to it." George paused for a moment, thinking of a way to start, and decided to keep it simple. "Hey, Cade, I'm still thinking about quitting my job."

"It's still that bad, huh?"

"Yeah, now they're talking cutbacks, and I just can't face the thought of firing part of my team. It's just changing too much, and I can't get my head on straight."

"It sounds like you've thought it through. I say go for it. You'll land on your feet. You've got a great background, and people like you. Whatever you decide to do, you're going to be fine," Cade said. "My advice is to start searching now. You're more marketable while you have a job."

"That's good advice, but don't be surprised if I end up as one of the casualties. I am going to start looking, though."

George and Cade tucked into their lunches, pausing only to catch up on the Cubs and Cade's family. Before George knew it, he was paid up and headed back to the office, thinking about résumé writing and preparing for interviews. To his surprise, he found himself excited.

I'm definitely ready for something different.

When George got back to the office, he had a voice mail.

Who leaves voice mail anymore? It has to be a salesman.

He was surprised to hear that it was the administrative assistant of his boss's boss. He wanted to meet with George at 3:30 p.m. George sucked air in between his teeth.

There it is. I've gotten myself fired. Maybe subconsciously this is what I wanted.

George survived till 3:25 p.m. and then made his way to the elevator. He stepped inside and pushed ten. He was alone.

The elevator seemed to go unusually slow. With each floor he felt himself grow more and more uneasy. Finally, the doors opened. He wandered the corridors and found Mr. Kirkpatrick's office. The administrative assistant showed him in.

"Good afternoon, George. Have a seat," Mr. Kirkpatrick said. George sat down and remained quiet. "It took some guts to send that e-mail. Do you think that was smart, George?"

George's stomach was tied up in knots. He heard himself say, "No, sir." He felt dizzy and detached, almost like he was outside his body, watching and listening to himself.

"It's rarely a good idea to go over the head of your boss. But I do appreciate your chutzpah. And in this case, it was a good idea. Because, George, after a couple of hours of thought, I think you're right. We've lost our way. We are so focused on financial performance that we keep shooting ourselves in the foot. We've—no, *I've*—been making bad decision after bad decision. That needs to stop now. Do you agree?"

Still hovering just outside his body, George heard the words that Mr. Kirkpatrick was saying, but he was having a hard time processing them. Mr. Kirkpatrick had stopped talking and was waiting. George began to feel anxious.

Say something. Say anything, George.

"I agree," he heard himself say.

"Good, George, because I was beginning to feel trapped. We're in a downward spiral. I cut costs, and our performance goes down. I've been searching for shortcuts, and it's not working. George, did you know I lost my father almost one year ago today?"

What? What does that have to do with it? Maybe he's just letting me down gently. But this doesn't sound like firing. No, this sounds like Mr. Kirkpatrick is agreeing with me. He felt himself snap back into his body.

"I'm sorry to hear that."

"Yes, he was a good man. He was a very successful man. And he taught me that it was his principles that made him successful. Principles like honesty, integrity, and compassion. He told me as long as I let my principles guide me, I would be successful. George, I'm going to make some changes around here."

Mr. Kirkpatrick rocked back in his chair but looked George straight in the eye. "I've been hearing about you for a long time. Your boss used to talk about you all the time as someone who could develop people and drive improvements. But I haven't been hearing that lately."

Oh crap, here it comes. I am fired after all.

"Maybe we've both lost our way. George, I have a proposal for you. I want you to do two things for me. I want you to teach and to coach."

"I'm sorry, but teach what and coach who? I don't understand."

"You would have to give up your current team, but I want you to move to Learning and Development and help me rebuild our ability to change. It's not a promotion, it's not more money, but it's a chance to make a difference. I want you to teach process design and process improvement. More important, I want you to help me change our culture. I want my management team to get reconnected with principles that matter. What do you think, George, are you interested?"

"What about my team? What about the layoffs?"

"Stopped, shut down, not happening. They're a bad idea, I know. You can help pick your successor, either from within your team or outside it. But your team stays intact. So, how about it?"

This can't be happening. Where's the catch? What's the saying . . . if it's too good to be true, it probably is?

"Is this for real, Mr. Kirkpatrick? Are you just messing with me?"

"I couldn't be more serious. And George, call me John. We're going to be working together on a regular basis."

"If this is real, if you're serious, then I'm more than interested, I'm all in! I'll knock it out of the park for you, John. Also, I do have the perfect successor. His name is Carl."

"Outstanding. Let me tell your boss, George. Just so you know, none of this is his fault. I've been putting ridiculous pressure on him for months. He's just been following orders. He'll be just as excited as you are. God, I should have done this months ago," admitted John. "All right, I'll have announcements going out Monday. Let's keep this quiet until then. You and I will meet once a week to work out this culture program. As to the process-improvement training, you're on your own with that."

"No problem. I got it."

"I know you do. Now get out of my office, George. I've got a lot of work to do," John said.

George walked out, still in shock. *Did that just happen? Is this one of those crazy dreams?*

When he made it back to his desk and spun around in his chair, he decided that this was most definitely real. Things never went this well in his dreams.

"Elena, it's George, I've got great news."

"Okay, spill it."

"I'm not going to be fired. I'm staying at United."

"Is that good news, honey? You've been so unhappy there."

"They're canceling the layoffs, and I'm taking a different role. It's not really a promotion or anything, but it's something I've very excited about. I'll be working on a culture program and teaching process-design courses. It's exactly what I'm looking for."

"That's wonderful! I'm so happy for you, honey. Why did the layoffs get canceled?"

"My e-mail to Mr. Kirkpatrick. Funny, he asked me to call him John now, how about that? I'm going to be working directly for him. My e-mail got him thinking and convinced him to change directions. Can you believe it?"

"It doesn't surprise me. I think it's easy for people to lose their way in corporate America, and if you have anything, hubby, you've got common sense."

"Oh, thanks a lot, that sounds like a backhanded compliment."

"No, I meant it as a compliment. You may be a worrier and a bit pessimistic, but you're always sensible and levelheaded."

"Still backhanded," George said.

"Okay, you're right, sorry. Let me try again. You're a shrewd businessman, an amazing father, and a red-hot, sensual lover."

"Better, especially the last part."

"I thought you'd like that last part. I'm proud of you, George. Especially that you had the courage to speak your mind and stand up for your people. I so glad it worked out for the best. Hurry home."

"Yep, just a few more hours. Good-bye."

"Good-bye."

The hours passed, and nobody stopped by to tell him that upon reflection, Mr. Kirkpatrick had changed his mind and oh, by the way, you're fired. By the end of the day, George couldn't wait to come back to the office.

He nabbed a seat on the train and sat back, thinking, *It still feels too good to be true. I'm excited about my job. When is the last time I've felt excited about my job? And with Amanda home and Alex doing better, almost everything seems to be getter better. So what now, do I get to focus on enjoying my life?*

CHAPTER 40

Born in the USA

July 3, 2014

On Thursday, George was a buzz saw at work. He felt incredibly motivated. He started working on a transition plan for his team, outlines for a couple of training courses, and notes on a culture program. Ideas were flowing, and he was amazed at the progress he made during the day.

Just after lunch, the phone rang.

"Hello, this is George, United Property Insurance."

"Hi, honey, it's your wife."

"Oh, Elena, how's your day?"

"Wonderful! It's my turn, I have great news. Alex was officially given the all-clear. He still meets Dr. Rao a few more times over the next month."

"That's fantastic. I was so worried about him."

"Wait, it gets better. Amanda got her hard cast removed today and got a walking cast. She still has at least four more weeks in her walking cast and regular rehabilitation sessions, but it's going to be so much easier for her to get around now."

"Wow, you weren't kidding about the good news," George said.

"Well, we can celebrate all our good news with fireworks tonight. Lynn and I are planning on getting there a little early to get a good spot. We'll bring some snacks and drinks."

"Awesome! I'm looking forward to it."

"See you tonight. Love you."

"See you tonight, Elena. Love you."

Late that afternoon, a group-wide message describing an upcoming culture program, headed by George, and including a heartfelt message from John Kirkpatrick, recognizing his prior mistakes and his intention to drive positive change. George thought his candor was impressive. In the back of his mind, though, he found himself wondering when the other shoe would drop. He hoped to see Shiloh on the ride home— they hadn't spoken since Wednesday—but his stop came and went.

Today's another day worth traveling back for. I should call Shiloh and tell him how well things are going. But at the moment, I could do without that craziness.

At home, over a light dinner, he asked, "Elena, what are the plans?"

"Well, I've got Alex putting together a cooler right now with drinks and snacks. Amanda is finally getting her shower for the day. You, sir, are responsible for finding blankets, mosquito spray, and the boom box. They are synchronizing the fireworks to a mix of classic rock, which I'm very excited about. The fireworks start at dusk, which Alex has targeted around nine eighteen p.m., according to some website he found."

"Sounds like a fantastic plan. I'd better get busy."

They left the house around seven thirty and arrived early enough to get a great spot. Alex helped George spread out the blankets. They had just finished when Cade, Lynn, and their two kids arrived. Isaac was a sophomore in high school, and Beth was in sixth grade. They were close enough in age to Amanda and Alex that they'd always had fun together, but the gender difference had kept them from being best friends, especially as they got older. Still, the families always had fun whenever they got together.

"So, George, tell me about the new role," Cade said.

"It's exactly what I wanted—what I needed, I guess. I'll be in Learning and Development, doing organization design and delivering process-design training. And I'll be working on a culture program. I'm really excited about it. I really thought I was going to get myself fired."

"I'm glad you spoke up for yourself, George. Maybe I should follow my dream and apply for the DJ job at the strip club."

Lynn slugged Cade in the shoulder. "Not funny, Cade," she said.

Both families broke out the snacks and drinks and caught up as the crowd filled in around them. As dusk turned to darkness, they cleaned up the cans and wrappers, and George passed around the bug spray.

A couple of loud test fireworks went off. Elena tuned in the radio and then snuggled in front of George, leaning back into his chest. George had a moment of déjà vu but couldn't quite place it. He searched his brain for a stretch and felt just on the edge of pulling up a memory, but he gave up when Alex announced that it was nine fifteen and the fireworks would be starting any moment. About five minutes later, the radio simulcast started in with Bruce Springsteen's "Born in the USA" while the fireworks launched at what seemed to George a fairly rapid pace.

I wonder how many people know that's more of a protest song than a patriotic one? The crowd doesn't seem to care.

They all joined in with the requisite oohs and ahs. George hugged Elena and just enjoyed the show. It seemed that every year Crystal Lake had to outdo the prior year.

That's Chicago's "Saturday in the Park." Clever, it mentions the Fourth of July. I'm having major déjà vu here. Chicago . . . it's that outdoor Chicago concert at Poplar Creek. Wow, that was before kids. It was an evening concert, and we sat on blankets. Life was pretty simple back then.

George leaned forward. "Elena, do you remember the Chicago concert we went to?"

She turned back to him with a large smile, "Yes, it was wonderful."

As the fireworks bloomed and boomed, punctuating songs he felt he'd known all his life, his mind drifted to his traveling list. By the time the finale filled the entire horizon with light and smoke, he knew his next two destinations. George was already grieving for the end of what had felt like a nearly perfect day.

When they got home, he did a quick search on the Internet. He got ready for bed and set Shiloh's app on his watch. He was delighted when it worked; it was nearly too far back, but the Adjustor accepted June 6, 1992. He tried to ignore the feeling of anticipation and focus on falling asleep. Eventually it worked.

CHAPTER 41

Saturday in the Park

June 6, 1992

George awoke feeling no sickness at all. In fact, he felt wonderful; he looked at the clock and was amazed to see it was 8:30 a.m. He gazed at Elena sleeping next to him, her long blonde hair spread across the pillow.

I slept in. This is the furthest back I've traveled, twenty-three years into the past. I feel so healthy, so young. And she's so heart-achingly beautiful. We've only been married a few years. We only dated for about a year before we married. It was probably a mistake; we didn't really know each other. It was such an adjustment for both of us. The love was exciting and intense, but so was the anxiety and the insecurity. I swear she took everything I said wrong. And she felt like I never listened to her. We were constantly talking past each other. Wow, I need to be careful. Those were delicate times. I could screw things up for this George.

After she woke up, he spent the morning tiptoeing around their conversation. This put Elena on edge. She could sense something was different. He tried to relax, but it was almost a disaster. Time had wiped out the details of the day before, and when he guessed wrong for the third time, Elena threw her hands up.

"George, do you even care? I've been planning this day for a while. I swear you're back to not listening to me again. Maybe we should just call off the concert. Do you even want to go? I know it's not one of your favorite bands."

"No, Elena, it's not that. I really want to go. I'm just having a hard time remembering our plans. I know we've been talking about it for a while, but I'm just a little spaced out today."

"A little?"

"You're right, I'm a complete space cadet. I'm sorry. Really, I'm sorry. We can't cancel, we'd be letting down Lynn and Cade. I really do want to go. Please forgive me, honey."

Holy cow, this is a nightmare. Wow, do I appreciate the connection Elena and I have now. Our relationship might not be as fiery, but it's so much stronger. I've been taking for granted the trust and respect we have for each other. I'll be so relieved when it's time to head to the concert.

Poplar Creek Music Theater was an outdoor concert venue in the northern suburbs of Chicago that seated about twenty thousand people. Its upper section was a grass bowl, and its lower section had seating. For Chicago's Twenty-One tour, George, Elena, Cade, and Lynn had chosen seats in the grass bowl, partially because they were cheaper, but more importantly because the best way to experience an outdoor rock concert was to sit on blankets under the open sky.

They arrived a good hour before the concert was supposed to begin, which was probably an hour and a half before the concert would actually begin. They snagged a good spot in the center and settled in to enjoy the perfect summer day. Elena and Lynn spread out blankets and unpacked their picnic of cheese, crackers, and fruit while George and Cade played Frisbee.

"Cade, come cut the cheese! You're good at that!" called Lynn. She giggled, getting a laugh from Elena as well.

"No can do. we only have about fifteen or twenty minutes of 'bee before the crowd fills in."

"Fine, play your Frisbee, but you should know you're not in college anymore," said Lynn.

Cade was right. Within fifteen minutes the crowd was too thick to play safely. George and Cade gave up and flopped down onto the blankets to gobble up the snacks.

"Okay, boys, you had your fun, but before you eat all the snacks, you've both got a job to do," Elena said.

"The Moody Blues need us for roadies, don't they?" asked George.

"Nope, we need you to go buy us wine."

Cade stood up and performed a formal bow, with a flourish of his hand. "Your wish is our command, my ladies."

Cade and George traversed the grassy hill, avoiding blankets and people. As they waited in line, Cade advised, "You should just buy a Coke for yourself, George." He carefully showed him the top of a flask.

"How'd you get that in?" asked George.

"I have my ways. Only the finest Canadian whiskey for you, George!"

"You're all right, for a freakishly tall guy. Thanks."

They bought the wine and Cokes and headed back up the hill. It was decidedly more difficult to navigate the hillside, as the crowd had filled in even more. They presented the wine to their appreciative wives, Cade doctored up the Cokes, and they spent the next forty-five minutes chatting and finishing the snacks. Then George and Cade had to make one more wine run before the concert started. As the band took the stage, Elena sat in front of George and leaned back into his chest.

The Moody Blues opened the concert with "I Know You're Out There Somewhere." They had not only had the standard guitar, bass, keyboard, and drums, but also a brass and string section. Justin Hayward and John Lodge sang about life, love, and dreams, performing "Your Wildest Dreams," "Isn't Life Strange," and "Question."

This group is so talented. Despite being such a large band, they have so much chemistry. The lyrics almost seem handpicked for everything I've been going through. Like they're just here to sing to Elena and me. Between the strangeness of traveling, the whiskey, and the grandiose, orchestral music, it feels overwhelming.

As the afternoon turned toward evening, he thought about Shiloh's story about how unlikely life, civilization, and this very moment were. He hugged Elena and let the music wash over him. It was unlike anything else he had felt in his life.

The Moody Blues played their final song, and the short intermission broke the spell George had been under. The girls made their way to the restrooms, and the boys made another trip to the concession for a final glass of wine. Despite the long lines, they all made it back before the headliner, Chicago, started.

Chicago opened with "Saturday in the Park," which was the perfect song for the afternoon and the crowd went absolutely crazy. They followed with "Chasin' the Wind" and "Does Anybody Really Know What Time It Is?"

It seems more than coincidence that a band named after the Chicago Transit Authority is singing to me about whether I should care about "what the time was that was on my watch." I swear it feels like they're singing directly to me. It's the whiskey. God, my head is spinning.

When the band broke into "If You Leave Me Now," Elena moved up next to George and kissed him. The sun had gone down, and one by one, the stars were beginning to appear. Waves of emotion and images of his life together with Elena swam through George's mind, overwhelming him. Serenaded by Chicago, they held onto each other and swayed in the warm, breezy night.

CHAPTER 42

Sunday Bloody Sunday

July 4, 2014

George woke on his own without his alarm, but checked his watch, still feeling the urge to make sure he had returned to the present. He remembered a quote he'd read long ago, "Any sufficiently advanced technology is indistinguishable from magic." It was from one of the classic sci-fi writers, Asimov or Arthur C. Clarke or the like.

I guess I'll still check every time. I think it's a fear of getting stuck in the past—though Shiloh said I'd be okay as long as the watch wasn't damaged, right? Why don't I have a hangover? I feel good. Oh, right, this body only had a few beers at the fireworks. Somewhere, another George is waking up, confused and hungover. Will he remember the concert? Or will he just have a blank spot or some vague memories? It's making my head spin. I should ask Shiloh about that the next time I see him.

George looked around his bedroom, studying the pictures on the walls and the dressers.

Back when I first met Shiloh, I was thinking how comfortable my marriage was. That we had lost passion and intensity. I forgot how insecure we were in the beginning. Everything was so awkward, so fragile. If my traveling is teaching me anything, it's that I tend to glorify the past. I'm lucky to have a strong marriage that is still romantic after all these years. Maybe this is what the traveling is all about?

George thought about getting up, but lounged in bed instead. It was something he rarely did anymore—just enjoying the peace of the morning.

I'm feeling really, really good. My kids are going to be all right, work has nearly miraculously turned around, and I even think I might be figuring out this travel business. My last couple of travels have felt right. I think it's not the events that are critical, but the relationships. Only one thing is bothering me. I want to ignore it, but at the concert, I promised myself I would deal with it.

He looked over at Elena. She was snuggled so deep in the covers he couldn't see her.

When was it? A Sunday, about ten or eleven years ago. It was a week before Alex's birthday—his fifth birthday. We had bought him some toys, books, and clothes, but I wanted something special. Something to commemorate the day that he could keep over time. I decided on a baseball card.

George closed his eyes.

Somehow I talked Elena in to letting me give Alex the middle name of Ernest, in honor of my hero Ernie Banks. I remember learning about him in elementary school. My teacher told us about Ernie's life.

Ernie Banks grew up in Texas, from a modest upbringing. His dad bought him his first glove for less than five dollars. He wasn't even playing baseball when he was discovered. A family friend saw him playing fast-pitch softball for a church and connected Ernie with a team in the American Negro League, the Kansas City Monarchs. But life threw him a curveball when he was drafted into the military. He was assigned to the U.S. Army and stationed in Germany. When he was discharged, he returned to play with the Monarchs. It wasn't long before his superior play led to him being recruited to the Chicago Cubs. In the majors he met a player that influenced his drive and determination. That player was Jackie Robinson. Ernie went on to be a coach for the Cubs. He was not only a wonderful player and coach, but also an amazing person. In fact, people eventually gave him the nickname Mr. Sunshine.

The day Ernie Banks visited my school and spoke in an assembly, he became my childhood hero. He also made me a lifelong baseball and Cubs fan. I dreamed of playing for the Cubs, and while I never made it past college ball, it did lead to a trip to the South Side to buy a baseball card.

George stared at the ceiling, replaying the events he tried so often to forget.

With two kids and one job, we were pretty much just getting by. I figured I could get an Ernie Banks rookie card for practically nothing and maybe someday it would be worth something, like a Mickey Mantle. But the Banks rookie cards were already so expensive, especially in the northern suburbs. So I called around and found a card in my price range—a 1969 Topps card advertised in mint condition. Not a rookie card, but it would do. It was at Charlie's Cards and Comics down in White Sox territory. I still remember talking with Charlie. Even on the phone I could tell he was a character.

Charlie's was on West Seventy-Ninth Street. George had mapped out the route, but he still got lost on his way. He found the shop and parked behind the store. Charlie turned out to be a gregarious but dodgy character. The card was far from mint, with a crease running through it and a stain on the back. Charlie had tried to sell him a half dozen other cards, but George only bought the Ernie Banks card—and that only after Charlie agreed to throw in a dozen comic books. George's reading had greatly improved as a child due to comics, and he thought the Richie Rich, Casper, and Donald Duck issues might get Alex more interested in reading.

As he left the store, he first heard and then saw what he would later read was a fight between two rival South Side gangs. George was confused, but his brain immediately picked out handguns. He almost turned and fled through the alley to his car. But he paused for a moment when he saw a small boy down the sidewalk, maybe ten or fifteen feet in front of him. The boy was frozen in place, holding a grocery bag. Time stood still as he looked at the boy and then down the street toward the commotion. One teen was pointing a gun at another teen. More concerning to George, the small boy was also in its sights. George's brain told him to go grab the kid, but fear gripped his body. He tried to move towards the kid, only to find he had taken two steps backward.

Fear overwhelmed him, and he retreated into the alley. Then he stopped, breathing hard, and turned to back for the kid— and a series of gunshots and shouts sounded. After a second or two, George peeked around the corner. Gang members were running off in all directions, leaving one teen in colors down in the middle of the street. The little boy was also on the ground, groceries spilled all around him. George remembered seeing an orange still moving, rolling toward the gutter.

George thought about going to the boy, but panicked again and raced for his car. Forcing himself to concentrate only on driving, he got lost again on the unfamiliar streets and nearly broadsided another car, but eventually found his composure and the highway.

I've played that scene over in my head a thousand times. A couple of days later I read that that Tommy Gritchen was rushed to the hospital in critical condition and later died. I could have saved that boy. How often do you have a chance to save a life?

He tried to convince himself that there wasn't time, but his brain wouldn't be talked out of it. He'd told Elena and later Cade about the event. They both tried to help him get past it, but it never left him. George once again pushed the memory to the back of his mind. He would enjoy his day off, his happiness, and his family. Then he would set Shiloh's app and return to a Sunday long ago to face his life's biggest regret.

CHAPTER 43

Tommy

August 3, 2003

I don't think I'll ever get used to being in another time and a younger body. Am I nervous or excited? I can't tell! I need to get up and out of the house before Elena or the kids wake up. I don't want to do any explaining and screw things up.

He dressed and went down to the kitchen and searched the cabinets for a map that included South Chicago. *I miss the GPS. I'd even settle for MapQuest. I guess today I do it the old-fashioned way. I got lost last time, so let's make sure I know this route.*

George left a note for Elena, explaining that he was running to South Chicago to pick up a baseball card for Alex's birthday. He grabbed his old Cubs cap and made it out before anyone else woke up.

It's too early to head down to Charlie's, even with the drive. I'm going to treat myself. The Coffee Cup should still be in business. I remember bringing Amanda and then Alex there on Saturday mornings to let Elena sleep in. I loved that tradition. It felt like losing a friend when it closed down. But today is 2003 and the Coffee Cup is still very much in business.

He enjoyed a leisurely fried-egg breakfast and amused himself by reading the eleven-year-old paper. After he paid, he went back to the car, checked the directions one more time, and headed for Charlie's Cards and Comics. This time he didn't get lost. He parked in the same spot behind Charlie's and waited. After about fifteen minutes, he went through the alley and looked out into the street. There was no sign of a gang—the street was completely empty.

What if I missed it? I should have researched the time of shooting. Once again, I'm not really prepared. I'll just stay put in this alley. Just look natural. Yeah, right, just some middle-aged white guy, hanging out in a South Side alley on a Sunday morning. Can't get any more natural.

"Hey, mister!"

George turned around and saw three gang members walking up the alley from behind him.

Damn it. They must have entered the street from this alley. So unlucky.

"Mister, what you doing on the South Side with a *scrubs* hat on?"

George was too stunned to respond. This was not what he'd planned. Another one of the boys stepped forward.

"Hey, you got to pay a tax to come down here. How much you got on you?"

"I don't want any trouble," George said.

Wait a second, I recognize that boy. His picture was in the paper, he's the gang member that got shot. What was his name?

"Your name's Mike, right? Mike, you need to get out of here. There's going to be trouble, and it's not going to end well for you."

Mike scowled. "You threatening me, rich man?"

He reached under his shirt and pulled a pistol from his waistband and pointed it at George, who went from nervous to panic in an instant.

"No, please, you don't understand—you're going to die today."

The teen turned to his friends, the pistol still pointed at George. "Man, this dude is just asking to be shot. He tells *me* I'm going to die today."

In a flash one of the other boys stepped forward and shoved George hard. Unprepared, George went down hard and struck his head on the brick wall. His vision went from blurry to black, like an old TV turning off.

George's eyes were still closed when he heard the gunshots. He snapped his eyes open and saw an empty alley. His Cubs cap was lying nearby. He heard more gunshots and shouts coming from up the street. He sat up quickly and felt dizzy. His face felt sticky . . . there was blood on his forehead, probably a cut from hitting the wall. It didn't seem to be bleeding now, though. He put one hand on the wall and carefully stood.

I was out. Shit, so woozy. Where are they?

He heard more commotion and shouting. Keeping a hand on the brick wall, he made his way down the alley toward the cross street. He carefully peered around the corner and saw a familiar sight. Gang members were running off in all directions. Mike was down in the street. He looked to the left and saw Tommy on the sidewalk, holding his chest. The same orange was rolling across the sidewalk.

Without thinking George ran toward Tommy. It wasn't far. As he ran up, Tommy looked at him. He was still alive.

"Someone hit me or something."

George reached in his jeans pocket and pulled out his handkerchief. He moved Tommy's hand away and held the handkerchief against the gunshot wound. There was a lot of blood.

Tommy's voice was quivering. "I was carrying the groceries and there was this fight, and then someone hit me and knocked me down. My mom's going to be mad about the groceries."

"Don't worry about the groceries, Tommy. We'll get them picked up."

Out of the corner of his eye, he saw the door of Charlie's Cards and Comics open. Charlie looked out and down the street, where Mike was lying.

George yelled, "Call an ambulance!" Charlie's head turned, but seemed to pause. "Now!" cried George. Charlie disappeared back inside his store. For a few moments the street was quiet. George just held the handkerchief against Tommy's chest. He didn't know what else to do.

"I'm real tired," whispered Tommy.

"Don't go to sleep, Tommy," George said. *Keep him talking.* "Hey, who's your favorite baseball team?"

Tommy managed half a smile. "The White Sox. They're going to win it all this year."

"Who's your favorite player?"

"Frank Thomas."

"Oh yeah, the Big Hurt. Hmmm, 2003 . . . let's see, they got Carlos Lee, Ordonez, yeah, they are pretty good this year." In the distance he could hear sirens.

"Mister, am I shot?" Tommy had figured it out.

"You're okay, Tommy. Yeah, you got nicked, but you're going to be all right. Just relax. Hey, the Sox are good this year, but they're not going to make it out of the division." George babbled on, the first things that came to his mind. Tommy frowned. "But you know what? In two years, they're going to win the World Series! They're going to beat the Houston Astros in four!"

"How could you know that, mister?"

"Call me George. Tommy, I'm serious. The White Sox will win the Series in 2005, and Frank Thomas helps them get there. It's his last season," said George.

The boy squinted his eyes.

"It's true, I know, because . . . ," George paused. "I know because I'm from the future. I came back to save you. You got to hold on and keep fighting so you can see the White Sox win it all."

Tommy managed a full smile. "You're full of shit, mister."

George laughed. The sirens were getting louder. George was relieved to see a police car and an ambulance turn the corner onto the street. A policeman stepped out of his car and said something into his radio.

Two paramedics emerged from the ambulance and began to walk toward Mike. George cried out, "No, over here. This boy's shot, but he's alive."

The paramedics pivoted and ran toward George and Tommy. One of them took over from George, putting pressure on the wound and talking to Tommy, while the other ran for a stretcher. Tommy's eyes got big. The policeman returned with the other paramedic and the stretcher. George could sense their urgency and concern.

As they lifted Tommy onto the stretcher, George leaned over him and smiled. "Remember the Sox, Tommy! Keep fighting!" Tommy's eyes were still large with fear, but George thought he heard it. They lifted him into the ambulance, and it pulled away as a second ambulance and two more police cars arrived.

George stood alone for a few minutes, somewhat in shock, as the police examined Mike. After the paramedics took over there, two of the policemen came over to talk to George. Their name tags identified them as Officer Callinan and Officer Keis.

"What happened here?" asked Officer Callinan.

"I don't know, some sort of gang fight. It happened so fast. This boy was just an innocent bystander. Is he going to make it?" asked George.

"Did you see the shootings?" asked Officer Keis, ignoring George's question.

George had to think for a moment. He had his first time, but not this time. "Uh, no. I was in the alley over there by Charlie's when I heard the gunshots. When I came around the corner gang members were running everywhere. By the time I got to Tommy, everyone else was gone, except for Mike over there." George down the street, where the paramedics were covering the teen's body with a blanket.

"How many gang members were involved?" asked Officer Callinan.

"I'm not exactly sure. There was maybe three on one side and four on the other? Around seven in all?" explained George.

"All right, sir, we're going to need for you to come to the station so a detective can ask you some questions. Can you give me your identification, so we can complete some paperwork?" said Officer Callinan.

George reached for his wallet, but it was gone. "Crap, they took my wallet."

"Who took your wallet?" questioned Officer Keis.

"Those teens, before the shooting they pushed me into the wall and I blacked out for a couple of minutes. They must have taken my wallet while I was out," George said.

"What were you doing here?" asked Officer Callinan.

"I came to save the boy," blurted out George. As soon as he said it he knew it was a mistake.

"What?" said Officer Keis.

"I mean, I came to buy a card at Charlie's. A baseball card . . . for my son. And I ran into some gang members in the alley. They pulled a gun on me and one of them pushed me. My head hit the wall and I blacked out. When I came to, the shootings had already happened. I ran over to save the boy—the kid they took in the first ambulance," George said. *Good recovery . . . I hope.*

Officer Keis examined George's head and called over one of the paramedics, who asked George a few questions and applied some salve to the cut on his head. He told George to watch out for concussion symptoms, but cleared him to go to the station.

Thirty minutes later George was in a dingy interrogation room talking to a Detective Benson. The detective had just asked him to describe his whole morning a second time.

"Look, sir. Do you guys not believe me or what?" asked George.

"It is a stretch that you came all the way down here to buy a baseball card, you have to admit," offered Detective Benson.

"What else would I be driving down here for?"

Detective Benson looked George over, "The same thing every other middle-class guy drives down here for: drugs."

The detective tossed something onto the table in front of George. It startled him. It was his wallet.

"We found this on Mike. We think you drove down here to buy some drugs and then got rolled by these boys. That's what we think."

Oh shit. That does make sense.

George started talking fast. "No, sir, I just drove down to buy an Ernie Banks baseball card from Charlie's. It's for my son's birthday. He'll be five years old in a couple of days. His middle name is Ernest, named after Ernie Banks. You can call my wife. She'll tell you the same thing."

George could see a change in the detective's face. Just then another detective came over and whispered into his ear. He shook his head.

"What? What's going on?" asked George.

The detective paused, as if deciding whether to say anything. "It's the little boy, Tommy. He didn't make it."

"Damn!" George put his head down on the table. *I failed. Again. How do I live with this?*

Detective Benson looked him over. "You really did try to save him, didn't you?"

"Yeah, hell of a lot of good it did."

"Hey, most people would have left. They just would have turned the other way and disappeared. If you hung around and tried to save that boy . . . well, that's something." Detective Benson cleared his throat. "I am going to call your wife to check your story, but I'm pretty sure it's going to check out, I know when a guy's telling the truth. I'm sorry for the hassle, Mr. Hartdegen."

The detective left, shutting George in with his thoughts.

It took George about thirty seconds to decide.

I'll try again. Hell, I'll keep trying till I use up my last three travels. I'm saving that damn kid one way or another.

CHAPTER 44

How to Save a Life

August 3, 2003

Déjà vu again. Get used to it, George. You've got a job to do.

He had searched the Internet to learn as much as he could about Tommy and the shooting. In addition to the facts of the shooting, he had tracked down and memorized Tommy's home address and phone number.

What if I just make a call or head straight down to Tommy's house? How would I explain myself without sounding crazy? I've got to keep it simple. Keep the morning the same, but wait in Charlie's shop instead of the alley. You know where they're coming from now. As soon as they walk by, find Tommy. Get him to safety before the shooting starts. No heroics, no explaining, just simple.

He left the Cubs hat behind and headed for the Coffee Cup. This time, to really shake things up, he had the buttermilk pancakes. As the morning wore on, his anxiety grew. The first time he'd lived through this day had been bad, but between the altercation in the alley, the accusation of a drug deal, and meeting Tommy only to lose him again, it had become one of the ugliest days in his life.

The first time I had guilt; now I have guilt and a keen sense of failure.

At least he was beginning to feel like he knew the route to Charlie's Cards and Comics. Traffic was light again, and he made good time. He parked behind Charlie's and made his way to the store. He didn't want to be in the alley when Mike and his entourage came through. He had time, so he bought the Ernie Banks card again. Charlie gave him the same bad deal for the creased card, throwing in the same bunch of worthless comic books. But this time George had him add one more baseball card. Charlie put it all in a small plastic bag.

"Mind if I stick around and just browse through your comics, Charlie?"

"No problem. If you find anything else, let me know, I'll make you a deal you can't pass up," replied Charlie.

George laughed and found a rack of comic books by the window. If his timing was right, he had about fifteen minutes before Mike walked by on his path toward doom. In the meantime, George perused the comics. This seemed to be some sort of science fiction section with no particular organization. Most were in rough condition, and there didn't seem to be more than one comic book from any series. Charlie's wasn't exactly the Bloomingdale's of used comics. He flipped through a couple: *Bad Company, Tank Girl, Heart of Empire.* The complexity and variety of art styles were surprising. He had read a few Superman and Spiderman comics when he was a boy, but these were more geared toward adults.

George checked the street, but it was empty. He looked at his watch and estimated that he still had about five more minutes. He picked up another comic, titled *Crisis on Infinite Earths*. A few months ago he would have considered it ridiculous, but now it hit a little too close to home. He continued down the row and came to a handwritten sign that read *Graphic Novels*. *Huh,* he thought, *I thought those were a relatively new phenomenon.* He glanced at a few: *Titan, The Silver Surfer,* and *The Shadow.* He wished he could bring one back to Alex—his fourteen-year-old Alex.

He was just about to go back to *Crisis on Infinite Earths* when he glanced up and saw Mike and his friends walking past the window. He had almost missed them. He went to the door and stepped out into the alcove to watch the boys continue down the street. A few seconds after the teens passed an alley, Tommy turned out of it and walked up the sidewalk toward George. At about the same time, the second group of teens arrived on the other side of the street. Mike and his friends had seen them and were crossing the street to confront them. It was happening faster than George had expected.

George stepped out onto the sidewalk.

"Hey, Tommy, over here, hurry!"

Tommy looked at George and stopped walking. He seemed confused. Behind him the two groups had already begun shouting at each other. George panicked. His plan had been to get Tommy to run into the store with him. He didn't want to step out of the alcove. Up the street, the shouting was escalating quickly. Without thinking, he took off at a run toward Tommy. For a moment, he thought Tommy was going to turn and run the other way.

"It's okay, Tommy."

Tommy looked like he was debating running away from the strange man in the street, but he paused long enough for George to reach him. He put his arm around Tommy and began to lead him back toward Charlie's shop.

"Those guys have guns. We have to hurry."

Two or three steps later, George heard gunshots. The next thing he knew he was falling, pulling Tommy and his groceries down with him. It felt like someone had punched his upper thigh. He hit the sidewalk hard as terrific pain shot through his body. The next few seconds seem to happen in slow motion. George looked at Tommy, who was staring up the street. A few more gunshots went off, and George half expected to see Tommy get hit. He looked up the street and saw Mike go down to one knee then all the way down on the street. The remaining teens took off in all directions.

George looked down at his thigh. The orange from Tommy's groceries rolled up against his leg, picking up a red streak. Blood was oozing from the wound, and George retrieved a handkerchief from his pocket, groaning, and pressed it against the wound. He almost passed out from the pain.

"Are you okay, mister?"

"Not really. I need you to go inside Charlie's and ask him to call an ambulance," George managed.

His breathing was rapid, but couldn't slow it down. Tommy paused for a moment and then took off at a full run for Charlie's. George continued to press on his thigh despite the pain.

That didn't go exactly as planned. God, it hurts.

A few minutes later, Tommy came back out of the store and jogged over to George.

"Okay, he's calling the police." Tommy watched George and looked at his thigh. "Do I know you, mister?"

"No, Tommy, but I know you. It's a long story, but I came to save your life today. You owe me one, so you've got to make me a promise."

My whole leg is going numb. No, my whole body is going numb. I don't think this is a good thing. I think I'm going into shock. Hold on, George.

Tommy squinted his eyes at George. "What promise?"

"You've got to promise to listen to your mom and be nice to people. Promise that you'll make your life count."

"Okay," said Tommy, sounding confused. George could hear sirens in the distance.

"Pick up your groceries."

He reached over, picked up the orange, and wiped it off on his jeans. He handed it to Tommy, who reluctantly took it.

"You're going to want to wash that off when you get home."

As Tommy continued to pick up his groceries, he asked, "How do you know my name?"

"I told you it's a long story, Tommy. But you can call me George. Hey, I got you something. Grab me that bag I dropped."

Tommy grabbed the plastic bag and handed it to George. With one hand George found the extra card he had found at Charlie's. He was careful not to get blood on it. He handed it to Tommy.

Tommy took it and turned it over, examining it carefully.

"It's Frank Thomas. He's my favorite baseball player."

"Yeah, you keep cheering for the White Sox. Who knows, maybe you'll be a baseball star one day," George said.

Tommy shook his head. "Naw, my mom says I'm going to be a lawyer. Cause I'm so good at arguing."

George was shivering now, but he managed to laugh. "You will make a great lawyer, Tommy."

The sirens got louder, and then George saw a squad car turn the corner. It pulled up near George and Tommy. Two officers got out; one ran toward George and the other toward Mike. George recognized Officer Keis.

"What happened here? Are you shot, sir?"

"Gang shooting, a bunch of teens fired at each other, I got hit by a stray bullet. Where's the ambulance? I think I'm going into shock."

"I told Charlie to call an ambulance, but I heard him ask for the police," explained Tommy. George scowled.

"They always send both. An ambulance will be here any second." Officer Keis dropped to his knee to examine George's leg. "There's no exit wound, but I don't think it hit bone. It must be a small-caliber bullet. Keep pressure on that."

Officer Keis stepped aside and began talking into his radio. Officer Callinan had finished examining Mike and made his way back toward George. He hustled over to Officer Keis shaking his head.

"That one didn't make it. He probably died instantly."

"How's this guy?" he asked.

"I saw much worse when I was in 'Nam," Officer Keis replied.

Officer Callinan frowned. "You were never in 'Nam."

Officer Keis smiled, talking loud enough for George to hear, "I'm trying to distract him. He's going to be okay. It looks to be small caliber. I don't think it hit a bone, and there isn't enough blood for an artery. Get a blanket from the trunk."

As Officer Callinan retrieved the blanket, the ambulance arrived. Officer Keis waved it over and went to the driver's side door to speak to the driver. The paramedics retrieved a stretcher from the back of the ambulance. They wheeled it over and lifted George on it. One of them began to dress George's gunshot wound.

"We need to get you out of here pretty quick," explained the paramedic. "We need to get some fluids in him!"—that directed at his partner—"and they'll need to remove the bullet at the hospital."

"Wait, he saved me," said Tommy. "He pushed me out of the way, and the bullet hit him instead of me."

"Is that true?" asked Officer Keis.

"Yeah, I finally saved him." said George.

Officer Keis looked puzzled but said, "Way to go, man. Hang in there, you're going to be fine."

He turned to the paramedics.

"Okay, get him out of here. We'll send a detective to the hospital later."

They began to wheel him toward the ambulance.

"You be good, Tommy."

"I will, mister."

"George, it's George."

Tommy nodded his head. "I will, Mr. George."

CHAPTER 45

The Grand Illusion

July 7, 2014

George didn't have to look at his watch to know he was back to the
present. The pain in his leg was gone, though he felt groggy. He
checked, and there was no sign of the gunshot.

*At least, somewhere out in the multiverse, Tommy is
waking up. I wonder what happened to him. Did he grow up to
be special? Or did the South Side get to him? The other George
has some major recovering to do. I hope he believes it was worth
it. It already doesn't seem real. Traveling is like dreaming: the
more time that passes, the less real it feels. No gunshot wound. My
back and knee sure ache, but that's just my normal middle-aged
body.*

Just over an hour later, George watched Shiloh board the
train, wondering when he would see duplicate T-shirts. Today he

was treated with, *I obey Gravity, it's the Law.* George pictured a pile of dirty shirts in a small one-bedroom apartment.

I have no idea how Shiloh lives. Is he neat? Is he a slob? I still know so little about him.

Shiloh slid into the seat next to George, removing his headphones. "I love Styx, what a great band. So what did you do in 2003?"

"I had a fantastic breakfast and bought a couple of baseball cards and comic books."

George paused for dramatic effect.

"Oh yeah, and I saved a life. A kid named Tommy."

"I saw it took you two times. Rookie."

"You noticed that, huh? Well hey, I'm almost an expert now. Honestly, I had an opportunity to save this kid back in 2003, but I didn't. And yeah, it took me two times. But it was worth it. It's something that's been bothering me for a long time."

"So do you feel better?"

Do I feel better? "Uhhh, sort of. I guess, I don't know. As you've told me, it doesn't change our past. But I'm still glad I did it. It's just that after a while, the travels don't seem real anymore. Shiloh, how do you know it's not just a complex dream or some sort of delusion?"

Shiloh leaned forward and his face lit up.

Here comes a speech. Let's hope one of these gives me some clues about Shiloh.

"George, you're already living an illusion in this life. Reality is far, far from your perception. Your illusion is that you believe you see, hear, and understand all that is happening around you. You think the world around is simple and understandable. You couldn't be more wrong."

Am I finally going to learn what this is all about?

"I'm all ears, Shiloh. Explain."

"First, you perceive that you are on flat, solid ground. Obviously, you are not. But despite the fact you know the earth is curved, you still perceive flat ground. As to the solidity of the ground, you are sitting on a layer of mantle almost eighteen hundred miles deep. Of that mantle, everything below about a hundred miles is hot. And hot means mechanically weak and highly viscous. Beneath that is over twenty-one hundred miles of core, most of it molten rock. So, basically, you have a thin layer of ridged plates, floating and shifting around on layers of a weak and liquid center. You are far from the safety of solid ground."

"Impressive facts, but I pretty much knew that." George knew he sounded disappointed.

"Fair enough. Let me continue. You also perceive that you are motionless. You aren't even close. You may know that the earth is spinning at a thousand and thirty-seven miles per hour. You might even understand that it orbits the sun at around sixty-five thousand miles per hour. Maybe you've read that the sun's orbital velocity around the core of the Milky Way is around five hundred thousand miles per hour." Shiloh took a breath. "But all of that motion is just a rounding error when compared to the speed at which our Milky Way Galaxy is moving. Now *that* speed works out to be an incredible one point three million miles per hour. So you're far from motionless—you're spinning and rotating and being flung through the universe at an astounding velocity."

"You freak me out with your photographic memory, Shiloh. I don't think I had any idea how fast the galaxy was moving. But I did know that it was moving. So, I'm still not sure I'm following your point."

"You think you understand the world directly in front of you, right? Wrong. Visible light is less than one percent of the electromagnetic spectrum. Ninety-nine percent of the spectrum is beyond your perception, including radiation, radio waves, microwave, infrared, x-rays, and gamma rays. Human hearing is just as limited, with a range of twenty hertz to twenty kilohertz. Bats can perceive up to two hundred kilohertz. Other animals, such as whales, can perceive down to ten hertz. If we could sense lower frequencies, we could hear things like earthquakes, volcanoes, and some types of extreme weather. In addition, our brains only process a small portion of our visual and auditory inputs. Therefore, you perceive very little of what's going on around you."

George wasn't buying it. "Again, seriously amazing statistics, but I still believe I have my hands around the most important parts of my reality. I get what you're saying, but it's not like my reality is like a dream."

"Not like a dream, but maybe like a video game or a simulation. You see, some scientists believe that our reality is actually just a hologram. Some of the math associated with black holes suggests that our universe is two-dimensional information rendered in three dimensions. In addition, in quantum mechanics, there is a concept called wave function collapse. It is based on the fact that you cannot know the spin and position of quantum particles simultaneously, so some attributes of quantum particle attributes, like position and spin, are only probabilities until observed. The implications of this are staggering. Some scientists believe this to mean that the universe is only real when observed. Think of it as a video game. A video game only renders the portion of its world visible to the observer. It only draws what the gamer is seeing. Some scientists believe this is how reality works." Shiloh saw the look on George's face. "I'm not making this up. Go read about it on Wikipedia or in any advanced quantum mechanics book."

"I'm not sure I can get my head around what you just said. Are you telling me that some scientists believe our world isn't real? It's just a projection or something?"

Shiloh raised his eyebrows. "They don't know. They're still trying to figure it out. My point is that your travels to alternate worlds and timelines are every bit as real as this world. What happens in those worlds is just as important as this one. They are all equal. It's important you know that. You saved that boy. It happened. It made a difference. And I'm happy you used your travel for something so unselfish."

"Shiloh, why don't you just tell me what is going on? Why don't you tell me the big secret?"

Shiloh examined George's face, looking deep into his eyes. "I will, George, but you're not quite ready yet. I'm sorry."

"Oh, I'm ready. I'm crossing dimensions, reliving my past, getting shot, saving lives—how can I not be ready?"

"You have a big decision to make, but it's not quite time yet."

"What decision? Christ, just tell me. At least tell me something."

"Okay, I lied. But I needed to keep things simple. I needed you to keep an open mind and make your own decisions."

"What the hell are you talking about?"

"I am a traveler. But obviously I'm not staying here one day, I'm here for the rest of my life. And I've had help. I was sent here. I didn't invent the Time Adjustor; I'm only using it."

I knew it! I was right. "Who sent you and why? Why me?"

"It's too soon to tell. You've got a little further to go on your journey. Just know that the people who sent me are good. They want to help. You've come a long way, George. I can tell you that your life matters. It can make a difference. Just remember that good can come from every tragedy."

"I've learned that. I know Amanda is going to be okay. I understand that Alex needs to find his own way, he's not me. I've learned not to let fear control my life. I'm ready, Shiloh."

"I'm sorry, George, but you're not quite ready. Look, you didn't even think about trying to save Mike. Every life is important."

The gang kid?

The train slowed as it approached Shiloh's stop.

"What? I was supposed to save Mike? Wait. How do you even know about Mike? Why wouldn't you tell me to save him if that's important? This is bullshit, Shiloh. I was just beginning to feel like I had things figured out."

"I saw the dates you traveled, and I looked up the newspaper articles. I don't know if saving Mike or Tommy is important. The point is that every life is precious and I'm betting that you didn't even consider that Mike's life might be important."

George put his hands on the back of his head and groaned.

"Hell, Shiloh. What am I supposed to do, try to save everyone? A man can only do so much in a day."

"Don't beat yourself up, George. It's wonderful you saved Tommy. I just want you to think about it. I've got to go. Just remember—no matter what life throws at you, it's an opportunity to grow."

CHAPTER 46

Doctor, Doctor

July 10, 2014

George glanced over at Elena. He'd had a bad feeling about this appointment all week, but he didn't show it to Elena. He kept coming back to Shiloh's comment about good things coming from tragedy. He could have been talking about anything. A national tragedy or even some horrible global event, or a just friend or coworker. His family had already had their share.

> *Please be early-onset menopause. That I can take, I think. Whatever it is.*

George tried not to drum nervously on the beige consultation room table. Was this the same one in which they'd heard about Alex? Discussed Amanda's eye? They all looked the same. It had been a good week. Work was amazing; it was refreshing to look forward to each day. The kids were happy to be back in school.

Life was settling back to normal and happy. *Except.* Except for the shadow cast by Shiloh's comment about George's journey. The moment Shiloh had said that, George had thought about Elena's doctor appointment.

After all, I am a world-class worrier.

Just when George was about to retreat to the waiting area to retrieve a magazine, the door opened. Two doctors entered. They had been seeing their family doctor, Dr. Jones, for more than ten years. The other doctor was a woman. George didn't recognize her.

Two doctors can't be a good thing. What the hell is going on?

"Elena and George, this is Dr. Canon. She is one of the top gynecologic oncologists in the nation. You might guess from her presence that this is a serious situation. In fact, I have tragic news for you. Elena, you have cancer. To be precise, our initial tests show that you have ovarian cancer in both ovaries, and we believe it has spread to your pelvis and abdomen."

He paused for a moment to let it sink in. George heard the words but struggled with the meaning, his mind not wanting to accept the information. Elena let out a small gasp. George looked over at her. She appeared pale and fragile, like she was fighting to keep from breaking down. He instinctively put a hand on her shoulder.

Dr. Jones continued, "I'm going to ask Dr. Canon to explain your situation and our next steps."

He turned to Dr. Canon, who said, "Mr. and Mrs. Hartdegen, I'm sorry to have to meet you under these circumstances. I'm going to walk you through the details of ovarian cancer and your options." She looked at their faces. "This must be quite a shock for both of you, so please stop me if you have questions. You will likely not remember all of this, but we can go back over the information at any time, as many times as you want."

The doctor paused, but George and Elena were silent. Elena stared into the distance, trying not to make eye contact with anyone.

"I'll start with the basics. Women have two ovaries, one on each side of the uterus. Each ovary is about the size of an almond. They produce the hormones estrogen and progesterone, as well as ova. Ova are eggs. Ovarian cancer starts in one ovary and then usually spreads to the other. It then advances to other parts of the pelvis and finally to the abdomen. We consider the ovaries to be stage one, the pelvis stage two, and the abdomen to be stage three. When cancer is found outside the abdomen, it would be referred to as stage four. Do you have any questions so far?"

I have about a thousand questions, but none I can string together into a coherent group of words.

Elena now had an impatient look on her face. She was staring at Dr. Canon but, like George, seemed unable to ask a question yet.

Dr. Canon continued, "I have reviewed the blood tests and the transvaginal ultrasound, and as Dr. Jones has stated, we believe the cancer is in both ovaries, has spread to the pelvis and is likely in the abdomen. At this stage, we would diagnose the cancer as stage three. We have a series of additional tests that will need to be performed."

What the hell? When did Elena have an ultrasound? Why didn't she tell me?

"Treatment involves surgery and usually chemotherapy. The surgery often includes removal of both ovaries and fallopian tubes, the uterus, and the omentum. The omentum is tissue attached to some of the organs in the belly. We would also like to perform some biopsies of the peritoneum, which is the lining of the abdominal cavity. This may lead to additional surgeries to remove any metastases larger than one centimeter. This improves survival rates as it increases the effectiveness of chemotherapy."

Elena fumbled with her purse and pulled out a tissue. "I have a question," she said.

"Absolutely," Dr. Canon replied.

"How long?" Elena whispered.

Dr. Canon looked at Dr. Jones. He nodded.

"This is a serious cancer. It has one of the worst survival rates. In general, for women with stage-three ovarian cancer the survival rate is between twenty and forty percent. As to your question, the period of time is difficult to predict. A rough guess for stage three would be anywhere from three months to five years. I have to be honest, though. I didn't like what I saw on the ultrasound. In this case, I would lean more toward three to six months. We'll know more after the additional tests and the biopsies."

"I want a second opinion," blurted out George. Elena turned to George and frowned. "There has to be a mistake. Elena has been thin her entire life, she exercises and eats healthy, and she has never smoked. This just has to be some kind of mistake."

Dr. Jones responded first. "You're welcome to get as many opinions as you like, George. In fact, I encourage it. But, I suspect the opinions will only vary slightly in the treatment approach."

Dr. Canon added, "While smoking and obesity do contribute to ovarian cancer risk, there seems to be a significant number of cases, as much as twenty-five percent, that are simply genetic predisposition. We still have a great deal to learn about cancer, but it can occur in healthy people. I'm also not trying to discourage other opinions, but the blood test and ultrasound were quite definitive."

"We'll fight it them. Whatever it takes—surgery, chemotherapy—we'll beat it." He looked at Elena. "Right?"

"Yes, whatever gives me the most time with you and the kids."

George noticed she was fighting back tears again. So was he.

"There is research indicating that positive attitude and a strong will to live have a statistical impact on survival rates. I do encourage you to be positive and proactive in your treatment program. With the surgery I described and chemotherapy administered both intravenously and directly into the abdomen, the survival rates have improved. The other good news is that there is a multitude of resources for you. We can connect you with counseling, support groups, and a variety of material contacts that will help you become educated and choose your best options going forward," Dr. Canon explained.

Meetings consumed the next several hours. Elena and George discussed treatment programs, scheduled appointments and tests, and reviewed insurance coverage. It was a whirlwind, and it was draining. Somehow, Elena stayed focused and held it together until the drive home, when she finally allowed herself to cry. And then she launched a plan of attack. She outlined how and when they would tell the kids, who else needed to be contacted, and a list of other items they needed to start thinking about: financial planning, help with housework, and other areas of support. George offered to quit his job. Elena dismissed that offer and ordered him to go to work on Friday, get his things in order, and apply for a three-month family leave. They eventually collapsed into their bed, exhausted, where Elena allowed herself one more cry.

CHAPTER 47

Do You Realize

July 11, 2014

George waited until Shiloh was about to sit down. Then he stood up and hit him in the face. Shiloh's head snapped to the side, and he staggered but kept his balance. Another man stepped toward George.

"Hey, mister, what's your problem?" he asked.

Shiloh recovered quickly. "It's okay, sir. I probably deserved that. It's fine. We're fine."

The other man glared at George, who had slumped back into his seat. He looked at Shiloh, who gave him one final nod, and continued on down the aisle. Shiloh sat down beside George.

"You knew, Shiloh. You knew all along, and you didn't warn me. We could have caught it sooner. It might have saved her."

"What's going on, George?"

George was shaking his head. "Don't mess with me. You knew Elena had cancer. You just told me I had further to go on my journey. You told me I had another tragedy coming. You knew."

"I'm so sorry, George. I'm so sorry. I didn't know. They told me you would lose a person close to you. I suspected it was Elena, but I wasn't sure. And I didn't know how. If I knew who and how, I would have told you."

"It's all bullshit anyway, Shiloh."

Shiloh was taken aback. "What?"

"It's bullshit. Your whole neat, tidy explanation for the universe, for life, and for everything—it's crap. Order plus chaos equals evolution and growth. It's a tired old Chinese philosophy. Zen, yin and yang, it's not exactly original thinking. You've just recycled some thousand-year-old philosophy and spiced it up with a bunch of Internet crap. Life is precious because the conditions on the earth are so rare. More bullshit, Shiloh: life evolved on the earth to be a perfect fit because of the conditions, not the other way around. And we're all on this magical journey of complexity toward some mystical end that you can't tell me about. You know why you can't tell me? Because you don't know—because it's crap! You know what I think? I think we live our lives through the pain and the suffering and then we die and then nothing, darkness. And what happens to the human race when our sun explodes, or we blow each other up with a nuclear bomb? Again, Shiloh: nothing. You want to hear my philosophy on the end of this magical journey for this universe, for all your multiverses? Nothingness—a dead, useless vacuum; that's what I think."

George was practically yelling. Other riders were turning in their seats to stare. George didn't care.

"It's okay, George."

George ignored him. "I still don't know what you are and how I've been able to travel. But you know what? I don't care anymore. I don't care because none of it matters. Nothing I've done has made any difference. I still don't know if my own kids are going to be happy, if their lives are going to have purpose. Mine certainly doesn't. And there is nothing I can do to save Elena. I almost have superpowers; I can goddamn travel across dimensions, but nothing I do will make any difference for Elena."

His eyes filled with tears, and his voice cracked.

"It's all right to be upset," Shiloh ventured.

"I had thousands of days with her, Shiloh, thousands of days, and I wasted most of them. I fought with her, I ignored her, and I took her for granted. Now I've only got one or two hundred left, and I've wasted thousands. It's not fair. Your crappy universe is total bullshit." He was barely able to get the words out.

"It's not fair, George, and it's okay to be upset." Shiloh leaned over to hug George. George recoiled, but Shiloh just leaned in further and put his arms around him.

George lost it. He sobbed uncontrollably. Nearly the whole train car was watching them now.

"You're right: you can't change this future or past, but you still have one hundred days with her, George. You still have a hundred days."

CHAPTER 48

I Will Survive

July 14, 2014

Elena was a flurry of activity in the days after their meeting. She made lists upon lists; she made phone calls and wrote letters. She wrote at a furious pace, and when she explained what she was doing, George was upset. She was writing letters for the future. She wrote letters for the kids' graduations, for their wedding days, and for the births of their children. She wrote and wrote and wrote. George felt it was giving up. It was an acceptance of her death, which he hadn't accepted. "I already know that I'm going to die," she explained, "it's just a question of when." One night George flipped through the envelopes. There was one for him labeled, "Open after my funeral." It was sealed. He put it back with the others.

Amanda and Alex took the news hard. Elena had insisted on telling them right away. George and Elena tried to focus on the treatment and the care that Elena would receive, but as soon as the kids heard *cancer*, they were devastated. Elena later told George that she'd already scheduled another counseling session for Alex.

How is this fair? How can all this happen to one family? God, I want to just drink. Just fall into depression, it would be so easy. Don't I deserve it? Don't I have the right?

He'd been approved for family leave—in fact, as soon as management heard the news, they sent him home and told him they would take care of everything.

He threw himself into cancer research. He searched through website after website, but they pretty much all had the same information: difficult to detect early, low survival rates, surgery, chemotherapy. Much of the research centered on early detection. Some focused on gene therapy, but any breakthroughs seemed to be years away. He made a list of questions for the next doctor appointment, but he felt like he didn't even know what to ask. He decided to call Shiloh. He had something he needed to tell him anyway. George retreated into his office and closed the door. Shiloh answered on the first ring.

"Hi, George, how are you?"

"Hanging in there. Hey, I wanted to apologize for my breakdown on the train and for hitting you. It was uncalled for."

"George, I hate to be the one to tell you, but you don't have much of a right cross. Seriously, though, it's okay, with everything you are going through. I don't blame you. I'm sure I've made things more difficult during such a rough patch in your life."

"Yeah, it's been quite the roller coaster. I just hate being so helpless with Elena's cancer. Every day, I want to fight it. I want to help her. But it seems like there is nothing I can do. Cancer is so evil."

"Can I tell you a little about cancer? It might not help you fight it, but it might help you understand it a little more," Shiloh said.

"Definitely. I'll take all the help I can get."

"You need to first understand what cancer is and what it isn't. It's not a thing, not in the way that bacteria or a virus or parasite are a thing. Sometimes it can be caused by carcinogenic viruses like hepatitis B and C, but often it's more complicated than that. The field of medicine has been developed over thousands of years to fight things in the body. We've gotten good at killing bacteria and viruses, and even helping the immune system fight off infections. But cancer is not an infectious agent that you can attack. It's essentially a failure in the body's processes. Your body has these amazing processes going on, such as DNA replication, DNA recombination, and even DNA mismatch repair, to replace and repair cells throughout your body. In cancer, something goes wrong with these processes, and this breakdown can spread."

Shiloh paused. George had a blank steno pad and a pen in front of him. He stared at the lines.

"Are you there, George?"

"I'm here; I'm just listening."

"I thought I lost you. Now, these processes are unbelievably complex. We still don't completely understand them. We've made progress, but science still has so far to go. Have you ever heard of protein folding? It's this miraculous process where the body takes random protein strands and reforms or folds them into usable structures. I can't begin to explain to you how amazing this process is. Somehow the body knows just the right solvent, pH level, concentration of salts, and temperature to coax the proteins into forming into the right usable molecular shape. In fact, they believe that in some processes certain molecules are used as 'chaperones' to help the proteins become structured into a particular tricky state. Just think about that. Your body has these perfect little microscopic laboratories that create just the right mix of chemicals and temperatures to create the building blocks you need to repair your body. Isn't it amazing?"

"Yes, amazing. Keep going."

"So with cancer, medical research and treatment have to deal with something very different. It's not about fighting a pathogen. Treatment has to either fix the broken processes or remove them so that they won't spread. Or, best yet, prevent the body's processes from breaking down in the first place by eliminating carcinogens, such as those in tobacco. There will be breakthroughs, George. But it's going to take time, and it requires a fresh look at the problem."

George put his pen down. The pad was still blank. "Shiloh, isn't there anything you can do for Elena?"

"All I can do is to encourage you to be there for her. And to make the most of every day you have with her."

You just hit this guy for no reason and he's still here. You have no reason to doubt him. "It's frustrating, but I guess I understand. Thanks for talking with me, Shiloh. And again, I'm sorry for hitting you. Although I did pull that punch. And for what I said. I didn't mean any of it. You've been a good friend."

"Thank you, George, that means a great deal to me. When is her surgery?"

"It's in three days, on Thursday. I'm scared."

"The surgery is going to go fine."

"Thank you for everything. I'll talk to you later," George said. "Good-bye."

CHAPTER 49

Time of Our Lives

When the doctor spoke to George after the surgery, she told him there was good news and bad news. George asked for the good news first. The doctor explained that the surgery had gone flawlessly. Then she explained that they'd removed several tumors from the abdominal cavity, but they didn't like what they'd seen, and aggressive chemotherapy would be necessary after Elena had recovered from the surgery.

Elena recovered quickly. She was home within four days, and the chemotherapy treatments wouldn't start for another two weeks.

Word had spread quickly, and George was overrun with offers of help. Neighbors, friends, and coworkers reached out, offering all kinds of support. Many people stopped by to see Elena, but it was often awkward and reserved. Cade and Lynn, however, stepped up with care and enthusiasm, and it was always relaxed and genuine.

Lynn organized their friends to drop off a different dinner every night. But the most valuable thing was her friendship. She spent long periods with Elena, just talking and laughing.

Others stop by, but they're never comfortable. It's like they're afraid of catching the cancer. Or maybe they're just worried they'll say something wrong. Well, it does make it easy to sort out our best friends from our acquaintances.

Meanwhile, George thought about the next one hundred days. One evening Elena found an invitation on her dinner plate. Between clip art of a movie camera on one side and a box of popcorn on the other, it read:

You're Invited
to the
World Premiere
of
"Time of Our Lives"

Starring Elena Hartdegen
Produced by George Hartdegen

7:00 p.m. Sharp
Hartdegen Theater (Basement)

That evening Elena, George, Amanda, and Alex all headed down to the basement. George had set up a small concession stand table with popcorn, soft drinks, and movie candy. Once they had all helped themselves to the snacks and sat down on the couch in front of the TV, George stood.

"Welcome, everyone, to the world premiere of the new hit movie *Time of Our Lives*. It's produced by a relatively unknown but extremely creative guy with the unlikely Hollywood name of George. More importantly, it stars the supremely talented and heartbreakingly beautiful Elena Hartdegen. I hope you enjoy the show."

George sat down and hit the play button. He had spent every spare minute over the last week assembling every photograph and video of their life he could find. When he'd first loaded it all into the editing software, it was over fourteen hours long. While the editing was tedious and time consuming, he had enjoyed sifting through the countless events and memories. He struggled with many items he had to cut, but he wanted it to run less than one hour. George had also pored over Elena's extensive CD collection and loaded several hours' worth of music that he knew she enjoyed to fit the family videos. About halfway through the editing he almost gave up. It just didn't seem to be coming together the way he'd hoped. However, by the time he had it down to an hour and seven minutes, he was extremely happy with the final product.

The video began with photographs of Elena as a baby, then a small girl. She was a beautiful, blonde-haired, tiny version of herself. Even from the photographs you could tell she was an energetic child and full of life. The video moved quickly on through her adolescence and young adulthood. Amanda and Alex were surprised to see some homecoming and prom pictures of their mom with various boyfriends. The photos switched to college, and then to photos of George and Elena dating. The first actual video was the highlights of their wedding.

As the videographer's camera panned past family and friends along the aisle to the first of the bridesmaids entering the sanctuary, George pulled his attention from the video and looked over at Elena and the kids. Elena was smiling through tears.

I think I did good. The kids seem to be fascinated with the wedding clips. I'm not sure if they've ever watched them before. Look at how thin I was. Look at all that hair.

The video moved on to the reception, at which both George and Elena seemed to have had a little too much champagne. After the wedding came photos from their honeymoon in the Caribbean, to the tune of Elton's John's "Island Girl." They both looked amazingly young and skinny. Next up was a vacation to Colorado with another couple.

"That's Johnny and Kim," George told his kids. "They were our good friends in college."

First Amanda and then Alex appeared: first pictures at the hospital, then videos of birthdays and Christmases. Sly and the Family Stone sang "We Are Family." The kids seemed to grow exponentially as the videos and years flew by. Everyone laughed as Amanda tried awkwardly to crawl and then later walk. She hadn't been a particularly coordinated toddler.

Such great years. And I spent so many of them fretting about fears that would never happen. I should have been living. I should have been happy more often. If your fears eventually come true, all the more reason to enjoy the now.

They watched their lives together unfold on the TV. Amanda was crying now, and George thought he even saw some moisture in Alex's eyes. As Elena watched the children as babies and preschoolers, her tears became a steady stream.

The video finished with clips from Amanda's party, everyone shouting "Arrrrr, matey!" and squinting. As the last song faded out, they all sat for a moment together, emotionally spent. Alex broke the silence. "I had forgotten so many of those good times."

"You weren't even around for half of those great times," George joked.

"Seems to me that I showed up at just the right time. You guys were spoiling Amanda," Alex said.

"Let me tell you, the baby years were no Saturday in the park. Amanda was colicky, and you, Alex, had ear infections constantly. You both were crying more than you weren't. It was brutal, right, Elena?

"Yes, and I wouldn't trade those baby years for anything. Those were my favorites," Elena said.

"Who were those boys, Mom? The one you went to homecoming with was cute," Amanda said.

"Hey," George said.

"I'm surprised you put those in there, George. Well, Amanda, that was me finding out who I didn't want to spend the rest of my life with. Most of my dating was about learning who I didn't like. That boy was cute, but he was a conceited brat who was only interested in one thing."

"Well, you can't blame him for that. I was the same way, only interested in one thing: your mom's cooking," George said.

Elena smiled at him. "Looks to me like you've enjoyed my cooking over the years just fine, hubby. But you do have a hidden talent as a director. That was wonderful, even if it did make me cry too much. Thank you, George." She was tearing up again.

CHAPTER 50

Centerfield

"Where are we going?"

"*We* aren't going anywhere. Lynn and I and our kids are going to a friend's pool. You, sir, get the day off," Elena said.

"I don't need a day off," George said.

"We haven't been apart for fifteen minutes since the diagnosis. You need a day off. I need a day off. Call a friend, go golfing."

"It's a weekday; all my friends are working."

"I don't care, George. Go to a museum, read a book, watch TV—just take a break."

"Okay, but try not to get too much sun today, and make sure you don't eat junk food. Are you allowed to get in a pool yet?"

Elena began unconsciously tapping her foot. "George."

"All right, all right, sorry. Go to the pool, enjoy your George-free day. Tell Lynn I said hi."

George's iPhone said the weather was going to be perfect: 76 degrees and blue skies all afternoon. He called Shiloh, who wanted an update, so George explained that the surgery had gone well and she was getting stronger every day. Shiloh loved the idea of a break and made him promise not to ask more about traveling. Instead, George would teach Shiloh, for a change—all about baseball.

George headed downtown and from there jumped on the Red Line. It took him to Wrigley right on time. He didn't see Shiloh right away, so he picked up the tickets at will call. A few minutes later he spotted Shiloh, who looked strange without his usual tweed jacket but wore a shirt displaying a picture of a cat and the words *Plays with String Theory.*

George smiled and thought, *He'll fit right in at the Wrigley bleachers.* He shouted, "Shiloh, over here!"

Shiloh did a full 360-degree spin before he zeroed in on the sound of George's voice.

"Oh, there you are! I wasn't sure if I was in the right place."

"You're in just the right place. Let's head in and find our seats."

George handed Shiloh his ticket, and they headed for the stadium.

"You know, the Cubs haven't won a World Series since 1908," George said as they handed over their tickets. "They've won divisional titles like twenty or twenty-one times, but only won the World Series twice, once in 1907 and then again in 1908. Back in 1945, the Cubs made it to the World Series and traveled to Detroit, where they won two out of three games. Most people thought they had it wrapped up, but when they returned to Chicago for the final four games, something odd happened. A bar owner tried to bring his goat into the game. P. K. Wrigley ejected the goat and his

owner from the game because of the smell. On the way out, the
man placed a curse on the Cubs. They lost that series to the Detroit
Tigers and haven't been back since."

"They haven't won in a hundred and six years?"

"Nope. They've come close, broke a lot of hearts, but
they've never even been back to the World Series. It's the longest
championship drought in all of professional sports," George said.

"And yet all these people still come to watch them try?"

"Yes, they do. Every year, they keep hoping."

"That's wonderful."

George stopped at a booth and bought Shiloh a Cubs hat.
Shiloh thanked him and promptly put it on. They found their
centerfield bleacher seats and settled in under the bright sunshine.
During the national anthem, George looked over at Shiloh. He
was smiling and singing along. He already seemed to be into the
experience.

"Today's a special day. It's a cross-town rivalry," George
noted. "The Cubs play the Chicago White Sox."

"In soccer that's called a derby."

"Let me present my case for baseball. It's not actually as
ordered at it may seem."

"I'm listening."

"So, to start with, the managers are constantly adjusting
the lineups. Just the pitching rotation is as much an art as a science.
The batter order is also very important. Then during the game,
the team can play aggressive or conservative. They call conservative
play 'small ball.'"

"Why?"

"Because they're not going for home runs and big hits.
They're taking a lot of pitches, bunting, and giving themselves the
best chance to get a run." Rowdy fans were filing into the bleachers

around them. Players took the field for stretching and warm-ups, running sprints and playing catch. A few vendors were already working the stands, shouting, "Beer here!" and "Hotdogs, get your hotdogs!" George could tell that Shiloh was having a hard time focusing on him. There was a lot to take in.

Shiloh kept his eyes on the field as he said, "Okay, so there's a lot of strategy, but it's all built around a pretty rigid structure. There's even lines where the players have to run, right?"

"Well, yeah, I guess, but even the ballfields vary. They don't have to be the same size and shape. They each have a different feel. You just have to trust me, there is more variability in baseball than you think."

Not long after the umpire yelled "Play ball!" the White Sox went out ahead early with an opening walk, followed by a home run. They followed up with three long fly balls, all of which were caught. The Cubs responded with two base hits in a row, followed by a strikeout. The White Sox pitcher gave up a walk, loading the bases. The crowd got loud, and people were standing when the next batter stepped up. George watched Shiloh take it all in. The Cubs batter hit into a groundout double play, and the entire stadium seemed to groan together.

After the pitchers settled down, the middle innings turned into a pitcher duel. There were a few hits here and there, but neither team threatened to score. George flagged down a beer vendor and ordered one each for Shiloh and himself. Shiloh seemed to enjoy it.

During a lull midway through the fourth inning, George felt a question rise up out of him. It wasn't the kind of question you asked in the bleachers in the middle of a baseball game, but he couldn't stop himself.

"Shiloh, what about God? Are you religious?" *I'm keeping my word; this isn't about traveling, sort of.*

"I both appreciate religion and am disappointed in it."

"What are you disappointed about?"

"I'm disappointed that some use religion as a tool to control people and to wield power. I'm disappointed that some people commit evil under the cover of religion. I'm disappointed that some use religion to keep people in ignorance, to prevent learning and growth, and to debate the scientific process. And I'm disappointed in the perception thing."

"Perception thing? I don't understand," George said.

"Okay, let me explain. In the 1940s and 1950s, everyone outside the United States thought the USA was John Wayne. But even John Wayne wasn't John Wayne. Now the world thinks the USA is some crazy cross between Bill Clinton, Barack Obama, and the Kardashian family. The truth is that our country is three hundred and twenty million different people, all with different beliefs, hopes, and dreams. It's the same with religion: people base their perception of religions on a few people and events. Millions of people fear Muslims because of a relatively small group of leaders and fanatics. And some people turn away from God and religion because of the actions of a few greedy evangelists or pedophiles. The reality is that each religion is made up of millions of devoted people who are making the world a better place. So I appreciate faith: people's ability to believe in more than they can see. There is great beauty in that. I appreciate that people can believe in a greater purpose and see that there is more to life. I appreciate that many religions have the humility to recognize that they cannot understand the mind of God. I appreciate that there is a structure to spread positivity and love and compassion. I think organized religion can do great good, but religious leaders have to be humble and have the strength to reject the evils of power. It's part of society and part of the complexity of the human existence."

"Do you believe in God?" pushed George. He looked around and realized that the Wrigley Field bleachers were quite social during the middle innings. There were lots of conversations going on, and no one seemed particularly interested in his and Shiloh's.

"Do you remember when I spoke to you about how unlikely life is? How perfect the conditions of the universe have to be for life to exist, and how the more complex life becomes, the more fragile it becomes? I believe that if people saw the math, the statistics associated with the mind-boggling odds of the universe's journey to get to this complexity, they would have a hard time not believing in God. Do you remember the second law of thermodynamics?"

"Uh, I used to, but I think I've forgotten," George replied.

"The universe wants entropy and hates order and complexity, and it's basically a miracle that life, people, and society exist at all. And while physics may explain how the universe works, it doesn't explain why it's here or what will happen."

"So you *do* believe in God?"

"I didn't say that I did or I didn't. Let's just say that I think it's unlikely that all of this happened randomly. And I think that if there is a God, he's probably a Cubs fan. Shouldn't we be watching the game, George?"

I never get the whole story from this guy. George stopped pushing, and they turned their attention back to the game. The White Sox had just hit a long fly ball that became the third out in the top of the seventh inning, stranding a base runner.

George turned to Shiloh with a grin. "Time for the seventh-inning stretch!"

They both sang along with "Take Me Out to the Ball Game," and George didn't mind that Shiloh was too loud and a little off key.

After the Cubs went three up and three down, at the top of the eighth inning their pitcher gave up a single to the first batter. After he followed it up with a walk, the Cubs manager came out to make a pitching change. The new pitcher got them out of the inning, but not before giving up a run. It was White Sox 3, Cubs 0.

In the bottom of the eighth, the Cubs' lead hitter started them off with a double. A sacrifice bunt advanced the runner to third base. The next three batters failed to bring home the runner after three consecutive groundouts ended the inning.

"They're bringing in their closer!" George said.

"What's a closer?"

What's a closer? He really doesn't know baseball. "It's a pitcher that you bring in to finish off the game. They're good at getting outs and keeping the other team from scoring."

"Why don't they bring them in right away?"

"Oh, they're only good for an inning or two. They can't throw as many pitches as a starter, but they usually pitch a lot more games."

The Cubs pitcher made George look good by getting two strikeouts and a fly out. Shiloh looked over at George and nodded as if indicating that he now understood. The first Cubs batter finished a long at-bat with a single to right field, just over the second baseman's outstretched glove. The White Sox pitcher followed with a strikeout but then walked the next two batters.

The stadium was roaring now, and everyone stood as the Cubs' batter came to the plate. He took the first two pitches for balls as the White Sox pitcher continued to struggle.

"There is nowhere to put him!" yelled George over the crowd.

Shiloh seemed confused. "What?"

"I mean a walk forces in a run."

Not wanting to give up another walk, the White Sox pitcher threw a fastball right down the center of the plate. The batter swung and made perfect contact. Everything seemed to go into slow motion as George heard the crack of the bat. He saw the ball rise up straight toward their seats. The White Sox centerfielder took off in a sprint for the wall. George tried to follow the path of the ball but lost it as it passed from shade to sunlight. The centerfielder pulled up as he reached the warning track; he seemed to look right at George. George saw a flash of motion to his right, and everything seemed to return to normal speed. The crowd had exploded, and he heard someone yell, "Walk off grand slam!" To his right, Shiloh was holding his new Cubs hat in his hand and staring down at it. George peered inside it and saw the baseball.

"Nice catch, buddy!" yelled a Cubs fan a couple of rows in front of them. Shiloh took the ball out of the hat, turned around, and tossed it about four rows up to a small boy who looked about six or seven years old. For a moment George thought it might hit the little boy directly in his face, but at the last moment, the boy's father reached out and barehanded it. He handed it to the little boy, who went from fear to delight in an instant. Shiloh turned around and put his hat back on. After a moment, people started filing out.

"Why are they leaving?" asked Shiloh. "There are still two more outs."

"No need: the Cubs already won. The game is over. Hey, nice catch, Shiloh!"

Shiloh just smiled, and they joined the crowd shuffling to the exit. After things quieted down, George looked at Shiloh and said, "You know, the boy you tossed the ball to was a White Sox fan."

"How do you know?"

"He was wearing a White Sox shirt, and his dad had a White Sox hat on."

"He still seemed happy to get the ball?"

"Oh, he was!" said George. "That was incredible, Shiloh. I think the dad was just a little confused. But you made that little boy's day. What did you think of the game?"

"It was wonderful. I see why people love baseball so much. It has a great deal of tradition. I still think soccer is a more perfect game, but I understand baseball better now. Thank you, George."

"Do you think the Cubs will ever win the World Series?"

"Yes, maybe sooner than you think," said Shiloh.

As they got out to the street, they shook hands and parted ways. Shiloh told George he was going to go for a walk and explore Wrigleyville. George told him he needed to get back to Elena and his family. As they split up, Shiloh yelled, "Thank you, George!"

CHAPTER 51

Time in a Bottle

Elena had been cleared for exercise, and she and George walked every day, for longer and longer stretches. Summer was still in full gear, and they had to walk in the morning or late in the evening to avoid the heat. George kept trying to keep the conversation light, making small talk about the past or current events, but she kept bringing up the future. George realized she was subtly trying to prepare him for a life without her. He refused to go down any such path. Eventually they reached an equilibrium, focusing on the kids' futures but avoiding references to her potential absence.

George loved having the extra time without work. He stayed on top of the finances and medical bills. They had family game night on a regular basis, and George planned movie nights and bowling nights. To George's delight, Alex participated without a fight, and Amanda and Alex got along perfectly—they'd never been closer. Some nights, after walking, George made a fire in their backyard fire pit. Occasionally, they all talked well into the evenings; other times they just enjoyed the fire and the evening in silence.

One day, George overheard Lynn recommending that Elena create a bucket list.

"I've already finished my bucket list," Elena said.

"You're either lying to me or to yourself," Lynn replied, sounding sad.

George thought, *She doesn't need a bucket list; she's going to get through this. Why do I keep telling myself that? One hundred days. I need to face this. I need to make sure whatever time left she has is everything it could be. Help her get the most of out her life.*

Later that evening, he caught her away from the kids for a moment and said, "Elena, I overheard Lynn today ask you about a bucket list."

"Hey, you can't listen in on our conversations! That's girl talk, not meant for the male ear."

"Elena, maybe you *should* make a bucket list."

"George, I've already done everything I've wanted in this life. I went to college, I got married, I had kids, and I've lived a full life. I'm sorry to say this, but the only things left that I want in my life, I don't think anyone can give me."

"Just try me. I'll do anything. I'll find a way. What do you want?"

"Oh, George, I know you would. I'm sorry. Let's just drop it."

George sensed that she didn't want to discuss it further, but he couldn't give up. "Elena, just tell me what else you want in your life. What about a trip to Europe? You've always wanted to go to Italy."

Elena frowned. "George, my chemotherapy starts next Monday. I'm going to be sick. I can't travel, and I don't want to sightsee anyway. I don't want to be on crowded buses and in small hotel rooms. It's not going to be a fairy tale ending. Do you understand?"

It caught George off guard. Elena had obviously thought more about the next couple of months than he had. "I'll ask the doctor if we can delay for a while. Maybe we can put off the chemotherapy for one more week."

"George, that would take away the one thing I do want. I want time. I want to be here with you and the kids as long as I can." She began to cry.

"You know what?" she finally said, angrily swiping at her blotchy face. "I do have a bucket list. I want to see my kids graduate high school and college. I want to see them get married. I want to watch Amanda hold her baby. I want to hold my grandkids in my arms. I want to see what kind of adults our kids become. Time, that's what's left on my bucket list. Can you give me that, George?"

Speechless, George watched her anger turn to sadness. Her head dropped, and she leaned into him. He hugged her tight as she continued to cry.

"I'm sorry, Elena."

She took a few deep breaths and finally said, "Oh, George, it's not your fault. I'm sorry I yelled at you. I know you're trying."

George held her tight, not sure what to say. After a few moments, Elena seemed to pull herself together.

"George, there is one thing I do think you can give me."

"Anything, Elena."

"You can help me find peace. You can help me make sure that you and kids are going to be all right without me. You need to accept that I don't have much time left. I'm not saying that I won't fight. Believe me, I'm going to fight for every day. But at some point, I want to go with grace and dignity. The chemo is going to be ugly. My support group has warned me. It's going to get hard. And I want to know that you can deal with it. And that you are going to be strong for the kids. Can you give me that?"

It was George's turn to cry. *Christ, George, she just asked you to be strong. Get it together. She's right. I need to help her. I need to help her fight, but I can't keep ignoring the reality she is facing.*

He took a deep breath.

"Elena, I will find a way. We'll face it together."

CHAPTER 52

Fall on Me

"There is a dizzying array of options and combinations of chemo drugs," Dr. Canon said. "But what you need to know is that the main challenge centers on the aggressiveness and dosage of the drugs."

George looked around the stark exam room, trying not to stare at the only thing on the wall, an unsettling cross-section of a uterus.

"I like the sound of aggressive drugs, if that gives me the best chance," Elena said.

"Well, more aggressive drugs and dosages can keep the cancer at bay, but they can have devastating side effects. On the other hand, dosages and treatments that minimize side effects are less effective in stopping the cancer from spreading."

"What about a middle ground?" George asked.

"It exists, but I have been thinking about a fairly aggressive drug and dosage. It would be a two-drug combination that would be administered intravenously. The dosage is more of an art than a science. It's affected by a variety of factors, including age, gender, weight, and disease state. It fact, even metabolism and genetics can impact the drugs' effects."

Elena pursed her lips. "Whatever I need to do to buy as much time as possible. I can handle the side effects."

How about remission? Is that too much to hope for?

"There would be three treatments over a six-week period. The good news is that this chemotherapy can be administered out-patient, at your home," explained Dr. Canon.

That is good news. Every day we stay out of this hospital is a good day.

The side effects from the first treatment hit Elena hard and fast. She had constant nausea, followed by vomiting and diarrhea. This quickly became an issue when combined with her loss of appetite. She went from a bundle of energy to complete exhaustion. Within a week after the first treatment, Elena was in the hospital with malnutrition and dehydration. She was also showing signs of anemia.

I researched, I listened to the doctors, and even Elena warned me, but I wasn't prepared for chemo. I was ready for her to be tired, for hair loss, but not this. Seeing her like this, every day . . . . The emotional toll is just as taxing as the physical demands.

The kids were trying, but they had become sullen and irritable. The family outings and game nights ended. Alex retreated more and more into his room, and George didn't have the energy to deal with him.

With a combination of intravenous iron and a number of antinausea, antidiarrhea, and other medications, Dr. Canon was able to get Elena strong enough to return home. Just keeping track of her medications became a major effort for George.

He also found himself constantly reminding her to drink and eat more. While she did get moody, George was impressed with her attitude. Despite it all, she remained strong and positive, especially around the kids. Her main complaint was that she didn't like being so dependent on George.

Visits from neighbors and friends declined even more. George could sense their shock when they first saw Elena. She had lost weight, and her hair loss was noticeable. They struggled to make conversation, and it was often Elena who found ways to break the tension with jokes or questions. There were exceptions; Lynn and Cade were constant companions. George could see Elena's face light up each time Lynn arrived, bringing movies and playing cards. Elena enjoyed their conversations the most. Lynn and Cade also took Alex and Amanda out to dinner with their kids occasionally. Just as Elena was starting to recover from the first round of chemo, the second round loomed on the calendar. The nausea finally seemed to have passed, and Elena was eating better, getting herself around the house, and even going for short walks with George. On the Saturday before the second treatment, George talked her into going out to a family dinner. He invited Cade, Lynn, and their kids as well. They went to an Italian restaurant, where they shared large heaps of pasta, several bottles of chianti, and endless stories and memories. It was a magic night. It felt like old times, with lots of loud conversation and laughter. Elena seemed to forget about her cancer for at least that night.

Round two brought the swift return of the nausea, vomiting, and diarrhea. Two or three days in, however, Elena experienced tingling and numbness in her hands and feet. When it spread to her arms and legs and became painful, she got a return trip to the hospital. Dr. Canon called it peripheral neuropathy and explained that, unfortunately, it wasn't uncommon as a side effect. She suggested they dial back the dosage in the third round, and George and Elena quickly agreed. It took longer, but Elena was able to return home again. This time she had lost all of her hair and even more weight.

CHAPTER 53

Moondance

George stroked Elena's face and whispered her name. Her eyes fluttered open, and she said, "George, what's wrong?"

"Nothing is wrong. Everything is wonderful, but I need you to wake up and follow me."

"What time is it?" Elena whispered.

George glanced at his Apple Watch. "It's two forty-two. Come on."

Elena swung her legs over the side of the bed and paused again. "Two forty-two? George, why am I up at nearly three in the morning?"

"Shhhh, no more questions, just follow me." George helped Elena stand. He took her by the hand and led her out of the bedroom. The house was dark and quiet. "Watch your step," he warned as they reached the staircase. She followed him down the stairs and toward the back of the house. He paused at the French doors that led to the backyard patio, looked at Elena, and smiled.

Then he opened the door and led Elena out into the night.

Hundreds of candles blazed all over the patio. The fire pit was burning strong as well. It was an absolutely perfect night. A warm breeze caused the candles to flicker, carrying smell of the neighbor's honeysuckle. They gazed up at the sky overhead, where the full moon glowed among a sparkling sweep of stars.

"Oh, George," she gasped. He walked over to the corner near the house and bent over. A moment later she heard soft music, it was Van Morrison singing about the stars and a fantabulous night.

He walked back to her side. He stared into her eyes and put his arm around her. They began to dance. They didn't speak, just slowly swayed to the music and held onto each other. Another gust of wind sent the candles flickering again.

The song ended, and Mr. Morrison began to sing about "Crazy Love." George whispered to Elena, "Look up." He stopped swaying and held her as she looked up at the night sky. The Perseids meteor shower was at its peak. Elena gasped as one after another streaked across the sky.

"You see, Elena, even the stars fall for you," he teased.

She caught him into another slow dance as "Into the Mystic" played, and once again George felt like the music was written just for them. With the stars falling around them, the candles dancing in the wind, and Van singing about mystic love, George felt like he could whisk Elena away to another time, another place. But, eventually, he felt Elena go a little unsteady in his arms. He picked her up and carried her back into the house. Without pausing he carried her up the stairs and into the bedroom, where tucked her back into the bed, kissed her on the cheek, and whispered, "I've always loved you, Elena."

She smiled and replied, "Thank you for the moondance, George."

CHAPTER 54

Amazing Grace

"Hello?"

"George, It's Shiloh."

"You're calling me?"

"Yeah, how is she?"

George looked out the French doors into his backyard. A breeze sent ripples through the leaves on the trees and puffed ashes out of the fire pit onto the brick pavers.

"Not that good. But they have lowered the dosage of the third treatment, which has helped. She still had nausea and vomiting, but she got past it quicker. The pain and numbness in her hands and feet haven't completely gone away, but at least they don't seem to be getting any worse. Her biggest complaint now is what she calls chemo brain. She has difficulty concentrating and she can't seem to remember anything. She's even struggling to read."

"What do the doctors say?"

"They are waiting to see how this round of chemo goes. Afterward they'll do an MRI, and I guess we'll go from there."

"How are you, George?"

George wandered into his office and stared at a row of books, reading the spines but not comprehending. "Oh, I don't know. Tired. Numb. I'm trying to make the most of the time, but it's hard. I just want her to be cured. Shiloh, I still don't believe you. That you can't help. I've been thinking about it. If there are so many parallel worlds, one of them has to have found a cure for cancer. Right?" *Come on, Shiloh, give me a miracle.*

"George, you have to believe me: I can't help. I'm so sorry. You're right, there likely is a world where they have cured cancer. In fact, I'm sure there is. But I have no way of finding that world. And even if I could, and even if I could get you there, it still wouldn't help."

"Why?"

"Because you can't bring anything back, remember? Not drugs, not research papers, nothing but your consciousness."

"I'll memorize it."

"George, the cure to cancer is not going to be something you can memorize. I'm sorry. Please stop asking. I feel terrible. How are the kids?"

Sure, change the subject. Oh hell, I believe him, I just don't want to. "The kids are all right. Amanda has been reading to her at night. It's pretty special. When Amanda was little, Elena loved to read to her. Now it's Amanda's turn. Before the cancer there was some tension building between them—they were starting to get on each other's nerves. Now all that has fallen away. I think it's really helping Amanda to deal with the cancer."

"How about Alex?"

"He's doing better. I was worried about him; he was retreating for a while. But he's been focusing on his music. I think it's helping him get through it. I think he's dealing as best as any fourteen-year-old would."

"Okay, well, hang in there, George. Keep on keeping on."

"I will. Hey, I do appreciate you calling. Thank you."

"Good-bye."

Two weeks after Elena's third treatment Dr. Canon scheduled a follow-up MRI. The news was not good. The cancer had continued to spread through Elena's abdomen. They discussed a number of potential options, but Dr. Canon was honest. They would all substantially reduce Elena's quality of life while offering little chance to extend it. And that was the best potential outcome—an unknown amount of time at a high cost. After a painful couple of days, they decided to do nothing. While George wanted to push more, he remembered the promise he had made to Elena: to help her have her peace and dignity.

After that, George decided that he would focus on her last remaining wish, peace of mind. He went through Elena's lists. He made sure their financial affairs were in order. He scheduled another appointment for Alex. He helped Amanda apply to college and for scholarships. Later, he sat with Elena and went over it all. It felt so trivial when compared to Elena's ordeal, but it seemed to help her.

Not long after that, Elena began to have severe pain and other complications. Dr. Canon prescribed a regimen of pain medications and a hospice nurse so Elena could remain at home.

One afternoon George found Alex in her room, softly playing his guitar for her. She later told George it was the only thing that made her forget the pain. She grew weaker, and on a Sunday afternoon, the hospice nurse recommended they call the priest in for last rites. Elena had been in and out of consciousness but she seemed alert as the priest spoke to and over her. Three hours later, with her family at her side, Elena found peace.

CHAPTER 55

She Goes On

The days leading up to the funeral were a blur. George was overrun. People reached out to express their sorrow, to check on him, and to offer help. George knew he had a multitude of preparations and decisions to make, but when he met with the local funeral director, he had quite a surprise. Elena had already met with him at some point and had made most of the plans and decisions. George could only shake his head.

Thank you, Elena.

The wake was one of the hardest things George had ever done. Amanda and Alex made a couple of photo collages to set out. George gave the funeral director the *Time of Our Lives* to play on loop. Elena's support group had put together a table on ovarian cancer and various ways to support research.

The visitation was an endless barrage of emotion. George had spent the previous day going through the invitation list, trying to figure out who everyone was. He had always been horrible with names, and it was a shock when he realized that Elena wouldn't be there to rescue him. People tried their best to make it easy for George and the kids, but inevitably someone would tell a story and the emotions would come flooding back. George appreciated that Elena had touched so many people in so many ways. But at some point, he went numb. He shook hands, thanked people, and answered questions, but he wasn't completely there. Thankfully, the funeral director and Lynn staged a break, pulling George and the kids into a back room for some food and rest. It gave George the strength to get through the remainder of the day.

That night George slept as deeply as he could ever remember. If he dreamed, he couldn't remember it.

At the funeral the next day, the parish priest welcomed everyone and gave an opening homily. The church choir sang "You Raise Me Up."

Amanda had written a poem for the ceremony—quickly and without any help. She wasn't happy with it, but George told her he loved it. She fretted until George told her Elena would have loved it.

Amanda walked to the podium, pulling out a sheet of paper. She looked up and began to speak.

"'My Mom,' a poem."

Amanda took a deep breath.

"My mom gave me life. Then she made it special. She nurtured me, she fed me. She taught me to walk, to talk. I think later, some days, she regretted teaching me to talk."

Amanda paused as a ripple of quiet laughter spread through the crowd.

"She read to me every night when I was little. She encouraged me to run and to jump. And she picked me up when I fell. She gave me a Band-Aid when I bled. She explained boys to me, or at least she tried." There was more careful laughter.

"She helped me face my fears. She encouraged me to take risks. And again, she picked me up when I fell. She pushed me out of my shell. But she made sure I stayed grounded."

Amanda paused again.

"And when I lost the vision in one of my eyes, she pointed out that I have another. When things were darkest, she showed me light. She's always kept me facing forward. I'm furious that she has been taken from me. But I'm grateful she has been there for me. I'll miss her always."

Amanda's voice began to quiver. She took a moment to fight back her emotions.

"And I'll never forget her. I love you, Mom."

Amanda folded up her paper and returned it to her pocket. She stepped down from the podium, and by the time she got to her seat she was sobbing.

The priest stepped forward.

"Amanda, thank you for your strength and for that wonderful poem. Next, George and Elena's son, Alex, and his friend will perform a song."

The church became still as Alex and Jeff prepared to play. Alex adjusted the mic, and the silence suddenly became pronounced to George. He noticed the sporadic coughs and quiet whispers that just a moment ago had been background noise. He was nervous for Alex. In all the commotion leading up to the funeral, he had never had a chance to listen to the song that Alex was going to play.

Alex leaned forward into the microphone.

"I'm Alex, and this is my friend Jeff. We're going to play a song called 'She Goes On' by Crowded House. This is for you, Mom." His voice cracked slightly when he said the word *Mom*. In the silence, Alex looked over at Jeff, and they nodded a silent one, two, and three. They began to play.

Pretty soon you'll be able to remember her
Lying in the garden singing
Right where she'll always be
The door is always open

Alex's voice was soft and innocent, but the speaker was turned up and it rang out through the church. Within three lines of the song, George was dumbfounded. He knew Alex had become an excellent guitarist, but his voice was nearly flawless. George had once heard a musician's voice described as "perfectly compatible with guitar," and that's what he heard in Alex's singing.

This is the place that I loved her
And these are the friends that she had
Long may the mountain ring
To the sound of her laughter
And she goes on and on

George had never heard of the song or the artist before. But as the lyrics told a melancholy story, he knew it was perfect. As Alex sang, "she goes on," he was overcome with emotion. Tears fell as he thought about living the years ahead with just Elena's spirit and memory. He decided to print out the words later, frame them, and hang it in his home office.

In her soft wind I will whisper
In her warm sun I will glisten
Till we see her once again
In a world without end

George looked around the church. Every eye was on Alex and Jeff. He saw quiet tears everywhere he looked. He returned his attention to Alex and was surprised with what he felt. He was proud. He was proud of Amanda's courage. He was proud that Alex had found a perfect way to remember Elena. Proud that Alex and Jeff had the bravery to express themselves in front of everyone.

I hope you're hearing this, Elena.

When the song ended, Alex and Jeff quietly returned to their seats.

The priest nodded to George, and he stood and walked to the podium. George feared this moment most of all. Nothing he had thought of seemed to be worthy of it. Eventually, he'd run out of time and had to accept the short, disappointing paragraph he had written.

"I have a friend who has been trying to teach me that death is a necessary part of life—that we can learn from every tragedy. But I have to be honest with all of you: I'm struggling to see how any good can come from Elena's death."

George noticed a lot of uncomfortable shifting in the audience. This wasn't starting well, but he didn't care.

"However, I can say, without a doubt, that a tremendous amount of good came from her life. I heard it from all of you yesterday. She touched a lot of people, more than I knew. You heard it from her children. And you will hear it from me. She gave more to this world than she took. She gave me strength. She made my house a home. She made me want to be a good man. She gave me my children. She helped us all get through tough times. And she made the good times wonderful. She was the love of my life, and like Amanda, I'm grateful for the time I had with her. Thank you all for coming, for your well wishes and your support."

George wanted to say more, but he had no words. As he returned to his seat, he heard Elena's voice in his head.

It's okay, George, don't worry. You did fine.

CHAPTER 56

Across the Universe

"George, what I'm about to tell you may seem unbelievable. I just ask that you keep an open mind and listen to all of it before you make up your mind."

George smiled. "Ah, Shiloh, you've sent me to alternate dimensions. I doubt there's anything you can say that I won't keep an open mind about."

"Okay, good. First, as I told you, I'm a traveler like you. I was sent here. Except obviously I'm not just living one day: I'm living a lifetime in your dimension, your world. I destroyed my Apple Watch when I arrived, and I'll remain here until I die."

"Wait, so then what happened to the Shiloh who was in this dimension?" asked George.

"Good question. The moment I destroyed my watch, the Shiloh from this world ceased to exist. I permanently took over his consciousness," Shiloh said.

"So you killed him?"

"In a sense, I guess. It's complicated. You see, he was just about to experience a fatal, fluke lab accident. That's why they picked this dimension for me. So I guess you could say that I replaced or killed this Shiloh, but he was about to die the very next day—while I knew to avoid the accident. It was a difficult decision for me, but ultimately I decided the good outweighed the bad. It's one that every traveler has to make."

"So who are *they*?" George asked.

"I was getting to that. *They* are the first people to discover this ability to travel. They became great explorers, visiting thousands and thousands of parallel worlds. Even though many of the worlds are similar, some are different. Some are more advanced. They found civilizations that had reached far greater developments in science, mathematics, and philosophy. They learned much about the multiverse and about the journey of complexity we're all on. But they learned one alarming thing. They couldn't travel to many of the dimensions because life—or at least intelligent life—had ended. The parallel worlds were destroying themselves at an alarming rate. It was a thousand different things: nuclear war, bioengineered viruses, runaway nanotechnology. With the help of other worlds, the first travelers did the math, and the probabilities were not good. And the multiverse is all about probabilities. By studying enough types of worlds, they determined that given enough time, there was a strong possibility that every single dimension in the multiverse would end up lifeless. So they set out to change that. Are you following me so far?"

"I think so, but you were right. It does all sound a bit far-fetched," George said. *Although it feels right.*

"It's going to get more unbelievable, so hang on. They began to experiment with changing other dimensions. They would travel to a world where war was about to break out and prevent it. Unfortunately, even when they changed major events, they only delayed the inevitable. If you develop a cure to a pandemic, another virus eventually takes its place. When they assassinated a leader who dragged the world into war, another leader would rise up and start the war, just a bit later. By accident, they discovered that it wasn't changing events that made the difference, but rather changing *people*. It was people who spread the message of love, compassion, and growth. It happens in different ways, through art, religion, education, or even politics. It could be leaders or great historical figures, but most of the time it was people like teachers, parents, and artists. It was smaller acts of kindness, or the teaching of a religious figure, or a selfless act by an individual that changed that world's viewpoint. They called these people or events 'sparks.' Sometimes it would take a single spark to get a civilization past a danger point, and other times it took hundreds. The keys are positivity, teaching, and growing— it's never technology. So they set out to change the odds that life will succeed in the multiverse. They enlisted hundreds of worlds to help them research and develop plans to create sparks throughout the multiverse."

Shiloh paused for a breath. "It's not easy; you can't send books, or computers, or research. You can't communicate between dimensions. And you can travel for either a day or a lifetime, and nothing in between. So they developed plans and trained thousands of travelers. The travelers have to memorize everything. And they have no proof of what they are. They travel to other dimensions to convince and train other travelers, spreading the sparks out through the multiverse and hopefully tipping the odds."

"How did you get picked?" George asked.

"Every traveler is picked based on research and analysis of similar worlds with similar histories. Each must have the opportunity to make some difference that matters. And each one must be able to travel to another dimension where the local version of themselves is about to die. They must be able to memorize information about the travelers they are to enlist. I think my photographic memory helped me get chosen. And each one must be willing to live their life over again."

"Live their life over again?" George asked.

"Yes, they have to change something in their life, live it better, and make some sort of difference. And here's the real kicker, George. They don't tell you what it is that you have to change." He looked George straight in the eye.

That makes no sense. "Why wouldn't they tell you? That's insane."

"I agree, but I don't know why. Unfortunately, there's a lot I don't know. You see, I am a fourth-generation traveler. I'm not from the world that created the plan, and neither was the traveler who trained me or the one who trained her. Everything is based on memory and word of mouth. I don't believe my traveler had any idea what my spark is. However, I have a theory. I believe that if they're too prescriptive, it won't work. If you were simply following a script, the act—or art, or whatever good you did—wouldn't be genuine and it wouldn't be a spark. It has to be free will. So they don't tell you."

"So what have you done? What's your spark, Shiloh?"

Shiloh took a deep breath. "I'm a teacher, and I believe that's my spark. I teach physics, and I'm trying not only to be the best physics teacher I can be, but also to encourage and inspire my students. Because the spark might actually be created not by me, but by one of my students. They might have a scientific breakthrough that helps feed the world or provides low-cost energy or something. I have to tell you, George, it's a little daunting, not knowing. I don't know if I am making the difference I'm supposed to make. It can be frustrating."

"I'll bet."

"But I'm also training my third traveler. Maybe for me it's training the travelers. I was assigned four: my first one declined, my second started her journey several years ago, and you are my third traveler."

"Wait, what?" said George.

"Isn't it obvious? You are my third traveler . . . or, I should say, candidate. The travels you've been taking are training. Single-day travels build flexibility in your consciousness. I've been building up to this for some time, George. Teaching you, training you. You were identified in the master plan. Somehow you or someone you influence has the chance to make a difference in the world. Your life can literally change a world. What do you think? Are you up for it?"

I'm a candidate? I'm supposed to save the world? Come on.

"Whoa, whoa, up for what? I'm confused right now, Shiloh. I'm sort of hoping I'm in the middle of one of my crazy dreams."

"This is no dream. I'm asking you if you're willing to travel to another dimension and relive your life. You're actually lucky. You'll be a fifth-generation traveler, and it ends there. You don't have to train anyone."

"I'm not feeling lucky. You're asking me to travel, prevent my own death, stay there to relive my life, and somehow do it better?" asked George.

"That's precisely what I'm asking. I guess technically the first travelers are asking you," said Shiloh.

"Can I change anything in my life—my job, the town where I live, anything?" asked George.

"Yeah, you always have free will. You can change anything, but George, you may never know which changes make a difference. So don't change just for change's sake; follow your heart about what you think will matter."

"Should I have saved Amanda from her accident? She lost an eye, but it got her interested in medicine and accepted into Northwestern."

"Since you already did save her once, I would say yes, you could save her again. As for whether you should, I don't know. You're going to have to follow your heart."

Follow my heart? These people figured out interdimensional travel, and their best advice is follow your heart?

"What about Alex and his drinking incident? It nearly killed him, but it sure woke me up. I think our relationship changed, and he has blossomed. Do I change that?" asked George.

"George, I don't know, I wish I did. You're going to have to make your own decisions. My own advice is to mostly think about changing yourself. But this is just me, it's nothing I was taught as a traveler. They don't tell us what we should or shouldn't change."

"What about Elena?" asked George.

"I think you can buy her time. I'm not a doctor, but you could make sure she was tested early and often. I just don't know if it will ultimately save her. She may still get cancer—it seemed to me that her cancer was largely genetically based."

"So there is a chance I would have to live through Elena's cancer and her death again. I don't know if I can do that, Shiloh," choked George, tears coming to his eyes.

"I understand, and I don't blame you. It's your choice. No one is going to force you. I will say that while you might have to live through her death again, you do get to live through her life again. And I think, if you consider it, it might be worth the price."

Wait, hold on. "And in this new life, when I die, that's it? What about my kids? What about Amanda and Alex in this life?"

Shiloh nodded. "It's hard. This is my biggest concern. But you can make plans. You can make sure they're taken care of. I know you have friends who would treat them like their own. I'll help if you like. I'll make sure they always have everything they need. George, the greatest minds in the multiverse think you should do this. That you make a difference in saving a world. You have to at least consider it."

"So let's just say there is a little more love in this other world, and humankind finds that balance between order and chaos. And we don't destroy ourselves with nuclear war or rogue biotechnology. And we continue on this journey of evolution and complexity. What happens at the end? What do we become?"

"Something wonderful." Shiloh smiled. George decided his crow's-feet made him make him look a little like Santa Claus.

"Really, that's all you're going to tell me? 'Something wonderful'? We never get to see it; we never get to know it?"

"You get something better."

George bit. "What's better than the meaning of life, the purpose of the universe?"

"You, George, get to see the mountains, and the seas, and the valleys. You get to live on the edge of the knife, you get the heron, you get the moondance, and to watch your son's birth again. You get the Magical Mystery Tour, the journey of life, and . . . George, you get rock and roll. Not every human that walked the planet gets rock and roll."

George just stared into space, so Shiloh continued. "So, you know what, I bet, on your last day, when you look back on both your lives and your journey, it will be enough."

"Shiloh, I don't think I can't leave my kids. And it won't be my life. As you said, it's a parallel world. It's not the same Elena; I would basically be cheating on my wife. And I'm still me; I'm don't know if I can live another life any better than this one. It doesn't matter, I can't leave Amanda and Alex."

"I understand, George, take all the time you need. I don't ask lightly. You have to know that I understand the burden I'm placing on you, because I carry one myself. But I wouldn't even ask if I didn't believe that you have a chance to help a civilization, a world, and the very multiverse itself."

Sure, just give me a cape. Shiloh and these parallel world scientists have no clue what they're doing. If they did, they wouldn't have picked me. A chance to save the very multiverse itself? What bullshit!

CHAPTER 57

The Letter

George sorted through the envelopes. At first he couldn't find the one he was looking for. The second time through, he found it. It was titled, "To George: Open after my funeral." He closed his eyes and took a deep breath. He opened the envelope and removed the note. He began to read, hearing Elena's voice as clearly as if she were in the room.

> *George,*
> *Thank you for choosing to spend your life with me.*
> *Thank you for being my best friend. Thank you*
> *for never questioning my decision to stay at home*
> *with the kids. Thank you for the thrill of falling*
> *in love, the joy of children, and the comfort of a*
> *happy marriage. You, Amanda, and Alex made my*
> *life richer.*

*I know you will do great with the chil-
dren. Please help them to remember my life, not my
death. Encourage Amanda to be brave and bold.
She is smarter, stronger, and more beautiful than she
knows. Please let Alex find himself. I know you're
disappointed he doesn't love sports as much as you,
but you need to know that he has the best parts of
you. He is inventive and driven and creative. Those
things come from you, George.*

*I hope you can love again. I want you to
know that I do want you to love again; there is not
enough of it in the world. It will never change what
we had, and I want nothing more than for you to be
happy for the rest of your life.*

*Thank you for the movie of my life, my
moondance, and helping me find dignity and peace.*

My Love Forever,

Elena

CHAPTER 58

She's Gone

"Thank you both for being there for Elena and for our family," George said, feeling every word in his heart as he faced Cade and Lynn over the kitchen table. "I can't tell you how much your friend-ship meant to her in the end."

"She was like a sister to me," Lynn said.

It seems like yesterday the four of us were sitting at this table making pirate jokes. How do I ask this of them?

"I'm afraid I have to ask more of you both."

Lynn and Cade looked at each other. "Anything, George. You just say it," Cade said.

"Well, with Elena gone, I've been working on our affairs. I'd like to ask the two of you to be Amanda and Alex's guardians if something were to happen to me. It wouldn't be a financial burden: Amanda received an insurance settlement for losing her eye, and Elena had a life insurance policy. They haven't paid the latter out yet—apparently it takes some time. I have one as well, and we have equity in our home. Anyway, there would be more than enough to support the kids, their college, their weddings . . . ." George felt a wave of emotion wash over him; he tried to cover it up with coughing, but it only made it worse. Cade put a hand on his shoulder.

"Jesus, George, are you okay? I mean, don't tell me you're sick too? Is there—"

No, I'm not okay.

"Cade," interrupted Lynn. "What he means to say is that we would honored to be Amanda and Alex's guardians."

"Yeah, absolutely, no question. But it will never come to that, will it, George?"

"I'm sorry," he managed. "I still can't seem to get through a conversation about Elena without breaking down. I never realized how much I would miss her."

George took a few breaths to pull himself together. "I'm fine. I'm not sick. But if I've learned anything over the last three months, it's that anything can happen at any time. With what our family has been through, we have to be prepared for anything."

"Sure, you need to be prepared, but Cade is right. It won't come to that. So, what about now? Do you and the kids need any help?" Lynn asked.

"No, we're all right. I mean, it's tough, but we're dealing with it. The kids are pitching in around the house. I think we're all looking for some kind of normalcy. Amanda's out of her walking cast, and Alex still has a few more sessions, but Dr. Rao still says he's doing great. I started back to work, and it's going well. School starts soon, and then we'll all be so busy we won't have time to think about anything else. I'm kind of looking forward to that."

"George, you know there are support groups. Also, you might want to think about hiring a housekeeper," Lynn said.

"Thanks, Lynn. Elena used a support group, and I could tell it helped her. I'll think about it. But I don't know about a housekeeper. I think it's a good thing that we all have to pitch in. I think it's been good for Amanda and Alex."

"Just don't be afraid to ask for help, George. You have a lot of friends who are ready, willing, and able."

"I know. We're lucky. I just appreciate that you're willing to be guardians. The kids are pretty self-sufficient, but they've both already been through so much. It gives me peace of mind." George stood up and hugged them both.

CHAPTER 59

Promises, Promises

George stood over his Apple Watch with a hammer in his hand, wavering. All his life he'd felt like he had a strong sense of what the "right thing" was. He didn't always act on it, but he knew. But now he had no idea. He was in the basement in his workroom, the watch balanced on the flat part of the large metal vise mounted on his workbench.

If I break this watch, the real George in this world will not return. He will no longer exist. I'll never return to my real life. But I'll have another lifetime with Elena, and with the kids. A chance to live my life better, to make a difference. They picked me, I'm meant to do this.

George swung the hammer tentatively; it struck the watch lightly and bounced off. The watch appeared unharmed. He remembered, what seemed like a long time ago, Shiloh talking about how well made it was.

It won't be easy to live my life over again. Every day I will feel the pressure to live this life better than the last. I'll still make mistakes, I'm not perfect—I'm still me. But at least I won't take Elena for granted. I know what it's like to be without her.

George looked down at the hammer in his hand and then glanced at the watch.

It still feels like a cheat, living my life over again. Didn't Shiloh call it that once, some sort of cheat on the universe? Why am I doing this? Is it really to save the world? Am I just running away from my current life? From facing everyday life without her. The responsibility of the kids on me alone?

"What are you doing, Daddy?" asked Amanda. George about jumped out of his skin.

Turning to look at her, he said, "I don't know, honey."

He set down the hammer and picked her up. He brushed the hair from her face, staring into her two perfect eyes.

Here's the truth: I can't leave my Amanda and Alex. I can't run away from my life. If I can't even deal with my current life—how can I live another better?

George picked up his watch and slipped into his pocket.

"I guess I'm making a decision, Amanda panda."

"What kind of decision?"

At three years old, Amanda was the queen of questions. She could ask them all day, and often did.

"A tough one."

"Why is it tough?"

"What's going on down here?" asked Elena, walking into the room.

"Oh, I was just fixing the cord on this old drill. It was worn down to wire, and I'm lucky I didn't electrocute myself," replied George, showing Elena his repair job. "I'm a master with electrical tape."

"Well, aren't we lucky to have such a handyman around? Mandy, you know you're not allowed down in Daddy's workroom." Elena took Amanda from George.

"It's okay, she was just checking up on me."

Elena set Amanda down and said, "Mandy, run upstairs. I'll be up in a minute to make you breakfast."

"Okay, Mommy," said Amanda as she marched off.

Elena planted a big, wet kiss on George's cheek. "Good morning," she said.

Well, that's not making my decision easier. "Good morning. Elena, I have something strange to tell you." *How do I say this?*

"Okay?"

"I had a nightmare last night. We were much older—the kids were in high school. You were diagnosed with ovarian cancer. I know it's only a dream, but please make me a promise."

"You're right, George, this is strange."

"I know, but I couldn't be more serious. Please promise me that when you get to forty, you'll get checkups for cancer every year."

Elena looked into George's eyes. "You are serious, aren't you?"

"Yes, I am. God, I miss you." He wrapped his arms around her.

"Miss me?"

Crap! Careful, George. "I lost you in my dream, and I couldn't stand it. Hey, let's have a perfect Saturday. Forget about chores, forget about housework. Let's take Amanda on a picnic or something."

"All right, what's gotten into you this morning?"

"Nothing. I just want to spend today like it's my last day with you. Humor me. I'll be back to your normal George tomorrow."

"Okay, then you can start your perfect day by making breakfast for Mandy and me."

"Deal," he said. He grabbed Elena's hand and walked her up the stairs.

CHAPTER 60

Come Together

George looked out the window into the backyard. It was sunny but windy. Fall was coming to an end. Amanda sat on the old tree swing, just swaying back and forth, her feet never leaving the grass. George walked out the French doors into the backyard.

I haven't seen anyone on that old swing for years. I hope it's still safe. He called to her, "Hey, how are you doing?" as he examined the ropes and the branch above. *Still looks fine after all these years. Seems like yesterday when I was swinging Amanda and her feet couldn't even touch the ground.*

"I don't know."

"Amanda panda, talk to me."

"You haven't called me that in a long time."

"I know. How are you doing?

"I miss Mom."

"Me too, Mandy. How are you feeling?"

"When will it stop hurting?"

Oh boy, how do I answer that? "I don't know. Maybe not for a long time, but we need to keep going. Mom would want us to keep going."

"Yeah, I guess. But, Dad, I'm scared."

"Scared of what?"

"I'm scared of going through life without Mom. Whenever I had a problem, she always knew how to fix it."

George moved behind Amanda, and she lifted her feet as he gave her a gentle push.

"The great thing about Mom was that she never tried to fix our problems, even when she knew the answer. She always helped you figure out how to fix your own problem. So, that means . . . you have the answers inside of you."

"Yeah, but she's not here to help me find the answers."

The wind kicked up again, scattering leaves across the yard. Amanda's hair flew in the breeze.

"She'll always be there, inside you. Whenever you have a problem, you'll hear her voice, helping you. I felt the same way when I lost my parents—damn, I still do miss them. But I just recently realized that they're still with me. Every time I struggle with a decision, they're in the back of my mind, offering me advice. We just have to learn to listen. And don't forget, I'm here too."

"I know, Dad. I don't mean for it to sound like that."

"I know, Mandy. It's okay. If Mom were here, what problems would you tell her about?"

"I don't know. I guess that I still feel like a kid."

You ARE a kid. "What do you mean?"

"Dad, I'm seventeen, I've never had a real boyfriend, I don't go to real parties . . . I mean, even my little brother got drunk before I did."

"And you think that's a bad thing?"

"My friends call me gullible. I need to grow up."

"Mandy, you have your whole life to grow up. Growing up is overrated. Trust me, with college, it's going to happen soon, whether you want it or not. I say hold on to your innocence as long as you can. Don't be in a hurry. Besides, after what you've been through the last three months, you've dealt with more than a lot of adults have. You're more grown up than you think you are."

"I guess. I just don't know what I want to do with my life. My friends all know what college they want, what majors they want—they have it all figured out. I have no clue."

"So what do you think Mom would say?"

"Oh, she would say that none of my friends really know what they want, that I need to give myself time and to listen to my heart. She would tell me to make a plan, but be ready to change it."

That's my girl. George stopped pushing Amanda and walked around to her side. "See, she is there, inside you," he said, putting a finger on her belly. "That's exactly what Mom would say."

"Are you worried about Alex, Dad?"

"Oh, yes and no. Just like you, he's been through so much. But Dr. Rao is helping him. And Alex and I talked for over an hour last night. I think he's doing really well. His music and his drawing are a great outlet for him."

"So are we going to be okay, Dad?"

"Yeah, kiddo, I think we're going to be okay. As long as we stick together, we're going to be all right."

"Shiloh speaking, how can I help you?"

"Shiloh, it's George."

"George, how are you, how are the kids?"

George was at home, sitting at his desk. He looked at a family picture. It had to be at least five years old.

"Shiloh, I didn't stay in the other dimension. I didn't break the watch. I couldn't leave my kids."

"I know."

"So I failed. All that planning, them sending you here, you leaving your other life, the watch, the travels, it was all for nothing. Am I in trouble with your time lords, or time police, or whatever they are?"

"No, George, you're not in trouble. And they're not time lords, they're just people with advanced technology trying to make a difference."

"Then did you fail, Shiloh? Did I ruin things for you?"

"No, you didn't ruin anything. It's always free choice. I never could see you leaving your kids, I always thought you would stay. But I had to let you decide."

George heard laughter from the kitchen. His kids were playing a card game together. "Well, I feel like I let down the universe, or the multiverse or whatever you call it."

"No, you stayed because you love your children, and that's what it's all about. Maybe you're meant to stay in this world. I believe that if you follow your heart, you've made the right decision."

"I appreciate everything you've done. I want to be your friend."

"We already are friends," Shiloh said.

"Yeah, but I want to you come over to dinner, meet the kids. Watch a movie with us. And you can teach me more about physics and rock and roll and maybe even soccer."

"Well, I guess that's fair, since you helped me appreciate baseball. That sounds great—I'd love to meet the kids. I feel like I already know them."

"Tonight, come have dinner tonight at six. Maybe I can get Alex to play some guitar for you."

"That sounds great. Pick me up at the train station?"

"Absolutely. Text me when you're close. You sure I didn't screw up the universe?"

"I'm positive. See you in a couple of hours."

"All right, see you soon."

CHAPTER 61

Graduation Day

June 19, 2020

Amanda walked up to the podium. When she reached the microphone she paused, looking out across the audience. A hush came over the crowd at Ryan Stadium. George waved.

> *Did she see me? I can't tell. She doesn't look nervous, but she must be. This place looks more like a rock concert than a commencement ceremony—so many people. I wonder what she's thinking? Remembering marching bands, football games, and college friends, or just trying to focus on her speech? I can't believe she didn't let me help her. She wrote it so quickly.*

"Good afternoon," Amanda said, and her words echoed across the stadium. She squinted into the late morning sun. The sky was clear other than a few seagulls drifting over from Lake Michigan. "This is an ambitious graduation speech, even for

Northwestern University. Why? you might ask. Because in the next few minutes I will answer three questions: the meaning of life, the key to happiness, and the secret to success. Impossible, you say . . . we will see. Let us jump right in, no holds barred, to 'the meaning of life.' I believe it can be summed up in just one word: *balance*."

She paused.

"I can sense your disappointment." Amanda gave the crowd her best smile.

Well, she certainly caught their attention right away. I wish she hadn't gone so grandiose. God, I'm so nervous for her.

"But this isn't the balance you might first think of. It is not average, middle of the road, or in between. This balance is the thrilling, death-defying balance that a tightrope walker perched between two towering skyscrapers must maintain. It is the skillful, perfect harmony of a skier rocketing down a mountainside," said Amanda, increasing her volume.

George looked to his left at Lynn and Cade. They looked nervous as well. He looked right. Alex had a smirk on his face, and Shiloh was grinning ear to ear.

"You see, life thrives on that razor's edge between chaos and order. Too much order, and life is stagnant and cannot change or evolve. Too much chaos, and life is overwhelmed. In this vast universe, we have found this perfect balance. Earth is, as scientists have coined, in the Goldilocks Zone—not too hot, not too cold; not too big, not too small. If you follow the path of evolution, you'll see that the evolutionary winners are the species that adapted, that used this balance to change. So, the meaning of life—change, adaptation, balance between chaos and order—is what made our particular branch of the evolutionary tree successful after a half billion years.

"Okay, so the meaning of life equals balance: one down."

Did Shiloh help her write her speech? Or has she really been listening to us?

"Next up, I will attempt the answer to what is the key to happiness? What are some of the most joyful, exciting activities that you can think of? Music? Art? Sports? What do these have in common? I submit to you that music is the perfect representation of our need to exist in between order and chaos. In music, the perfect progression of notes—that is, a scale—is boring! It's too much order. And totally random notes and sounds are awful. But the artists who find that line between order and chaos create pure beauty. Green Day, the Flaming Lips, Radiohead, even going all the way back to Mozart and Beethoven, they all find that perfect place between simplicity and complexity. So, what is the most successful form of music today? Rock and roll, which is just a representation of order and chaos! Rock—order, roll—chaos . . . make sense?"

George looked around the audience and saw nodding heads.

"Now think about competitive sports: a structured set of rules and guidelines inside which anything can happen, leading to an uncertain outcome. What's the most thrilling? What about a close game that's down to the last few minutes with everything hanging in the balance? How about the underdog overcoming impossible odds to succeed? Again, it's that tipping point between structure and uncertainty. Or take the most perfect example: surfing. It's literally riding atop a chaotic wave simply using skill and balance. It's the kind of thing we find joyful, exciting, and fun. So, the key to happiness equals finding the ideal balance between chaos and order. That's two down, one to go." She looked out into the crowd and paused.

I think she sees us.

Amanda gave a quick wink.

She does see us.

"Finally, what's the secret to success? It's the easiest one—believe me! First, what is success? Is it family, wealth, fame, or health? Can you have wealth and fame and still have a happy family and be healthy? Don't look to Wall Street or Hollywood, because I don't see many happy and healthy folks in the long run there. And can you stay healthy and maintain a strong family without some money or success? So what do the keys of life and happiness teach us? I submit that the secret to success is also balance—but again, not balance as in the perfect balance between love and money; it's still the balance between order and chaos. The ability to change, adapt, and grow—to look at life's challenges as opportunities. It's the ability to overcome adversity, pain, and even death, and not just to get past them, but to learn and grow from them. That is what leads to happiness. So the secret to success equals balance. Hmmm, all three have the same answer—bet you didn't see that coming."

Oh boy, she actually thinks she has it all figured out. She listened to Shiloh and me, and now she believes she understands everything. She has so much more to learn—she doesn't know she's just beginning. We have our work cut out for us now.

"I know what you're thinking now: I just described Zen and yin and yang. The Buddha already had this all figured out way back in the sixth century. True, but he never tied it to rock and roll! Seriously, let me give you an example to make it real. When I was seventeen, I lost vision in one of my eyes during a car accident. That horrible event, in the long run, gave me more than it took. It gave me an interest in medicine, and it helped me get into medical school in this university. Neither would have happened without the accident. Then, shortly after my accident, my mom died from ovarian cancer. That tragedy pushed me to explore medical science and participate in cancer research, and ultimately to my involvement in the cancer research breakthrough you have been hearing so much about. It's why I stand up here today, giving a commencement speech. It will never make up for losing my mother—she was an amazing woman. But I've tried to honor her by making something good from her death."

Visions of Elena passed before George's eyes. He felt tears forming and his throat tightening up, but he fought it off.

"My dad taught me that chaos, destruction, and death are a necessary part of this universe. And while we don't have to like it, we must use that to learn and grow. He taught me that with love you can not only overcome anything, but you can also use chaos to grow and change. So, I challenge each of you to find that death-defying balance in your lives. Push yourselves to explore, create, learn, and constantly change. Push yourself to the edge, but don't cross it. Stay grounded and spiritual, and love your family and friends. Learn from mistakes, challenges, and tragedies. Make every loss count. Join me in this journey. Together let's create something wonderful. Thank you!"

The momentary silence caught George off guard. Then he heard a handful of individuals clapping. This quickly turned to widespread applause, which grew until it became thunderous. Then the entire audience stood.

CHAPTER 62

In My Life

July 24, 2058

Shiloh made his way through the hospice. His bad knee was acting up again.

Getting old is a bitch.

He had visited many times before, so he knew the drill. His long white hair was in a ponytail. He wore jeans, and today's T-shirt read *The physics are theoretical, but the fun is real.* He glanced into George's room to see if he was sleeping, but he was sitting up in bed, watching old-time television on the wall viewer. As Shiloh stepped in, George turned off the viewer.

"Shiloh, how are you? You're looking more and more like Gandalf every day!"

Shiloh stroked his beard. It was white, matching his hair, and while it was growing longer, it wasn't quite Gandalf length yet. Nevertheless, he was happy with it.

"All we have to decide is what to do with the time that is given us," he said in his best booming Gandalf voice. "Ah, it would be more impressive if I had a flowing robe and a staff. Unfortunately, people think I look more like Santa than Gandalf."

"No, it's perfect—you make a great Gandalf."

Shiloh sat down on the chair next to the bed. George looked terribly thin and frail. It caught him off guard. Trying to cover his worry, he asked, "How are you, George?"

"This is the end, Shiloh. Sorry to be so blunt and dramatic, but I'm afraid it's the truth. My ticker is just about through. The doctor said I have weeks, maybe even days."

"I'm so sorry. But weren't they looking into a transplant? Is that still a possibility?"

"No, I'm ninety-four years old, for Chrissake. I would never make it through a transplant. I take more medication than a heavy-metal band. Besides, I don't want some manufactured heart they grew in a lab. I'm ready, Shiloh. I've lived a full life."

Shiloh took a deep breath. He'd known this was coming for some time, but it still wasn't easy. "I understand. You have lived a full life, and what a life! You should be so proud."

"Well, I guess I have no regrets. Or at least no major regrets. Proud . . . well, I am proud of my kids. I guess I'm happy with my life. I'm just not sure I can point to anything I have done that's made a difference. Shiloh, do you still wonder if I made a mistake not staying in the alternate universe?"

"No, George, I think you did the right thing. I'm sure it wasn't easy to give up a chance to relive your life and to be with Elena again. But you were right to stay. Your kids are amazing. Just think how many lives have been extended by the work your daughter has done! Who knows what would have been lost if cancer was still the killer it once was? Think of all the children who have had full lives because of Amanda's work. And I think anyone you ask would say that society is better off because of Alex. I guess we'll never know how many lives he's touched with his music and writing, but I think it's millions."

"Thanks, Shiloh. I'm just happy they have been able to stay grounded through their success. Success is a dangerous thing."

"That's how you've made the difference: by being there for your children and your friends. That's more than enough. It's what matters." Shiloh studied his face, trying to see if he believed. He wanted George to be at peace.

"Well, I did stay for my kids, but I also stayed because I was still afraid. I wasn't ready. It's taken me a lifetime, Shiloh, but I'm no longer afraid. And I've learned a few things. It almost took me a century, but I think I finally understand."

"Understand what?"

"I've learned to be grateful. I learned to appreciate everything this universe has given me. For my kids, and for meeting you, Shiloh. And for my time with Elena. I've learned not to underestimate the power of tragedy. I learned that not only does the universe need conflict and challenges to advance, but I do as well. And now I understand that the past is not as wonderful as I remember and that the future is likely better than I fear.

"Hey, I had the most amazing and vivid dream last night. I need to tell you about it. It was like the kind I used to have back when I was traveling."

"That's strange. The vivid dreams typically only occur right before or right after you travel," Shiloh said.

"It started with you and I on a stage. We were dressed in military-style jackets and pants—the Beatles' Sgt. Pepper outfits. Yours was yellow and mine was light blue. We were in front of an enormous crowd; it went on as far as I could see. We both had matching Stratocasters, and you were wearing circular rose-colored glasses. I guess you were supposed to be Lennon, and I was McCartney. I was really nervous in front of this enormous crowd. Someone was yelling from behind me, and I turned around and it was Ringo sitting behind a drum set. He was yelling, "Plug it in, laddie, plug it in." So I see my guitar isn't plugged into the amp. I plug it in, and a screech of feedback rips through the speakers. Ringo rolled his eyes at me. I remember thinking how cool it was that Ringo was rolling his eyes at me."

Shiloh stared at George, listening intently. He wondered if George was making this up or if he actually had this dream. It did sound like the kind of dream you would have as a side effect of traveling. He allowed himself a sliver of hope.

"You tell me to play 'In My Life.' The crowd goes quiet, and I'm terrified now because I don't know how to play guitar. Then we start playing. The words come flowing out. Shiloh, you and I are in perfect harmony. All my nervousness goes away and I'm completely at peace. It was amazing. I look down at hands, and my fingers are expertly finding the chords."

George paused for a moment. Shiloh was mesmerized. "What happened next?"

"So I look out into the audience and I start to see people I know. My parents are there. Elena and the kids are there. I see all of my friends and neighbors. My childhood friends are there, and they're all still little kids. I realize everyone I've ever known in my life is in the audience. It's so strange. We finish the song, and the crowd goes crazy. Ringo and George Harrison join us in front, and we bow together. The crowd goes crazy again, and we march off the stage in single file. Backstage, we can hear the audience chanting, 'Encore, encore!' They won't stop. It's loud, but you look at me and yell, "One last song!" So we walk back out onto the stage and play

'All You Need Is Love.' The whole audience is singing along, and it sounds wonderful. I'm singing directly to Elena, and she's singing back at me. Then, at the end of the song, a curtain of mist comes rolling in and everything fades away. That's it—then I wake up."

"I love that dream, George. You had that last night?"

"Yeah. Well, this morning. I woke up feeling the best I have in years. It felt like everything was right in the universe. Except one thing. I miss Elena, I still miss her every day. Shiloh, I have a final confession to make to you."

"A final confession?"

"I want to travel again. I only used nine travels—I have one left."

Shiloh smiled knowingly. "Why do you want to go, George?"

"I never regretted my decision to stay in this life, but lately I got to thinking. My kids are grown; my life is ending . . . it's too bad I can't go back now. And then it came to me: I never used my last travel."

"So you want to try to make a difference in another world, to create more sparks?"

"I'll be honest. I wish I knew how to be a hero. And I wish I knew how to create a spark or even what a spark is. The truth is, I want to go back for selfish reasons: to see Elena again and because I want to keep learning. Like you said, Shiloh, I'm just at the beginning. I want to keep growing. What you've taught me has changed my life. You made me want to get off the river. Is it still possible? Can I go back?"

"I have a present for you, George," Shiloh said. He pulled out a small white box and handed it to George, who looked at him wide-eyed.

"Is it? So, wait—this was the plan all along? You've always known I'd eventually choose to go back?"

"No, but I've always hoped you would. There's no definitive plan; it's always been your choice. And you've chosen wisely, all along your journey. This time it's a one-way trip, but you already know that. So tell Elena I said hey. I'm so happy for you, George. And if you're ever on a train, and the guy next to you looks lost, ask him how he is. Tell him what you've learned. Maybe the multiverse does have a chance after all."

The End

Acknowledgments

It all started with comic books. When I was in second grade, I was in the lowest reading group, and it made school difficult for me. That summer, I discovered my older brothers' comic books. I started with *Richie Rich, Casper,* and *DuckTales.* Then I moved on to *Superman, Spiderman,* and *Batman.* I was hooked. I worked my way through a thousand or so comic books in that one summer. When they tested us for third grade, I moved from the lowest reading group to the highest, and I've loved to read ever since. So, I send my thanks to Stan Lee, Jim Shooter, and other great comic book writers who captured the imagination of millions of kids.

Next, I would like to thank my parents, Ray and Dolores Kuhn. Although I was their seventh child, they still had the energy to teach me strong principles and the value of hard work. Our childhood was chaotic but wonderful. My parents always put their children first, and I'm grateful for their love and guidance.

This book simply wouldn't have happened without my lovely wife, Melinda. She read the first chapter and told me to keep going. She went on to read every bit I wrote, half drafted, out of order, and full of errors, and her feedback saved me from great embarrassment. She tolerated me when I was obsessed and encouraged me when I felt like giving up. She gave me unconditional support, always. She's my muse and my rock and the love of my life.

Writing is a lonely process, and I craved feedback. Thank you to my beta readers: Tyra, Maureen, Carrie, Rob, Louise, John, Pat, Jason, Brian, Arley, Christy, Tony, and Joe. Your encouragement and reassurance often came along at just the right time, and your honest feedback was important to this book and to me as a writer.

A big thanks to Neil Finn for allowing me to reprint the lyrics from "She Goes On." If you don't have a copy of Crowded House's *Woodface* in your music collection, run over to iTunes and pick it up right now: it's a fantastic album.

Thanks to my excellent editor, Kellie M. Hultgren. It cannot be easy to edit a first-time author, but she treated me with patience and diligence. She was candid and direct with her feedback, which is difficult to take, but so valuable. Thanks to Wendy Weckwerth for the final proof edit, Tyra Brosseau for the author photo and Athena Currier for the internal design and the creative cover design. Thanks also to my publisher, Lily Coyle, for being gentle with a virgin writer, putting up with my endless questions, and giving sound, practical advice.

I cannot predict how this book will be received, but I do know that writing it has helped me tremendously. If you ever thought about writing, *do it.* Right now: go to your computer and begin today. It will remind you how much you need to learn, but It will also show you the universe as you've never seen it before.

Go forth and create a spark!

Kevin A. Kuhn, November 22nd, 2016

Shiloh's Recommended Reading

Pinker, Steven (2011). *The Better Angels of Our Nature: Why Violence Has Declined.* Viking. ISBN 978-0670022953.

Singh, Simon (2005). *Big Bang: The Origin of the Universe.* Forth Estate. ISBN 0-00-719382-3.

Kaku, Michio (2014). *The Future of the Mind: The Scientific Quest to Understand, Enhance, and Empower the Mind.* Doubleday. ISBN 978-0385530828.

Merton, Robert K. (1973). *The Sociology of Science: Theoretical and Empirical Investigations.* University of Chicago Press. ISBN 0-226-52091-9.

Christian, David, Brown, Cynthia, Benjamin, Craig (2014). *Big History: Between Nothing and Everything.* McGraw-Hill Education. ISBN 978-0073385617.

Greene, Brian (2011). *The Hidden Reality: Parallel Universes and the Deep Laws of the Cosmos.* Alfred A. Knopf. ISBN 978-0307265630.

Shiloh's Recommended Listening

Tears for Fears. "Everybody Wants to Rule the World." By Olzabal, Roland, Stanley, Ian and Hughes, Chris. Somerset, UK: Fontana/Mercury/Phonogram. *Songs from the Big Chair.* 1985.

Joey Ramone. "What a Wonderful World." By Thiele, Bob and Weiss, George David. Sanctuary Records Group. *Don't Worry About Me.* 2002.

The Moody Blues. "Question." By Hayward, Justin. London, UK: Threshold Records. *A Question of Balance.* 1970.

The Church. "Under the Milky Way." By Kilbey, Steve and Jansson, Karin. Australia: Arista. *Starfish.* 1988.

The Pixies. "Where is My Mind?" By Francis, Black. Boston, MA: 4AD. *Surfer Rosa.* 1988.

The Beatles. "All You Need Is Love." By Lennon-McCartney. London, UK: Parlophone Capitol. *Magical Mystery Tour.* 1967.

Styx. "The Grand Illusion." By Dennis DeYoung. Chicago, IL: A&M Records. *The Grand Illusion.* 1977.

The Flaming Lips. "Do You Realize??" By Coyne, Wayne, Drozd, Steven, Ivins, Michael and Fridmann, Dave. New York, NY: Warner Brothers Records. *Yoshimi Battles the Pink Robots.* 2002.

The Beatles. "Across the Universe." By Lennon-McCartney, London, UK: Regal Starline. *No One's Gonna Change Our World.* 1969.